EVERYONE'S TALKING ABOUT
KATHERINE GOVIER

"Govier has a distinctive writing talent. While she will inevitably be considered the newest star in the Canadian women writer's firmament, her unusual technique should set her apart."

—Marilyn Brown, *Edmonton Journal*

"Style, vitality and insight are the attributes of a good writer, and these Govier has in abundance."

—Claire Harrison, *Ontario Revue*

"Govier has a clear and effortless style. She handles shifts in time and place and juxtapositions of past and present with confidence."

—Geoff Hancock, *Toronto Star*

"Katherine Govier... will prove herself one of the real writers of our time."

—Jane Rule, *Globe and Mail*

Going Through the Motions

Katherine Govier

SEAL BOOKS
McClelland and Stewart-Bantam Limited
Toronto

*This low-priced Seal Book
has been completely reset in a type face
designed for easy reading, and was printed
from new plates. It contains the complete
text of the original hard-cover edition.*
NOT ONE WORD HAS BEEN OMITTED.

🦭

GOING THROUGH THE MOTIONS
*A Seal Book / published by arrangement with
McClelland and Stewart, Ltd.*

PRINTING HISTORY
*McClelland and Stewart edition published September 1982
Seal edition / November 1983*

The author acknowledges the generous assistance of the Ontario Arts Council and the Canada Council.

"Halfway Down" from *When We Were Very Young* by A.A. Milne reproduced by permission of The Canadian Publishers, McClelland and Stewart, Toronto.

"All of Me" by Seymour Simons and Gerald Marks © 1931, Bourne Co., New York, N.Y. Copyright renewed. Used by permission of Bourne Music Canada Limited, Toronto. Administered by Gordon V. Thompson Limited.

For John

CONFIDENTIAL

Ministry of Correctional Services for the Province
of Ontario—Probation and Parole Services

Pre-Sentence Report

Prepared for:

His Honour, Judge G.W. Grimsley

Old City Hall, Toronto, Ontario

Prepared by:

Miss D.J. Ritter, Probation Officer

1240 Bay Street, Suite #506
Toronto, Ontario

Basic Information

Name:	Joan Sincere
Address:	27½ Baldwin Street, upstairs, Toronto
Date & Place of Birth	21 October 1949, Edmonton, Alberta; age 30 years
Marital Status:	Single
Previous Record	No criminal record available
Charge	Assault
Plea	Not Guilty
Date of Conviction	2 June 1980
Date of Remand	23 June 1980

1

Family Background

Joan Sincere, the offender, was born and raised an
only child in a large home in suburban Edmonton.
There was nothing in her upbringing to suggest trouble. She had holidays at the lake, braces to straight-
en her teeth, and dancing lessons. Although she was
considered a happy child, she describes her home as
"oppressively normal."

The mother is fifty-five, works for local charities,
and is president of the Philharmonic Society. The father
was a successful businessman with a large photograph-
ic studio. Joan began ballet lessons at five and from
that year on spent twelve to sixteen hours a week at
the dance studio. Ballet was all she cared about: school,
neighbourhood friends, family outings meant nothing.
Her only recollected fights with her parents involved
whether she should stay home and do school work
or whether she would be allowed to perform in local
shows. Her friend and aunt remember her as a disciplined, intense child who attracted imitators.

The offender's problems began with puberty. She
was tall for her age and appeared older. She was "boy
crazy," her aunt says, and attracted attention by wearing a padded bra and a great deal of make-up. At sixteen,
against her father's better judgement, she was allowed
to go to England to the Royal Ballet School. Away from
home, she became rebellious and headstrong. Despite
discipline problems, she was accepted into the ballet
company at seventeen, but left almost immediately.
She explained to her parents that she was fired because
she had become overweight.

In fact, the offender was pregnant. She did not wish
to have an abortion, although the operation would
have been legal in England. She chose to have her child
and give it away. Her family was never informed of
the birth. The offender spent some months in a refuge
for unwed mothers and other problem girls, and then
began to support herself in London doing commercial
dancing. She first appeared in chorus lines and musical comedies. After several years, these jobs led her to
the more lucrative job of stripping.

According to the offender, stripping was ideal for her.

She arranged her own bookings, created her own routines, and made a good income. There is no record of her being in any sort of trouble during this time. However, after eight years, in July 1978, she decided to leave London. Returning to Canada, she wished to be far away from her parents for fear of embarrassing them. She settled in Toronto, where the incident leading to the assault took place.

Employment

Mr. Herbert Spanatakis, manager of the Coliseum on Yonge Street, describes the offender as a spirited performer. He feels, however, that she had lately become a trouble-maker. He refused to employ her after the incident. Arlene Olsen, a friend of long standing, says the offender's current unemployment is atypical. Erratic employers and sudden dismissals are in the nature of her profession. Yet the offender has kept body and soul together, as it were, this way for a dozen years.

The Offender as a Person

The offender enjoys excellent health and does not use drugs or alcohol to excess. Her friends call her a survivor. The offender's aunt feels that the woman's criminal behaviour is symptomatic of a deep-rooted psychiatric problem. The offender certainly has a forceful personality and to meet and talk with her is to be for the moment persuaded of her point of view. I speak for myself; despite her obvious moral weakness and the gap of understanding that must necessarily exist between a woman of her experience and someone like myself, I was moved.

(At this point, Your Honour, the investigator respectfully injects her own assessment in a manner perhaps more candid than orthodox. My reason for so doing is that I feel that the popular conception of her occupation makes the offender easy prey to false interpretation. I wish to be fair. Please bear with me if I seem to betray feeling.)

To go on, I should say the offender co-operated from the outset in the preparation of this report. Her own account of her past is substantiated for the most part by others. When led to discuss her recent actions, however, she quickly becomes unreasonable. The offender shows all signs of a woman who is coming undone; in my view, the years of borderline existence have taken their toll.

She is self-indulgent and seemingly without shame. She talks incomprehensibly about life under a microscope. Perhaps this fantasy comes from being watched so much. As well, in the nether world of which she became a part, she acquired a superstitious dread of ill fortune. Her main adviser seems to be a fortune-teller who predicted the death of her father. There may be some justification, however, in her paranoia. Since the publication of a newspaper article and photograph at the time of her arrest, she has been plagued, she claims, by obscene telephone calls. A knife and other weapons have been left at her doorstep. On the day of her interview she sported a large facial bruise which, she said, was given her by a friend.

Conclusion

The offender is regarded by all who know her as intelligent and talented, although of an inflammatory nature. This is the first time she has come to the attention of the authorities. It must be added, however, that in the matter of the assault, she shows no remorse. But as the provocation was unique, there is no reason to believe she will repeat the act.

Again, with your leave, Your Honour, I digress slightly from the facts. It is my view that the offender represents not a legal but a social problem. Her problems arise from her efforts to support herself rather than slip into dependence on the state, or worse, fall in with a man who encourages illegal methods of earning. She is clinging to the edge of respectability by her fingertips. If we come along and punish her, we are stamping on those fingers.

This case, I suggest, inspires one to meditate on the circumstances of the individual, the artist, among us. Her behaviour is constantly motivated by the belief that she can "be herself" and "express herself" in her daily life. One can see clearly that Miss Sincere is deluded. Yet is not this delusion—that circumstances conspired to demean us and that no one appreciates our true worth—a universal one?

In the assault itself, the offender claims to have been defending her dignity. It seems to me that the same impulse that got her in trouble can be used to help her. I believe she has great potential for the future if she can be persuaded to settle down in a stable life. This could be a turning point. She might find more suitable employment and become a better citizen. In short, the offender can be saved.

For this reason, lenience in sentencing might be worthwhile. I respectfully submit that the offender would benefit from a thorough psychiatric assessment, followed by any treatment considered necessary.

D.J. Ritter (Miss)
Probation/Parole Officer

CHAPTER ONE

The paramoecium is a soft-sided, one-celled creature, visible only through a microscope. But how expressive it is, how fluid, how perfectly adapted to its world! Shaped like the sole of a slipper, it lengthens or swells as it navigates. Its fluted edges are trimmed with hairs, hairs that beat in the inter-cellular spaces, to drive it along past other little life stations. These hairs are its adornment, its mobility, and its defence. With these hairs the paramoecium can catch a grain of alien matter and hold it; it can gradually pass the matter along, dance it from one hair to another as grass seems to pass the wind along its blades. Then the paramoecium, reacting with some complex instinct, may discharge the particle into the nowhere between cells. Or, if it is hungry, it may keep the grain of matter, caressing it down to the indentation that is the paramoecium's gullet. There, it consumes the grain. Envelops it, takes it in, and the other becomes paramoecium.

Think of these mysteries and of the beauty of the paramoecium, Joan told herself. Think—she'd gone before the show to sit with Alex, an old friend, and his buddies at a table in the tavern and she'd fallen into conversation with a man called David. He'd asked her about her work. "It's not worth talking about," she said. "You talk." He said he was an amateur scientist, and he'd started telling her about the paramoecium. She had felt an affinity with the creature, if you could call it one. Perhaps it was the business of the hair-like legs. She too relied on legs to attract her neighbours, to draw them in, and then, if necessary, to get away from them. Or perhaps it was because the paramoecium reminded her of a childhood dream, a nightmare she supposed, except that it was very simple and there was no recognizable element of horror in it. The dream returned to her still, even now, as she sat on the edge of the chair in the storage room downstairs at the Coliseum on Yonge Street. The room served as her dressing-room; her suitcase was open on the floor and five pairs of shoes were spread around her feet.

In the old dream there was a mass of something alive, a growing elastic mass. The mass could break into pieces and remain alive no matter how small its parts. In the dream Joan had become an army of little selves and staked herself out around it, pushing and prodding it to make it into some kind of shape, something recognizable.

Putting on her stockings, as she was doing now, brought the vision back. Her pink flesh went into dark silk like sausage meat into its skin. There the raw material was, encased, with a seam up the back, slippery, shapely, transformed into something marketable. Her whole life she had been pouring herself into similar encasements.

"So," she said to herself, "you had a dream about growing up."

She lifted her right buttock from the chair, felt for the back garter, and snapped the stocking to it.

It had been a scary dream because she had always failed. The plasma would overflow and threaten to swallow her; before the catastrophe she had always woken up. Now she was an adult. She had no more such terrors, not while sleeping, anyway. And when she was awake she could handle them. She had given birth to a child of her own, and she earned a living as a dancer, sometimes a good living, sometimes not so good. The other leg went easily into the stocking, the dark rim at the top stretching over the muscle in her thigh.

Silk stockings were so much nicer than the black net ones that cut into the balls of the feet. Even nylon was preferable to those, but silk was nicest and Joan kept using them even though they cost a fortune and ran easily. She liked to have the best. Sometimes Herbie, the manager, asked her to wear the black net for a change. Herbie was a little too interested in the girls' routines, but he was basically a good guy. Just as well, too, because in the last week, in a fit of pique, she had dispensed with her agent, which left her at Herbie's mercy. She was no longer so sure it had been a good idea, although it had felt wonderful at the time.

Thinking about tantrums, she'd indulged in several lately. Earlier this evening she'd had a screaming match with Gina and Candy, the other strippers, because they'd borrowed her nail polish without asking. Now they weren't speaking to her. Too bad. Joan was a solo act and she could go it alone.

In the case of the agent, going it alone meant that instead of enduring the once-removed insult, instead of grinding her teeth at Marty's impotence as he dealt with obnoxious employers, she could be affronted directly and in person by these guys. A melancholy set of alternatives. But then, life was full of these sorry choices. For instance right now, her choice was between a corset worn with a wraparound nylon skirt and pink satin hot pants with a bra. The corset was sexy but it all came off at once, so you had to drag out the bottom half to make the act last. The bra was more fun to work with but the matching hot pants were ugly. She chose the first, and her mood improved slightly.

She picked up the backless, boned corset. Bending forward to fit her breasts into the cups she caught a glimpse of herself in the faint silver of the mirror. A dancer who didn't like looking in mirrors wasn't worth her toe plasters. She liked it still, and could still feel the ticklish fun of dressing up, of putting on satins and sequins and feathers, and watching it all turn her into one of those animals advertised on the sign outside, "Exotic Dancers."

Shoes were last. She hesitated. She reached for the heavy black character dancing shoes with the Cuban heels, from Agnello and Davide on Oxford Street in London. They were meant to go with the costume she wore, but they killed her feet. She could wear her soft silver slippers meant for the little girl number if she felt like it. Or the sling-backs meant for the evening dress number, or even the antique ankle boots. She could forgo shoe conventions and no one would know. There was no teacher out in the audience, no critic lurking in the doorway to say she wasn't maintaining her standards. Only she would notice the cheat. But no. She picked up the painful black ones and buckled them on.

She was dressed. It was time to go out. She pulled the black Chinese kimono with the painted dragon on the back that she used as a cover-up off the nail in the door.

She had never got used to it, not in ten years. She would never get used to it. Slipping out the door of the storage room clutching a robe around herself, ignoring the arched eyebrow of the guy entering the men's john next door. She crossed the hall and opened the door to the low-ceilinged bar room. Acrid smoke hit her nostrils. Then came the smell of beer, that ageless yeasty odour. And after that, the voices, voices like a gang of burglars bursting into her thoughts.

"So I tole the bastards, I said. . . ."

"Where's the can in this joint?"

" 'Scuse lady, move your ass." By the time she reached the music booth, Joan felt submerged in another element, a humid cloth of smell and voice and flesh. And then the eyes hit her. Wary eyes, afraid to be caught, insulting eyes, some of them even friendly eyes, but curious, every set of them. As she put her head into the booth to find the tape, the eyes of the bar attacked, like darts into the paramoecium.

But paramoecium had become mammal by then. This little smattering of life had on her glitter and her heels; she had armed herself further; she was complex. There was no way past the defences. She would entice them, but it would be for her own purposes. They were her victims.

Inside her spotlight, her plastic bubble, she could control everything, but the bubble was transparent. The eyes remained. And Joan said to herself, as she had said to herself yesterday and the day before, that she'd been around here too long.

* * *

UNDER THE LOW ceiling, square tables, mostly of men. Men all at angles, leaning back in their chairs, or bent over fingering their beer bottles. They crowded one side of the tables, facing the stage; a mournful chorus before the crumbling Greek temples on the walls. They were decent, ordinary people. God knows what they were doing there. And where was Herbie?

"The lady wants to dance again." One man began to push his palms together, like a baby. "Off, off, take it off."

"Hey come on outa there." An arm went around Joan from behind, the fingers trying to get a grip on her flesh through the tight satin, and slipping.

"Whassa matter, can't you talk?"

There was Herbie, edging his way through the tables, symbol of control, stage-manager, bouncer, money-taker.

"Ready?"

She nodded, pointed to the tape she wanted, held up three fingers for three minutes, and cut back across the floor and out the door.

On the other side, in the hallway, she put her hand on the doorknob and swung her leg to warm up. She caught her right heel in her palm and lifted it high over her head, straightening her knee beside her ear. Arm stretched overhead, she jerked the leg once, twice, three times. She turned around, switching hands on the doorknob, and pulled the other one. The left leg had never gone quite as high: as it unfolded over her head there was a little ping in the hamstring, and pain. Still it went higher than almost anyone else's leg ever did. She looked at the high instep, then let her eye roll down the shin, the inside of the thigh. The right was stronger but the left was prettier. Long, lovely leg, my favourite, she thought.

Her music started. The first set was the romantic one: Roy Orbison singing "Only the Lonely." She took off her dragon coverup, waited eight bars, checked her hairpins, opened the door, and entered the room with her head high.

The guys had barely left room for her to get to the stage. She slid between tables and ran up the three steps: the stage was so rickety it shuddered under her feet and the decorative velvet ropes around its edges quivered. The tape seemed too slow; it must have developed a slur. Machines have personalities; they learned to thwart you just like accompanists did: both wanted to start slow and end fast when they played for a dancer. To compensate for the lag, she doubled up on her first set of *chaîné* turns. Whipping the edges of the pink skirt up and down, Joan made a circle on the little stage. She felt the eyes come again to roost on her, like a flock of waxwings on a berry tree in winter.

Three songs. Ten minutes dancing, a slow strip-tease, for fifteen dollars. Do that four times a night for sixty dollars, and five days a week makes you three hundred. No deductions, no tax. Sounds good until you do it, until you have to face the faces out there. Lately she'd been going into a cold trance while she danced, repeating to herself that it would only be ten minutes before she could skip out the door wearing next to nothing, dragging her marabou and bits of satin, leaving behind the leers, the smart-ass remarks, even the applause, with relief. She stopped centre stage and began to do fan kicks.

Right leg, left leg, circling in front of her nose and dropping behind on the off beat. Up and up and up, sixteen times. And then a sideways glide, twitching her hips, letting her hands make S's over her shoulders, down her breasts and stomach. She noticed that Alex and his radio friend were gone. Good. It was easier with strangers. Looking behind her, she could see the image she left, fabric whirling in the shape of her skin. The flesh-eating birds were moving closer in: she could not be still.

At the break in the music she went to the corner of the stage, turned her back and loosened the tie of her skirt. One had to be careful to avoid the comedy of a stuck fastener. The second song was a little faster, the Beatles'

"In an Octopus' Garden." If Herbie was in the mood, a blue light would start to weave around the stage. He was in the mood. She began to dance, unwinding her skirt and pulling it up like a cape around her shoulders. She circled her neck with it, and her bust, and then let it slither to the ground. Quickly she unhooked the corset and whirled out of it too, her bare breasts slipping forward, into the spotlights. She was down to her bikini and garter belt.

It was time to take off the stockings, but she didn't feel like it. She delayed the moment when she would go over to that stool in the back corner of the stage, unbuckle her shoes and snap the garters, then peel down the dark silk. Stockings could be fun if she found something alive behind those red eyes. Some audiences were conducive; this one gave her a bad feeling. She finished the song without taking off anything more.

It was the second break in the music. Joan turned her back and eyed herself in the mirror on the back wall of the stage. She had to get her nerve up for the risk, for the unknown reaction. What would they have for her tonight? Cheers, hoots of derision, thumping on tables? Sometimes they had nothing. That was the worst, when you dropped your pants and there was no response.

"C'mon, what'cha waitin' for?"

The last song was the raunchiest; usually Joan did a floor show. Leaving her back to the audience, she stuck her heels wide apart, bent forward, and shimmied. She was showing them legs split like the points of a compass, fringe moving over the moon of her cheeks, the narrow seam of her G-string. For a long time there had been fun in mooning the world, fun flaunting what she had, in being lusted after. That was the reason the girls she'd trained with had called her a real commercial lady, a walloper. Now it wasn't fun, and she hated faking.

Suddenly she turned and took a run to the front of the stage, careful to keep out of grabbing range of the front tables. She slid down into a split. As she did, a man got up for a better view. Usually, Joan felt safest on the floor. The flat surface was like a partner. She pressed her weight into it, stretched, rolled, and curled her legs.

"C'mon, let's have it!"

"Show us what you got!"

But today, she couldn't relax: something was wrong. Herbie had put the tables too close; the space didn't feel right. Looking up, she could see the hovering figure of a man. He got into her light. It happened sometimes, men got up to touch the dancer. To grab the dancer.

It had happened to Joan before and she knew what she was supposed to do. The dancer is meant to be a good sport according to the rules of the strip joints. But Joan's rules were not those rules. Hers were the rules of a childhood spent in the ballet studio, of the line of cygnets, of the impenetrable unison of the corps. She was not to be touched, not to be interfered with; she was apart, an entertainer. And she was not in the mood for games.

The drunk wavered toward the stairs and put his hand on the ropes. He was coming up on stage, and that was making Joan very angry. His mouth was wet and crooked.

"C'mon baby, let's see your pussy," he said.

Joan swung her hips around and scrambled to her feet. She strutted away from him around in a circle to the back of the stage, and kept on dancing. Then she realized she'd made a mistake: she was trapped between the drunk and the mirror. She had to move forward and there he was, jumping in front of her, throwing open his arms. She wanted to push him but she had to keep on dancing.

"Hey, won'cha come and sit on my face?"

That did it. Joan bared her teeth in a wide smile, stepped into a half-turn, wound up with her trusty right and kicked him squarely in the chin.

His head snapped to the ceiling. He stood absolutely still, as if he'd been called to attention by God. Joan kept the grin and did more kicks around in a circle, the gap of white thigh between ruffle and stocking-top slashing through the blue light. She had kicked him viciously. She was shocked. Think back, she told herself. Run it by slowly.

The man's chin was at a height of approximately five

feet. It is impossible to strike that height with a light foot. There is effort involved in raising a leg the first quarter arc of the distance from ground to ceiling. But then, as a foot rises to the ninety-degree point, it grows light, becoming its own propellant. From there on up, the foot flies like a rock on a string. She had jumped on both feet, and then let one foot fly. The heavy black shoe gained momentum as it rose. It was moving fast when it connected with the man's chin.

Joan danced on, her hands playing on her belly in a nervous effort to distract eyes from the man. Out of the corner of her eye she saw that he had not fallen over. He was holding his jaw with his hand. Blood was coming from the cracks at the side of his mouth. He staggered to the ropes. But this was not a boxing ring, it was barely even a theatre: the ropes were hanging on cardboard. He leaned on them and pitched over the side onto the floor.

Now the men were on their feet, shouting, rushing to him.

There was no way Joan was taking anything else off. Still wearing her bikini and garter belt at the end of a show? Herbie would freak. Maybe they'd get her under the Unfair Business Practices—the stripper who doesn't. Just at the right moment, the tape began to speed. The singing voice got higher and mechanical. *"Voulez-vous couchez avec moi, ce soir?"* sang Minnie Mouse. Joan's final turns were so fast her hair went round like a tail and got in her mouth. She didn't fancy being on the floor when the music ended: instead of the usual splits she finished with a fast bow. On the last chord, she snatched her skirt and corset from the floor and darted down the steps, between the tables, pulling the door fast behind her. She was out.

JOAN PRESSED HER back against the door, hands behind her holding the knob. Her breath was coming in ragged puffs, but she still had enough air in her to run. Surely they wouldn't follow her. She listened: it was too quiet behind her in that room. The men must be ministering to their wounded friend. She crumpled her skirt up against her chest and sprinted to the dressing-room.

The sweat was cool under her arms, in the archways beneath those wide, proud shoulders. Beads were cooling too in the valley between her breasts, small breasts without fat, conical breasts propped up on muscle. She was glad she kicked the man. He got in her way and insulted her; he wasn't going to get away with it.

At times like this, all the indignities of her job swept over her. There had been a sympathetic man once, manager of a Legion hall somewhere. "Look," he had said, "I can see you're unhappy." Unhappy? He'd just broken a two-week contract because, he said, her breasts were too small. He thought she was hurt because he didn't find her sexy. It would never have occurred to him that she simply needed the money. "Look," he had gone on, an expression of stupid concern on his face, "you probably hate men." His face had furrowed at the thought of this unnatural attitude. "And I can see why. You'd be the type of woman that a man might treat bad, you know, because you're not very, you know. . . ." His hands had carved a voluptuous curve in the air. Very . . . you know.

Every stripper had to suffer comparison with the perfect you-know. She was supposed to acknowledge this fantasy of perfection that she was not; it was part of the exchange between stripper and audience. You showed your poor excuse for a body and instead of adoring you, they let you know how far off the mark you were. "No tits!" "Fat ass!" "She's a dog, a turkey." Joan had learned to pay it back with mockery when she saw them aroused in spite of themselves. Sometimes the men felt sorry for her, a further humiliation. "I don't mind a flat-chested woman myself," the Legion man had said. "I could be nice to you. I'm a married man, but I do have affairs." And sometimes they were hostile in a straightforward manner; they intended to do her harm. Like tonight.

Joan laughed, dizzily. So many propositions, so many insults. She'd let it get to her. She was definitely showing signs of wear. She took off her shoes, leaned back on the chair and stuck her feet up the wall, letting the blood run back to her head. And then she began to shake.

She clenched her teeth. She held her stomach, as it began to ache. Dimly knowing that one of her attacks was starting, and so it would end, Joan brought her legs down and carefully took off the precious stockings. Then she walked through the closet and opened a plywood door to the makeshift shower. Thanks to Herbie's obsession with cleanliness, the girls had their own wash-room. She turned on the hot water. Then she took five steps back and fell onto the chair again. Curling her legs up in a ball, her breasts pressed against her knees, Joan began to rock.

The voice that came out of her at those times was high. It was as if she were a child lying in bed at night, afraid of the dark, calling for her mother on the other side of the wall, but not calling loudly enough for her mother to hear. She hadn't wanted her mother then; she didn't want anyone now. Mothers were a drag, and a lover was never there when you needed him. She rocked more. The panic was coming. She was alone; no one could help her; she couldn't carry on.

It was one of those times when the great bubble over Toronto burst, when all the trapezes snapped, and her aerial act collapsed. She was an aerial act because her life had no floor, and no back-up. It was arduous and full of danger, and if she stopped one day and asked for a reason to go on, the answer would be that there was no reason.

Simple obligations—to undress, to face the man with the cut mouth, to get herself home to bed—were now impossible. Why should she go home anyway, when there would be no dinner in the oven, no one waiting for her, no love letters under the doormat? Once, Joan had disdained such comforts. She had made her life float, so she was not tied down to the world the way other people were. Most of the time she felt she had it the best way. And then there were times like this.

Minutes passed. Curled in her ball, Joan didn't make a sound. She was suspended, waiting for the fall.

Then as the wire was folding under her, she began to

fight for control. She gave herself small reassurances. She always finished a show, even though this time she hadn't managed to get her clothes off. She always had money somehow or other. She had friends, a dog. But those attachments were feeble to the trapeze artist in free fall. She plunged past it all, into the brilliance of pure fear. (It was delicious, exhilarating. A long ride going who knew where.) Pure pain was the same brilliant flash. It was only the small doses of pain and fear, a twisted ankle, a hurled knife, that were unbearable.

It began to recede. Now Joan sat up with her eyes open. She knew she could dull it further by describing it. What could she call this feeling? Emptiness? Perhaps just fatigue. She slowed her breathing and relaxed the muscles around her heart. Her hand flattened on the seat beside her. She put her feet down slowly and heavily, like someone walking in a net. Testing. Testing. A warm body would have been nice, she would have embraced another body and drawn it to her, feeling the heat of it, but there was no one.

The cooling steam from the shower, still pounding in the bathroom, crept over her shoulder like the breath from some huge being. She had to get these clothes off and get into that water. She would promise herself not to worry about anything until she had eaten.

The shower was running boiling hot and the bathroom was in thick fog. Naked, Joan could just see the deep pleat in the side of her thigh, and the two tight valleys running down from her breasts to her waist and below, fading into the small mound of belly that was always there, no matter how much weight she lost. She was in good shape. For thirty, she added these days, crossing her fingers. She put a shower cap on her long hair, gunpowder brown, someone called it once: the swatch of it lay in a heavy S in the clear plastic at the nape of her neck.

Feeling her way toward the taps, she turned the shower to lukewarm and stepped in, backwards, as she always did, protecting her sensitive parts. She let the water drum on her shoulder blades and began to plan what she would eat. Often she had an omelette late at night. You hit the high spots occasionally when you worked the clubs, eating caviar from big dishes on the table, but most often you landed in greasy little roadside joints where the only thing you could trust was the bacon and eggs. She had a lot of bacon and eggs. Joan saw her body as a machine for turning foodstuffs into Joan Sincere, therefore she ate fresh greens, tomatoes and liver for stress, almost no sugar and lean meats. She took vitamins B and E, kelp and calcium pills. She hated junk food. And yet. Tonight the meal which would most console her was a cheeseburger and chips.

Cheeseburger and chips! The thrill of the forbidden from childhood, when a potato was judged to be such a low animal that it was not allowed in the house, and Joan was soberly asked to consider all that went into a meat grinder before she bit into a meat patty. Back home, sin had been going to the Waffle Shop after ballet class for chips and gravy with a cherry Coke. Wonderful thought. Too bad she couldn't share the sin with someone tonight. Alex and his friend, that paramoecium man, but they had gone. Or Arlene, for old times' sake, if she wasn't tucked up across town with her useless husband and his wretched kids.

Joan soaped herself all over. The anxiety attack seemed to have passed. She wouldn't have another for ten days or so. In the mean time, she'd find life agreeable at the very least, and maybe even good. She'd almost forgotten what the attack was all about. She sudsed her pubic hair energetically. She was always washing. The girls were all always washing. If it wasn't their bodies or their hair it was their costumes. You can only do so much washing and ironing before glimpsing the absurdity of life. They glimpsed, and winked. All the perfumes of Arabia, Arlene used to say, standing at the sink in their London flat, shall not sweeten these smells.

Soap bubbles filled the bottom of the shower stall. Joan turned off the water. Silence, and steam: she emerged from the cloud, stepping over the metal sill and searching with her foot for the mat. There. She felt for her towel on the rack. There. She wrapped herself in it and thought how, more than anything, she wanted to sleep. She looked in the mirror, rubbing the steam off with her hand and then standing on tiptoe and leaning in so she could see herself almost full length.

Her legs, as she looked down at them, were straight pillars, the colour of dust. She couldn't remember now if she'd ever been really white. As a child, had she not been olive, a greenish pigment that stayed, although her parents complained she didn't play outside enough? There were white triangles around her pubic hair and breasts, while her stomach showed the remnant of last summer's tan. Her face was pale as soap. It was white because she wanted it white, even as her hair darkened from blonde to this metal shade. She had begun at ten or so to put on heavy make-up for fun, and then to remove it with cream, leaving the cream on to block the sun. It was a face that had been erased every day. She wanted nothing to be written there.

She walked through to the dressing-room. There was a knock on the door.

"What is it?" Clutching the towel around her.

Louder knock.

"Who's there?"

"Can you come out?" It was a man's voice, unfamiliar.

"One minute please." Joan dropped the towel and spun around to reach her socks, her underwear, her sweater, and her jeans. She pulled her fun fur off the nail on the wall and pushed her feet into high-heeled clogs. Her eye make-up was streaking down her face. She dipped her finger in her coconut vitamin E cream and rubbed under her eyes, gaping into the mirror. "Who's there?"

The door rattled alarmingly. "Ya bust my jaw, ya know."

It was him. Joan stuffed her costumes into her bag, getting ready to make a break for it. She opened the door a crack.

The wide, leaning drunk stood there. His eyes were

red, his shirt hanging out of his pants. There was dried blood on his chin. He seemed to have a Hungarian accent, but perhaps this was because he had no front teeth.

"It was an accident. You're lucky you didn't get hurt. Getting up there on the stage like that. You can't expect...."

"You kicked me on purpose."

"Oh, don't be ridiculous." Joan couldn't get past him, so she began to shut the door. The man put his shoulder to it, but she had strong arms; she was squeezing him out.

Then she saw the cop. He was standing a little way back in his blue, boxy uniform, with his cardboard-stiff hat pushed back. His face looked pudgy and recently shaven; his expression was sheepish. His hand rested on his belt about three inches away from his holster.

"You broke my bridge," the man was shouting. "I paid a thousand bucks for it." He shouldered the door. The hinges began to splinter.

"Oh, get stuffed!" Joan wanted to fight but she was watching the cop. His hand left the belt and reached for her shoulder.

"C'mon, lady. I'm going to take you down to the station and ask you a few questions."

"Get your hand off me."

"You going to come quietly?"

"For what? I haven't done any—" The hand came back, rougher this time, to her shoulder.

"Let go," she said. "I'm coming."

They passed back through the bar: the injured party, swaggering; Joan, bag in hand, clogs slapping against her heels, her hair tucked into the collar of her fur coat; and the cop. A man leaned from his table to touch Joan's leg. "Hey, brute, take me home with you!" Another man winked at her, his cheek resting in his palm, laughing up his sleeve.

As she went out the door she saw Gina and Candy sitting behind the bar. Herbie stood beside them, next to the telephone. The girls waved. Herbie lifted his hands and shook them by his ears. It came to her that this was all his doing.

"My nice clean club," he shouted. "How could you do this to me?"

She kicked a table leg. "This is a dump," she screamed, "a dump!"

They were out the door then and into the street, down the side-walk and into the waiting squad car with its red light on top. If she did say so herself, it was a superb exit.

CHAPTER TWO

The trouble with David's friends was that they all thought they were so smart.

David was sitting at a table in a downstairs tavern on Yonge Street. It was smoky and faintly sinister, with gloomy murals of Greek ruins on the walls, but it was supposed to have the best-looking strippers in town. David wouldn't have known or cared if that were true. The Coliseum had become the bar of choice of the CBC radio people, and it was inevitable that he should go there once, at least.

It wasn't all bad. Already he'd had a fifteen-minute conversation with a stripper named Joan Sincere. He'd never met a stripper before. And she had done something to David that he'd thought only poetry and cameras could do: she'd made him see his element new, in sharp relief, as if for the first time.

Across from David was Charlie, as close a buddy as anyone in the corporation: they drank together and watched ball games, and occasionally they had real conversations. Tonight, however, his mood was supercilious. Next to David was a story producer named Ellen who kept leaning over him and asking him to take her dancing. He'd known her for years. Why had she all of a sudden turned on the juice? It depressed him. Spotted around in the next few tables were Alex, a lawyer whom he'd known for years, a couple of television reporters, and a cameraman named Martin. Martin had lost his job.

"So I said to him, you know I'm getting the feeling this is personal. And he said we've got to look after our own. So I could see the feeling was I'd quit and no one who'd walked out of CBC Montreal was going to get back in here. . . ."

His complaint was drowned for a minute as Ellen excused herself. "I've got to go again. I know I've been up and down all night. Right back."

"So I pulled out my Bic, poured oil on the bridge, and lit it." Martin leaned back in satisfaction. It was an old story: he'd left the corporation for good several times already.

"Who's she phoning?" Alex leaned over the table to hiss in his ear. "Aren't you going to carry her off tonight? You could, you know, she's making it very plain."

"She's calling her husband."

"Husband? I thought Gord Riley was the great love of her life." Alex was obsessed with minor celebrities; he tried hard to keep up on media gossip.

"That's a distinction that's getting increasingly hard to maintain," said Charlie. The guys all laughed. Ellen was a metallic blonde and definitely used goods. However, none of them were above giving her a whirl. The laughter acknowledged this fraternity of fallibility. Then the conversation broke up into pockets again, several of them talking at once, no one really listening. There was an election in the city. One of the hopeful politicians had come to Martin and asked him for advice on how to be interviewed on television. Martin had set up a chair and pointed a camera at him and put him through his paces in the living-room.

"Mostly I had to keep telling him to sit still. That's the main thing. Just don't move around."

"These gays have got the ward sewn up, they've got the politicians wound around their little fingers. You know there's three hundred thousand of them in the city now? It's not that anyone cares, but when they take over the ward, when we're subjected to gay values—" said Charlie.

"What's an example of a gay value? You're such a gay-basher," David said, "you trying to prove you've got latent tendencies?"

"Don't get me started."

"You should go home to your wife."

"Hey, look at this." Martin had a pamphlet printed up by one of the candidates. He began to read from it. "I was born, schooled, and married in this ward and have practised dentistry here for twelve years. This is where my roots are. . . ."

"This is where my root canals are, he means."

The laughter broke out again, loudly, just as Ellen appeared and wedged her way through the chairs to nestle in next to David again.

"He's not home," she murmured in his ear.

They all had opinions, and they all talked about who was screwing whom. David was sick of opinions and sick of gossip, so that pretty well wrapped things up with this gang. They had to have opinions—Charlie, for instance, was hired for his opinions and it took some effort to keep drumming them up. Opinions were kept up with a maximum of drinking and a minimum of thinking. Opinions and office affairs. David disapproved of both. He did not voice many opinions. Whenever he had one, he was simultaneously willing to entertain the idea that his opinion was ridiculous. When people came on David's radio show and stated firm beliefs, he danced around them, making clever transitions and conditionals, saying, "Do I understand you to mean . . ." and "It follows from your point that. . . ." That's what *he* was hired for.

"I should probably get going," he said to no one in particular. Ellen leaned closer to his arm. He didn't want to be there. He'd had a nice chat with the stripper and that was enough. Before he met her all he knew about strippers was that they didn't make good radio. Sure, he might go down to a basement bar and have a hamburger served by some chick without her top on, but that wasn't a stripper. Real strippers were a little different; they weren't oversexed tarts. They were, according to this woman Joan, entrepreneurial females with artistic leanings. Some of them hated taking their clothes off, and did it more because they didn't think they were sexy than because they did. Some of them were straightforward exhibitionists. Joan, he figured while watching her talking, was somewhere in between.

"So is she the whore with the heart of gold then?" Charlie could tell David wasn't all there tonight. He ribbed him because he was jealous, probably; she was a good-looking woman.

"You're so out of date, Charlie. You've lived in the suburbs too long. Strippers aren't whores. Most of them are fine-arts students from York University trying to make their tuition fees."

"And most whores are housewives from Don Mills."

"Whose husbands work at the CBC and never come home at night."

"Well, we've got to keep pace with inflation, don't we? Jennie keeps telling me she wants to get out of the house." Jennie was Charlie's wife. Charlie never brought her around. She would have killed too many of his good lines.

"Anyway that's not it at all. She's just a regular woman. Alex has known her for years. She's a dancer. She used to be with the Royal Ballet in London." That was a bit of a lie but David didn't care. Charlie wouldn't know Margot Fonteyn from a go-go girl.

"Don't tell me you believed that? You're going soft."

"Don't panic. It's no big deal." The last thing David wanted was for his friends to suspect anything was a big deal.

"O.K. O.K. So I wonder if she's a good lay."

Again David laughed lightly and waved a hand, implying by the gesture that "a good lay" was the farthest thing from his mind. He didn't want to talk about Joan and he didn't want to talk about sex. Sex in these circles was the kind summed up by eye rolling, or so awful that you wanted to forget about it. Or it was with your wife. At last,

Charlie read the signs and shut up. He took out his tobacco to roll a cigarette.

Meeting the stripper had reminded David of something, and that was the distinction between real people and media people. Media people didn't really do anything; they just talked about what everyone else did. Whenever you needed a testimonial, for instance, on hair tonic or sex therapy, a media person was suspect: you had to get a housewife or a ball player; a real person. Joan was real. She was out there living by her wits, she was beautiful, she might even be talented for all he knew, and she did the one thing that the rest of them just pretended to do—put herself on the line to make a dollar.

Ellen clung to David's arm. She had been still and intent during the conversation about Joan, but it had not discouraged her. David sighed. He pried himself loose and sat back so he could have a look at her. In profile, she looked like a hawk. She always wore something shiny over her breasts, so that they shimmered like water. She wasn't a tramp, but she'd been around; her body looked tight and athletic, knowledgeable. There would be a certain cachet in having an affair with Ellen. Men didn't mind following one another there.

Perhaps he should take up her offer. If he laid Ellen it would show he made the grade with these people even when he didn't try. But he did not want to get involved with Ellen. He was free but he was not free.

He had never been in this conundrum before, this little corral without fences, made of his own surprising compunctions. What was happening to him? His pattern with women had established itself twelve, perhaps fifteen years earlier and had not changed. He found one, wanted to possess her, and pursued her. He fascinated her without committing himself and before long *his* desire to possess her became *her* desire to possess *him* and then he could escape. David knew he was doing this; he had even become angry with himself about it. He wasn't a sexist. He liked women. He even liked ugly women: he'd had great talks with some and then was dismayed when they became romantic. Neither had he come this far in life without falling wildly in love several times; he was not a misfit, but still. Lately there'd been nothing. He wasn't letting himself get into anything.

Ellen and Charlie were insulting one another.

"O.K., portly, I'll admit to that. But isn't portly sexy?"

"Not with cigarette and beer smell, too."

It was getting late. David's mind wandered within its wandering. David thought about sex, not the act of, but the nature of. He was conscious that his body was tense, hard, and full up with itself. There was no space inside it, no relaxation. This was very different from the bodies of women. The stripper's, or even Ellen's for that matter. Sitting beside the stripper he had been conscious of her body. She was rounded, but light; she was like a wishbone, like a harp, a sea shell. Her body seemed contented, self-sustaining. It had been built around a centre, and that centre was a space. It seemed to him, anyway. Women would probably hit him if they heard what he was thinking. He knew guys who thought of women simply as a hole to fill. That wasn't what he meant, at all. He just thought it must be very different to know that your body was not chock-full at any moment, that there was space for the organs to drift a little. He jerked himself forward. He had just realized that his stripper was getting ready to go on. He had to get out of there.

"Look Ellen, I'm really beat. An' I've gotta work in the morning. I'm going to get out of here." He hated the look of insult on her face, so he leaned over and kissed her on the lips lightly. Then he patted her arm. "We'll do this again." He put his hand flat on the table and turned a big open grin at the group. "A great night folks, but I'm on my way."

AT HOME, DAVID turned on the light in the bathroom and greeted his low-down face. "You couldn't just let Ellen know you weren't interested, could you? You had to give her a crumb so she'd keep making you feel good." And, he might have added, you were too chicken to stay and watch the stripper.

David had a mole under his left eye, half-way down the cheek. It was a raised, light-coloured mole, and with the cast of his long eyelashes on thin cheeks, it made him look delicate. He had the face of a mime. If you painted it white and put a Ping-Pong ball on his nose he would look just like Bip. But the delicacy ended at his neck. He had sharp bones, heavily muscled, and big hands and feet. As well, he had observed lately the growth of more body hair. Since his late teens, he'd had a large sandy mat on his chest, like the hair on his head with a bit more red in it. Now that hair had gone over his shoulders and across his back from one collar-bone to the other and had even begun to grow over the small ridges of his hip-bones. Very macho. All he got for that was a lot of gay men smiling at him in bars.

He had begun, three days before, to grow a beard. He liked the shade on the lower part of his face. He liked not having to shave, and he liked looking disreputable.

He leaned down to brush his teeth.

In bed, David did not sleep. He had thought he was very tired, but as soon as he put down the book he was trying to read, a biology text entitled *Life of Invertebrates*, his eyes stuck open and his mind began to rattle off bits of the day's conversation. He turned on the light again and looked for another book.

On his bedside table were *The Hite Report on Female Sexuality; The Canadian Establishment*, parts I and II; *A Distant Mirror: The Calamitous Fourteenth Century; An Anthology of Twentieth Century Poets;* and Burke's *Language as Symbolic Action*. Usually one of them could be counted on to put him to sleep.

David loved facts, and loved sinking his tired brain into their numbing multitudes. By day, information was his business; at night it became his soporific. He picked up *The Hite Report*. Female orgasms: at first he'd been disinclined to believe that more could be created by a political movement called feminism, but now he was more or less convinced. It was Ellen's view that men were becoming intimidated by women's knowledge of their own sexuality. "I've spent my whole life fighting off men," she had said that night, throwing back her head and hooting. "But now, if I want one, I have to wrestle him to the ground."

David realized, of course, that he was implicated. She had been sitting with her chair half drawn up to the table and the spotlight from the ceiling had come down on one side of her face. He saw the face in his mind and it turned from Ellen's face to the stripper's. Joan. She was a beautiful, flawed creature. Beautiful with her high, domed head, her Egyptian profile and full lips. Flawed because there was a twist to her mouth, to the bottom half of her face. She looked like someone had taken a swipe at her once, when she was young. She looked as if she were holding her jaw stiff because otherwise her chin would tremble. Even when she laughed, the crooked look didn't go away: one side of her lip pulled back a little higher than the other. He read on.

"Only twenty percent of these women said they never required foreplay to achieve. . . . " It was not what he wanted to read. He wanted romance. He put away *The Hite Report* and flipped through the poetry. Here, some Irish stuff, Seamus Heaney remembering his mother. "And here is love, sunk past its gleam in the meal bin. . . . " Wonderful.

It was now 12:55 by the clock beside his bed. The telephone sat on the table, in the reddish glow of the digital clock, easily within reach. It had push-button dialing for extra speed. It was red, he liked red. His hot line from the days of fevered womanizing. Joan had given him her phone number. It was written on a white paper coaster and sat on the bedside table. She said she wanted to see some paramoecia. "My etchings?" he'd said, laughing.

"No, really," she'd said.

"My fame then," he'd said. "That's what appeals to you." That's how dumb he was. He couldn't believe she was truly interested in what he'd been saying.

She had got up from the table suddenly and turned her back. She was wearing a silk kimono with a dragon on the back, over a pair of jeans. She had a lovely back, an expensive-looking back, perhaps because it was broad and very proud. He could not understand how she gave the impression of such high standing in the world. She couldn't have much money.

He had offended her. That line about the etchings. And the one about being famous. They weren't even his lines; they were borrowed from his friends. He didn't even know why he'd said them, but there she went. So why should he care? Was he going to take her out? Take her to bed? It seemed a bit of a juvenile fantasy, to contemplate undressing a stripper. Maybe they'd have a relationship. He imagined what his mother would have said. Then he laughed at himself, conjuring his mother to put the stripper in her place. He was not exactly a virgin himself. You can't return to go every time you meet someone exciting. So why not start where he was, where they both probably were, close to the end of innocence, with next to nothing to lose?

Joan Sincere. He'd assumed it was a stage name, but she said it wasn't. Perhaps this dancing was an extended adolescent rebellion. Convincing himself that he and she were all wrong made it easier to pick up the telephone. He would arrange to meet her after her show tomorrow. He did not want to be one of her public, but to have her alone, knowing that her body was a spark of lust for hundreds of men, knowing that she was a symbol. That appealed to the academic in him.

He picked up the paper coaster and then the telephone, and pressed the little tune that would reach her voice. There was no answer.

CHAPTER THREE

Joan rolled over in bed. It was morning. She peered at the clock. Late morning; in forty-five minutes it would be noon. Joan had been an early bird as a child. Working nights and sleeping late had perverted her natural wont to get moving when the day was fresh, and it still bothered her. By noon she might have come down with the flu or pulled a muscle, but in the morning, especially if the sun was out, she felt she could do anything. If she didn't get up soon, she'd have missed her best time.

Today there was a sharp wind rattling the bare grey branches of the chestnut tree outside her window. She knew that tree well: living on the second floor made her feel that it was her closest neighbour. There were swellings on the branches that had to be buds. Could have fooled me, tree, I thought you were dead. Rudy put his paws on the edge of the bed and pushed his nose in her face. His tail had the rest of the body in thrall, intense wagging making even the grey curls over his nose tremble.

"How's the dog?" She had been too depressed last night even to walk him. "You want out, don't you?"

Joan swung her legs down from the bed. It was a high bed, with a tall curved wooden headboard and foot, and it reminded her of a boat. She'd bought it for thirty-five dollars from the Crippled Civilians when she'd first come to Toronto. The dog too was second-hand: she'd found him in a pen at the Humane Society and named him after Nureyev. He danced impatiently in the hall, his toe-nails skittering on the hardwood.

"O.K., O.K." She pulled on a faded chenille housecoat and tied it in front of her as they raced down the steps to the street door. As Joan opened it, Rudy shot out from under her feet, his eye on a black dot across the road. The squirrels were coming out of hibernation. This one was still sleepy: Rudy had caught it completely off guard. He rushed up behind it as the squirrel was standing on its hind legs, midway between two trees, coming so close he had to skid sideways to avoid bumping into it. Then he leapt back and barked: he didn't want to catch that squirrel, only to chase it. Belatedly the squirrel flew to a tree trunk, a sudden curved dart through the air. Rudy took one last leap after it, and then panted around the trunk, tongue hanging out, again the dripping-jawed pursuer.

Upstairs, Joan put the telephone jack back in the wall. She'd taken it out when she came in last night. Something had told her it was going to be one of those nights. When she'd first arrived here the crank calls had frightened her. The breathers, and the ones who asked if they could come over and perform indecent acts, even the seemingly innocent wrong numbers, they all frightened her. People didn't do that in England, the phones were too expensive. She'd got the dog to make her feel safe and only realized later that *she* would have to look after *him*, and that the danger had been mostly in her mind.

She put on a record of Strauss waltzes to get her moving. She'd been dancing in her sleep, and her muscles were tense. Now that all the containment, the binding of hair, the bandaging of feet, was excised from her life she sought it in sleep. Sometimes it was simply an exercise, a *rond de jambe en l'air,* for instance. She would see only the foot from the bent knee making a perfect half circle to flick the standing calf. Just that geometry rendered. She used to think that if she could master the technique, she could live her life perfectly.

THE FIRST DAY at ballet class her mother had held her hand. She had been five years old; she had straight legs in white woollen leggings, and almost white hair sitting on the velvet collar of her coat. She considered herself a miniature, fully made person. Mother in her felt hat, Joan

in the buttoned-up coat with matching skirt, the two of
them had gone to an old grey building downtown, behind
the bus depot.

To get to the door where the ballet school was, you had
to cross a lane where the buses came out. There was a red
electric sign. DANCER, BUSES LEAVING. She had thought it
was put there especially for little girls. Only when she
learned to read properly, maybe two years later, did Joan
realize that the letter G was broken; it wasn't DANCER but
DANGER.

But the first day. Two hands, gloved hands, no doubt,
her own and her mother's, four feet, one clicking sharp
long pair, one padding small pair. Mother had a girl who
wanted to dance. Mother had wanted to dance herself,
when she was a girl. She had gone around to the ladies
she knew, the forbidding ladies who marshalled the sym-
phony and the theatre guild, and asked them where she
should send her daughter for lessons. The recommenda-
tion was Miss Levy. That's why they were walking up to
the Bugle Building, where the studio was.

Inside the front door an elevator with a lattice of metal
strips stood open. Mother had handed her in to the old
man; the lattice clanked shut. It was frightening the
letting go of hands. Mother had always said Joan was very
independent. Perhaps Joan had insisted on going up alone.
Mother had never seen through a bluff.

After the class, she had shunned the elevator and
walked down the stairs. It was a very long, steep set of
stairs, with red linoleum. The door at the top of the stairs,
behind Joan as she descended, was the kind of glass you
couldn't see through, all rough and bubbly like ice that
had melted and frozen again. Her mother's hand had
reached from the bottom to take her back. She couldn't
remember what she had done behind that door, but it
must have been all right, because her mother's hand was
squeezing hers: it was warm. There was a wide lady, Miss
Levy, behind Joan at the turn of the stairs.

"She'll be fine. She's very quick."

"Did you hear that, Joan? You're a good girl."

". . . small for her age?"

"... thought she was only three or four ... very intelligent. But ..., good feet, the legs ... long neck ... spurt of growth one of these years."

It was her first taste of being a commodity, of being talked about in the third person while she listened. She loved it. She wanted to be good, for her mother. That took no effort, normally. She and Mother were like one person, and Mother was easy to please. But she also wanted to be good for Miss Levy, for all the adults who would discuss her.

In that long second-floor studio there was always a beam of sun. It fell along the hardwood floor, where the dancing was, showing up the scuff marks and the resin stains. At first Joan saw only the floor, and Miss Levy's lower body. Thick black skirt, rounded calves, and on the floor precise feet in new—always new—pink kid slippers. Without ribbons. The students had to wear black, with ribbons, but the teacher could do what she wanted.

The teacher's feet were plump pods of power. When they weren't hopping like beans, they stood still. Above the feet hung the clouds of her deep voice, a voice that filled the air as no voice had before, a voice with authority rolling in it. Later, Joan would lift her eyes to the small, rotund body, the waving arms, the short thick black hair that cupped her forehead and tucked behind Miss Levy's ears. She would see the whole of that compact, sausage body overbalancing on tiny feet. She would see the face etched against the light of the windows: black eyebrows set wide apart, moving separately and defiantly as she spoke, brown eyes in purple hollows, a pale mole with a hair in it on her chin. Miss Levy's face was black and white and shadows, like an image blown up by a projector. Her voice was simply God's.

"Ready, and!" The pianist would strike, sudden as a machine. The room would fill with notes, not music, just notes pounded out in a rhythm imperative enough for the vague, five-year-old bodies to understand.

"One, two, in front, behind. Arlene, stop, stop, STOP."

The pianist would lift her fingers from the keys mid-phrase; she seemed to draw the notes back into silence.

"Arlene, straighten your supporting knee. How many times have I. . . ." Arlene would jimmy her feet around. The others would freeze, the pianist's hands attending, bird-like, over the key-board.

"Ready, and!"

They'd begin again. Miss Levy would sigh, and her feet stuffed in their pink slippers would begin their march down the line of little girls. "You're so soft, so unformed. We'll have to work hard to make you into something," she'd say.

It was true: in this place Joan and the others were not completed articles. Over the years Miss Levy would take her stick and poke a buttock here, a thigh there, lift the underarm at the bar to show where the muscle had to grow and become firm, and where it must turn out, lift up or tuck under before their bodies could even classify as something to work with, before they were even clay. At the moment they were nothing. Dust, with a destiny.

So, there had been mother's gloved hand reaching up the staircase for her. Come out, get away while you can, get away from the dark lobby of the old building, away from the elevator rattling like the witch's cage of old bones. Run away with Mother along the hallway to the outside and the ordinary world.

She had grasped the hand, and had gone with her mother, and yet it seemed, as she revisited the day that she had dropped her mother's hand and run back upstairs, that she had disappeared behind the frosted door where hundreds of little girls had disappeared before her.

MUSIC FLOODED HER bare rooms. Joan went into the kitchen and picked up the campers' flint she'd been using to light her gas burners since her landlady had refused to repair the pilot light. She turned on the gas, flicked the flint to make a spark, and a circle of flame ruffled into existence. She reached for the kettle.

She loved the view from her kitchen window. Baldwin was a tiny street, two blocks long. To the left, a house sliced in half, its mirror twin knocked down. The surviving half hung beside a hole in the ground, its exposed wall showing beams and old plaster. Someone had been going to build there but had thought better of it.

On the corner across from the half-house was the Frenchman's house. It was old, red brick on the front and rippling Insulbrick on the side. There were three round windows on the third floor with green trim, like three drooping eyelids. It had a white veranda with spool trim where the Frenchman sat in a straight-backed chair and watched the neighbourhood. The wind had carried trash up against the fence, blocking the sidewalk. Loose mongrel dogs, and Rudy, burrowed in the piles.

Down the laneway beside the Frenchman's on weekday mornings there would be a little parade of Chinese children going off to school, each child under a black umbrella for rain, snow, or sun. If Joan stood up close to the window and looked down she could see next door where the old Chinese man who ran the milk store was stacking folded cardboard boxes outside his front window, neatly, neatly. Joan stretched her arms sideways and back. The shadow of the house fell across her window in the morning now that the sun was coming as much from the south as from the east. She could see herself reflected over the street.

It was that filthy time of year again. In April people in this city began to expect spring, especially those who'd read poems and nursery tales written in England. All through April the locals complained about the brisk winds, the sleet, the greyness, as if spring were unaccountably delayed, as if this had never happened before. But spring never came until May. It didn't pay to look ahead, Joan had found.

She turned back to the kitchen, found the coffee tin and put four spoonsful in the filter, and then realized that she had placed an empty kettle over a flame. Ritual tasks, things that she did every day, she could forget in a moment of blankness. Concentration had never been Joan's strong point: fortunate then that she had so few distractions in the kitchen. Just think if she had a husband and children and was frying eggs, grease spitting, the dog under her feet, slipping utensils under the barricade of hubby's newspaper. She would no doubt stab herself or someone else. She was an accident waiting to happen, her father used to say.

Suddenly she could hear barking. And a voice shouting. "Bad dog! Bad!"

She put the kettle down and ran for the stairs. Perhaps Rudy had killed a cat. She would have to deal with the wrath of neighbours. She opened the door and felt a rush of black fur past her knees. Peering into the sunlight, she could hear Rudy's panting in the dark stairwell behind her. She began to laugh.

"Think that's funny, do you?"

The voice was sour. It came from the old grey-haired woman pushing a pram on the opposite sidewalk.

"He's harmless enough. Just chasing squirrels."

"I've got a little boy in here. I wouldn't want to take him out of the buggy with a vicious dog like that loose."

"Oh heavens, Rudy wouldn't hurt a flea." He'd proven that: fleas feasted on him. Joan had a suspicion the old lady had nothing in the pram anyway. It was that sort of neighbourhood. She probably lived out of brown paper bags and slept in laundromats; she patrolled the surrounding six blocks regularly. She must have pinched the pram on a previous beat; however, the residents of these streets—elderly Chinese couples, art students and mysteriously idle middle-aged men—didn't put that sort of thing out for the garbage.

"There's a law against that, I should think," the old woman went on.

"What?"

"Dogs like that."

Now Joan saw that the bag lady had a stone in her hand. Joan had a moment of flashing rage, and then the rage gave way to pity. Rudy was growling beside her knee. Two frightened, dependent creatures, house pet and scavenger, with no one to chase but each other.

"Are you throwing stones at my dog?"

"He bit me."

"He doesn't bite."

"My leg, look."

From thirty feet Joan could see nothing but large rubber boots.

"What did you do to him?"

"He came up and sunk his teeth into my leg. I was just trying to get away." But the woman's voice was losing conviction. No harm was done.

"I'm sure he wouldn't bite you, unless you started it," said Joan with finality. She turned back indoors, shutting the door again. There sat Rudy wearing his look of endless willingness to please. He was an actor. Maybe he didn't deserve her defence. He'd never bitten anyone before, but then how many bag ladies did he know? Perhaps the old woman was telling the truth, perhaps her pet was the kind of beast who went around sinking his teeth into the legs of helpless old ladies. She looked at him searchingly. If he'd bitten the old lady, he chose wisely. The authorities weren't going to go after him.

Unlike his mistress.

"Eh, Rudy?"

Joan padded back upstairs. She resisted speaking to her dog in complete sentences. Complete sentences would have been a sign of madness. Asking him for agreement was merely companionable. Too bad she didn't have the dog's sixth sense for vulnerability. How was she to know that the drunk she kicked was the sort to trot out his lawyer and his dental work and get the cops to slap her not only with assault but with wilful damage to property?

"You and I are really cruising for a bruising, aren't we? Shopping for a surprise, aren't we?"

He rubbed his head on her knee. Rudy was her child, and she said of him what had been said of her over the years.

As Joan was pouring the coffee, the telephone rang. She

looked at it with distrust, decided not to answer it, and then couldn't bear the suspense. She picked it up and held her nose.

"Hello?"

"Joan Sincere?"

"No, it isn't."

"Joan, it's Herbie."

She let go of her nose. "Oh hi, sorry, I was expecting another call."

He didn't laugh. "How are you feeling, Joan?"

"Fine, thank you. Why, am I supposed to be sick? Maybe I should think again. I was feeling O.K. until you called."

"That was quite a little upset we had last night."

Joan waited. He had something up his sleeve. Quiet, persistent Herbie. Herbie who played the *père de famille* with the girls at the club. Herbie was a bit ruthless.

"We've never had the police in here before."

"Why'd you call them then?"

"Quite a scene, yup, uh-hum."

"What happened after?"

"The girls filled in for you. Did an extra show each. I was glad you went quietly, yup, uh-hum. Things went smoothly after that."

"Smoothly? Hell, Herbie, I got busted for assault."

Silence.

Joan felt tears coming to her eyes. Fat lot he cared.

"'Sa shame. Joan, listen. I'd just like to say this to you, because you're not just one of my girls, you're a friend. 'N I'm your friend. I like to think. Anyway, get yourself a lawyer. This guy is really angry. You know how it is, in front of everyone, to be embarrassed. I think his friends were laughing at him. You know."

"Oh sure, I know. I should feel sorry for him. Is that all you can say, Herbie?"

"I'm sorry, Joan. Yup, uh-hum."

"Herbie, you're a weasel." He probably didn't know what a weasel was. "You're a vicious rodent."

Silence proceeded from the telephone. Then he began

to bleat. "Is that all you can say to me, Joan? Have you no pity for me, your loyal employer, for whom you make these problems? *Joan*."

"What did I do to you? I'm in shock, Herbie."

His voice changed suddenly, went smooth and confidential. "I know you are, sweetie, and that's why I called. Take the night off, why don't you? It'll be good for you. I don't want more publicity, you know what I mean? Let's have it die down. Come back Saturday night, O.K.? And we'll call it at that, O.K.? You don't mind. Just remember whose side I'm on. Bye-bye."

He hung up. Whose side, sure. Damn and triple damn. She slammed down the receiver.

The phone rang again. She picked it up. "Hello?"

A husky whisper. "Hey baby, do you give blow jobs, too?"

She slammed down the receiver again and then took it off the hook. Why did all the sickies get her number? It was all coming back now. Last night, the shouting, the feeling that her trapeze had collapsed. She could feel her neck getting tense. She needed a pill.

Joan loved pills. She loved them so much she didn't let herself take pain-killers or tranquillizers because she didn't think she'd stop once she started. Instead, when in distress, she took vitamins. She could get a mellow high from three bone-meal tablets and a warm cup of milk and even feel that she was doing something good for herself. She went to the refrigerator and opened the door. Inside were two rows of jelly-brown bottles with white screw caps. They were full of red, white, and yellow lozenges. She reached for C. Potent B. Kelp. Iron. She gulped them down with water, two of each kind, sent them sailing down her throat like missiles to the interior. Then she poured herself a cup of coffee.

It was now noon. Sure enough, the day was ruined. She wandered down the hall to her living-room just as the waltzes ended. Landlady, bag lady, her life was ruled by these stingy old cows. Not to mention Herbie, who as den mother seemed to be an honorary old lady himself, bossy, possessive, and ultimately traitorous. Her ballet mistresses had been the same way, from Madam back to Miss Levy. She flipped the record over and as the waltz struck up again tucked herself into the corner of her couch, pulling her feet in after her.

The bag lady reminded her of Miss Levy, actually. There was something in the way the eyes flashed sideways in that sodden face, something about the vigour of those eyes buried in a thick pad of flesh. Miss Levy had been a bag lady of sorts, drinking too much, living off the easy talents of the young, circling them, chiding them, claiming to be protecting them. People always asked about one's mother and father and thought that when they knew, they had all the clues to one's personality. No one ever thought to ask about one's ballet teacher. The part of Joan that was made by Miss Levy was as hard as a toned muscle inside her, and safe from understanding, because now no one knew it was there.

JOAN HAD GONE by herself on the bus to ballet class after the first year. She had put her slippers in a purple bag with yellow cord; it was a bag that had once held her father's whisky. Two nights a week after school and on Saturday mornings she stood at the bus-stop. In the field behind her, children played baseball and in winter made pies in the snow. Joan was the smallest in her class and always had to be in the front of the line; she was not good at games. The other children pointed at her when she boarded the red and yellow bus.

"Joan's a goody-goody."

"Going to your belly lessons?"

She would put her ticket in the box and sit sideways, facing the driver with her back to the playing field. The bus made a loop through the neighbourhood. The houses were stucco and stained wood, flat-roofed, spreading. The driveways were wide enough for two cars. The next stop to Joan's had been the end of the line. There the bus waited for five, sometimes ten minutes. Joan sat still in her seat, thinking of nothing, emptying her mind clean of the spelling bee, the tick her dog had got at the lake, and her best friend's new bicycle. She was becoming the other Joan.

The other Joan liked the nine o'clock Saturday morning classes best of all. She wore her white tunic with the red belt, her black cotton tights and white socks, her hair tied in a bun and covered with a net. Ballet classes were mainly intimidation and grief, to which was added, as she became older, the pressing, painful necessity of forcing the body in ways it did not go. But she loved the classes. She loved the separate world that lay up the red linoleum stairs. That world had its own language, the mispronounced French for the names of steps—*plié, fondu, battement tendu, dégagé*. She stood with one hand on the *barre*, and then turned around, held on with the other hand, and did the second side. She rarely made a mistake. She was eager to submit to the clockwork of it, the pounding of the piano and the counterpoint on the floor made by the end of Miss Levy's cane.

"Ready and, one-two, one-two."

Ballet's world easily overtook the everyday. Its costumes, its movements were infinitely more interesting than tartan jumpers and knee socks for games of tag. She never missed a lesson. She never broke the code. "Yes, Miss Levy. No, Miss Levy." "Thank you, Miss Levy," when she was corrected. The curtsy after class, as if for the queen, she loved. She began to consider herself special, a stranger in the school yard. Miss Levy, who frowned and shouted and stamped her feet, was, nonetheless, the beloved bestower of all this magic. Joan's own mother was reduced to chauffeur, laundress, and seamstress.

"Ready and, one-two, one-two, now hold, one-two. . . ." To this day she counted things in fours and eights. Steps along the sidewalk to the red TTC sign, stairs across the pavement to the streetcar island, her own voice as metronome. Everything had to be measured, balanced, symmetrical. Even her body.

The Royal Academy of Dancing, whose syllabus Miss Levy followed, liked to measure a child's proportions before taking her into its examinations. At six, Joan had measured up as ideal. She consisted of four parts of equal length; top of head to shoulder, shoulder to hip, hip to knee, knee to heel. Four parts: if they were equal at the age of six, it was said that the child would grow up to have the classical proportions of a ballerina. Joan had been proud of her measurement; her glory was to be a child with four parts of equal length, a child who could remember the exercises and live by the rules.

Only once did she remember being late for ballet. It was on a Sunday. A few girls had been asked to come and try for a part in the Christmas show. At noon Joan had left her house with fresh tunic and tights, her slippers, character shoes, and extra pins in case her hair fell down. She sat for ten minutes on the bus at the end of the line first looking at her hands, and then at the wide lawns silvered with the first thin layer of snow. At twenty minutes to one she had arrived at the Bugle Building. The lights were on in the downstairs dressing-room. It was not the one Joan was used to; it was where the big girls dressed. Under the door Joan could see light in the studio, too, and voices. She could hear the piano. Joan tiptoed into the dressing-room and took off her clothes.

It was an honour to be in this room; it was an honour to be asked to come on a Sunday. None of her friends were here. Had she made a mistake? Dancers were in the studio already, but she thought she was early. Did she make a mistake about the time? She sat and waited. There was a wooden shingle on the wall with a cartoon of a fat man running. The caption read: "Ve get too soon old and too late schmart." She did not understand the sign, although the word "late" felt like a spitball aimed at her.

She looked at the ballet photographs, too, which hung on the wall. They were ancient shots of the stage at Covent Garden, full of matchstick-size women in white tutus. Joan always leapt immediately into every painted stage set, every black-and-white photograph of a famous ballerina sinking feathery to her knees. "You have glamorous dreams," one of the other girls had said to her once, disapproving. This had been a meaningless criticism to Joan. What were dreams for, if not for glamour?

It had to be at least one o'clock now, and no one else had come. Trembling, Joan had stood up. It was in a moment of silence between piano and voice, and the floor creaked under her, and Miss Levy's voice rose above the partition.

"Who's there?"

"It's Joan."

The door opened. Miss Levy's square body massed dark against the wall of windows at the far end of the studio. All the other girls were there, dancing already.

"You're late." Miss Levy's scowl was dreadful.

"I thought it was at one."

"I'm disappointed in you, Joan. I take my Sunday to come in and give you girls a chance to perform and you can't even get yourself here on time." She shook her head and turned away, leaving Joan in the doorway. "I thought you weren't coming. The best parts for the show have all been given out. You'll just have to sit on the side."

Joan had sat cross-legged under the *barre* and cried. She'd cried until she couldn't stop hiccupping. When Miss Levy couldn't stand it any more, and took her up on her lap on a chair at the front of the room, it was even worse. At home, no one embraced her when she cried, no one used the warmth of a lap to comfort her. From Miss Levy especially, the warmth felt indecent. The others rolled their eyes at her when Miss Levy wasn't looking. They knew something Joan didn't know, that a part had been saved for her. But Miss Levy was not about to stop the punishment so soon.

"You've let me down, Joan. What would you think if you came one day when I said I'd teach you and I wasn't here? What would you think? It's the same thing to me if you don't come."

But it isn't, it isn't, Joan wanted to say. You're the teacher and I'm only one of the students. You're a grown-up and I'm only a child. You have to be here. But she would never have argued with Miss Levy.

By the end of the class, the punishment was over. Joan had a part in the show, and the girls had opened ranks to let her in again. The pianist had tried to make her smile. She talked with her eyes, saying, "I'm with you, poor dear." The pianist, too, had to be careful; the teacher might just as easily turn her wrath on her. The sympathy between them was a conspiracy of the powerless.

Victims, however, make unreliable allies. They might wink and cheer one another, behind the tyrant's back, but if Miss Levy turned, the girls would freeze. For a solo, even for a smile of approval from Miss Levy, they would have walked over one another's faces. These things were understood; that was the way it was.

THE CHRISTMAS SHOWS had been the beginning. When Joan was seven she'd played a Dutch girl and a link in a wreath; when she was eight she did her first solo as a mouse. Her father hadn't liked it.

"Why is she going to her dancing again? She went yesterday."

"It's the rehearsals for the Christmas shows, dear."

"We agreed she'd take classes, but you never said she'd be gone every night. What about her school work?"

"School work is no trouble for her, dear. She never brings any home."

"I don't like all this fooling around."

"Why shouldn't she have the fun of performing if she's going to have all the class work and exams?"

Her father had come to see one of the shows. He said he enjoyed it, but the truth was he didn't like to see her with make-up on and her hair sprayed, dancing in thin tights with people watching. Funny, how Howard Sincere and Hannah Levy had sparred. Joan had been forged between their opposing fires, each a distant, disapproving, possessive love. Even she understood that the fights were not about performing, really; they were about who owned Joan.

Miss Levy's hospital shows at Christmas were the centre

of her year. She got a roster of charities to assist and the
dancers trouped out to cheer the inmates of various local
institutions. Rehearsals went on for weeks. Miss Levy was
proud. Perhaps she thought that somewhere it would be
recorded if she, Hannah Levy, formerly of the Sadler's
Wells Ballet School (teaching division), was allowing shod-
dy work to be presented on the auditorium stage at the
Veteran's hospital in Alberta. She changed entrance steps,
exit steps, drilled and drilled the students to keep their
lines straight.

Each time one child caught the measles or skipped class
to go skating, it was a quake in Levy's firmament. Didn't
they know what joys awaited if they'd only work at their
dancing? It was not impossible to find talent in a city in
Western Canada, not impossible at all, that was the sad
thing. There was talent enough, but where was the dedi-
cation? Finally she would say that there was no more time.

"That'll have to do, I suppose," she'd say. "Dress rehearsal is next Tuesday. I can't change it any more." She'd
heave a massive sigh. "I would have given you something
more exciting, but you won't work, will you?"

It was up to the children to look guilty then; they
dutifully hung their heads. This let Miss Levy off the hook
for lack-lustre choreography, for the seventy-two *chaîné*
turns in the middle of the dance that were so very dull but
that neither the army veterans nor the Indian children
with tuberculosis were going to notice.

When show day came, the dancers turned their fluffy
tutu skirts inside out in hat boxes. Joan carried a black and
yellow Stetson box with a braided rope handle. They met
in the lane beside the Bugle Building to take a chartered
bus to the hospital. Arriving at the service entrance, they
would enter through the kitchen and be hustled away
somewhere to change before show time. When they heard
their music start, they formed lines in front of the cramped
and cranky faces of the sick people and danced, danced,
danced. Quickly it would be over, they'd rush to change,
and the bus would take them back. Maybe they and the
patients had dreamt the whole thing. It seemed they must

have: Mother's car stood in the line of other cars waiting to collect the children, white exhaust rising from the tailpipe in a long train into the black of midnight sky. Joan had never been allowed out so late before.

One Christmas Miss Levy's group was invited to open the new mental hospital at Ponoka. This was a place where you could be locked up for life, where the patients were sick in the head and did wild, unthinkable things. But it was an invitation to perform, and therefore irresistible.

For Ponoka they had to get on the bus before noon. There were twenty-five dancers, the eldest fifteen and the youngest seven. Twenty girls and the rest the strange sort of boys who happened into ballet classes—the tall, awkward one with shoulder blades that stuck out the back, the little soft one with blond hair and glasses, and Tommy, the perfect dream, at twelve the heart-throb of the dancing school—fell into the vinyl seats of the bus. Miss Levy patrolled the aisle. Would they behave properly? Had they remembered their crêpe-paper-wrapped hoops, their tap shoes, their candlesticks?

The bus drew out of town past the used-car lots and along the Calgary trail, under a gaudy blue sky, past the grain elevator with JESUS SAVES written on the side. The sun bounced off a thin, hard layer of snow that turned the fields into marble. The children talked about the trouble they had keeping the bows in their hair, about the presents they were counting on getting for Christmas; they were little princesses and princes rolling out for a visit to the commoners. Miss Levy's jujube profile bounced before them in the sideways seat.

From the back entrance, the new mental hospital looked very little different from the other institutions they had seen. But the halls were so long you couldn't see their ends; the building had wings and more wings, and on each connecting door there was a lock. A nurse led the band of children, each of whom lugged his own costumes and props. She unlocked each door in front of them and stood by as they walked through. Then she locked it behind them. Fifty more steps, and she repeated the same operation. Stage by stage they proceeded into the depths of the building, its tile walls and antiseptic floor sparkling despite the blood and guts Joan was sure spilled there every night.

In the infirmary, the dancers dressed for the first show. There were bars over the windows. Everyone was very quiet until it was time to go on. Miss Levy stood in the wings. There was a real orchestra pit for the pianist, and the stage was the largest they'd ever danced on. The children were so far apart that they lost their formation. Miss Levy waved her arms and made faces from behind her blind, but it was no good; two girls crashed and fell over.

For her solo Joan wore a red dress with a sash. She danced and mouthed the words to the "Good Ship Lollipop." Because she was standing still during the song and looking straight over the footlights, she could actually see the crazy people. There were hundreds of them and they were grown-ups. The close-cut, docile heads were the heads of men as old as her father. It shocked her that they were not children. Where had they been before the hospital opened up and created them? Had they been living in the town, walking on the streets? Overnight, they'd been gathered from their hiding places, enough of them to fill up this huge new building.

After the show, the troupe was locked in the infirmary again to wait four hours until the next show. The nurses gave them tiddlywinks to play with. Joan carefully placed the edge of one plastic chip against the other and pressed to make it hop. As the nurses watched she played the game with great seriousness, to show that she was not crazy.

After the evening show, they did the grand finale that they'd practised in the studio but never had space to perform. All the dancers paraded across the stage in pyjamas, singing "Santa Claus Is Coming to Town."

"Stay in your red dress," Miss Levy hissed to Joan. "And stand out in front of the others."

Out in front, all alone, Joan looked sideways at Miss

Levy in the wings. The teacher was moving her feet from side to side, making little circles with her hands. This was a test: Joan was supposed to dance. But just make it up? Without being told what to do? She looked over the lights to the crazy people's heads. Their mouths gaped enthusiastically.

"You'd better not shout, you'd better not cry, better not pout I'm telling you why, Santa Claus is coming to town."

Joan started moving her hands back and forth in circles, and then she slid her feet from side to side. "He sees you when you're sleeping, he knows when you're awake." She did a little spin and stopped facing the audience, found she had an extra beat in the bar and pointed a foot forward. From then on it was easy. She repeated the same thing on the other side. It was such fun, it seemed too soon when the music ended and the clapping began.

Miss Levy walked to the centre stage and took Joan's hand. The other children moved forward and took hands too. They bowed all at once, just as they'd practised. The crazy people put their hands together over and over. Joan could tell she'd done well. Miss Levy kissed her ear.

A nurse stepped out from the corner of the stage. "One of our patients has prepared a speech to thank the dancers," she said. "That's it, Mr. Michaels, you may come up now."

A man made his way from the first row of seats to the stairs at the side of the stage. He was dressed like Santa Claus, and he walked like a baby, proudly, watching each foot poke ahead of the last, legs barely visible in his huge red suit. His head was swollen at the top. It looked like an upside-down pear sitting on his shoulders. As he walked, his pointed Santa hat fell off. His hair was shaved on his scalp; he looked pock-marked and grey. His eyes and mouth, as he came up the stairs, were soft and watery, bleary. He was coming right for Joan. She could tell he planned to lift her up and kiss her. She could read that look a mile away. She gripped Miss Levy's hand. Don't let him, she prayed.

Miss Levy offered Joan's hand to the crazy man.

He took it. His palm was slippery with sweat, but his touch was the most absolutely gentle thing. It was light; it was terrifyingly gentle; it was like death coming out of the dark and into the spotlight. Joan stood, her arm stretched up to where his hand cupped hers, and everything in her stopped. The man accepted his applause. Then he began to talk. At first he was careful but soon his words became slurred. He lost track of his prepared speech. Joan could tell without looking at him that he was just saying anything he could find in the jumble of his head. The nurse's mouth stiffened, and she rearranged it while staring at the inmate. Joan could see she was ashamed of her patient, and even hated him.

Suddenly the Christmas show was very sad: poor Santa could not remember his instructions, and he would get in trouble. Joan could feel what he felt. She wished she could draw the man away from the blankness of the footlights, lead him around in the waltz from "Alice Blue Gown," take him on the "Good Ship Lollipop.". Joan could feel the lump in his throat, the fear fluttering there, the horrible effort of making shapeless lips form precise sounds, of having to work with a body that dull and stupid, that far from beauty. She felt the sweat on his palm slip on hers. She wished she had never seen the man, but now that she had it was as if she would hold him by the hand always and he would become a part of her.

JOAN SIPPED HER coffee, cooler now. If she thought too much about the past, she'd lose her nerve for the present. She took the record off the turntable. It was time to do some laundry, go to the market, to the bank, maybe make a little search of the old-clothes shops. Drum up a sense of urgency.

The sun was nearly high enough now to disappear from the kitchen window. She put her cup in the sink and looked at the clock. She gave herself half an hour to get out of here. She sorted her laundry, got into a pair of jeans, made a list. Then, with one foot lifting Rudy away

from his perennially hopeful stance at the door, she ran for
the College car.

CHAPTER FOUR

David was sitting at his desk at 354 Jarvis Street. The
radio building, as it was called, was old, ugly, and gothic
with green paint in the halls. It used to be a private girls'
school; David still felt that if he came in on a week-end, he
had probed a secret part. It was not yet the week-end,
however. Only Friday, and David sat with his door slightly
ajar. Not enough to invite anyone to drop in, exactly, but
enough to let anyone who was wondering know that he
was there, and working.

David had grown sensitive to the opinions of his peers
about how hard he worked. Staff announcers were considered to be boring stuffed shirts with melodious voices who
had landed by luck in these cushy jobs from which they
could not be removed, while the real creative forces of the
place worked on six-month contracts, competing for limited funds. David had first come to the corporation five
years ago, hired to host an afternoon children's show on
radio. He'd rapidly moved around to the music shows, the
intellectual shows, and finally the early-morning current-
affairs show. He'd been a modest phenomenon: he had
eclectic knowledge, lively enthusiasm, and a golden voice.
As the rest of the staff gained respect for him, he lost
respect for the whole game. If he could succeed this easily,
mustn't there be something missing? If he could pass for
knowledgeable, mustn't the rest of them be a bit dim?

The problem of being appointed, or appointing yourself,
a voice, was that you had to be vain to withstand the pot
shots, the inevitable times you made a fool of yourself.
David was not that vain. On the other hand he was too
vain to allow that he was working in a worthless system.

He was trying to think of a way out of this maze, something more to aspire to. The broader his knowledge became, the greater his skills, the less he felt he was fit for this job. What he really wanted to do was pursue his hobbies to the point of excellence. Learn to do difficult shots underwater, electron-microscope photography, something like that. Maybe write a little poetry.

The hands of the clock moved around to twelve. He had to meet the producer and remote crew of a local television show. It was one of these afternoon shows that took up community problems. "Our business," the producer had told David while trying to talk him into doing some interviews for them, "is to worry about whatever is affecting the quality of life in this city." All radio people were supposed to aspire to positions in television. David wasn't sure he did. He certainly did not aspire to be in the business of worrying. He headed for the parking lot, where they waited.

There was the van, there the cheerful researcher in her silk shirt and jeans, there the producer with his can of Coke. They got into a car; the white van bearing its blue circle with orange spikes followed them out of the lot. On the way to the location the researcher briefed David, handing him the green sheets with her pre-interview questions. You have to be an idiot to flub this one, her smooth hands said. We've covered you from all angles. The researchers were professionally soothing; they all looked as if they'd gone to private schools, and they wrote in fat, upright script.

They were heading for a block of co-operative apartments in the downtown core, where the tenants were protesting. A boulevard café had opened up, using the common space between the building and the city sidewalk. The tenants' organization wanted it closed. The noise, the garbage, the liquor being served right where their children played made them angry.

"So we're talking to the president of the tenants' union?"

"Oh, no. He wasn't a good talker." She deftly raised the

green sheet from his hand and presented another. "This is the guy, George Allenby."

David scanned it. "But he's in favour."

"The producers thought it was better. He's in a wheel-chair. There's about a dozen people in wheelchairs in the co-op."

"A dozen out of two hundred? Why are they in favour?"

"They like cafés on the sidewalk because they can roll right in; they don't have to be lifted upstairs or anything."

"You've got to be kidding."

"No, I'm not kidding." He looked at her in disbelief, until she went on. "This is important stuff, David. The whole idea of combining residential and commercial establishments in these new inner-city developments is coming into question. It's the survival of the cities as places to live that's threatened. Don't you see?"

"I do see. I just don't like our angle."

David brooded for the rest of the ride.

They pulled up outside a new row of town houses built of raw-looking red brick. A clutch of people standing on the corner eyed the CBC vehicles with suspicion. As David stepped out of the car, he saw two wheelchairs lying in wait at the entranceway to the houses. The cameraman shouldered his equipment and headed across the street to get long shots of the row of houses; the sound man handed David a microphone. A wheelchair spun out of the door-way, its spokes catching the sun.

"David, this is George Allenby. This is David Calder, who'll be. . . ."

"Won't shake your hand." Allenby scowled. His hands were clutched tight on the arms of his chair, and his stomach was round and slack in the centre of it.

"That's O.K. You don't have to talk now, you can wait until the camera's ready."

David watched the crippled man out of the corner of his eye. He'd probably fallen off an oil rig when he was eighteen, or played chicken in a Camaro on Lakeshore Boulevard. Poor bastard: the last twenty years or whatever it had been of resting on calloused haunches, looking at things from the height of three feet, had not been good for his humour.

"Let me just clip this on your jacket, would you?"

Allenby jerked violently as the man leaned over him, and his scowl deepened. He looked into the distance. Having been appointed spokesman in this altercation seemed to justify his deep resentment of the world.

"Turning spring, isn't it?" said the researcher.

Nothing. Good talker, was he? Maybe Allenby was saving himself. Very well. If he didn't talk on camera they'd get the president of the union. Surely he'd be in the crowd. The camera moved closer, and suddenly, without waiting to be asked, the man began to speak.

"I've got no time for these union folk, they do nothing but bother us all. . . ."

"Excuse me, Mr. Allenby, could you just wait a minute before we start. The camera isn't quite. . . ."

". . . come to my door, expect me to sign these papers against the restaurant. Never said nothin' to me before that, never invite me over for a drink. Takes me a while to get to the door. I'm not signing no paper for them. I'm not going to stop a guy from making a buck. Last summer they had tables all along here, me and the guys just came down the elevator, went right in. Now they want to close it down."

David signalled distress. The camera had moved right in on Allenby.

"If you ask me, these tenants are crazy. They want to stop the whole world 'n make it impossible for a guy to go for a beer. I'm not having anything to do with them."

"Thank you. We've been talking to Mr. George Allenby, who—"

"Hey, those cameras, they're rolling, right?"

"Yes."

"O.K., well I want to tell the politicians and voters in this city that they suck, all of them. Get my drift? You suck!" Allenby's hands flicked forward on his wheels like the tongues of snakes, and he began to spin away.

David looked quizzically at the producer. He was making circles with one hand beside his head. "There's many an unforeseen angle on the problems of residents in the downtown core..." he began. They'd edit down to practically nothing anyway.

The van dropped him at the radio building, and he ran back up to his office. He wanted to pick up some files and take them home, and then get his camera and go out to the Beaches. There was a piece of paper on his desk. It was a note from Charlie. "Pick up today's *Sun*. Isn't that your hoofer from last night?"

He shut the office door behind him. He wondered what the note could mean. He'd forgotten all about calling Joan. Was she advertised at a club somewhere, or mentioned in a gossip column? On Jarvis Street he'd stop at the first red newspaper box.

JOAN HAD GONE to the Dressmakers' Supply on Bay Street. It was one of her favourite places in Toronto, across the street from the Mercedes-Benz "pre-owned" car sales. On the main floor were huge spools of ribbon and fur trim, plumes and tassels; on the second floor were the fabric flowers, hat forms, sequin strips, and hundreds and hundreds of jars of beads. Painted beads, crystal beads, wooden beads, pearl beads. It was solace for Joan to browse amongst all of these fine points, the details of her profession. She'd spent a thousand hours, probably, in the last ten years, sewing beads onto bras and bikinis, sewing marabou trim on négligés. Not many people could say that. She bought a Velcro fastener for her cut-offs and had a conversation with a sales clerk about how to wash sequinned garments without causing the colour to run.

On the way home she transferred from the subway to the College streetcar and then fell into a reverie of costumes over the years. That lime green sheath that unzipped on one side—where had it gone? When she focussed on the street again, she was past the Chinese and Portuguese section. She stepped down from the car into daylight and ordinary things came into dazzling focus; the blunt end of the streetcar as it swayed on its way, the blue sign of her bank two blocks behind her on College. She walked slowly back toward it.

Joan had always liked banks. She'd opened her first account with earnings made from dancing when she was twelve years old. She'd never closed it. It was bad luck to close a bank account; it was like shutting off a possibility. Now she had five scattered in Canada and England.

Joan was good with money, so good that people thought she was being kept by a man. No one had ever kept her, not since her parents did when she was a child. Her financial habits had been acquired over more than a dozen years of living week to week, close to the bone. The secret of her money management was that all of her money was disposable. She regarded everything but rent and telephone as luxuries. All her luxuries were of equal importance: fresh vegetables, new records, pantihose, taxis late at night. If her one hundred dollars a week ran out before Friday, when she scheduled her visit to the bank for the next withdrawal, then she didn't eat, shop, or ride for a day or two. Simple.

All in all, her version of poverty wasn't so bad: there was nothing Joan wanted particularly that she didn't have. She'd enjoy the odd visit to a big house, an expensive restaurant, a day on a sailboat. But she had no desire to make any of those things her own. They had been there in her childhood, and she hadn't owned them then: it was not so very different now. Having few possessions meant she was never implicated by her surroundings.

At the bank there was always the same news, the same small, steady amount of money going in and out. She had a business record in a big floppy book with carbon paper inside it to write down her earnings. She would watch the neat tally made by the computer in her passbook, and leave with a small fan of bills.

"Miss Sincere. And how are you today?"

A white-haired man with an unidentifiable central Eu-

ropean accent had run the current-accounts department
for as long as Joan had gone to this bank. The old man was
a curiosity; the younger members of his sex were all
managers and women had a monopoly on the tellers'
spots. He'd landed in this middle position and stayed
there. He was big and bent, and made eager, mouse-like
beckoning gestures with his hands when Joan came in the
door. He took an interest in Joan's finances because he
knew she was a dancer, and he extended to her all the
old-world respect accorded to artists. He addressed her in
a loud whisper.

"Miss Sincere, I see your picture is in the newspaper."
He was smiling, but his hands kept moving, worried.

"What newspaper?"

"You haven't seen? It's a big picture. Right at the top of
the page." He shook his head at her. "That's a lot of
trouble for you. Now the man will make you pay."

A pulse made itself felt in Joan's throat. Herbie's telephone call. "Any *more* publicity," he had said.

"Are you sure it's my picture? I haven't seen it."

"Oh, it's a very nice picture, don't you worry. I could
show you but—but—I have not got my paper. Probably I
left it on the subway." He moved his hands on the desk,
regret in their bent fingers. "Please don't worry. I am sure
you were not at fault."

"A man was in my way. I had to keep dancing."

"I see, of course." He nodded, and the hands lay still
again. Then he placed them further out and leaned between them across the desk. "Please, come and see me if
you have a problem with your cash flow."

Joan smiled and bit her lip, wanting to escape at the
first sign of sympathy. She went to the counter and wrote
out her withdrawal. The computer ate the number of her
account and ruminated, then emitted a buzz, and began to
type with its little teeth a white page to lie on top of the
other white pages of her passbook. The teller opened her
drawer and drew out the bills. Four beige, one purple,
and two blue, the same every week. Joan opened her

wallet and slipped the bills into place. The old man looked up from his desk as she went to leave.

"Good day, Miss Sincere. You be careful now."

She began to blush. It had been a curse in her childhood, this ferocious blushing when she was called to task for something. It covered her neck, her ears, and her face in a deep magenta wash. She'd learned to control it; it had been years since she'd had a bad blush. But now that it had begun there was nothing she could do. Heat radiated from her face as she pushed through the revolving glass door into the street.

There was a red metal box, but no copies of the *Sun* were left. It must be the *Sun:* no other paper would run a picture. It was four o'clock in the afternoon now, and the sun was at the blinding spot in the west. College Street was clogged with cars, but her little street going south was absolutely still. Joan had no job to go to tonight, and nothing else to do. The expressways would be lined with people getting away to the quiet with their loved ones for the week-end. She would be putting in a zipper for a strip job she didn't even know if she had any more, and walking the dog.

She put up a hand to shield her eyes from the sun. In the glare, the houses disappeared; she didn't know which way was safety. She juggled her bag, her purchase, the wallet she still held in her hand. She turned her ankle, and walked on, painfully. Only one more block. Rudy would be lying against the door waiting for the sound of her key in the lock to dislodge his dreams. Once she got in, she would lock the door behind her, unplug the telephone, have some tea, and put on a record. What would it be? Beethoven. "The Appassionata." Something sad and wise.

She came to her sidewalk and turned up it quickly; she was so close to safety that she had to make it now. She went past the car pulled up on the curb in front of her house without looking at it. Then she heard its door open. A man stood up and a palm slapped on the car roof.

"Hey! Aren't you speaking to me?"

Caught! She turned back. Who was it? Oh, the golden tones. The same ones from the tavern last night. David. She was angry at him for stopping her in the escape inward, to anonymity. "You scared me."

"I'm sorry, I thought I'd drop by for a visit." He got no answer. He held up a hand with a newspaper in it. "I found your street here."

"Oh, no. Please." She turned to go into the house.

"Are you really upset?" He came around the car and caught her elbow from behind. A sore lump rose up her throat and burst in her mouth as they touched. He was so close. She could feel the warmth of his chest even through his tweed jacket. Little explosions of relief were going on in her throat. It wasn't so much that it was *him*, but that he was a human being.

"Don't touch me," she muttered, trying not to cry.

"Don't what?" he said, putting his arm around her shoulders.

"Nothing."

They leaned together, walking up the walk. Joan was sure the Frenchman was watching from his window. She looked at the sidewalk, that way she could disguise her unstrung emotions. What they said didn't matter either, really, it was just the tremor of vocal chords, the touching of one voice to another, like a limb, a banner.

"You O.K.?"

"I'm in shock."

"Are you going to ask me in?"

"If you want."

There it was. On the third page, at the top. In fat black type, the words STRIPPER PACKS WALLOP. The picture was three inches high. It was an old one, from her kick-line days at the London Palladium, one her agent used to distribute. Herbie must have given it to the newspaper last night, the bastard. The shot was taken from below stage and showed a mile of leg, a round, satin-cased rump and, beyond a ledge of bosom, a tiny head. The head was sleek and wrapped in chiffon that ended in a spray at the back of her neck. Her knee was raised, and she was looking over the head of the photographer. She looked like some breed of warrior peacock, with her eye on a victim.

"If I didn't know better, I'd swear it wasn't me."

"Oh come on, it's you. It looks just like you. Don't you recognize yourself?"

"Sometimes I have trouble."

She turned away from the newspaper. She felt sick.

"What's the matter? This is great advertising."

"Advertising? It's not advertising, it's slander. I feel humiliated. Everyone's going to see it."

She picked up the newspaper again and held it in front of her. There were only three lines of type. *Joan Sincere, 30, of Baldwin Street, a stripper who works at the Coliseum, ran into a little interference last night when an unidentified admirer wandered onto the stage. He came away with injuries to his face and upper body, and damaged dental work to boot. Joan has been charged with assault and wilfull damage to property. Where's your manners, Joan? He only wanted to sign your dance card!*

"Oh my God."

"They charged you, eh?"

"How did they get this story?"

"There was probably a crime reporter at the police station."

"I feel sick. This morning, even while I was lying here sleeping, people were reading this, rubbing their dirty thumbs over my picture, crumpling it, leaving it on the park bench. It's like I'm a criminal."

"Not yet. That comes later, when you're convicted." David seemed to be taking the news lightly.

"Thanks a lot. I'm just going to have to leave town. Get out of here. Go to Montreal to live. Back to England, anywhere."

"Remember what you told me last night? That you wanted to translate yourself into another medium? Well, you've made it already. You're in print. Look at it positively. Joan, I bet in the long run it will be good for you."

"But no one even asked me." She tore the newspaper in half with one wide jerk of her arms. "It's a lie. It's my name but it's their story." The page with her picture floated to the kitchen floor. She put her foot on it. Her foot was more than the size of her whole body, in ink. She twisted her foot, tearing the paper. "There, got you, *got* you." She twisted back and forth until the sheet was shredded and the picture gone.

David and Joan sat side by side on bar stools, looking at each other through the hanging plants in the mirror behind the counter. Joan had disguised herself with an Afro wig and round pink glasses. Then, as they walked down Beverley Street to Queen, she had found what copies she could of the *Sun* in the red boxes, bought them and torn them up. All three of them.

Now she was on her third vodka and soda. She drank vodka and soda when she intended to get drunk because she kidded herself that this particular mixture, being colourless, had few calories. David was slowly working on his second Bloody Mary. At last, with the aid of her disguise, Joan could talk.

"I can't imagine why you even like me," said Joan-with-wig.

"You're tough."

"Yeah."

"I had the feeling I irritated you last night. Something I said."

"Probably. I can't even remember. But I like the—thing— you told me about." That was true. She remembered. This man brought a sense of calm, of order.

"Paramoecium."

"Yeah." She smiled for the first time that afternoon. "And what did you like?"

"I liked your—I don't know—your mind."

"Not many men have loved me for my mind." She laughed; it was like a cough.

"No," he said. "Actually more women do that kind of

thing, fall in love with a mind. Or what they think is a mind; they fall in love with the words that come out."

"God! I hardly even know you. All I know is that you talk pretty, and you've got a mole under your eye. It looks like a tear that froze half-way down your cheek."

"What else do you know about me?"

"That the lady next to you was trying to get you into bed."

"Not bad," said David. He drew back a little. He wanted to throw her off balance. "How many men have you been to bed with?"

"Are you trying to take advantage of my drunken state?"

"Absolutely not. I'm just trying to put things in perspective."

"Oh."

"Well?"

"I don't know. Maybe thirty."

"Thirty? Good God."

"And a couple of women. Is that too many?"

"It certainly puts things in perspective. Thirty! I'd say that's almost promiscuity."

"Promiscuity? I haven't heard that in years. How many women have you gone to bed with?"

"Oh, I can't compete with you. Maybe twenty," he lied. "And two point two men."

"Twenty. Is that all?"

"I don't know. I don't notch a stick."

"Maybe I overestimated. Maybe it was only five and it just *felt* like thirty, you know what I mean?" She put her fists out and began striking off one finger after another. "Oh, and him. Eech. Then there was . . . that's twelve . . . maybe there were only a couple of dozen."

David was counting on his fingers. "The only one I can't seem to remember is the first one."

"I bet you had more than me. You're the promiscuous one."

"I'm older than you. I deserve more."

"I bet I started earlier, though." She peered into the mirror and patted her wig. "This is a dumb conversation."

"O.K., O.K. But tell me, how many of those men were you in love with?"

"Are you serious?" She turned to face him with her lips parted.

"Yeah, how many?"

"You mean really in love, so that I'd spend my life with them? You mean like in love, forever and ever, happily, all of that? Well never, obviously. Here I am alone at thirty."

"Come on, surely you had a big romance that went on the rocks, a broken marriage, something. A past, you know. You've been in love, I can tell."

"You cannot. How?"

"I can just tell, it's like the glass is broken on a clock, something like that. Once it's happened, you can see how things work inside."

"You're nuts."

"How many times did you *think* you were in love then?"

"For how long?"

"More than a week."

"Once."

"Who?"

"You wouldn't know him."

"Who?"

"Joe Blow."

"No."

"In England. Tell you what, if I ever decide I'm in love with you I'll tell you about the great tradition."

"It's a deal."

They leaned into each other's shoulders. David pulled a curl in Joan's wig. "How could two people like us fall in love? You, the great man-hater, me the great woman-hater? I don't even believe in love. It's a line, a capitalist plot. The only reason people go in for it is that their lives are hopeless, they're politically powerless, and they need to be distracted."

"Oh, God."

"No really. I think people should just be good friends, don't you?"

"Friends?" Joan's mouth dropped around the lip of her

glass. She looked up into the mirror to compose herself and didn't recognize the round head. She looked like the little girl from the Henry cartoons. She was shocked by what he said. She'd assumed David was like everyone else, looking for love. Or facsimile.

"C'mon, David, go easy on me. I lost my job, I got busted, and I got into the newspaper. I've had a bad day. I can't afford to lose any more illusions."

"No, it's good for you."

"Hah!" She leaned over her drink watching the ice cubes. They were small and lost, oval instead of cubic after the fifteen-minute bath in vodka. She listened to David: that practised voice, a bass purr working on the side of her neck, her ear.

"Most women are so simple. So trusting. So dumb. Like dogs wanting to be loved. You should be beyond all that. Don't tell me you're a romantic, you want to look up to a man?"

"Something like that." David was trying to goad her with a confession but it wouldn't work. She was thinking about Joe. Joe Blow, whose name wasn't really that at all. Her first man, her initiation. It's true, she did look to men to teach her. What had Joe taught her? That it was possible to treat a lover like an enemy. Possible to lie, deny and betray a lover, and spend your time in other people's beds, even though your cells were crying out his name.

Not that her cells were crying out for Joe. She didn't know what they cried for now, she'd stopped listening. This man and that, probably not thirty of them. She'd never replaced the first one. Not that she'd wanted to. The thing she liked about this David was, come to think of it, that he didn't seem at all like Joe.

"So you think we should just be friends, do you?" The vodka was taking over large areas of her brain. The mirror looked like the liquid in the glass, with blobs of ice floating in it where the heads had been. She put her elbow on the counter, jarring her funny bone. She was probably speaking too loudly too. "You know I don't fuck my friends."

*   *   *

It was later, but still not night. David was leaning against the pillows, the hair on his chest moving slightly in the breeze that came in the window. It was very cool in the bedroom, but there was sweat on their bodies. Lovely sweat, clear and sweet-smelling as a dew through which they'd travelled. It had been slow and suspended, the motions familiar yet astonishing. It was impossible to remember what making love had been like before, impossible to remember even now, five minutes after the fact, what making love had been like this time.

David had taken Joan back to her apartment. Immediately she had gone to lie on the bed.

"I just need to rest a minute," she said. "Don't go."

The room had lifted around her ears. At first she thought she'd be sick, but she found herself getting used to it. It was as if she were on her back in a bath and the water was jogging her temples. She would move carefully, so evenly that she would not break the surface.

The beginning had been uncertain. It had been a long time for Joan, months. There were all the clothes to get rid of, the wig too. She blew in David's ear and laughed. She touched his penis and it moved. It felt like a certain kind of satin, the kind that didn't shine, what did you call it? Peau-de-soie? She ran her hand down between his legs where the terrain was hairy, and played with his testicles. She was only thinking about making love really, feeling the tips of her nipples begin to tingle and her thighs draw tight together as they always did when she was aroused, and then he took her. Whole. He got on top of her, clamped his arms around her, and his thighs; the surprisingly wide muscles of his chest closing around her as he thrust into her, finding the place.

His violence, his grasp made her still. He was like some enormous insect drawing juice from a plant. The violence surprised him too perhaps. Its end had been the same as its beginning: sudden, shattering. Now they rested, heavy and white.

"What time is it?"

David leaned over the bedside table where he had laid his watch, face up, just for this purpose. "Quarter to seven."

"Oh, it doesn't matter anyway, I don't have to work tonight." Her weight was sinking slowly into his. Her head jerked once. She was asleep.

David stayed propped up with two pillows behind the small of his back and the silky, feline head half-way down his chest. She was half-turned to face him, her arm around his waist, her breast pressed against the hollow by his hip-bone. She seemed to be trusting, truthful, but of course that was another illusion.

He did not want to sleep. He felt like watching over the scene. He was the man and the watcher of the man, the mind in the clouds directing. He would have liked to be God then: the two of them needed protection from the dangers that were creeping toward them through the walls.

CHAPTER FIVE

There is a special way the waves look, in the early evening before the sky is quite dark and when there is almost no wind. The water is firm and muscular, green and grey. It throws no great crests; it stirs, thickly. David walked along the boardwalk from Kew Gardens toward the Balmy Beach Canoe Club, looking out at Lake Ontario. He passed a woman with her Borzoi and then several teen-age boys with radios blasting from their bikes. It was the middle of the week-end: few people were alone.

The waves fascinated him. Their foam broke the same way every time. The breaking began low along the sand, at the far left of his vision. At first it was just a kernel of

white, exploding from the narrow edge of the triangle
where a shelf of water angled in against the sand. The
little comet sped back along the top of the wave leaving a
widening tail of white. It sped as if it were shot from a
cylinder of steam until it reached the end of the swell, and
then it dropped into a pool of foam.

So the breaking of a wave was not a simple overflowing,
a horizontal fold, but a linear thing. It was a star shooting
through space, a missile. David was thrilled with his
observation. Knowing that changed the wave forever. He
would have loved to catch it on film, but his camera
seemed inadequate. He lowered it and continued to walk.

Joan had woken up at nine o'clock the night before and
kicked him out of her apartment. She said she wanted to
be alone. He understood the idea, but he wished he'd
expressed it himself. He did not lay claims on people, and
he had educated his nearest and dearest not to lay claims
on him. They tried, mind you, even still. His mother,
calling from her Montreal apartment. His father, patheti-
cally trying to remain young for his new wife, in a bungalow in Etobicoke. Even his sister in San Francisco who
wrote him letters now and then and signed them "Bitsy."
He liked to think of her as Elizabeth, now that she had
grown up. "Bitsy" had been a red-haired, soggy-bottomed
thing who followed him. He wanted no letters from her.
Elizabeth as a grown-up was someone he was prepared to
communicate with, however. She did not understand. The
women in his family told him he was hard, but it was
simply that he did not want to be responsible for any
dependent creature. And he told them—or did he? Did
he only rehearse telling them and really say nothing at all?
—that he had to be hard, or else the whole gang of them
would collapse on his shoulders.

Hardness notwithstanding, sometimes he felt sorry for
himself. He reached the end of the boardwalk and turned
back toward the city. A jogger passed him. There was the
woman stroking her Borzoi, dog and owner stopped in the
middle of their walk for a moment of closeness. I am
available, the woman seemed to be saying. See me lavish

affection on this dog, lean and hunched. See what love I could offer, if humans were not so everlastingly difficult.

He had spent the whole day alone. It was most unusual for David to do that. He had many friends and not much free time, and he rarely said no when people asked him to dinner. As a single man he was much in demand. He imagined a weekday. He walked down the halls of the CBC and people stuck their heads over partitions. Hi, David. How's it going? It was that way everywhere. On general principle, he liked people. But these days he was tired of society.

As a boy he'd been some kind of recluse. The science club, the debating team, that sort of thing had kept him busy. Square, square, square. His mother had been his best friend. He was not at all adventuresome. He even had to be told how to masturbate. He and another boy— he could see the close-cut red hair, the bullet-shaped head now—had been talking about how you did it with girls. You can do it by yourself, you know, the boy had said. Just go home and try. He'd gone home and faced himself in the bathroom mirror over the back of the toilet. He had liked it, but he had known he shouldn't do it. Some things you can just tell.

He'd loved to watch the girls when they came back from gym class, their hair wet from the shower. He had thought one touch would be fatal, that he would be felled. He had thought he would never grow up and lose this vulnerability, but he had. Inch by inch, square by square, his inner graph had filled with the thicker blood of manhood. He was hairier, heavier, stronger than he had ever imagined he could be.

When he was a teenager, the family had hired a man to work around the yard one spring. The man was European, with a curl over his forehead and a wide, heavy frame. He used to stop David as he was on his way to school. "How many times can you do it?" he'd ask. "I can do it five times in one night, five times. My wife says I'm an animal." The man smiled proudly. It frightened David, it was an image of something unknown that was expected of him, something, he was very sure, beyond that which his parents were prepared to demonstrate.

It was true what he'd told Joan, he could not remember the day he'd lost his virginity, nor the circumstances, nor the individual with whom he'd shared the moment. He started counting from the first time he made a success of it, which was sometime later, around his twenty-third birthday. Finding his way among the girls, he had found his way among the boys as well. Suddenly it became easy to joke and stand about in hallways with fists in your pocket. He'd begun to enjoy the bravado of men. "Oh yeah, I planked her once," or "Boy, did I get a hot one last night," was play talk. It didn't have to be true, it was like the five times a night, just talk. The talk was code for something like "Isn't it a bit rough, having to be the man? We must build each other up for the task." That insight had brightened up his life, had made people much less frightening.

He'd been alone since the night before, when he'd left Joan. He was not accustomed to being asked to leave a woman's bed. Still, that morning he got up feeling splendid. The window in his bedroom over Palmerston Avenue had been open just the right few inches. He could hear voices speaking in another language. The voices made clucking noises, like pigeons in the eaves. It might be Korean, it might be Portuguese, it could be anything in the polyglot West Annex. He found it soothing to be in a place where the outside language did not connect with the inner one.

He showered without shaving. Although he'd begun to hate his prickly, dark chin, he'd give the beard another week. Standing at the kitchen window, he saw a starling, its beak loaded with dead grass. It was nothing to look at, just a yellow-orange beak and a lump of greenish-black plumage with spots on the wings, like oil on water. He sat—David assumed it was a he—his head turning this way and that, on the end of a bare branch. His load of building materials bobbed as he jumped to another branch. He sat there for a minute, looked around again and

jumped to another spot, a foot distant. He kept the vigil
minute after minute, patient, seemingly nonchalant, only
his load giving him away.

He was on his way to a secret place. If there were eyes
on him, cats' eyes, dogs' eyes, the eyes of larger birds, he
would outwait them. He would sacrifice his load of straw
and fly away. Certainly, if he had known there were human
eyes on him, he would have abandoned his plans. But he
did not know. He waited, not giving up, not going ahead.
The patience of the bird was exhausting. Perhaps he felt
David's eyes, behind the thermopane of the window.
Perhaps he would never complete his project.

And then, suddenly, he made his move, flying to a hole
in a tree five feet from where he'd perched. It was a
hollow where a branch had been. As he landed, another
yellow beak popped out of the dark hole. The mate
emerged, and flew off: when she'd passed him the starling
dropped into the hole himself, his straws bending as he
went in the opening.

David turned away. He felt an inconceivable gripping in
his chest at the thought of Mr. and Mrs. Bird building
their nest. Theirs was a conspiracy so profound that it
electrified them; it was their only occupation. For months
now they would build, lay, feed, and teach. And all the
while, they would be on guard against the discovery that
had already been made. Perhaps even now they had
begun to feel uneasy, sensing that his eyes had followed
them.

David thought of trying to get a photograph of the
starlings coming in and out of their nest in their furtive
necessity, but he decided against it. His life had become a
series of opportunities for photographs, some taken, some
not. Even when he didn't have his camera, he reacted that
way. There were moments of heat, warmth, and wetness,
of connecting deeply to another person, but there was
always this return to the still interior that stole from the
present tense, took it with a soft click, click, click.

All day David had wandered in the city, shooting pictures. The face of a woman selling bread at the St.

Lawrence Market came back to him as he stood on the boardwalk, in its thick features an outrage at the invasion that his camera represented. Her look was inside his leather case now. Some people smiled and posed, but they weren't the interesting ones. He had been shouted at, pushed away, had doors slammed in his face more often than he cared to think about. If David were called upon to defend his actions, he would have said to his subjects that it wasn't they who were exposed in the photographs, it was himself. Subjects were accidents. Take a shot of a drunk on a street corner, develop it, and you have captured an aspect of the photographer. Self-portrait.

He decided not to take a shot of the woman with the dog. She would say something to him and it would get complicated. He really did not want to talk to anyone.

This business of watching, of being a spy. It had become his adult habit. When he was twenty-one and having one of his stupid fights with his father, he had taken a dare to infiltrate the Canadian Nazi party. He wanted to discover valour. He wanted to prove that the Nazis did have evil intent, to prove that there was real danger in Canada. If he did that, he would not be a sissy; he supposed that had been the general idea.

David had called up the RCMP and offered his services. They must have thought he was some kind of nut, looking for a way to get hurt. They turned him down. Then he had gone to the Toronto police and they'd agreed to help. They fitted him with a little tape-recorder, and he'd gone and joined the party.

Those meetings. He thought of them still, whenever he looked into a small room filled with men and smoke. They were in an empty apartment over a Bloor Street newsstand. The men wore suits and had large pores, spotty skin, metallic voices, hairy knuckles. Each one had something unattractive about him. Sometimes their voices went right up to screams, and then died down again, mouths slowing in the clouds of smoke. At first he was sure the men could tell just by looking at him that he wasn't one of them. But as the meetings continued, he understood why

they didn't. Their vanity prevented them. That he—
young, blond, North American by birth—should be there
fed their dream of takeover; they considered it a step
toward success. They accepted him, told him their strate-
gies. By the time David had been there three times he
knew that it didn't matter what the group planned, or if
the plans were ever carried out, there was real danger.
David could have lifted handfuls of it from the air. People
were crazy: that was real danger.

The escapade had ended with a mass rally at Allen
Gardens. The Nazi party came out with placards, David
among them. The police were supposed to have photographs of David, to know that he wasn't one of them but
was just protecting his cover. The demonstration had got
out of control. There was pushing and shoving and David
got separated from the others. People shouted and threw
rotten vegetables at him. They hissed in his face and
shoved him. He came out of it with the worst beating he'd
ever had.

And what had he proved? That you could get hurt in
Canada. He'd won some bemused respect from his father,
perhaps. He'd got a permanent nervousness in large crowds.
He never talked about it. It wasn't something he was
proud of now, having been a police informer. But he
persisted in the habit of spying. Neither side of a battle
was safe. Spies, thought David, were not so much traitors
as cautious people, people who could see too clearly the
weakness of beliefs.

He walked further back toward the western end of the
boardwalk. Why these ancient histories came back to him
he didn't know. The last day at work had been distressing.
The sight of all those t.v. people dithering around a
misanthrope in a wheelchair made him wince. He found
his work bearable only as long as he remained detached.
That story would be decidedly more amusing, more illus-
trative of the weakness of the media, if it had not had his
face attached. The contradiction in his position did not
escape him. If the lady selling bread had no reason to be
angry because he used her face to say something, then

what right had he to his embarrassment when CBC used his face to sell the botched, off-base little items that passed as local news?

To test himself, he considered for a second quitting his job. He wanted a new car and his colour television was not yet paid for. And besides, he liked the access, he liked to know what was going on, even if he did not approve. One thing he had decided in his maturity was that he would never quit on principle. Quitting for a principle would be self-indulgent. If there were principles at stake, then he had to keep fighting. He'd only leave when he no longer had them.

Change lobsters and dance, Calder, he admonished himself. Appreciate the layers of meaning, the changing points of view ("repositionings" as the politicians called them), the lies, but don't call them that. Forget this allegiance to something called fact. To be in media was to be a student of media, not of life. Surely by now he could banish that most elementary illusion. The form is the story, not the content. It reminded David of the problem he'd had with academe. It was all form and no content there, too. When he had walked away from that world he had thought he'd walked away from the problem altogether. It was a time when he was not so equivocal. He liked to think of it. He *could* take a stand.

It had been a fall day in 1968 when he'd quit his doctoral program in dramatic theory. Around him clever, arrogant young men and women "critiqued" each other's papers. They built a floating island of theory; the waters of sense lapped at its edge. Those had been the days of easy money for graduate studies. But David decided he wanted to do whatever it was himself, not to look at what others had done. That afternoon the urgency had been as real as the leaves of red maple curling on the still-green quad. He had gone to his adviser's office.

"Dr. Ridpath. I have come to tell you that I am dropping out of the program. I am going to become an actor."

He had been astonished to hear his own words: he'd never acted in his life.

Dr. Ridpath swivelled outward in his chair and raised a stumpy leg to cross it over his knee. His pant leg slid up, revealing a wrinkled tartan sock. He smiled indulgently. "You look nonplussed, my man. Can I have the secretary bring in something for you? A cold drink? A coffee?"

In fact, David had felt he barely had time to stay, so intense were his ambitions, but he was polite.

"I'll have a coffee please, with milk."

They drank their coffee slowly, out of disposable paper cups encased in red plastic holders. Dr. Ridpath, surprisingly, did not ask David about his acting experience, an omission for which David was grateful. Instead, he reminisced.

"Strange you should mention it. There was a time when I wanted to be an actor."

"Oh?"

"The head of the department here actually wanted to be an explorer. Got so far as a flight over the Antarctic once, I believe." Dr. Ridpath chuckled. He was trying to be open-minded. He too had been foolish in his youth. "And, of course, there's old Dr. Waterhouse in classics, who will persist in writing those dreadful novels."

"I haven't read them."

"Oh well, they're, you know. . . ." Dr. Ridpath put his red plastic cup on his knee. He cocked his head, reaching for words. "Many of us have had these ambitions. It seems to me quite natural." He went on to describe those who ran for office, those who entered the priesthood, those who had wanted, reaching a little further back, to be firemen. Dr. Ridpath's voice became a little less kind; it seemed to David to develop a snide tone.

"I want to do my own work, not someone else's. I want to deal with the heart of the matter."

Ridpath had laughed. "And where, exactly, is that?" He paused. "I'm sure you'll come to see these desires as stages of rebellion. I know the field you're in is becoming increasingly competitive, David. Perhaps you're afraid you won't make it as a scholar. But I think you have a good chance, if you carry on. I'm sure you'll come to recognize as we all do here that the best vocation for an intelligent man is to be a professor."

Finally David escaped. Dr. Ridpath had turned back to the blotter on his oak desk, but he called after him.

"I'll keep my eyes open for your name on the playbills."

Well, David supposed, he had his victory over the likes of Dr. Ridpath. He had achieved his ambition, in a way. His name, if not on playbills, was known. The trouble was that having achieved it was very little different from not having achieved it. He was still in compromising situations every day of his life. He still spent his time talking about what other people did. Perhaps Dr. Ridpath had the last laugh after all: perhaps there was no heart in the matter. He looked at the lake. If someone were drowning he could save him and play the hero. But there was no one even in the water.

It was time for him to make a decision and go somewhere. He couldn't stand all night looking at the lake. He would have liked to speak to Joan. He thought again about the first night, only two days ago, when he'd gone down to the Coliseum with Alex and Charlie and Ellen. He wanted to remember everything that had happened, first Thursday, and then yesterday. He had never believed Rennick when he dropped the names of people he knew in show business, but that night he'd had to give him some credit, when Joan came out to say hello. He couldn't believe she was a stripper, she was so good-looking.

She was a long-faced woman with light brown hair pulled tightly away from her face. It blended with her skin and she looked almost bald, but he saw later that the hair was in a knot at the nape of her neck. She poked a thin hand at him. It was a transparent hand, olive-skinned. The handshake was firm. David was moved by the sight of that brave, shapely hand in his own.

The rest of her was very remote, however. They had sat around the little table in the thick air of the tavern. There were paintings of ruins on the walls, and in amongst them, plaster columns, and bits of mirrors stuck together in a mosaic. Joan's reflection was caught in the cheap decor; the bulb-shaped head, high round forehead and long scoop down the back of the skull into her neck, seemed to be lit from within. Her nose was long and rounded as well, and her lips were large. She looked sulky, spoiled, even, with her big gold button earrings and her long fingers with painted nails stretched out on the table-top. Rennick had started talking about some client of his who'd hidden her lover's body in the freezer: it was the sort of topic he assumed everyone took pleasure in. Joan had said nothing.

Right away, David had typed her: it was a bad habit he had. Dancer, he thought, can't talk, nothing to say. Still, she didn't look like the run of the mill stripper. Of course, never having met a stripper he wasn't sure what the mill run was like.

"You don't look like the average. . . ."

"I'm not."

He had been taken aback. "Clearly," he murmured.

"I'm a special case," she said sarcastically. "But then—" she'd looked around the club, her lip curled, "I guess we all are."

"Of course," said David. "Well, it's an unusual occupation."

"Aren't you going to ask me why I'm a stripper?"

"I might."

"I trained as a dancer, and I never had a chance to be anything else. I've been working clubs for ten years. Can you believe it?"

"It doesn't show." He had meant that to be a compliment, but it sounded wrong. She gave him a withering look.

"It will. Everyone takes a beating in this work. Used to be I could do a double booking six nights a week and enjoy it. Not now. I'm working too hard, and there's not enough money in it. Not only that but we're going out of date."

"Strippers? No, I heard they were coming back in. The new conservatism and all, doesn't that bring people down here?"

"It's not the audiences. There's always audiences. It's the industry that's outdated. I'm the material, the labour, the finished article. I have to do it all myself. There's no loopholes, you know what I mean? Everyone else works for a corporation, everyone has a union, everyone takes a day off with pay. You know what I mean?"

"I know what you mean," he said, laughing.

"I mean, think about it. It's so inefficient. I'm my own seamstress. I do the laundry, I badger the manager to give me hangers for the dressing-room, I dance, I come back and ask for my money, and I start all over. What do you call that in business?"

"Vertical integration?"

"I don't know. But that's what's wrong with stripping. We're too integrated, we're not economical. We need to be made into a new medium. I need to become technological, computerized, microfilmed, something. You know."

She leaned back and examined her finger-nails. "What do you do?"

"You managed to slip that in, didn't you? I—well—I work in radio."

"Yeah? Well, there you are, you can tell me how to do it."

"What you need is someone to invest a little money in you." Maybe she thought he was Darryl Zanuck: he didn't even get a chance to say he wasn't all that famous, most people barely remembered where they'd heard him. Her electronic fantasy was interesting. "Do you sing, or act?"

"Lots of strippers want to be singers. I'm not stupid. I know I'm tone deaf. And act? When I first came here an agent sent me for an audition. I'd been up late, I had bags under my eyes and my hair was dirty. They stood us all in a line like horses, they did everything but pick up our feet to examine the hooves. They said you, you're perfect. You know what I was perfect for? A harassed housewife." She laughed. "All I had to do was rub a wet shirt between my knuckles and say, 'It really works.' The soap, you know, works." She shrugged. "I couldn't do it. Wasn't convincing, they said."

David laughed. He liked her a lot. He was thinking that she was beautiful, but he couldn't possibly say that. "I used to want to be an actor," he said. "I could put you onto my agent; she was a genius. You can't just sit there waiting to be discovered." By the look on her face he figured he had her number. "A lot of people do that. They think they've got some magical quality that the world can't do without. But they don't stand for anything, they don't go out and do anything. I don't mean to offend you, Joan, but ladies like you are a dime a dozen."

The finger-nails jumped up, dancing lightly on the hard surface of the table. Each one seemed to be independent, each one an irate little person.

"I don't think so," she said. There was a silence.

"You know," she said, "one thing is, you get so you can size people up pretty fast in this business."

The smile slipped from his face. "You sizing me up?"

"I already did. You're an arrogant prig." As she said it, she looked in his eyes and laughed, invitingly, he'd almost say. Then she slid her chair back along the floor, ready to go. Her neck was rigid.

Of course, he was secretly afraid that he was a prig. He was afraid of all sorts of things like strange toilets and backstage rooms where G-strings lay among the grease pencils, afraid and fascinated. She knew all about those places and that made her superior to him, in his mind, a fact that he felt he'd concealed very well during their conversation. He was impressed. He laughed. "You're probably right."

The chair stopped moving. She fixed her large, solemn pupils on his face. "Yeah," she said. "I'm right all the time. It's just that I don't have many friends."

She stayed at the table a while longer, and let him buy her a ginger ale. She said she didn't feel like going on that night. "Why are we talking about my work?" she said. "It's not worth talking about. You entertain me. I bet you could tell me about a place I've never been, something really pretty you saw, anything. You talk."

He was touched, his heart twinged for her, little girl lost in a bad world. He'd begun to tell her about the things he'd seen in a slide under an electron microscope. He didn't know why he chose that, but it seemed to be right. He did love that world. He talked about the floodlit cells, about the way the paramoecium floated, peacefully, about the brilliance and economy of its system. Her eyes had left his eyes, lingered on the lower part of his face, and then turned to the wall behind him, but her imagination had stayed with him. He could tell.

When she stood up to get ready, she said, "That was really great. Thanks for the story." She'd held out her hand to shake his, and in it was the little piece of paper with her phone anumber on it. That was when he'd said that stupid thing about her being interested in his "fame." He'd nearly ruined it. She'd gone across the room and out the side door to where the girls dressed. He'd sat there, unfolded the paper coaster with numerals on it, and pocketed it. He'd sat for a few more minutes, and then decided to leave, thinking it was the kindest thing. It would have confused him to watch her strip.

But now he'd spent an afternoon with her, and had gone to bed with her. That—he would think about that part very carefully too, but not now. He had been thinking all his waking minutes today. Suddenly he was impatient with the old things in his life. He should do something, commit himself to a course. Make a decision, he said to himself. Dive in, even if there is no one drowning. You can't drop out of school, or quit your job. But you're crazy about this woman. Go and find her.

He began to walk quickly toward his car. Just one thing nagged at him. Under a lamp-post, he stopped and looked at his watch. It was still only nine-thirty. He'd have to go somewhere else for an hour and a half, and then pick her up after the show. Something told him it was still too soon to see her act.

CHAPTER SIX

Joan got off the streetcar, walked half a block and turned right in front of an even row of brown-shingled, semi-detached houses, two by two, very dull companions. She was in the east end of the city, half-way between Riverdale and the Beaches. It was nowhere; she only came here to visit Arlene. She could never spot Arlene's house until she was in front of it, because there was nothing to make it stand out from the rest. Number 408. She'd almost passed it again. She saw signs of digging already in the front flower-beds: Arlene was advancing the season this year, just to give herself a little more work. And then she saw her friend, disengaging herself from the lower limbs of a bush.

She saw Arlene before Arlene saw her. Bent over, the back of her cotton print housedress lifted in an arc to reveal the hard bulge of a dancer's haunch, she was working in the earth at the side of the house. Scratch, scratch, went a little tool with sharp metal fingers. Arlene's head was covered in a scarf, also printed cotton, but unmatching. Her feet were apart and well-balanced: she worked with one arm braced against the soil, the other arm—slim, with a cord of muscle raised like a wire under the forearm—raking the trowel up and down. She looked like a crone from a fairy tale, collecting faggots or whatever they did, an ageless scrabbler in the dirt. She was not beautiful. She was another kind of thing, an evocative thing. The ordinariness of her pose seemed to sing praises of all the life that went slow and dumb through working bodies.

Arlene's slow brown eyes caught Joan. She stood, pulling off her rubber gloves and pressing a hand down the side of her skirt to wipe it before removing her hair from her eyes. Joan saw the Royal Opera House at Covent Garden. The darkened circle and the glow of hundreds of little red-covered lamps and Arlene, doing pirouettes, those whip-like arms drawing the spotlight to her. This woman with her trowel had once been a swan on stage and thousands had admired her. Such people are mingled with the rest of us, before and after their moments of glory, thought Joan. The words "I love Arlene" came to her mind, surprisingly. Arlene was a quantity ripe for transformation. She could be utterly conquered by context. She had also once been an awkward girl standing at the bus-stop in Edmonton after a ballet class, begging Joan to be her friend.

THEY'D BEEN EQUALS, early on. No, not even equals, Joan had been better than Arlene—quicker, prettier, more expressive. She had easily maintained that lead, too, until they went on point. It was Joan's feet that had made her fall behind Arlene. Her ugly, battered feet. Often, over the years, Joan and Arlene had sat on benches side by side examining the damage to their feet, proudly, like men would display war wounds.

Joan had long, skinny toes. The second toe was longer than the big toe. Just like Anna Pavlova, Miss Levy had told her, and it hadn't held her back. From the beginning, this distinction singled out Joan for special, more than ordinary pain, and gave her the occasion to use greater than ordinary will-power. But now the feet had imperfections she hadn't been born with, imperfections she had created. The balls were padded with a thick callus, evidence that she had balanced her weight wrong, and the top of the arch showed veins popping, purple around the circles, and red marks of a host of blisters that had burst out of the toes over the years. Arlene's feet were different: her toes were as straight as if they'd been cut off with a ruler; they were thick rather than thin and the skin on them not transparent and tortured, but coarse, dead-looking.

It was as if all life in that end of Arlene had retreated up her ankles to avoid the punishment inflicted on these mute, obedient wedges.

Going on point had ruined their feet. To go on point was, in ballet terms, to become a woman. At eleven or twelve the whole class of girls had caught the longing like a flu. They watched the girls in the older groups rising magically on the tips of their toes and becoming angel, flower, bird. Arlene and Joan talked a lot about how it was done.

"It's all in the shoe. The shoe is wooden and it's so strong it holds you up." They were mystified, however, by the problem of the toes. Just how did your toes fit into that tiny cylindrical end of the satin slipper? Did you really stand right on the tips of them?

The shoes themselves were beautiful; tiny, heavy, and utterly stiff with a haughty arch. They were shaped like cocoons and covered with pale pink satin. The girls fingered point shoes in the dance stores. They put them on their hands and danced with them on the counter tops. But when the clerks came to help, they had to say, "We're just looking"; at best they could try on another of the soft black kid slippers of the uninitiated.

The older girls dangled their point shoes on ribbons, carrying them in and out of class. They usually had a clean new pink pair for going up on point and an old pair for "flat work." Old point shoes were broken down for flat when their arches had become too soft to stand on. Joan had watched the older girls begin to break their shoes, smashing them repeatedly against the door frame of the dressing-room. Some took a hammer to the toes, and then loosened the glue in the arch and ripped out the hard spine. Sometimes they put the shoes through a cycle of a clothes dryer, to finish off the job. The shoes came out of the breaking down process utilitarian and ugly, a dismal grey with lumpy toes and collapsed insteps.

Once, just once, Joan saw a beautiful used shoe. When she was twelve, a contingent from the Bolshoi Ballet had come to town. Some of the girls in Miss Levy's school were allowed to go to a master class given by the company. A venerated dancer who, people whispered, was over sixty, and still beautiful, like a monument, had brought out her shoes to show the girls. The shoes had been new the night before: now she was going to throw them out. They were still clean and pink, but the toe and the arch, hard as wood yesterday, were completely limp from one night's performance of "Swan Lake." You could see the form of the dancer's foot impressed in the satin: she had danced it into a soft fossil.

But it was the toe end that dazzled Joan. The size of a thumb print, it was the balance point that supported the weight of the ballerina's entire body. In school Joan had learned that you couldn't defy gravity, not on the earth: the expression describes an illusion. But women danced on the tips of their toes, and it looked easy. Someday Joan would do it, too. The perversity of it, the bizarre specificity of toe dancing no longer surprised her. It seemed instead like some of the other feats achieved by women. Miss Levy's steel will making dancing flowers out of a dozen clumsy older girls. The girls in turn putting on their make-up and curling their hair after ballet class, disguising their taut bodies in ruffles and lace to show the boys that they were, after all, just giggling and harmless, waiting to be caught. What did a grown-up girl become? She was an illusion within an illusion, a trick belying natural law.

Miss Levy guarded the littler ones' inexperience like a brood hen guarded eggs: she could make them wait forever. Too young, and not strong enough in the ankles, Joan and Arlene stepped around on *demi-pointe*, their toes bent at the ball of the foot. Although they had been warned not to, they tried the miracle in the basement, tried to stand on their toes holding onto a shelf, without the shoes, stabbing their big toes down at the floor. This was dangerous, Miss Levy said, their bones were still soft and could break.

It seemed unfair that the girls were kept in check. The boys had been "men" from the start. They did their feats of elevation at the end of regular classes, called out to perform slowly, grandly, with thunderous music as the girls stood by. They sneered at the girls who were waiting to go on point. But Joan, for her part, scorned the boy-men. They were to be without metamorphosis.

At last one day Miss Levy turned away after the curtsy, her black bulk filling up the doorway of the studio as the students clapped. The girls turned back to the *barre* to pick up their bags and heard the teacher's voice.

"You can buy some point shoes and bring them to the Saturday class."

As if it were nothing, as if she were saying, buy a sandwich and bring it to eat after rehearsal.

Silence was law in the studio. The girls froze, and Miss Levy permitted herself a little smile. She listed prohibitions. No Italian shoes, they wore out too easily. The shoe must be English, with the high vamp that was safer for beginners. And there was only one way to be sure of a proper fit. They were to place the foot in the shoe (nothing was too obvious to mention) and then set the toe down on the floor with a little weight on it: the fabric of the heel must be loose enough to allow only one finger to slide inside.

"And don't experiment before class, do you hear me?"

"Yes, Miss Levy."

In the dressing-room the girls threw themselves around with shrieks of delight, tangling their legs with the benches, pounding the walls.

Arlene and Joan went together to buy their shoes. The clerk must have known it was their first time: she was testy.

"Yes, it *is* your size."

"How can it be?" The shoes were only six inches long.

Joan slid her foot into the hard burrow. If it lay flat on the floor, she couldn't stand on it. Her foot was curled like a claw; the toes bumped against the hard sides. This was not a shoe; it was a foot's coffin. She couldn't believe she'd ever take a step in it. When Joan placed the toe down on the floor with a little weight on it, however, there was just enough slack at the heel for her finger. If Miss Levy said, it must be so. They bought the shoes and then pink satin ribbon to sew on for ties, and lamb's-wool to soften the inside of the blocked toes. They went to a department store to get the pink embroidery cotton for darning the toes.

Darning was a strange, secret ritual. Joan was to see it again and again, in every studio and rehearsal room she frequented, in bed-sits where the students in London spent their evenings, on trains and buses commuting to school. The darning was intended to save the satin from wearing out when it rubbed on the floor, but when it was first done on a brand-new shoe, it seemed like an unprovoked attack. All dancers did it differently. A sombre European girl made tight, hard beads of stitches in tight coils over the toes. Others made fat, overlapping loops like crochet stitches. Joan was taught by her mother to take small, neat stitches, each one shaped like a T, around in an arc over the toe and down along the underside of the satin pleats to the tiny leather sole of the slipper, making a keyhole shape which she filled with smaller and smaller stitches. She sat in her bedroom for hours trying to force the needle through the satin without getting it stuck in the wooden toe piece. By the time she had finished she had pricked her fingers and the beautiful satin shoes were already spotted with blood.

The next Saturday a dozen pairs of point shoes lay under the *barre*, small pink expectant things. When there were only ten minutes to go before the end of the class, Miss Levy ordered the girls to change shoes. They sat down on the floor and tied on the new shoes, then stood up and tried to walk. Joan limped stiffly in a circle, watching the others do the same. A metamorphosis had occurred, but it was a terrible mistake. Instead of turning into angels, the girls were changed into so many little bent ladies with bound feet. Miss Levy affected nonchalance, talking softly with the pianist.

"Facing the *barre*, please. Rise on *demi-pointe*."

She wanted them to rise half-way up on their toes to the

ball of the foot and force the shoes to break at the toe joint. They rose. Cracking sounds came from the shoes: Joan could feel the stiff soles shifting. And the hard walls of the shoe bore into her skin, protected only by the thin layer of her tights. Up and down, up and down, she wasn't even on point and Joan's feet hurt already.

"All the way up now, please."

She gripped the *barre* and pushed herself up to stand on the end of her toes. It was not a great moment. Standing up there hurt. For the first time, Joan realized that there was no magical key to lift the weight from her toes, no trick with mirrors to save her skin.

She'd been up and down from flat feet to point about four times when the pain became what she first considered unbearable. She sprang up once more, barely swallowed a scream, and dropped. Something must be terribly wrong.

"What are you doing, Joan?"

"Something's happened to my toes. They hurt."

"Everybody's toes hurt."

Joan could not believe that everybody's toes hurt the way hers did.

"I think they're bleeding," she ventured.

"Keep on," said Miss Levy and waved to the pianist. She did not allow for the possibility of quitting. Joan clamped her teeth on her tongue and sprang up and down for another sixteen bars of music, each time unable to believe that she had done it again. The pain grew worse. She redefined unbearable; there were further stages to come, each one beyond what she had imagined before. She favoured her right foot and then her left, but it was useless, they both hurt equally. To keep herself going, she tried to think of pain worse than this. In all of her twelve years, she couldn't think of a thing. The hardball that hit her in the nose when she was playing short stop. The scrapes she got when she went around the corner on the neighbour's scooter and slid off. Those things happened once when you weren't expecting them. This you knew exactly, in advance, and you had to keep doing it to yourself.

Then Miss Levy asked the girls to let go of the *barre*. She wanted continuous *chaîné* turns from the corner. The girls formed a line, all of them limping a little, some of them shaking. In a way the turns were easier than the rises, because you only had to jump on your toes once and then stay up. But it felt as if she were screwing her foot into a hole, taking the skin off it. Her feet were burning and throbbing inside the shoes. She felt sure there was no skin left, that she was working her way through the flesh and would soon be dancing on bones.

At last the class was over. Joan barely managed to curtsy before dragging herself to the dressing-room. Miss Levy looked after her with a smile. Joan remembered that smile. It was a damnably satisfied smile, a smile that said, I made you wait for it, now do you see why? Did you think this was going to be easy?

Sometimes Miss Levy came to the dressing-room doorway after class and stood with a hand on the knob declaiming on some issue of ballet deportment, some transgression of the dress code. But that day she disappeared into her office, leaving the girls to their grief. Moaning and gasping, they unwrapped the ribbons from their ankles and gingerly pulled their feet from the little pink prisons. Joan's feet were stuck to the inside of the shoes: she had to jerk them to dislodge them. When the foot came out, it was a crumpled, stiff thing, the toes stained with blood.

"Blood! Look!"

"Me, too!"

"Let me see."

They compared the damage. Arlene had no blood, only a few rubbed spots on her toes. Joan's feet were the worst in the whole dressing-room. She had to pluck the thin, drying skin of the tights away from her flesh. On her smallest toe blisters had erupted and broken, leaving the skin pushed back and stuck to itself like postage stamps to paper. The nail on her big toe had cut through the skin of her next toes. And worst, the second toes on both feet, the extra long ones, had been curled against the front of the shoe and were peeled raw, wet, like some kind of vegetable.

Joan was the centre of attention.

In the weeks following their initiation, the girls engaged in orgiastic discussions of remedies and prevention. To toughen the skin, rub the feet regularly with alcohol. Powder the inside of the point shoes to prevent sticking. At the risk of being considered a baby, devise a cap of lamb's-wool to be placed over the toes. And tape. Tape, tape, tape. The ultimate solution was to wrap the toes individually or in little bunches, in gauze and adhesive tape before each class. Some dancers did this so that each toe looked like a stiff little body cast protruding from the end of the foot. Then they stuffed their toes into tights and finally into the point shoes. The crushing was worse, but at least the skin didn't break. Sometimes they left their toes wrapped for weeks; finally when the tape was removed the toes looked withered and quite dead. As their new shoes were broken in, the pain became less. But then the shoes wore out; with a new pair the ripping and blistering began again.

The peculiarities of Joan's feet soon ceased to be of interest and the simple fact remained: at point work Joan was the worst in class. Miss Levy had no patience with this new, stumbling Joan who couldn't be counted upon to lead the line. It was the first sign that Joan's day was ending.

ALL THAT WAS long ago. Arlene would know how many years. She was fond of saying things like, "It's twelve years since we..." and "twenty years ago we...." It gave Joan the creeps. She hoped Arlene wouldn't do that today. She needed to talk, but she couldn't take any of that sentimental stuff.

Arlene came forward, arms open. "Joan! What a great surprise. You look wonderful. But you always do. I'm such a mess."

She reached for Joan's taut shoulders, taut body. A flush

of pre-tear pressure went through Joan's head. She gave her friend a peck on the cheek. "Actually I'm a wreck. How are you? How's your garden?"

"Thank God the kids are away at a friend's today so I can get something done."

"Don't let me take you away from anything." Joan felt irritated every time she came here and found Arlene occupied by her own life. It was totally unfair and she knew it. She excused herself partly by reasoning that Arlene's life was not good enough for her and partly by saying that on one of her rare visits, she deserved all of Arlene's attention.

"Don't be silly. Let's have tea."

Inside the house there was shadow, the clutter of toys, a record turning soundlessly on the turntable. Joan went to take it off as Arlene put the kettle on. Tchaikovsky.

"Have you been practising?" It was their joke. In the old days they used to check up, trying to catch the other out in efforts to break the tie.

"Oh no, I was just prancing around."

Arlene came out of the kitchen pulling the scarf from her head. She'd always known when Joan didn't like the way she dressed. Joan turned back to the record-player, biting her lips on the words, "You shouldn't wear kerchiefs. They make you look like a peasant."

Arlene graciously ignored her. "You know, I can't do a *grand plié*? I'm so out of shape."

"You don't look it"

"I know. I never looked it. My body doesn't change."

At eight, Arlene was thin, dark, the sad-faced girl who'd come out of the back row of the class to demonstrate a beautiful extension. Joan had been first incredulous, then jealous, then quick to ally herself with the newcomer who threatened her position as monitor. For years she had suspected that Arlene was a put-up favourite created only to spur her, Joan, on to greater things. Such was her conceit.

But who would have guessed Arlene had it in her? Those skinny legs—still skinny. The freckles on skin stretched tight over jutting crooked teeth. If they had been Joan's teeth she'd have been sent to the orthodontist. That lank, shiny black hair: there was Arab in her background. Arlene and Joan had planned their glamorous careers together in the top bunk of Arlene's family trailer parked in a tiny back yard behind a frame bungalow. They planned that Joan would be the ballerina and Arlene would dance too, but as a kind of handmaiden. Joan had the talent, they concluded, although Arlene was a good worker. At first Arlene had had trouble with weak legs, but she practised *jetés* on the way home from school, in the hallways after class, even in her sleep. She got so good at *jetés* that when visitors came to the ballet studio, Arlene was asked to do *jetés* all by herself. Years later, they were the first thing to bring her to the attention of the teachers at the Royal Ballet School.

A good worker. Now Joan could see that from the very first Arlene had set out to equal, then to surpass Joan, Joan who had it all. It would have been beneath Joan even to admit they were competing. But they had been, and Arlene had won. Her parents had sold their trailer and given up holidays to send Arlene to London. She had worked to get noticed, to get a place in the company, to emerge from the corps and become one of a handful of upcoming stars and then at twenty-eight had given it up to marry a slovenly pianist who wanted her to stay home and look after his awful children from a previous marriage. The pianist had decided to emigrate to Canada. To this Joan owed the fact that on a Saturday afternoon, having arrived in Toronto by her own equally irrational route, she could hop on the streetcar and visit her oldest friend. Sometimes she saw Arlene as a ghost from her childhood reappearing with inexplicable motive. Sometimes it seemed all they could do was compare fates. Whose choices had been worse? Whose fate less kind? But in fact, Arlene was a true friend, her only friend: with their history, they were the only ones who could understand each other.

When Joan arrived, Arlene would be working like today, or standing in front of an oven pulling out loaves of bread, or sitting in front of a sewing table with yards of draperies tumbling down the side. She would have asked Joan over for tea but then she would be too busy to talk. Joan would sit, watching. She felt that Arlene used her chores as a weapon, a shield. It had been different, once. Arlene had sought her.

Every day after class, she would come up to Joan. "Do you want to walk to the bus-stop with me?" But Joan had other friends to meet, noisy, confident, blonde friends. Only Arlene knew that there would come a day when the other friends weren't around, and Joan, who never could have walked to the bus-stop alone, would say yes.

"You're my favourite dancer in the whole class," said Arlene.

"Oh, thank you."

"You have a nice *attitude*. You can get your knee really high."

"Thank you." And as an afterthought, "You have a nice *arabesque*." It was true. Arlene was born with a good line.

Their conversations were technical, even when they weren't talking ballet.

"You're popular," Arlene said. There was something funny about the way her lips closed over her teeth—not quite. Joan stared at Arlene.

"What do you mean?"

"Everybody wants to be your friend. Everybody wants to be around you."

It was not flattery; it was simple observation. Humility had been Arlene's most attractive quality in those days. Humility, and the practical approach. She'd see a new watch or a pleated skirt on Joan and say, "Oh, that's good." Not "That's pretty," or, "I like that," but "That's good." Good for the purpose. The purpose being to achieve notice, to make a step ahead of the others, to matter.

Arlene put the teapot down heavily on the kitchen table, and hooked her foot around a chair leg, drawing the seat under her.

"You don't know how glad I am you came by. I really need to talk about something."

Tiny spokes in the skin were shooting out from the corners of her eyes, and a cleft had come on either side of her nose. Joan could never be sure she noticed the lines because they'd got worse, or because she was so worried about her own wrinkles that she imagined Arlene's growing. It was obvious, in any case, that Arlene was not happy. She had not been happy since Joan had first seen her in Toronto a year ago, but Joan didn't ask about it. She'd tried to talk her out of the marriage and when Arlene wouldn't listen, Joan had sworn to keep out of it thereafter.

Arlene put two bony elbows on the table and propped her chin between them. She closed her lips over her teeth and squeezed them, as if to keep the words in. But the words came out anyway, strained, drawn sounds.

"You know I can't handle these kids."

"Sure you can."

"No. Really." The lips struggled and reopened. "It's awful but I never really feel they're mine. I feel like I'm a servant. And Mick doesn't help, the way he treats me. I mean, I just can't seem to get through to them. For instance, you know what Mitzi wants now? Ballet lessons. I tell her she's not the right build, it'd be nothing but sorrow, but she wants them anyway. I supposed it'd be a way of getting close to her but—I just don't know. If you had a daughter, would you give her ballet lessons?"

"I have a daughter."

"Oh, that's right. I forgot, for a minute." Arlene stopped and stared at the table. Joan stared at the table, too, and the look on her face was baleful: no one understands me, it said.

"But I meant, really, I guess, if you were bringing up a child, and she wanted to . . . and you could see that it wasn't right for her, oh Joan, what's the matter? Let me get you a Kleenex, you know you haven't mentioned your daughter for years."

"You haven't asked for years."

"I didn't know you were in touch."

"We're not. The last time I heard she was eight, now

she's thirteen." Joan stared belligerently at Arlene. Arlene flustered for the Kleenex and more tea. Joan could bully so easily. She hated herself for doing it, but she couldn't help herself. She had got the habit. She didn't know why she was getting upset about Sara, when it was April. February 8 was Sara's birthday. Every February 8 since the year of her birth Joan had gone out and got drunk and cried because she'd given her kid away. Half the time Arlene had been propping her up. Once a year, every year, and that was the extent of her mourning. Today, however, she was furious because Arlene, who'd never even given birth, was playing mother while Joan, who could still remember the tearing in her pelvis, was childless. It was just more proof of how unattached Joan was. And how far down she'd gone, when she could envy poor Arlene her troubles.

"Well, does yours take ballet?"

"I don't even know." Silence. Then slowly. "If I were you, I wouldn't let her. It's too painful. I don't know. Unless she was so, so good that it would be a terrible waste if she didn't."

"Yes, but how can you tell at that age?"

"You can't."

"So what can you do?"

Arlene poured more tea. She manouevred nervously around Joan's cross words. That chippiness was the only sign that she was in need, Princess Joan had got herself into another scrape. Arlene would listen. It had always been that way. Joan outdid every problem of hers, winning —even in misery sweepstakes. There was no point in asking what it was: it would come out eventually.

"You know, I think I might give up the clubs."

"No kidding."

"Yeah. I can't stand it any more."

"I thought you liked it. I thought it was a cause with you. Stripping as the basic art form. People deserve sincerity, remember?"

"That was before."

"Before what?"

So Arlene really hadn't seen the newspaper. Joan relaxed her shoulders a little. "Before I got so old, I guess. I just don't think I can hack it any more. The clubs are getting so seedy. Most of the other girls aren't even dancers, you know. You wouldn't believe the things they do backstage. Borrow your stuff without asking. I got into a big fight there on Thursday night, actually."

"Did you lose your job?"

"I don't know. Not yet. They just told me not to go in last night." She couldn't bring herself to tell Arlene about getting busted. "But I've got to get out. I mean it this time. Before things get worse. I'm slipping. Doing dumb things."

"Like what? Tell me?"

"Like fighting. Getting drunk. And last night I got drunk and went to bed with a guy I just met. I haven't done that in ages. It's a bad sign."

"What are you going to do?"

She started to cry.

Arlene sat silently, unsurprised. Since they'd first left home together at sixteen it had often come down to this: the two of them, an Arborite table somewhere, a pot of tea. Out of money, out of favour, out of steam. It was as if their lives were big balls of thread. They sat and sat, and the ball was thick and hopelessly tangled, but finally it began to shift and one little strand drifted free until finally it was all rolling out again. Arlene had learned to await the unravelling. Joan had always leapt too fast, pulling and breaking things.

"Sometimes I can't believe this is my life. It's like I got on the wrong route somewhere, this was not where I was going."

"It's not over. You're only thirty."

"Thirty! Thirty's the end. You know I'm getting so I'm afraid to look in the mirror in the morning? Wrinkles, bags, grey hair—I'm scanning for it all the time."

"You always were pretty struck on mirrors."

Joan hiccupped, cried some more, and let Arlene pour the tea.

*   *   *

ALWAYS, IN THE studio, Joan had been presented with her image, feet turned to the corners of the room, body spinning, caught in the bleary silver of the back mirror, distinguished only by a slighter thigh or darker arm from the next girls. She sought reassurance in mirrors and found the opposite. A certain angle made her look heavy. Her chin sagged slightly. Her critical faculty was never as sharp as when she looked in a mirror. She was not perfect.

Once she had been perfect, but that little body of four equal parts had grown; its thighs and hips had swelled. Every pound that went on her in adolescence was eyed askance, for it became an addition to the load, to be regretted the way an extra bag loaded on a beast of burden was to be regretted as it set out on a long, uphill trek.

Joan had been on a diet ever since she was eleven. It was probably because Miss Levy herself should have been on a diet that she terrorized the girls so much about their weight. The diet was really just another way of looking in mirrors. It was a kind of sneak preview for mirrors, watching what went in to see what would become of Joan's body. She had seen her legs get long, her breasts go from dark gumdrops to full, fatless loops over her bony ribs. The face had filled out too. Before puberty she'd looked older, her face peaked and worried, the face of a mother at the top of this growing statue, the face of a sculptor inspecting his work. But then it began to want its own beauty. It had been a stretch of skin through which words and eyesight came only with difficulty, and then it came to life. Joan's eyes turned from hazel to dark brown. Her skin and lips became fleshy, warm, disobedient. She acquired a sulky, sensuous look. To Miss Levy the new face was a threat.

The girls had been on point for half a year when Miss Levy announced that she was going to choose two dancers from the class to do a *pas de deux* for the recital. It was to be a romantic duet with lifts. Of course it had to be danced on point. Since there were only two "men" in the class and one of them was six inches shorter than all of the girls even standing on flat feet, there wasn't much difficulty in choosing a man for the part. It had to be Vern.

If there were any justice, Joan would never have had to give Vern a second look. He was tall and scrawny with big ears. He was a creep, but he was indispensable. He had ten young women on their mettle to be chosen to dance with him. In the old days, there would have been no doubt that the girl chosen for the *pas de deux* would have been Joan. But since point shoes had been introduced, the hierarchy was threatening to crumble.

Sunday afternoon Arlene and Joan arrived together, before the other girls, and sat in the dressing-room giggling. Miss Levy waited in semi-darkness in her office. Fifteen minutes late, she opened the studio door and the girls filed in, point shoes clacking in their hands. Vern sauntered sheepishly out of the boy's change room. All of a sudden friends ceased to be friends: they were competing.

Miss Levy knew how to set a stage. Displayed in the back of the room was a blue velvet tutu, a short one with a stiff skirt and matching blue velvet pants. It hung like a piece of taxidermy in a plastic bag. The girls eyed it covertly. It would be worn by the chosen one: someone's mother would take it home for fitting. Aside from the tutu, there was only Miss Levy in the room, a strange, far-off Miss Levy who must be appeased.

"Good afternoon, girls. And Vern."

"Good afternoon, Miss Levy."

They took their places at the *barre*. Miss Levy asked for point shoes right after the *pliés*. Joan felt confident as she reached for her shoes, partly inspired by her previous successes in that room, and partly by the security of the taping around her toes. She looked at Arlene, sitting on the floor beside her, winding the shoe ribbons around her ankles, her buck teeth showing slightly under her lips. She did not think the part, nor the tutu, would sit well on

Arlene. Surely this time she could get away from the pain and really dance on point.

Miss Levy gave them a long warm-up on point, rises, and *barre* work, *bourrées* up and down the floor, *posé* turns. Arlene led the line. Behind her, Joan started out strongly enough, but before long the pernicious rubbing inside her shoes began. She clenched and unclenched her foot, working to adjust the taped caps of her toes.

When her second turn to dance down the diagonal came up, she sprang onto her right foot and felt a slash like a knife cut across her toes. She faltered. Then she started again and made the long journey from one corner to the other. There was an ugly shock of pain each time she stepped. She knew that Miss Levy was watching, and Vern, too, from his saturnine position at the back of the room.

"Are you having problems?" Miss Levy's voice, though it came over Joan's back, seemed to have been with her all the time.

"No, not really," Joan muttered without turning her face to the teacher. She knew it was rude, but she was afraid she was going to cry.

"Look at me when I'm speaking to you."

"Yes, Miss Levy."

"Is something wrong?"

"No, Miss Levy."

"Well, carry on then."

Joan carried on. She felt the curious eyes of her classmates. Each girl was working in her own glass cage. Arlene would not be exactly hoping for Joan's downfall, she would not dare to hope for that because it might have brought bad luck on herself, but she would be holding her breath against the other's success. Joan made a decision that she would beat them all. She would dance through whatever pain came to her. She would let it sear up her legs and into her head, but she would carry on. She believed confusedly that if she danced long enough, she would come out the other side of pain, emerge into freedom and weightlessness, and then dance as long as she

liked. She tried to see that place ahead of her. The pain of
each step brought her closer.

Miss Levy called a break, pulling Joan out of her trance.
The girls put on their sweaters and sat under the *barre*,
damp and shaking, not looking at one another, while Miss
Levy worked with Vern.

He was insufferable. He was as far from a hero as
anyone could be. Judging by the steps Miss Levy was
giving him, his role in the *pas de deux* would be minimal.
He had to stand with one foot in front of the other, walk in
a circle, perform certain manly lunges with his arms up
like brackets for the girl to twirl between. He got sixteen
bars of music to himself, for leaps. When he began to
practise his *tours en l'air,* Joan was jealous. She could have
done them better if she hadn't had to wear those shoes.

Miss Levy asked Arlene to dance with Vern.

Joan watched as the two stood side by side, and Arlene
rose on her points, pirouetted, and inclined with careful,
imperfect grace. The girls all sighed: it was so romantic.
Miss Levy cut the performance short, however. She wasn't
entirely pleased and Joan could see why. There was something *too* matched about Arlene and Vern. In the light of
day they were comic partners, bringing out each other's
freckles and buck teeth.

"You try, Joan."

"Yes, Miss Levy."

Joan got up and walked to the centre of the room. Vern
was smirking at her. Miss Levy gave her a series of turns
and *bourrées* to do, ending with an *arabesque* holding
onto Vern's extended, branch-like arm.

"Ready, and. . . ."

The piano began. Joan reached for Vern's arm and
began. She rose on her points and felt the pain return. It
was caused by the weight of her flesh. She blamed the
pain on the new hillocks of fat over her hip-bones at the
side, on the softness in her upper arms and breasts; all of
these changes were hardly noticeable except that they
added ounces and finally pounds. Now all that weight bore
down on her toes. She hated her flesh. Miss Levy had

warned her—every pound made things worse. Try carrying a pound of butter, she'd said, and see how easily you can dance. Her body seemed to be pounds and pounds of butter. She wished she could have stayed the way she was at eleven, all frame with no chassis, all bone and muscle and childish straight lines. Some girls seemed to be able to keep themselves from maturing, at least until the day they stopped dancing, when the repressed fat would burst out all over into great hard bulges like Miss Levy's.

Joan sucked in her breath and reached for Vern's arm.

"She's grabbing me 'way too tight."

"Start again."

Joan went through the steps, furious at her body because it felt so heavy, so dead. Tears were standing over her eyes. Her feet were throbbing. Finally a warm wash seemed to cover her.

"Try again. Joan, you're too tense." Again. Joan clutched Vern's arm harder, hating the dance that made her need him like that. She stumbled.

"What on earth is wrong, Joan?"

"It's my feet."

They all looked down at once. There was a lot of blood. It was soaking up her tights from the slippers, making ragged red peaks on her pink calves.

"Oh, my goodness," said Miss Levy.

As the room regarded Joan's messy, inefficient instruments, she was ashamed. "I'll go and wash them."

"Arlene, will you help her?"

Miss Levy's voice was cold. Joan listened for some recollection of tenderness, of her status as favourite. Nothing. There was only a savour of punishment.

"And then come back, Arlene, and learn your part. The rest can go."

Joan wasn't going to cry, then or ever, about the point shoes. She wasn't worried about the *pas de deux* or about the blue tutu. There would be other parts for her, she would work harder, lose weight, make herself hard and fine and without fluid. It was her first loss to Arlene, and her feet were skinned and blistered, but when she left the studio she felt a mean kind of triumph. She had found her will. She could have danced until she was blood-red up to the neck; the pain had finally become irrelevant. It was Miss Levy who had cracked first, and Joan's body was unbroken, hers alone.

DANCING HAD MADE Joan a wanderer. She had lain in bed at night reading ballet books and floating above her mattress. Miss Levy said Joan had to go away if she really wanted to dance. She knew she really wanted to dance. That meant only her parents remained to be convinced. Joan wouldn't mind leaving them. She had already left them years before, when she was very young. She had left them when she left off believing in their kind of life. Joan would find a way, and she would go.

There was a girl who'd "gone" from Miss Levy's school several years before Joan. She had been the star pupil. Her photograph hung outside Miss Levy's office. The girl stood in a perfect second *arabesque*, shown in profile. She wore a red tutu and red shoes: the pink ribbons were tied so tight they made indentations in her ankles. The leg was at exactly ninety degrees, her arms firmly ahead and her eyes lifted over her hand. On the back of her head was a tight knob of hair and on the front of her head fixed button eyes, hooked to the future. Joan thought the star pupil's legs were a little short, but there was one thing she obviously had and that was vision.

Arlene, too, was determined that she should go to England. It seemed unlikely: Arlene's family could not afford to send her. They had sustained each other in the fantasy, however, each secretly believing that only *she* would make it, but needing the company of a friend in the dream.

Miss Levy had rarely addressed Joan by name since the audition: she acted as if the girl had intentionally failed so as to wound her. Even when Joan's point work improved as her feet toughened and she became more adept with tape, Miss Levy indulged in the long punishment.

"The front girl should step to the back of the line; her timing is wrong," she'd say. "The second girl may lead." The front girl would have been Joan, and the second Arlene. Once in a while the reverse would happen: Joan would be signalled, impatiently, by Miss Levy to take over the lead, or to demonstrate an *enchaînement,* since she could put the steps together faster than anyone else could. Miss Levy would watch disconsolately while the other girls tried to do it, and then turn away.

"Show them, Joan," she'd say, looking out the window.

Miss Levy could refuse to watch her, but she couldn't stop Joan from dancing well. She could leap higher than the boys and sometimes, when she stood by the *barre* to warm up, she had surging moments when she could feel her limbs becoming articulate, losing their heavy dumbness and coming to life in the new animal she was.

She had gained a licence to express herself. That a fifteen-year-old girl moving from the tyranny of home to the boredom of school and back again, gratefully, to the tyranny of dance, should have uncovered a self to express amazed even Joan. But it had happened. She had grown rebellious by obeying all the rules. Perhaps it was in her chemistry, in the adultness of her body. Joan connected the new power with her bushes of hair in unexpected places and the breasts that bounced when she moved.

"Hold them up," Miss Levy would instruct. "Don't let them bounce. There are muscles there, you can control them." Miss Levy herself had a monumental bosom. No matter, however: her dancers weren't meant to indulge in these things. Obedient Arlene had remained in the form of a leprechaun, and Joan felt sorry for her. Joan liked breasts on principle, but thought hers were a funny shape, being conical and pointing out to the sides, like wall-eyes. She bought a bra with padding in it to round them out. Miss Levy for once had not had the nerve to interfere. The padded bra was the beginning of her escape.

Joan talked Arlene and the others into going to the Waffle Shop to have chips with gravy and cherry Cokes after class, a practice strictly forbidden by Miss Levy.

Getting away was always a problem. Arlene would stand by the door, holding her satchel of shoes and tights. Joan stood in front of the narrow dressing-room mirror, wearing her padded satin bra.

"Just a minute, wait a sec." She was already expert at drawing the black line around the bottom of her eyes, even though in school it was said that if you wore eye-liner that way you were a slut. She put on lipstick and back-combed her hair. She had Estée Lauder perfume, borrowed from her mother's drawer, on her temples and the hollow over her collar-bone. When the last bit of make-up was patted down with powder, the tubes packed in the fishing-tackle box she now carried all the time, Joan would put on her shirt and jacket. Finally she would snap her leather riding gloves over the back of her hands as they all watched.

Once Joan was ready, the girls would exit the studio in a clump, Joan pressed into their midst. They'd demonstrate combinations on their way down the hall—"Step *ballonné*, *ballonné*, *ballonné*," someone would say, and the right leg would sweep out and then snap back toward the knee three times as they passed Miss Levy's office. When Miss Levy looked up with irritation at the noise and the rush-ing, they protested: "We're just practising, Miss Levy." Not once did she catch a glimpse of Joan's made-up face.

Outside the glass door, the girls clattered giggling down the long staircase. Under the arcade and out of sight, should Miss Levy happen to glance down from her win-dow, Joan would imitate the teacher's ponderous walk; toes turned out to the corners of the imaginary box she always said you were to envision around your feet, slowly rotating head scanning the room from side to side, lips pressed together.

There was no pity for Miss Levy now that her students were old enough to fight back. They amused themselves by making up stories about the teacher's life. When she came into the classroom sterner than usual, walking with her cane, and holding her neck stiff, turning her whole body to turn her head, they said she'd been drunk the night before.

"Be very good today, girls. I have a sick headache." Behind her back they rolled their eyes. Once Joan had brought up Miss Levy's favourite smoked meat sandwich on rye from the restaurant downstairs and overheard her on the telephone. "I don't want to talk about it now," she shouted, and banged down the receiver. From this incident, Joan created a violent boy-friend, and entertained the others in the Waffle Shop with descriptions of how the man made attempts on Levy's squat person on a sofa.

Meanwhile, the teacher mounted her own offence. One Monday night Joan came to the studio from school as usual, stopping in the wash-room in the hall to scrub her face and take the back-combing out of her hair. The girls were ready and warming up for ten minutes; Vern was at the end of the *barre* making wisecracks. Finally Miss Levy came in.

Approaching with small steps, her kid slippers hissing slightly on the hardwood, sticky with the resin from the box in the corner, she made no greeting.

"*Pliés*," she said. "Ready, and." Her voice sounded flat. Drinking? Sulking? Had they forgotten something? The pianist looked inquiringly over her shoulder. Miss Levy hadn't stipulated the *plié* exercise she wanted.

"*Pliés!*"

The girls snapped their feet into the first position and raised their right arms to the side, holding the *barre* with their left. It was going to be a bad day. They drew up their thigh muscles, ready to go. Then it started.

"You are dancers," said Miss Levy.

The pianist took her hands off the keys just before the initial crash. The girls' knees quivered at the beginning of the bend and then stayed up straight.

"Tell me, what do you come here for, day after day?"

The old rhetorical question. No one moved. No one wanted to get into trouble by answering, even if the answer was dictated.

"You come here because you're dancers. You're trained

to become artists. You must remember that. You have your profession to live up to. You aren't common street girls who can wander about in public embracing your boyfriends, covered in make-up. What do you think I spend all this time on you for, so you can stand on a street corner with your hip out?"

Miss Levy particularly hated the stance girls affected with one leg bent and the hip cocked to the side. She said it created saddle-bags of fat on the side of the thigh; she implied that it led to moral degeneracy.

"Last Saturday," Miss Levy began again, "I went out for a walk on Jasper Avenue and what did I see? What do you think I saw? Anyone? I saw one of my own girls dressed up like a hussie and hanging on some boy's arm." She turned her back on them and looked toward the windows at the end of the front room, as if to remind them of the evils beyond. "I think we can all guess who it was."

The objects of the attack remained still and tensed, looking straight ahead at the *barre*. It could have been any of them but it was most likely Joan. Saturday after class Joan had gone downtown with a boy from school, wearing her eye-liner and her lipstick and her gloves with the holes in the knuckles; they'd strolled among the stores and then went home on the bus. Joan's heart began to beat in her throat. Her face grew very hot, that uncontrollable blush. She stared through the head in front of her, wishing Levy would fly out the window, wishing everyone else in the room dead on the floor, for being witness to her humiliation.

And then Miss Levy began to cry. Her thick lower lip, rimmed with the row of tiny black hairs, began to tremble. Her voice rose half an octave and began to shake. "I just never thought I'd see the day when one of my own girls. . . ." She walked away from them then, toward the window. She stood in front of it, solid black and shot through with the glare of the glass. She looked like a stone guard at the entrance to a tomb.

Her eyes were fixed on the alley below. When her girls were young, she'd been the good witch who led them to the rarified realm of ballet. She had cast herself in opposition to the colours and the noise of the city streets. Now the girls were almost adults. Miss Levy had fought this battle with others before them, and except in the case of the goody-two-shoes in the red tutu hanging in her frame in the hall, she had lost. Each loss she would explain as the failure of *girls,* not of *art,* but the toll against her mounted; art must have seemed in jeopardy. Joan understood, and saw as well that Miss Levy was not going to give up her fight. The light hit the pane of glass; dust was reflected. There was a teacher in the window, looking back into the room saying, stay forever in the studio with me, don't grow up. If you do, you defy me.

Very well, I defy you.

The silence was long.

The pianist tried to catch Joan's eye, an idiotic smile on her face. Joan looked through her, too. She had decided to look through them all from then on.

"What do you have to say for yourself, Joan?"

"I'm sorry, Miss Levy." A craven apology, bitterly given.

"Ready, and . . ." said Miss Levy, turning back to face the class. Her voice began to soar again. Perhaps she thought she'd won, for the moment; she was fool enough to enjoy lip service. The pianist's hands were raised over the keys. "*Pliés* in first, second, fourth, fifth, and fourth crossed. . . . And if I *ever,* ever catch one of you again, I'll expel you. Your parents would agree. You can never be too careful in this world, never. When you're a dancer, you've got to watch your behaviour in public all the time. You represent me, you represent my school, you represent the profession. I won't have it, do you hear, I won't have it! Ready, and. . . ."

Finally, the music started.

"SO WHAT HAPPENED with this guy?" Arlene was saying.

"Oh, he was just a guy I met at the club. And then he came over. We had a few drinks. Quite a few. One thing I remember. He said there was no way a man who hated women, like he did, and a woman like me who hated men, could get together. Hah! And you know the dumb thing? The only reason I ever had any time for him was he told me about this microscopic animal, this cell, called the paramoecium and I loved hearing him talk." She began to laugh, and a tear splashed onto the table.

Arlene put out her finger and dabbed the spot of water. She lifted her finger and looked at it, glistening on the tip.

"How now? What do we have here? And what shall I do with it? Shall I blow it away?" She put the finger to the edge of her lips and blew. The moisture vanished. "Aw come on, it doesn't sound so bad. He wasn't a rapist was he? Or a pervert? You can't fall apart, Joan. You know I'm counting on you to enjoy your life for both of us. You can do anything you want, if you just keep on. I know you can."

"I used to think that. But God, I'm afraid of turning into one of those awful old dancers who's fat and drunk and bitter and sits around talking about how if only her agent hadn't screwed up on the New York trip they'd have it all, you know what I mean? If I start getting like that, I want you to shoot me, O.K.? Shoot me. Promise?"

"O.K. I promise. Let's go for a walk. I have an idea."

Between the Greek cafés on the Danforth there were cheap stores where children's shoes and overalls hung bleached in the windows. Past an army surplus store there was a small, pink-lettered sign. *Destin. Salon de Thé. 2nd. Flr. M. Darling.*

Fortune-tellers were a bad habit with Joan and Arlene. Back home in Edmonton, the common view was that the only people who went to have their tea leaves or their palm scrutinized by the fraudulent Gipsies of the town were the weak, the lost, and the artists. Miss Levy frequented readers. Her favourite had been down in Ciro's café. Joan and Arlene followed their teacher there, sat in the next booth beyond the curtains, and watched her tuck herself into a nook to wait for the lady with the fringed scarf and thick painted lips.

Ballet people were superstitious. A hair on your sandwich meant you were going to get sick; new shoes on the table-top meant bad luck. Talismans and charms helped protect you: a feather fan on the mantel, a locket with an old photograph, a used slipper. In London, too, the dancers went to the painted Gipsy wagons along Portobello Road. Away from home Joan and Arlene had begun to seek the dire predictions of old women with warts, wrinkles, deep clefts in their faces, and deep shafts of light falling into their eyes. But that was in another country. Today Joan was ambivalent.

The stairs were narrow and turned back on themselves twice in the climb. At the third-floor landing, black-and-white linoleum squares on the floor announced the start of Mr. Darling's turf. "Please knock," said a hand-written note.

The door was opened by a squat woman with short grey hair. "I am Vera. Come this way."

Vera led them past an open door to a kitchen, and then along a narrow hall hung with framed newspaper articles about lucky investments: one was meant to assume the successes had been made through tips from Mr. Darling. There were pictures of Mr. Darling shaking hands with dignitaries, celebrities.

"You are the lady who was here last week."

"This is my friend, Joan."

"Please, no names."

Vera gestured them to a table. Joan glared at Arlene. So she'd been here last week. It was a little too often to her mind.

The tea-room had a green ceiling and walls. White plaster curls and leaves festooned the corners and ledges; the place looked like a *petit four*. There were eight tiny tables with white table-cloths and wrought-iron chairs. There was antique china and a silver tea-set with a samovar. In the centre of the ceiling hung a crystal basket chandelier.

"Who is this guy? These are real antiques."

"His family's. See that portrait of the guy in the judge's gown? That's his father."

Now Joan noticed there were candles everywhere. Vera lifted a taper off the centre table and lit it. Then she walked around the room lighting the rest. In the corners there were wall sconces. On the mantel a series of candelabra, in a mirror display cabinet more candles. As she touched each one with her lighted taper, more shadows sprang into the room. Now the ceiling was stippled snake skin. The windows were painted black. The crone-guard shuffled to their side.

"I'll take your money. That's twenty-five dollars each."

"Twenty-five? It used to be twenty."

"'S twenty-five."

"But it's always been twenty." Arlene's voice was pinched, like a tenant being forced beyond her means. Joan looked away. Arlene drew up her purse resignedly, and Joan followed. Vera took the bills and went back down the hall to the kitchen.

In the corner, behind her, Joan could see one pane of glass that was not painted. She strained her neck to see out. They were across the street from a little island of park. There was the grey circle of an empty wading pool, a stone fountain with no water in it, and men in ski jackets talking under a tree that looked as if it, too, had turned to stone. The background sky was a deep rose grey, and the sun on its angle turned the edges of the buildings a sharp navy. A taxi, yellow and black and bright as a kite, pulled up below the window. A man paid his fare and got out, looking down the street as if he didn't know where to go. Joan did not want to be in this tea-room.

"What does Mr. Darling tell you about your future?" Joan knew well enough that this was not the question she should ask.

"Oh, things."

"And do they come true?"

"Yes."

"What came true that he told you?"

"You know I can't say, Joan. He tells you things about your past, too."

"About my past I already know, thank you."

Vera returned with teacups and pots. The cream she put in a little glass vase inside the cup. There was a bowl of white sugar lumps on their table. Both the women lifted their teapots and stirred the leaves at the same time. Poured the cream in, at the same time. Two lumps of sugar. Sipped.

Arlene drained her cup, put her right hand on it, turned it upside down in the saucer and spun it three times. Joan was facing the hall: she could see a small barrel-chested man wearing a brown leather jacket cross the hall and disappear into the kitchen. At once his reflection appeared in the glass of a large picture hanging in the hall.

"Is that him?"

"Probably, I can't see."

Joan watched in the picture frame. She could see the man move blindly back and forth between large white objects against the walls. She couldn't see his hands or his head, only the trunk and arms. He leaned into his hands, which were stretched out in front of him. His walk was steady, but slow, like a dance. Three steps one way, three the other. Perhaps he was readying himself for the messages he was about to receive, practising for his trance. There was a familiar shape to the movements; they reminded Joan of something. Suddenly he sat, and bent his head over something. Of course. He'd been making his dinner, and now he was eating it.

"This is ridiculous. I'm going to go. We've been waiting forty-five minutes."

"Don't get mad. You'll queer your readings."

"I've got to work tonight. I can't sit here forever."

At that moment, as if he'd heard, the man stood and strode out of the kitchen, exploding full face into Joan's watching glass.

"You can come in now."

Arlene pointed to Joan. Joan stood up, dropping her handbag.

"Take your teacup."

"Oh."

In the next room, Mr. Darling had taken a seat at a small rosewood table half hidden by a Victorian screen painted with herons. He gave Joan a long, unfriendly stare. Then he poured the liquid out of her cup, and dumped out the leaves. He had thick, very dark glasses and a face like a ferret, oddly narrow on top of that wide body. His shirt was undone down his chest and tufts of blond hair stood out. He wore gold chains around his neck and wrists.

"Have you got a photograph with you? It doesn't have to be you, but someone relevant."

She felt as if she were applying for a passport. She found her wallet. She kept no photograph of herself, but there was a small shot of her mother. She drew it out.

"My mother."

He reached for it.

"Is that all? It's too small. I can't read it. I have weak eyes. Whoever sent you here should have told you."

"Well they didn't."

"Then I wasn't meant to read a photograph. Have you got some keys?"

She dug out her keys, but as she placed them on the table his eye fastened on her ring. It was an old tiger's-eye she'd bought on Portobello Road.

"May I hold that?"

She slipped it off her finger. He grabbed it, and shut his eyes.

"There are people speaking in English accents. Stay away from them. You don't like being a loser, do you? Well, then, stay away from them."

Joan fell into the old habit of optimistic interpretation. If staying away from the English was wise then it had been good that she had come home to Canada.

"What does the initial J mean to you?"

"Nothing."

"A person born in January. A Capricorn."

"I don't know."

"Don't block me." He was practically shouting. "You're being obstructionist."

"I'm not."

"Initial J."

"Me, Joan. But not a Cap—"

"No, no." He jiggled impatiently in his chair.

"Joe."

"Joe. That's him. Stay away from him."

"He's not here. That's over."

"Over, but not finished. Stay away from him. He's a desperado. He'll never change. You should know, after all that happened. Did you lose a child? Were you supposed to marry this man?"

"Not marry. The child, yes." I know my past, Joan reminded herself. I'm not going to fall for his telling me what I already know.

Now Mr. Darling settled into a rhythmic weaving in his chair. He looked at his hands where they lay on the table, the tiger's-eye ring between thumb and forefinger. "They're telling me," he said. "They're telling me to tell you that you're in a black nimbus, a spiritual cloud. You're out of focus. What? Yes. A pattern, yes, thank you." He bobbed his head. "They gave me that word, the voices did. A pattern you got from this man Joe."

"That's not true. That was a long time ago."

"Don't talk back to me!"

He slammed his hands on the table and stood, shaking so violently that he made its legs rattle. He looked into her eyes, but his pupils were large and seemed not to take her in. "You didn't come here for the right reasons. I can see that, don't you think you can fool me. You aren't willing to listen to me. You came here to test me. You're a man-hater. I can feel it around you."

Joan pushed her own chair back from the table. "You know I get a strange feeling from you. You're the one who's hostile. Maybe I scare you. You should know you can't read a fortune for someone you dislike."

Mr. Darling lifted his hands and stepped back from the chair. "Don't you get personal with me," he shouted. "Don't you try that. It's not allowed. I won't have it. I won't finish your reading and you can't come back here for a year."

"Don't worry about it. I wouldn't come back here if you paid me. You better give me my money back."

"Your reading is finished," said Mr. Darling. As he was walking away Joan noticed that he had a twisted spine, and a hump on one shoulder. He was nearly blind and he stuttered; he was the lame, the halt, and the blind rolled into one. He left the room.

Joan sat at the rosewood table. She looked at the blue herons browsing on the silk screen. Their knees were lifted gently out of the water, their beaks raised to pick up the slightest hint of disturbance. She felt stupid. Really stupid. She'd done it again. She had got into a fight with a stranger. So *what* if he was trying to tell her what to do, she'd paid money for it. He didn't even know her. If he thought she was a person in a cloud, too bad for him: she didn't have to believe him. She wanted to have more of the reading. She certainly didn't want to wrestle with Vera for her twenty-five dollars.

She kept sitting at the table.

In two minutes Mr. Darling came back. "I said your reading was over."

"Well, I'm still here. I'm trying to decide what I should do."

"Don't ask me."

Joan laughed.

Mr. Darling came and stood right in front of her, but she wasn't going to be bullied into standing up. Standing up, she'd be half-way out of her position; she'd have started to retreat.

"Look, Mr. Darling, I didn't mean to offend you. I want to finish the reading. Or have my money back."

"You're not getting your money back. You insulted me."

"I didn't mean to. I hear you're very good, and I want to finish the reading. I'm here to listen. I really am."

Mr. Darling wavered, unsure whether to stand on the insult or fall for the flattery. He fell for it.

"Well, all right then, I'll just read your cards. But you can't come back for two years." He walked stiffly back to his seat and sat down, his head cocked defensively. "I'll try to re-establish contact with my voices."

"Fine."

"And I won't read you again for two years, understand?"

Joan nodded.

He began to weave again, both hands on her ring.

"As I was saying, you're in a bad pattern. Going from man to man. You're desperate." He opened his eyes. "No offence. I'm not saying you're ugly or anything. I mean," he shrugged elaborately, "Marilyn Monroe was desperate."

"Of course."

"My voices are telling me that you are in a pattern left by this bad man Joe. Your death energy is coming out. Take these cards and shuffle them, make them your own."

Now he picked up the deck of cards. "Place your hand on this and ask a question."

"Out loud?"

"Of course," he snapped. "I'm not going to read your mind."

"What work will I be doing in the future?"

"What do you do now? Do you have a job?"

"I'm a dancer."

"I see. Oh yes, you'll be a success."

"In what?"

"I see success. Lights all around you. How old are you now? The next two years will be peak, very good, but you can't waste any more time. You've got to get in focus. Put your left hand on this pile."

He cut the cards. "Questions?"

"What about a man?" She didn't want to admit she was thinking of David. It was unscientific and David would scoff.

"What man? Does he have something on his face? A mark?"

"A mole."

"Curly hair?"

"No, straight."

"Oh yes, so it is. Yes, I've got him. You're strangers. It's not an easy one. Try being friends. He doesn't know anything about these things, so you must start at the beginning. Don't rush. It will wait."

Mr. Darling's frenzy was slowing. His voice came out more easily. "Give me something else you carry. That's good, your keys. You keep that end. Yes. I can see. You do not know how to have a relationship with anyone. Man or woman. Especially man. You do not trust men. You have lots of horror stories in your past. I know, I know. You wouldn't believe the things people have been through. The things they tell me. But remember. The taker loses and the giver is repaid a hundred-fold, isn't that what the Bible says?"

Joan was astonished to find her eyes filling with tears.

"This man I keep going back to, this J. He hurt you so, you have not recovered. You must get out of the cloud. You must hurry. You have only the next few months. If you had come to me six months from now it would have been too late. You know what you need? You need a therapist. Go see a psychiatrist, a woman. Tell her you want to learn how to have a relationship so that you don't have to be either the queen or the slave."

He dropped the keys. Joan dragged them back to her purse, her heart pounding. She could murder Arlene. What happened to the good old-fashioned hocus-pocus? They had to find a tea-leaf reader who referred people to shrinks. Maybe she should have asked Vera if she took ROSEHIP.

"And, oh yes, there will be the sudden death of a man. You will be notified." With that, Mr. Darling looked up, and dismissed her. "Don't tell anyone about your reading."

"I'm sure I won't." Joan had meant to be ambiguous, smug, but she was shaken. She collected her ring and purse, and stood. Probably Arlene had primed him for the whole thing. She made for the door, passing Arlene, who stuck her head out the door of the tea-room.

"Aren't you going to wait for me?"

"No way. I've gotta get out of here."

She ran down the stairs and out into the present tense of fresh air. She'd spent her luxury money. What a sting! Go to these guys when you're down, and they zero in on your weaknesses. She felt worse than she had when she came. She wished she could forget it all, but she couldn't. She'd remember every word.

CHAPTER SEVEN

Joan was sleeping in a high bed with a curved headboard. A man lay beside her on his back. It was the beginning of May, but snow had begun to fall outside. So much snow fell that there were heavy drifts up against the sides of the houses, rounding all the corners, blocking passages. Looking out of her bedroom window she could see that there was a state of emergency in the city, so much snow had fallen. She heard a faint rumble of dump trucks coming to take the snow away.

When she lay down on the bed again, she saw that snow had come inside her room as well. The man beside her was covered with the snow that wasn't really snow but a white foam, clinging to his face and neck. What was it? Shaving cream? Chemical warfare? No, it was grief, age, that which could not be changed.

A dream Rudy, noble and full of grace, jumped onto the bed and began to whine. There must be somebody coming, a thief. She comforted the dog and faced the bedroom door. The door began to open. She could see the squat form of an old woman there in the doorway, with a pram holding a phantom baby. The woman had a light in her hand; a beam was directed straight at them. The light came up brighter, and Joan bit down on the snow to stop her scream.

The telephone rang.

The ring came from the world where Joan was supposed to be. Her face was pressed into a foam pillow. David's shoulder was beside her mouth. She forced herself up, her feet only just hitting the floor as Rudy, sleeping under the bed as usual, slid out, ready for a rapid escape.

"Hello?"

She was trying to keep her voice neutral, to keep the huskiness out of it while she made the immense effort of pulling her wits together.

"Joan?"

"Mother?"

"Is that you, Joan?"

"Mother!" She was still trying to think. Had she done something wrong, or was this a social call? "It's nice to hear your voice." Surprisingly, it was.

"How are you dear?" It was a very controlled voice.

"I'm fine, Mum, fine. Is everything all right?"

There was a pause. Joan's eye focussed on the kitchen clock. It was barely 8:30. Joan's mother did not routinely call at this hour of the day. She rarely called at all, since she had an old-fashioned disapproval of spending money on long-distance wires, but when she did call it was always later in the morning, around nine in Alberta, after Joan's father had gone to work. Every now and then, Joan and her mother had intimate conversations over these wires, each seated in the safety of a world of her own making, looking at her own trinkets and house-plants, out of range of the other's imperative.

They were no longer close. They were more like two nebulae in space. They could revolve in the expected patterns as long as they never came too near one another. If they did, they would collapse into each other's gravity, or explode.

It was six-thirty in the morning in Alberta and her mother had telephoned.

"Mother, are you all right?"

Joan listened to the silence, trying to detect the problem. Her mother would first try her own detections: she could tell if Joan was alone by the sound of her voice, and she seemed to be able to read sex instantly from the distance of 2,500 miles. When she did, her reaction was a swift hurt and apologies about being a bother.

"Were you still sleeping, dear?" Her mother's voice was wobbling.

"Not really, just dozing. I finished work early last night."

One of the fictions maintained between them was that Joan performed with dance companies, in musical shows and sometimes at conventions. Although it had been a decade since Joan had done anything other than strip, her parents continued to believe that she was a variety showgirl. That was as far as they were willing to go. Joan appreciated the fact. It gave them all privacy. Privacy allowed parents and child to maintain good impressions of one another.

"Dear." There was another pause. "Dear, I—really, there's only one way to tell you this. I can't even believe it myself." The voice faded and then came back. "He only went into the hospital two days ago, and I would have called but it didn't seem serious and now—it's all over."

Joan's mother never answered a question directly, didn't express things in logical order, and half the time forgot to tell you the name of whoever she was talking about. If you asked her if she was busy Monday she started to tell you the roof was leaking over the front bedroom. Often Joan was panting with irritation within two minutes of the opening of a conversation. Then she was sad because she was so annoyed: there had been a time when simple little things like pronoun antecedents were unnecessary to them.

"He? Mother, please. Who?"

"Your father."

"What do you mean it's all over?"

"He died, dear."

My father? You mean your husband? Dad? Dead? Howard Sincere? Joan struggled against incredulity. She wanted to tell her mother she was crazy, and bit her tongue.

"When?"

"This morning, around one o'clock."

"But he wasn't even *sick*," she argued.

"He had a little heart attack at work. And then—he had a bigger one."

"Oh, Mum, are you O.K.?" Joan was wailing now. "What did you do?"

"Your Aunt Beth is here. She'd just happened to come, for a visit."

Aunt Beth lived in Winnipeg. Joan had never liked her. Her mother went on talking.

"He lost consciousness. He never spoke to me again after the first time. He said, he said he'd be coming home in a day or two."

Her mother's voice was becoming child-like, soft at the edges of words. Meanwhile, Joan had to concentrate on her body. She had got a big cramp in her left leg, in the back. Hamstring. It was tightening; it became insupportable and she had to sit down. She could not reach the table, the telephone wire was too short, so she was sliding down the wall. She had not cried yet.

"Mum, I'm so sorry, I just can't seem to—to—think. I want to do something, I don't know what. What should I do?" Joan had lived in a world without family for so long she had lost her instincts for it. She rubbed the back of her leg desperately.

"Beth is here just now." Was that a plea or a rejection?

"Well, I'm coming home."

"It's not too far for you, is it?"

"No, no."

"Fine, dear, I'll come and meet you at the airport. He was the last Sincere, you know. Mitch was the only brother and he and Beth never had children. . . ."

"I'm a Sincere."

"Oh yes, dear, but I suppose, well, we always thought you'd marry and then if you had children they'd be something else. Just the name, I mean. He was the last."

"I'll get a reservation today if I can."

"We think the funeral will be Wednesday."

"I've never been to a funeral before." Now Joan was sounding plaintive. She was sitting on the floor. She looked around the wall and saw David standing in the hall, listening.

"Is there someone with you, dear?"

"Yes."

"That's nice. I'm glad that you're not alone," her mother said softly. It was the kindest thing she had ever said, Joan thought. She began to cry and her mother did too, and then Aunt Beth took the telephone and told Joan to make her plane reservations and call them back.

My father is a memory. A big, bushy-eyebrowed man with those thick layers of skin, a ruddiness from beer and the army, and hundreds of laugh lines around his eyes. Joan pondered it. She had not seen him for a year; she would not see him again now, ever. Since she was sixteen, he had appeared in her life only in visits in hotels once a year. In fact, he had become a memory long ago. That had been all right as long as she did not have to think she would never see him again.

David walked Joan back to bed, and began to rub her cramped hamstring. As she put her head on the pillow she remembered the old woman in her dream, and the snow, and the bright beam of light. The old woman had the face of the fortune-teller, Mr. Darling, a cold ferret face. That face could visit a healthy man overnight, and the next day he would be gone. Last night her father had been dying. No hairs had stood up on the back of her neck while it was happening. She had done her act as usual and afterwards had gone out for Chinese food with David. They had been laughing; she couldn't remember what had been so funny.

A kind of awe was filling Joan, the way the snow had filled the streets in her dream. People did die. She had seen the power. They died slowly or suddenly, losing their functions little by little, or all at once. Either way they vanished into that bright erasing beam. Howard Sincere had been whited out.

Rudy's paws were on the edge of the bed: he sniffed, recognizing pain. She patted the blankets. "O.K." He jumped up onto the bed and she put her arms around his neck, drawing him toward her, a crying towel. Her father was dead. Her father was dead. A howl came out of her throat, and she sobbed as if she were retching.

When she stopped, the room was still. The fact was growing cold already. It had been stated, it was true; astonishingly, the process of adjustment had begun. She tried to think back to the beginning, as the telephone rang, when she hadn't known. She couldn't. Her father had checked out. Gone and left the rest of them behind. She felt light, almost elated with this trauma, which was the worst that could be dealt to her, she thought, and here she was still cogent.

"What happened?" said David.

"Another redskin bit the dust," she said. It was an expression her father had used in jest, usually when someone got married.

The morning went by jerkily, without sense, like flash-cards spinning on a spool. Joan at the stove putting the kettle on to boil. Joan at the bathroom mirror deciding to apply an oatmeal treatment. David was watching every move she made.

"You should talk," he finally said.

"What can I say? What can I tell you? You didn't know him."

"I know he was your father."

Was.

"The fortune-teller said, 'There will be the sudden death of a man; you will be notified.'"

"They all say that. Now and then they've got to hit it right."

"Don't be flip."

"I'm trying to make you feel better."

"Well you can't." She wore her housecoat and the oatmeal which was stiffening on her face; she liked the mask, it felt tragic. She was cut off from her father, by his death. Cut off from her mother by the choices of both of them. She couldn't get a flight until tonight. By the time she got to Edmonton everything would be in place, covered up, unreal as her childhood. She went to look out the window.

She was surprised to see that the street did not look as it had in her dream. In fact the long-expected green had begun to invade. A translucent mist dotted the branches and fences; there were spikes of green in the yellow grass. When it came, summer would bring closeness, heaviness; the sky would disappear and those complicated skeletons of trees would turn into rustling fat mounds. She would feel closed in by summer when it arrived, but now she was only seeing its suggestions, a transparency.

"Joan are you all right? What would you like me to do?"

"Be like you are. Just stay, and be quiet."

She dressed in cord pants and a sweater with a texture like the oatmeal on her face. She took Rudy out and bought a paper, and then began reading the ads. That was what people did when they were going to change their lives, wasn't it?

"Look," she said, "a casting agency wants extras for a film being shot in Toronto."

"Try them," said David.

"Naw, it'd be a big four or five days work, that's the problem."

"You're scared."

"I might have to talk," she said. "You probably think that's funny, but it's a lot easier to take your clothes off in front of people than to actually say lines." She turned the page.

"I think you want to act. You just don't want to fail."

"Is that so?"

"Look, with your training, you're half-way there. Why not talk to Johanna, at Characters?"

"Another sleazy agent?"

"She's different. She'll tell you straight if there's a chance."

"Anyway I don't want you to help me."

He shrugged. "I'll leave her number."

While David began poaching eggs, she went further in the Help Wanted ads. Legal secretaries, foremen/women in a dry-cleaning plant, worm-pickers. Worm-picker. She didn't even know if she had the qualifications. It was terrifying. Now that she'd decided to stop stripping, she realized that everywhere else people had skills. She could always apply for a Manpower retraining grant: the government would probably love to get rid of one stripper and see her recycled in the economy in a blue cotton uniform and a hair net.

Nothing seemed to have her name on it. She put down the paper in disgust. She didn't even know if she had enough money to pay for her airplane ticket. For sure, she'd be broke when she got back. Furthermore, she was fighting another panic attack. Everything was slipping and sliding all around her. The walls, the floor, seemed to be on angles. She went to the telephone, made a face at David, and dialed. Even though this was Sunday morning, he'd be in his office.

"Marty? It's Joan."

"Joan?" He was going to play dumb and pretend he'd forgotten who she was, even though he'd given out her picture to the newspapers not even a week ago.

"Yeah, Joan, you jerk."

"Oh, Joan. Ya mean Joan Sincere, the hippest stripper of all who retired from the circuit only last week after a rousing send-off from Toronto's finest? Who I once knew in the old days before she got uppity? *Joan*, how are ya."

"The same, Marty."

Funny about these guys who pulled strings for her. They were the smart-ass, slow-burning types who held a grudge for half a century, but never lost their lines.

"So did ya decide to become a bank teller?"

"Who told you I retired? I'm thinking about it, that's all."

"Just a rumour, just a rumour. I'm glad to hear it's not true, Joan. Can't see you in a day job. Gotta stand all the time, I tell you, it's not normal. You're going to kill your legs. I can't see it. You're too good-looking to go straight, Joan."

"I remember when we met you told me I was too good-looking to be a stripper."

"I must'a been trying to put the moves on ya. No wonder you've got such a big head. O.K., Joan, what d'ya want?"

It was always like that, a standard two-minute chat-up and then a sudden dive. What do you want? She didn't know what she wanted. She was thinking about being too good-looking to strip. She thought of the strippers she knew. They were all cunning, knowing, sexy, but not beautiful. They had odds and sods for bodies: long skinny legs and long hanging breasts, some with tiny high buttocks and some with short deep thighs, some with backs and shoulders like men. The audience never let a flaw slip by. "What are you, a boy? You had a sex change? Oh lady, don't take it off, there's nothin' I want. Get your pension, lady." She could hear the voices all over again. She'd called Marty to see if he could get her some more work, but suddenly she'd changed her mind.

"I don't know. Just let's say I spoke too soon when I said I didn't need you any more."

"So are you looking for a new gig? You didn't want to stay at the Coliseum?" He sped by the apology, but she knew he heard it.

"I don't know if Herbie wants me. I mean, he's waiting to see how it goes. But listen, what have you got?"

"There's a classy new joint opening up in Yorkville, they're going to have male and female strippers. Might be able to get you in there, now that you're sort of *known*, you know, you could do a bit of a tough act."

"What if I wanted to do something different?"

"Ya mean like what?"

"Straight acting, like in a movie."

She arched her eyebrows over the receiver at David, who had put the eggs out on plates. He was reading the newspaper. He wouldn't catch her eye. He probably thought she was awful doing this on the day her father died. Could he understand that she had to make this kind of call *because* everything had changed?

Marty's laugh cut. "I don't get that kind of call too much."

"Well, I just thought I'd try it out. So you can keep in touch, O.K.?"

"O.K. kid, take it easy. Come down some time and we'll have a drink, eh? I'll see what I can do for ya."

"Bye."

She put down the receiver softly. She couldn't bear to hear a loud noise. Her energy was fading away quickly. She felt nauseous. The poached eggs sat wetly on their plates. She turned on David.

"So don't you have to go to work?"

"On Sunday? No. But listen Joan. I hate to say this, but if you're in the mood for making phone calls there's one you should make."

"What's that?"

"A lawyer."

"That's too much. I can't cope. Why don't you just get out of here? Leave me alone."

He picked up one of the letters that had been left at the door downstairs. It had a lawyer's mark in the upper left-hand corner. "You're going to court. Phone Rennick," David said. "He'll do it for you, don't be embarrassed. Everyone's got a friend. You need someone."

"He'll need to be paid and I can't afford it."

"I can lend you some money."

"No. I'll ask my mother."

"If you'd rather. But phone him." David had picked up his coat. "I'll go down to the office and come back at six."

Alone, Joan walked around the edge of the kitchen table. She kept her telephone books in a drawer. Slowly she approached the drawer, and then turned away. This couldn't be happening to her, it couldn't. She grabbed the fat sloppy book; its edges were darkened with dust. She found the number in the white pages. Alexander Rennick, Barr. 88 St. Mary Street.

"Hello?" A man's voice, probably Alex himself.

"Um—Alex Rennick, please." She'd expected an intermediary, but it was Sunday; of course he'd answer himself.

"Who is it?"

"Joan Sincere."

"Joan, it's me. You caught me working on Sunday." He sounded delighted.

"You left early the night you came to the Coliseum."

"Yeah, we did. I hear there was a little excitement."

"That's why I called. I need some, um, legal advice."

"Right."

Less than a year ago, when Joan had just got back from England, Alex had helped her recover some wages in small-claims court. The manager who owed her hadn't even showed up. Alex had said he only wanted twenty-five dollars for his services, but since then Joan had avoided him. She felt that any further social contact would be seen as repayment of a debt. Alex had grown up in the same neighbourhood as Joan, and he used to chase her home from school. She thought he was a creep. Somehow they'd kept in touch; she remembered meeting him once in a pub in Soho. What he saw in Joan she didn't know. Sin, she supposed. But that was unfair. Maybe he saw a little blonde, silent girl who stayed at the edges of the school yard and only loved her ballet lessons, a little girl Joan herself had tried to forget. She supposed Alex still harboured some kind of childish crush on her. Of course he was married with children now, and she was steadily going down in the world, but those things probably only enhanced it for him.

"This time you've got to charge me the full fee, Alex, or I won't let you defend me."

"I didn't even say I was willing yet, hang on. Let me start a file. Joan Sincere. I've always liked your name, Joan. If I hadn't known you all my life I'd have sworn it was a stage name."

"You're so original, Alex. Everyone says that."

"Hey, I saw you had a long chat with David Calder the other night. Did you two get together or something?"

"Put your timer on, Alex, this is business."

"O.K., O.K. So what did they get you for?"

As she heard the slow, cogitating rhythms of his voice, Joan could visualize Alex. He was medium height with straight brown hair, which was rather long and tended to hang in his right eye. He worked for corporations most of the time and titillated himself with the unwashed like herself. He also liked to hang around media types. He had the mentality of a groupie: probably the picture in the paper made him keen on taking her case.

She hung up the phone more sad than ever. There were still two days to get through before her flight home for the funeral. There was one more thing she could do. If she really meant to change her life, that was. But it would have to wait until tomorrow.

Monday she slept until one in the afternoon, a sure sign of depression. When she got up, she dressed to go out. An hour later she opened her front door and saw a knife lying on the mat.

She stooped. It was lying sideways right in the centre of the doorway, its blade facing her door at a perfect right angle. It was a very sharp knife with a wooden handle, a hunting knife, she thought. The paint was worn off, but she could see the handle had been green. She put her hand out for it and then drew back. It looked as if it had been put there on purpose.

The street door was always open. Anyone could walk up the stairs to 27½ Baldwin. She stood still. Rudy sniffed the knife without interest.

"What happened, Rudy, who came to the door?"

He jumped around in a circle and then put his front paws down and stretched backwards, arching his neck and letting out a long yowl. Usually he went into a frenzy of barking when he heard a step outside the door. Even the postman pushing letters through the slot downstairs was considered by Rudy to be unacceptably aggressive: he snarled and raged and jumped up to tear the pieces of paper as they came through. How had someone put the knife here without Rudy hearing? What if the person had tried to open the door?

The knife lay there, looking like a murder threat. Joan told herself she was not in a normal frame of mind. She wasn't about to call the police, especially when she was up on a charge herself. Perhaps the knife was a different sort of message. She bent down and picked it up. She looked down the stairs then and saw that the street door was ajar. There was a shadow moving behind it. Suddenly Rudy began to bark insanely, taking in breath between yaps like a drooling wolf. He shot down the stairs. Joan stood with the knife in her hand, ready to defend herself. Rudy knocked the door wide open as he ran through. In the lee of it was the bag lady.

The old woman stood without moving, showing no fear of the dog this time. Her eyes seemed to be tiny black beads under folds of skin. She had her pram behind her and was rocking it with one hand. On an impulse Joan carried the knife down the stairs.

"I found something dropped in front of my door," she said. "Perhaps you would have a use for it?"

The bag lady turned to look.

"It's a knife."

The bag lady nodded. "If you don't want it, you should put it in the garbage."

Joan dropped it in the city trash-can and headed up the street. She was carrying three fat shopping bags full of satins, ruffles, chiffon, beads, and sequins. She'd left a fortune in foot-gear in the bottom of her closet, but there was no help for it: no self-respecting dancer would wear someone else's shoes. She had her hair parted in the middle and done in knots over each ear, primly. In honour of spring, she had on her sailor shorts with the button closings on both sides and an oversized shirt with epaulettes. Her plan was to sell her costumes for the cash she needed for the plane ticket. She figured she had a couple of thousand dollars' worth. She was going to hit her friends first.

After twelve years in London Joan had left with five pounds in hand, a sacrosanct bank account with enough money to set herself up in Canada, and a trunk full of costumes. Most of them she'd made herself: they were her only valuables, aside from her sewing-machine, which she had sold in her last month in England. The ways of sewing costumes were folklore among the burlesque entertainers: how to cut a skirt from a yard and a half of fabric, how to hide a separating zipper down the sides of hot pants, where to find beads for putting on bras. When she started to work in Toronto, Joan's costumes were the talk of the business from Dundas West to Queen Street East. For years she'd regarded these costumes as money in the bank. Liquidating the reserve was an extreme that she'd threaten when things were very bad. But she never had. It would have been like the carpenter selling his tools, the fisherman his boat. It would pay the rent today but put her on the dole tomorrow.

She had to turn sideways to get on the streetcar at Dundas and McCaul; she led with two bags and pulled the other behind her. The clubs were mostly around Yonge and Dundas, so she got off after four stops and walked north. A poster on the door of Victor's said "Peaches Galore"—nobody she knew. From the looks of her she wouldn't care to spend a couple of thousand dollars on something nice to wear. Next along the strip was a down-stairs joint without a name. Unity's poster was up there, a black and white Xeroxed number that did nothing but make her look more hollow-eyed and ghoulish than ever. That girl wasn't keeping herself up. Joan went in.

After the spring street, the bar was cool and empty. A few men sat at the tables, each of them alone. The resentful, shut-out looks on their faces would not change, Joan knew, when the dancer came out to flatter them with her false offers. Looking across the room, Joan saw with surprise that there had been a bar put in along the side of the stage, so that people could sit within a foot of the stripper. They could reach up and grab her leg, and no doubt did. Unity wouldn't like that. This town was getting worse by the day.

Joan walked through the bar without seeing Unity. She

checked out the back room where the girls changed. She wasn't there. It was a low-grade joint. The basement walls were painted black with enamel, and there were fluorescent lights in the ceiling. A stripper with frizzy blonde hair was onstage, kneeling on a chair. A radio was on behind the bar. The announcer's voice came through her disco record. "The best hamburger meat made . . . there is no success like home cooking."

The stripper gave up on her routine and tried to get up a little chat with some of the men. "You're really getting your money's worth today aren't you, you've been here since before lunch." She oscillated her body very gently. "I keep waiting for something to happen, and nothin's happening." She looked exasperated. Suddenly she put her arms behind her back and with difficulty, grimacing, undid her bra. It swung down. She pulled down the shoulder straps and stuck it on the back of the chair. Her great white distended breasts had no noticeable effect on the men.

She oscillated some more. "What else is there?" she said.

"Your shoes," said a man.

"Oh, they've been driving you mad, have they?" She did not take her shoes off. Instead she stood up, turned away and pulled her panties to just above her knees. She turned around and then put one foot back up on the chair. She stayed there for a minute and then pulled her pants back on, without effect. She levelled her gaze at the audience once more, picked up her bra and walked off stage. Someone lifted the needle off the record.

"May the saints preserve us," said Joan to no one in particular. The disastrous number reminded her of something clinical, a resuscitation demonstration, for instance. Stripper as St. John's Ambulance volunteer. In case of emergency, don't lose your head, proceed with caution and an absolutely even pace. Coax but do not frighten the victim. Do all you can to keep him alive but keep away from his grasp. Exit with benign reproofs.

After her dance, the stripper had thrown on a housecoat

and was sitting at the bar. Joan went over and sat down
with her; they ordered beer. The bartender was propped
on the back legs of a stool behind the cash register reading
a gun magazine.

"You seen Unity?"

"Nah, she didn't show today. Supposed to start at two."
He shrugged. "Lucky the manager ain't been in. I won't
say nothin' but she's missed two shows already."

"That's not like her. Maybe she's sick."

"Yeah, well, she was here last night until late talking
with some guy, 'cause I saw 'er leaving with 'im. And that
ain't like her either. Hell, she's as likely to spit in your eye
as say hello."

"Tell her Joan came by, will you?"

"'f I see 'er I will."

The other woman didn't want to buy any costumes, so
Joan drained her glass and went back up to the street.
Squinting as she came back into the light, she turned
south. So far not so good. She'd go down to Maxie's where
Sugar Bush usually played. The costume bags were getting
heavy. What if she couldn't sell any? She was down to
about fifty dollars in the bank, and she didn't want to
borrow from anybody. Under her breath she ran through
all the swear words she knew, which took her about two
blocks further south.

Maxie's was on a side street south of Queen, next to the
squash club: it had a good clientele because the stock-
brokers and lawyers who went next door tended to drop in
for a drink after their work-outs. It was getting on toward
four in the afternoon; there ought to be some action there
soon. The sidewalk seemed like a conveyer belt, moving
backward as she stepped forward, holding her in the same
place. She longed to get back inside one of those dark,
cool basements with dim lights and drinks, where she'd
lived most of the last ten years of her life.

At the door of Maxie's she saw Unity, limping to the
stairs on spike heels.

"Hey lady, what'cha doing? You're missing your shows."

"Yeah, I gotta see Sugar. She's havin' a meetin'." Unity

pulled weakly on the heavy door and stood aside for Joan to go through. "You comin' too?"

"I don't know about any meeting, but I'm coming down. You don't look too great. What's the matter?"

"I dunno. I'm really spaced today. I just couldn't get it together to get down there."

"You want to lose your job?"

"I wouldn't mind."

"I know the feeling. I'm quitting, myself."

"Noooo." Unity gave Joan a long look. Joan gestured through the door and then followed Unity down the steps. Her hand on the railing, Unity walked painfully, like an old lady.

"Your knees bothering you?"

"Yeah, they're bad these days. I really oughta have that operation, but who can afford the time, eh?"

"Really oughta have a lot of things, right?"

"Right."

The place was full of men in blue suits with briefcases leaned against the table legs. Unity and Joan looked for a table against the wall.

"Afternoon ladies. What'll it be?"

"Double scotch on the rocks."

"I'll have a gin and tonic."

Unity's face as she leaned into the flame of her lighter was thin, peaky they'd call it in England. Crêpe-paper lines surrounded her eyes and lips, white crumples in the white skin. Unity was getting old. You never asked how old. She might be younger than Joan, or she might be thirty-five.

"Man, I'm so sick of this bullshit I tell you, I am so. . . . Like I mean, I met this guy last night. . . ." The sentence lapsed, as if it had never begun, as if the words had no particular meaning. It was a phrase like a lazy fish that had risen to the surface of a muddy pond. The waiter set a glass in front of her. She reached for it without looking at it. Her long fingers clamped around it rigidly. They were white along the bones.

Obviously it wasn't worth trying to have a conversation with Unity. Joan looked around the room.

There was Sugar Bush. You couldn't fail to see her, her head like a tiger lily in the darkness, that orange and black striped hair rippling as she talked, her head shaking like a rattle. She was sitting at the bar, twisting around to face some man. He looked completely bewildered. Sugar Bush was so animated most people went still when she got going, whether she was dancing or talking.

"Sugar! Sugar Bush!"

She didn't hear.

The waiter passed by, kicking over one of Joan's bags of dresses.

"Hey, watch it."

"Sorry. Is there something you want?"

"Give Sugar Bush a message, will you? Tell her her friends are here."

Unity hadn't looked away from the spot on the wall where she'd fixed her eyes.

"Unity, did you hear me? I quit."

"Heard you got fired."

"No, I'm quitting. That's it. No more dancing. I'm even going to sell my costumes. They're all here, see, in the bags."

"Geeze." Unity took a slow puff on her cigarette and brought her eyes back, with difficulty, from the hole they were boring in the wall. "That magenta négligé with the ruffled G-string?"

"Yeah."

"How much?"

Joan hadn't thought of how much. It occurred to her for the first time that her friends weren't going to be able to afford the costumes. She'd made her own in the first place because she couldn't afford anything else. She just might have a whole lot of unrealizable assets in that bag. They were worth a lot of money, but if anyone had that amount of dough they wouldn't be stripping.

"Maybe a hundred." It was worth more.

"Whew!"

"I need the money to pay my air ticket. My father died. I'm going home."

"Geeze, I'm sorry, that's too bad. That's a real shame." She sat quiet for a minute and then went on. "It's not that I don't have the money."

"I know, I know."

They were all terribly proud about money.

"You think I couldn't afford to give you what it's worth, don't you?" Unity drifted off again then, her hand still gripping the glass. She wasn't normal. Joan was getting impatient with this whole gambit. Then Unity spoke again, her eyes fixed on the wall.

"And so what'cha gonna do now, now you're finished with all this?"

"Don't know."

"Fuschia quit, did you know her?"

"I know who she is."

"Coupla months ago. Walked out of the Derby Hotel, said she'd never go on a stage again."

"What's she doin' now?"

"Cleaning houses."

"That better?"

"She says. Still hard on the knees, though."

They laughed together.

"Hey girls! *Ça va, mes copains?*" Sugar bounded up beside them and stooped to kiss both, on both cheeks. "Hey Joan, back among the living! Where ya working these days? Haven't seen you in an age. . . . Get me a gin, Teddy, will you, that's a boy, I love ya." With her crazy striped hair and her pink skin, her brown eyes that darted about, clear and guiltless, Sugar made everybody feel they should take their clothes off. Her legs were skinny below the knees and her hips wide; she had the floppy breasts and wide body of a tart rather than a dancer. What she did on stage was not so much dance as dangle, like the lure before the fish. Her giggle was the hook at the end. Sugar Bush could have turned on the sphinx. She ran a constant battle against tight-asses, stuffed shirts, and the women who hated her because she was sexy.

"You came for the meeting? That's great, Joan, we need you."

"What meeting?"

"We're going to get together, get some action on some of these bad manager problems."

"Joan's quitting," said Unity.

"Joan's *quit*," said Joan. "I haven't worked in a week, and I'm not going to do it again. They've seen my last, girls." She picked up her gin and toasted herself.

"A great little dancer like you? You're going to hide away that lovely body? You're not. You got a duty to womankind. Joan, you can't leave us. A duty to mankind, too. My God."

"Don't say that, you'll make me cry."

"You're not quitting, not serious, like?"

"Serious, like."

Sugar Bush put her pointed face in her two hands and her elbows on the table and looked hard into Joan's face, as if she were trying to fathom the flaw in reasoning that would make her do this crazy thing. "You gonna clerk in Woolworth's? What're you gonna do?"

"Oh yeah?" said Unity dubiously.

"I've got the name of a good agent," said Joan. She hadn't even known she was going to use that tip.

"That's great," repeated Unity with the same lack of conviction. Getting out was to her an utter fantasy. Joan's teeth set a little harder on her purpose.

Gina and Candy came in the door and flounced up the aisle between the tables toward them. They shrieked their hellos; all five kissed one another extravagantly and the waiter pulled up two extra chairs. One stripper alone in a bar always looked depressed. Two looked conspiratorial, and more than that became a competition. Joan didn't know why they'd be sceptical about her acting; they all did it all the time. The staginess of their behaviour grew exponentially with each addition to the group. Joan leaned back and watched.

They were four women who looked almost like any others. Everyday ladies, but each had odd touches hinting at their strangeness. They'd tell you, each one, they were just making a living. But this living? Why these four, and not the four ladies in the other corner, office girls, by the looks of it? The strippers were each a little more separate, as if drawn into the picture with a thicker black line around their edges. Brighter, in relief against the backdrop of the lounge, even when the lights weren't on them. The secretaries blended, with each other and the room. They made an art of blending. The strippers held themselves apart to be special. Candy's high blonde frizzy pony-tail and curled eyelashes, Gina's exaggerated pout in glossy vermilion, Unity's cavernous black eyes: they were like artists' conceptions of everyday ladies. Loners, hooked on being admired all the time, hooked on being the focal point of the desire of strange men, unwilling to be touched, unwilling to be real. That was their camouflage. They might take their clothes off but they never dropped their disguises.

"Hey girls, aren't you tired of being asked to upgrade your act, when you mean taking a few dance classes, and the manager means do more spreads?"

"Do you know, at the Derby things have got so bad there's a sign up saying if you still got your G-string on five minutes before the end of the act you'll be docked twenty-five dollars?"

"I'm only here, ladies, because I'm through with this whole number. You want to buy some costumes?" Joan felt uneasy. The union was a good idea but she couldn't get used to the idea of group action where she was used to going it alone.

"I asked Herbie about'cha and he said you were taking a rest," said Gina. Gina chewed gum; she looked like she had to chew gum or her jaws would lock with tension. Gina called herself an interpretive dancer. She got so involved in her own dramas that the audience was a terrible intrusion. When you asked Gina why she started stripping she'd say flatly, "I married a cocksucker." She never elaborated. Once she stepped in front of a man who had pulled out a camera and shouted, "Who are you, with that camera? Do I know you? Why are you pointing it at me?"

"Herbie, that bastard."

"He's not so bad."

"Thanks to him I'm getting sued."

A thoughtful look came on Gina's face. "Geeze." She shook her head and chewed her gum. "Can't win, can ya?"

"Hey, are you selling that black marabou stole you have?"

They picked up their glasses and moved back to the dressing-room. Behind the plywood partition, Joan bent over her bags and opened them up. The girls dove. Joan stepped back and watched. Ten years of her life went flying up in the air, like flames into the wind. A red stole and blue stockings, gold corset and G-string. That cancan skirt, lined with pink and yellow ruffles, she'd made that back at the beginning. It was a full circle and weighed about three pounds because it was all satin. It looked great with black silk stockings and a black backless corset. Candy tried it on. It was too tight at the waist.

"You can move the button over a bit."

Sugar found the best dress in the bag, the Charleston-style sleeveless silk that was tight to the hips and then had a long fringe that parted over buttocks and hung to the knees. And there was Joan's black Chinese robe to go over it, the one with the golden dragon painted on the back. A Chinese stripper in Soho had given her that. Joan snatched it.

"Hey, I want that."

Unity pulled out the pearl-encrusted underwear set that must have taken Joan a hundred hours to make. The bra and bikini were silver lamé with beads covering the cups and dropping down in strands from the bottoms. The pearls made a soft clacking sound as she held up the set, like little teeth. They would be beautiful on Unity. But she put them down.

"I'll give you seventy-five for the burgundy négligé. And I'd love to have these but I can't afford them."

"Take them now, you can pay me later."

"You need the money."

"Let's face it, where else am I gonna sell them?"

"Door to door in Scarborough?"

They laughed the rich, easy chimes of insiders. It was theirs to joke about the overweight, the uptight, the unsexed women in civilian life—wives and career types, proper ladies. Imagining such women in the pearl-studded underwear set, they opened their throats from their appointed position as anima, exhibitionist, free agent. They leaned on each other in laughter, all the while suspecting the other side was laughing harder in their warm houses with their children, looked after by their men. Their protection was the girls. Together they made a broken-up shattered crystal of a society. They were inside out and backwards, displaying what should be intimate and hiding what was ordinary.

"What am I bid for the black fringe?"

"Oh, I love that, dear. Just love it."

"I got it at Camden Passage before the old clothes barrows got too picked over. It's real silk. And I replaced all the old fringe with new. I love it too. Maybe I should keep—"

"No, I'll take it. I'll give you fifty."

"Fifty? Get serious. Eighty."

"Sixty-five."

"o.k. You got yourself a steal."

"Don't I look great, ladies? My buns hanging out the back there? I love it. Ummmmmm." Sugar stood with her back to the mirror and looked over her shoulder at the little white half-moons showing through the black.

"Sensational. You'll knock their socks off. I used to wear it with a sequined G-string. . . ." But it didn't matter. Didn't matter at all. What she needed more than memory was money to get her out of this mess. "Where's your wallet?"

Half an hour later Joan had four hundred dollars in cash, cheques, and i.o.u.'s. "You're really getting out?" Unity had said at the end, the disbelief on her face changing to complete incomprehension as she saw the costumes going out of Joan's bags and into theirs. "You think you can do it? What are you gonna be?"

"An actress if I can make it." Each time she said it, her dread grew. She was forcing herself to the gate. She was going to have to do something about it now.

"Be a lady wrestler. There's money in it."

"You're not going to become an ordinary lady, are you?"

"I might."

"It's not possible, ya know. I mean, you can sell your stuff, Joan, but you can't change history," said Sugar Bush.

When Joan left, Sugar Bush was pumping for group action against things that made life tough for the strippers, like managers who broke contracts and clubs with bad facilities. Joan wished her well. She took a backward look at Unity, dozing on a chair with her head dropping forward. The sight made her mad. She was on a fast ride down from here; the union ought to make a pension fund its first priority.

When she got home, she looked on the counter. Yes, David had left a piece of paper with the agent's number. Johanna, at Characters. She'd met a few of those; she supposed she was one herself now. Give David's name and she would get an appointment. Johanna. At least it wasn't a man. The name had a lucky sound to it. She didn't know what miracle she expected this woman to perform, but she dialed the number.

CHAPTER EIGHT

It was almost six o'clock and Joan was at the airport, her bulging overnight bag in one hand, the orange ticket envelope in the other. Everyone was going against her: she was buffeted by one clump of men after another, and then pushed aside by a stream of Japanese under the baton of a woman with a red cape. Joan rarely went anywhere in rush hour and when she did she resented it. The force of mass movement against her made her heart pound. She had even got to the point where she was afraid of large audiences clapping loudly. Her assumption was that when any crowd was mobilized it was against her; she was its victim.

Gate 85. The security checkers looked at her ticket and then ran her bag down a moving table.

"I've only got five minutes," she said.

"Better make it fast. You're at the far end."

The years in London had taught her how to run in train stations. She was always at stations at the last minute, as if part of her didn't want to go anywhere. Today, she dodged down the long corridor, cursing, her bag thumping on her leg. She reached the departure gate just as the attendants were closing the flight.

In the plane, she edged her way down the aisle, past the protruding shoulders of businessmen, bending the edges of their raised newspapers. She spied her designated seat. On the aisle, a woman smiled to herself over a stack of baby pictures. Proud grandmother, no doubt: Joan hoped there would be no need to chat. She clambered over the woman's knees and stuffed her bag under the seat in front. There was little in it except a green dress and shoes, a sweater and jeans. She didn't intend to stay long. Finally she dropped into her seat and reached for the belt buckles.

She'd made it, miraculously. There had been her usual last-minute scramble. She'd misplaced her wallet, the traffic was clogged, and in the car David had held her up with hugs and kisses. Now she was really going, strapped into a padded chair. She would do some serious thinking while in transit. It seemed appropriate for her: a moving vehicle could be her best point of view. As the plane began to speed down the runway, she accepted its force as it pressed her against the padded seat. She waited for the earth to drop away.

She was going to bury her father. The funeral was not a

death, however; that had already happened. The funeral was an official farewell to that which once was, a body. The gem buried in that body, the spark that fired it, the true father, had departed without fanfare when the flesh began to self-destruct. Dad had checked out on them and forgotten to take his body. It was left to the women to dispatch that. She supposed that if the truth were known, the body was what they had known best.

It was very primitive, very simple, this stock human beings placed in the physical. Joan more than most lived for her body and in her body, assuming that it would never fail to fascinate, never fail at all. But body was only a symbol. Dancers might misplace their centres, but ordinary people—civilians—were supposed to know better. She doubted that they did. When her own body began to go, so would people's grasp of who she was. And when she was buried it would be a case of mistaken identity, just as it was with her father. She'd hardly known the man himself.

But regrets were forbidden indulgences. That was a rule she'd made for herself when she first left her parents, the white stucco house with its square lawn and silver birches holding it down in one place, never to move, so that you knew as you grew up that it was your responsibility to walk away, since the door would never open on anything new. Now the plane had gained altitude enough so that Toronto was only an untidy spill of houses under its left wing. Joan closed her eyes. She had three hours in the air.

SHE HAD SPENT most of her life defying her father. She supposed that had caused him pain. Now he was dead, and even if she wanted to she could not apologize. But she did not want to ask his forgiveness. She did not forgive him for choosing to make himself an obstacle for her. He had wanted her to stay home, and give up dancing.

"She'll spend the rest of her life sitting around backstage without any clothes on, that's what she'll do. But don't listen to me. Do what you want to. You will anyway, you always do."

"Dad, that's not what dancers do."

"You don't know, Joan. You're too young to know what you're getting into."

"Well, how do you know? You don't understand anything about ballet. When did you ever go backstage?"

"Joan, don't you have school work to do? Leave your father and me alone to discuss this, please."

Somehow, after months, her mother and Joan had won the argument: Joan would be allowed to take the examination for entrance to the Royal Ballet School. Success had come from the fact that the ballet school offered academic courses and if, when she was eighteen, she wanted to do something other than dance, she would have enough education to have an option. Her father had been keen on options. There had been no such word in Joan's vocabulary. She'd closed her eyes on her father's face, closed her ears to his pleading. She embraced his image of Joan Sincere from Edmonton leading the bohemian life, sitting around in the nude playing gin rummy. It became her dream. If they thought she was bad, she would be bad.

Poor Dad. She had adored him and she'd never once pleased him. He had made the fatal error of trying to protect her. She had said goodbye to his protection with little regret, perhaps even with pleasure at the darts of pain in his blue eyes. It was so important to disobey him that she would have gone to hell if he'd forbade her. All he had done to her was expect her to be a normal little girl, to eat dinner at home every night, to walk under the street lights and not down the dark lane. He used to carry her on his shoulders from the skating-rink so that she wouldn't make her blades dull on the concrete. That was before Miss Levy forbade ice skating because it developed the wrong muscles.

When she was ten, they'd run relays in the back yard. "You could be an excellent runner, if you wanted," he'd said, searching for an alternative. But she hadn't wanted. At dance recitals, he frowned. Stood by, with his hands in

his pockets, when the ladies talked about talent. He didn't
want his Joan to be special, to stick her neck out, to make
the audacious move of attempting Art. Maybe it had
something to do with his own artistic impulse, frozen into
posed photographs. Or maybe he simply wanted to keep
her from getting away, to save her for mankind, for man,
more simply. For him and his successor, a husband. She
had fought him, thinking he'd wanted her to remain a
child, when it hadn't been true. What he wanted was
different, but just as unfair. He had wanted her to grow up
and be an ordinary lady.

He had not got what he wanted. That fact had been
acknowledged between them, and laid to rest. She had
thought it would make her free of him, but it hadn't. He
would be her father whatever she did; he had been her
father in spite of himself.

Together Joan and Arlene went before the examiner from
England, a grey pigeon whose every feather vibrated as
she searched for faults. Together they passed, and were
accepted. To have been the only one in the city would
have been wonderful, Joan often thought, but then she'd
have lost the comparing, competing, confiding that made
it real. Arlene and Joan were stuck together after that, put
back to back and measured against each other, bound neck
to neck in the starting.

Arlene was five foot three and would be lucky if she
made another inch: already she was taller than her mother, that squat moustached woman who stood over soup
kettles at her stove. Joan was three inches taller, five feet
six and threatening to grow more. It was a worry: Miss
Levy said they didn't like tall dancers in England. The
mothers put their heads together over the list of woolly
bloomers and socks demanded for the school. Joan watched
the ugly clothing go into the trunk with disinterest: already she and Arlene had agreed that they'd scrap it all
once they arrived in London and saw what the others were
wearing.

"You know, it's not going to be any picnic," said her

father, still manning barricades long since overturned. Women's talk about opportunities, and about how she had to "see" if she could make her dancing a profession, had beaten him, but he was being robbed of his daughter and he was never going to let them forget it. There were things her dad couldn't help her with, he kept reminding her. He couldn't do anything about the cold damp rooms, the bad food, the way they classified you the minute you opened your mouth. He had been in England in the war, and he knew. Joan only half heard him. Everyone had his experience in England, everyone had an opinion on what it would be like. The warnings meant nothing to her. She just knew the country would be hers when she arrived.

Street names from nursery rhymes—Drury Lane, Picadilly— and grey fogs through which the yellow light of Big Ben loomed, that would be London. Somewhere there would be big iron gates that would swing open in ecstatic welcome, bugles to sound, and someone, she didn't know who, someone to come down the walk, arms raised, draped in satins, and say, "Joan Sincere, you've arrived. Whatever took you so long?"

London. In that great, grey city Joan was a tiny black dot. She sat in the hall outside the principal's office on a small white chair, her feet crossed neatly underneath, beside the net bag of shoes and tights. The ceiling above her was a dome. Dancers passed by her, their knitted sweaters tied around their waists, their pink-clad legs rubbing like nervous fingers. Their voices bounced up to the top of the dome and down again in front of Joan.

She'd made her passage to England, and had been met at the airport by Mrs. Steadman, a connection of her mother's. She spent her first three days in an extra bedroom in Mrs. Steadman's house on Primrose Hill. The room smelled like gas. She had stood freezing in a queue, her shoulders hunched, her face pursed in a parody of Englishness. She walked miles upstairs and down in the underground, getting to the school on Talgarth Road. She'd been to several dance classes already, among voices that went on in a high rattle, saying familiar words in birdy tones she could not understand. And now she was waiting for the principal. She adjusted her feet, uncrossing them at the ankle and placing them side by side, her knees turned on an angle.

There was a constant river of traffic going by the school windows, and it was always either raining or about to rain. So this was London: rustle of rain and the nervous whine of cars on the road, the dark sky as she had come to class that morning and the gloom again overhead now, before she went home at night.

She was still trying to pop her right ear from the airplane ride. She sat there stretching her jaw downward and swallowing, as if she could manage to snap her surroundings into focus. Beside her, stairs led in a spiral down to the canteen. In either direction went two long arms of the building where the studios were: behind her another stretch of hall went to the dressing-room. In certain hallways there was a glass in the ceiling. There, you could see the grey clouds settling low and sometimes, if you were quick, a triangle of blue opening before more clouds rolled in and filled it. Those triangles seized Joan; they reminded her of home.

But now it was dark in the glass overhead. Absence of sun had been the first physical deprivation here. Along with sun had vanished deep armchairs and couches, steak and broccoli, Father's car; something called comfort which she had never really noticed before.

Her hands gripped one another, the nails leaving red rings on her palms.

"You may come in now, Joan." Hilary, the secretary, had opened the door. She held it wide for Joan to enter and then closed it behind her.

There was a graceful mahogany desk in the centre of the room: there the lady sat. They called her Madam. Madam was a refined version of Miss Levy. She had pink, fine skin and white hair, erect posture and a voice like a silver bell. Hilary came back to sit at her elbow, in a little side-car desk. Both of them smiled merrily at Joan. Then Hilary put her head down to some writing. Madam gestured to a wooden chair in front of her.

"How are you today, Joan? Have you made your adjustment from the wilds of Canada?"

Joan felt clumsy. She seemed to overflow her little chair, and her bag dropped on the floor with a thud. Madam stood, and walked in front of her desk. She looked too well-trained to go about in the ordinary world. She looked like an artefact, with perfect hands and feet taking her around her little ballroom, like the mice pulling Cinderella's carriage. She stood directly in front of Joan, her hand placed lightly on the desk. Her feet were in a loose fifth position, looking as if they too were resting weightlessly, ready for further flight, although not anticipating it.

"Yes, Madam."

"And do you have a proper room now?"

"Yes, Madam." Joan and Arlene together had a bed-sit in Earl's Court, if you called that proper.

"Very good. We're happy to have two of you together; it's most unusual, of course, to have two from the same school. In Vancouver, wasn't it?"

"Edmonton, Madam."

"And we do have great faith that you both will profit by your training."

Joan said nothing. There was a bomb to be dropped, it seemed.

"I've had a word with your teachers, Joan, and looked in on a class or two myself. Don't be so nervous, dear. It is quite routine that we have a few words with the new students, once they've had a week of class." She said *class* with a drawl so that it rhymed with "hoss," the way a Texan would say horse.

There were in all eighteen students in the final two years of the ballet school's program; most of the others had attended the school since age eight or nine. Joan and Arlene and two boys were the only newcomers. Numbers were kept down because of the limited placements possible in the company.

"It seems to us that there are some irregularities in the way you've been trained."

Joan's nails went into her palms again.

"There are some things I'd like you to correct as soon as possible. Your heels are too far apart in the first position. You must not straighten your knees so far, because they will become overextended. Keep your heels tight together and lift up the knee muscles where they are, don't force them back."

"Yes, Madam."

"Your hand is carried too high in the second arm position and the fingers aren't right. And there's something very odd about your head, often. Of course, these are only the things I've noticed so far. You'll have a great deal of work to do. It's strange, isn't it, that Arlene doesn't seem to have picked up the same affectations? However."

Joan didn't see why this woman, for all her good manners, should choose to dress her down in front of the secretary. She was already preparing to dislike Madam.

"I find it peculiar, you know. We've seen a number of dancers from Canada. There's only been one who was what I call great. Of course, you know who I mean. I don't understand why there have not been others. Do you suppose there is something in the national character which leads you to be very competent but not, how shall I say it, surpassing?" She paused. She couldn't expect an answer. "Perhaps you're here to change that, Joan."

Joan kept her chin high. She felt that Madam was trying to humiliate her, that secretly she knew Joan was exceptional. It was a kind of goad. There had been an incident, her second day in class, when Madam and an older man and a woman had turned up at the door of the dance class. The teacher was intoning in her flat, nasal voice. "One *two* repeat in *front*, repeat *behind*, three *four*!" The teachers were all a little mad; this one had a face set in a wide, glassy smile and her eyebrows arched up to her hair-line. She had dipped her head toward the visitors in mid-shout, and continued. "Turn around, please. We'll have the same on this side. Ready, *and*."

The girls did a half-turn at the *barre*. Joan kept her eyes ahead and her chin in but she caught a glimpse of the group at the door. The man put his head close to Madam's and whispered; Madam whispered something back. They were looking intently at Joan: she began to blush.

They started the exercise. At the *barre* the line of dancers was one creature, a multi-jointed caterpillar, moving determinedly in each limb but making no forward progress. It was a creature with one brain, moving to one beat, thinking only of the coming movement. The brain was in its knees, its feet, its arms. Knowledge passed down the *barre*. Joan was being watched; Joan was singled out; Joan was special. The creature moved as if to camouflage her. Within its many-limbed confines, she tried to show herself off. Her shoulders, held a trifle further back; her legs, extended straighter and higher to the side; her back arching more deeply as the extended leg swung around to the back. You had to look quickly to see her, but she was there, amongst all the imperfects, amongst the round shoulders, the heavy thighs, the flapping feet, and even the other half-dozen who were very, very good—a stand-out.

"You've got a little ballerina here," said the man, distinctly. Madam drew him back from the floor.

And now Joan faced Madam in her office. Both of them tensed, hands and feet poised. Joan cast Madam as the enemy.

"That will be enough for today, Joan."

"Thank you, Madam."

Another memory from the first year in London: the sound of Arlene crying in the dark, across the bit of floor that separated their single beds.

"Arlene?"

The hiccups and sniffing stopped instantly when she spoke, the way the rustle of a mouse halts with a human footfall.

"Are you awake?"

Arlene didn't answer. If she were homesick, she didn't say. Joan had refused to even feel her own homesickness, much less admit it. She lay there awake, still, until Arlene assumed she'd gone to sleep and began crying again.

They were friends on principle but something had pushed up between them in London, something greater than the usual competition for favour. It was that huge empty stage with sixty feet of air over it, with lights in the dome, with guy wires and electric cords and rows of suspended curtains. It opened upward, to the heavens, and outward to the people. It was a lover's leap to greatness. That stage meant one thing: you could let nobody get in front of you. If Arlene missed her home, she was lonely for the old Joan, too, because she had become someone distant, driven.

Saturday afternoons there was no class, and some days the students were given free tickets to the ballet. They studied the stage minutely, studied the dancers mercilessly, criticized the performance. They'd stand in front by the white columns arguing their favourite's merits. Joan would be restless. She'd leave the others where they turned back to the tube station and wander by herself, along the crooked streets, down to Soho. It was her habit to go where she shouldn't, mingle and watch.

Soon Soho became her favourite place in London. She loved its illogical streets, the oyster merchant with pots of yellow flowers over the door, the florists' and fruit stands, the barrows full of cabbages. She loved the windows in dirty bookshops, the funny pictures of wild-eyed men about to slap a lady's white-gartered buttocks. Inside, there would be lines of men standing in front of the book racks. You could smell food and garbage. You could practically reach out and touch the things that were so hidden back home. There were public baths, and pornographic films, and men who passed by and asked her if she would like to watch something with them.

It all reminded her of the summer fairs in a prairie town, where into the dusty roads and vacant lots the midway would suddenly burst. The freaks, the peep shows, the Lido girls with masks of powder and high-heeled slippers. There, the carnies always took your money. They would sell you ten wooden balls with weights in them and watch you try to knock the ducks off the shelf. They would entice you into the tent to see luscious dancers, and you would long to go, even though the sample sent out front had saggy thighs with bruises on them. In that world you were the perennial innocent, the prey, the game. In Soho it was the same. Joan was sure the people who worked there had magic beyond ordinary life, wisdom acquired from being on the bottom rung.

There were black marketeers selling whatever they sold, from America and the Middle East, and show-business stores like Frederick's of Hollywood, displaying black lace panties in the window. The panties fascinated Joan: they were shaped like a diamond with a red-rimmed hole in the centre of the crotch. Proper, respectable people walked by them all day without giving a second look. There were leather stores and places where you could buy every kind and colour of dance shoe. In the basements there were drinking clubs, strip parlours, shows, and more shows.

As Joan walked, late on a Saturday afternoon, the lights came on. There were yellow strings along the signboards, and neon words in the windows. At first the evening was blue; later it was black. She would walk slowly down the centre of the sidewalk, averting her eyes from men whom she thought Mrs. Steadman would have pegged for white slavers. She would be safe if she didn't look at them.

Week after week, she went down to Soho alone. She began to know the streets—Lisle and Wardour and Greek— and the people who lived there. There was a girl with a bleached-out nest of hair who was always out on Peter Street; she began to say hello to Joan. She would come out of a snack shop with her plastic handbag and a cup of tea and go to the staircase next door. That must have been where she lived. Sometimes men went up there; sometimes the girl came and went several times while Joan was in the area. She was a prostitute. Once Joan had recognized one, she recognized others. Then she began to see boys too. They sat at the bottom of the stairs and leaned in the pubs, younger, more saucy than the girls.

Walking those broken streets, so narrow that the taxis sat in rows plugged up without moving while the crazy people calmly threaded amongst them, who gave a thought to Joan, a curious girl-woman in sensible shoes? She was a girl who didn't belong there but who, when you looked up close, didn't belong back home in Edmonton, either. She walked past the forlorn Greek sailors moving in packs along the sidewalks, and the stumpy, red-faced newsagent packing up for the night. She learned how to make jokes with the barrow boys getting ready to push off from Berwick Street. They sold safes from the underneath pockets of their aprons, she discovered. Once a man opened his pants and showed her his purple bulge of flesh. Who gave a second thought, except that she came back again and, in a while, she was accepted among the sin sellers; even if she were not one of them she could move freely and unharmed. She had yet to go into the clubs that advertised dancers, although she longed to.

By nine o'clock on Saturday, before the Soho night had really begun, she'd be back on the tube for Earl's Court. And on Monday morning she'd be skimming the resined hardwood of the studio among the beautiful bodies in their nylon skins, their nets and bands, their elastic belts, and sweaters wrapped around themselves as if human beings had to be covered and tied all over, or else explode.

THE PILOT ANNOUNCED that they were beginning their descent, and Joan got up to go to the wash-room. She looked in the mirror, remembering that she was facing her family for the first time in years. What would they think, looking at this face? What would her father have thought, if he had seen it, the result of the life he so hated her to lead? She assessed her face. The top half was serene—high cheek-bones, still eyes, wide apart; the bottom half nervous, her mouth an oblique thin line pulling to one side, as if she'd been slapped. The fact that her mouth twisted up with emotion was not in her favour. It had always been her weakness, to feel things so much. And yet, she said, looking into her eyes, there are things to be proud of.

Speak up, Joan, her father would have said. If you have something to say for yourself.

All right, Father. You ran a photography studio by yourself; you taught me how to work alone. I, too, have earned my living, ever since I was eighteen years old. I've done what had to be done. I have been so poor that I had to go out on dates in order to get dinner. I have considered prostitution, but rejected it because I liked sex too much. I have stayed on my own small turf, I have an economy of a small scale, and it suits me.

She turned from the mirror, her speech concluded. She'd never expected, as dancers she'd known had expected, that life would change completely by a lucky chance. For instance, some of them might be looking to meet a rich man on this very flight. She'd had a rich boy-friend once, in London. He thought he could buy her, every last nylon and hairpin of her. She had experienced no greed, no great desire to have this wealth, dangled before her like a slippery négligé, drop over her shoulders. She had unearthed nothing even remotely like a secret glee, finding someone who could adore her and support her. There was only an overwhelming desire to get away. No, she was stuck with herself, stuck being who she was.

She could hardly call it personal integrity. It was more like pride. Hubris. She could not tolerate seeing her precious livelihood turned into a day's change for spending in the casino. She could not tolerate the contrast between herself and him. The rich man had turned mean in the end. He said there was nothing worse than a prostitute who couldn't be bought out of her vice, a prostitute who did it for the fun of it. It was no good Joan's pointing out that it proved a prostitute was exactly what she wasn't. He said ugly things and broke an old glass vase in her flat before he walked out.

Men had often turned mean that way with Joan. They

thought they could take her over and when they found out
they couldn't they wanted to wipe the floor with her. It
frightened her to think, for a minute, that those men had
something to do with her father. He had been a kind man,
a kind man who loved her dearly, but only on condition.
The condition that she conform to his ideal. She returned
to her seat, put her head in the corner and pulled in her
arms and legs tightly. She needed a nap to face what was
coming.

When the plane landed in Edmonton, Joan discovered
that the foot that was crossed underneath its mate had
gone completely numb and felt twice its normal size. She
lifted it down with clumsy, tingling hands, and banged it
weakly on the floor. The ping of blood vessels coming back
to life, the maddening buzz in her skin nearly made her
scream. If this little blood retreat, this mini-death, was
such a tantalizing agony, how was death itself?

Here was Edmonton without Dad. Joan had not been in
the city for fourteen years, since her first exit. It was like
going back to childhood and finding that one parent had
been erased. She did not know if she could bear it.

"Joan, dear." Her mother took her arm and folded her
hands over it. Joan's mother had the long-faced dignity of
many tall women. She wore glasses on a chain around her
neck and double-knit suits in one of three shades. Today it
was taupe. Joan looked at her and thought, as she had
often thought before, where did I come from?

"You're looking well dear, aren't you?"

Just the way her mother said it, Joan knew that this
time it was a mistake to be looking well. Either she was
not looking well and her mother was offended, or she
looked too well and her mother wondered what she was
up to.

"I hope you brought something else to wear."

"Of course I did, Mother."

"Aunt Beth has moved to a hotel. Some of the Sinceres

have come out now and she wanted to be with them. So it's just you and I at home."

"Oh."

It had been almost two years since they'd seen one another, just before Joan left London, and the illusion of close contact created by telephone calls only increased the awkward knowledge that they were now strangers. Strangers entrusted with a stack of formative experiences together, a residue of sentiment, and the ultimate responsibility for one another at times like this, but strangers still. People whose regular lives did not intersect. Now they walked arm in arm past the wide, empty public lounges. Already Joan could feel the great, deserted northern plain outside. The airport here was far too big: it had been built in anticipation of more polar routes but there had been none. Joan didn't know where they were heading, and she wasn't sure if her mother was used to driving. Neither of them mentioned the reason they were together.

The last time Joan had seen her father he had been wearing white shoes and a white belt for his trip to Spain. Mother, the thinking half of the duo, had stayed behind watching their embrace with a fixed, sad smile. Joan had kissed her too then, and they'd all patted one another's backs. Her parents were almost at retirement age, and they were touring now and then, to find sun and golf-courses. She'd joked and called them jet setters, but they still had their closed careful stance. Especially her father had looked wrong in the role.

Howard Sincere had the thick features and powerful trunk of a boxer. His hands and forearms had always looked wrong when he adjusted the focus on his cameras, too. They looked as if they should have been loading freight. He'd been a weight-lifter, a canoeist, a sportsman in his youth, but then he chose to start a photography studio and spend the rest of his life creating stillness. He'd enshrined half of his city in poses of cliché perfection, all accomplished while not saying a word. The photographs, lined up and fading in the store window, had been just as silent, just as stubborn, just as determined not to reveal what was underneath, not to show off or to be ostentatious. When she was young, Joan had adored her father's studio. Even then there was a feeling of broodiness, a faint whiff of what he repressed. He had seemed to be' such a happy man. But as he grew older, the wrinkles cut deep into his skin and the great snapping brown eyes moved slowly as if it hurt to let in the world.

Joan and her mother drove through the outskirts of the city. It was almost nine o'clock at night but the sky had not darkened; northern summer nights were endless. The city should have looked smaller, after London and Toronto, but it didn't. It looked confusing, like a scrambled board game. There was a store she knew, there a hotel, there a street that captivated her with a sense of old friendship, but at their end would be a new, confusing thoroughfare. In her old neighbourhood the bus loop looked tiny. The houses were lit inside, so smug, so separate, so happy to be what they were and no more. There was the house where she'd grown up, enormous with its high staircase, its empty rooms, its picture windows to the back yard. There had been terrors outside; that juniper bush at the front door where the bogy-man hid, that long walk with the garbage to the dark at the back gate. Now the terror was that her home seemed so foreign.

Joan and her mother spent the next day in rapid orbit, answering bells, making arrangements. They were bewildered by their new relationship. A wife without a husband, a daughter without a father, what shape were they to take? The triangle was reduced to a straight line. They pitied each other. They feared open hostility.

"The limousine is coming to pick us up at one o'clock, dear. I hope you'll be ready."

"Of course I will, Mother."

"Would you like a cup of coffee, Joan?"

"No, thanks. I don't drink it after breakfast."

"Oh, aren't you noble?"

And then they were in the limousine, drawing up in front of the white pillars of the Forest Green Funeral Home. Inside the front door, Aunt Beth was a shadow.

She wore black. Nobody wears black to funerals, now, David had said.

David had not met Aunt Beth. She was small and so buxom that she seemed to stand forward on a slant, like a bird about to peck. Her hair was thin at the crest: through its wave you could see the rounded top of her head. And she was most decidedly in black. She regarded Joan's green dress balefully. Joan's mother, in gold and grey, apparently passed.

"I think we should step into the waiting-room," said Aunt Beth in a reverential tone. She took Martha by the arm.

In the small, pastel room Joan looked at her finger-nails and tried to imagine how she had offended Aunt Beth. Since her arrival, the woman had barely managed to look Joan in the eye. Beth had remarked darkly that she had heard a lot about Joan lately. There was only one thing she could mean by that: the newspaper article. Hadn't some-one already said to Joan that it might go on the wire and run all over the country? Her father had always said to her that her sins would find her out.

Aunt Beth seemed to have forgotten Joan for the mo-ment, however. She was sitting on the edge of her chair reviewing strategy with Martha. They had already chosen a closed coffin, cremation, and burial of the urn of ashes. But Aunt Beth wished to run it through again. They repeated the plans, nodding. Everything would be all right. There would be no space here for unseemly dis-plays, no time for silence.

Pain, before it came to the surface in Joan, began to sink under the soft landslide of words. Like a load of fine earth poured onto a wooden box, Aunt Beth's words muffled the scream inside. It had been like this always. A dune of propriety had built up, covering Joan to her knees, to her waist, to her chest. She had now exactly the feeling she'd had at sixteen, that she had to escape. Before suffocating, she had made her break. There would be free movement, real expression in art. But that too had proven false, performance on stage being as much a lie as performance in life.

The calm now was a pre-performance quiet. There would be reassurances all around, and then silence, as imaginations began to work. Now no one spoke. The first guests must be entering the chapel. In minutes the family would go through the front door. Five minutes before the curtain went up there would be a crisis, a tantrum; one minute before it went up peace would be restored.

"Where's my handkerchief? Martha! Have you got one? Joan," Aunt Beth hissed frantically.

"Oh, I forgot. How could I have forgotten?"

"Are there any here? Kleenex, oh dear, not Kleenex, hasn't anyone got any handkerchiefs?"

Joan's mother began to cry. Aunt Beth began to cry. Joan felt panic rise.

"Oh Mother, don't cry yet. Here, let me help you." Even she. Joan, was play acting. She searched in her purse, and found the large wad of Kleenex she'd taken from the bathroom at home. "Will this do?"

"It'll have to," said Beth, grimly.

"Thank you, dears. I had thought I was all through crying. But it looks like I'll start again." As if there were some shame involved.

They all repaired their cheeks. The organ began to pump, squeezing out moans to cue the mourners. The door to the chapel was opened. Straining for relevance, the attendants adopted faces from soap opera. Joan and her mother and Aunt Beth were led to sit in the first few pews, parading in front of the friends and relatives already gathered. Joan saw no face she recognized, and didn't look again. She sat facing the front, and turned her back to see the pallbearers.

Two men were in front, her father's fishing buddies. Behind them were two neighbours. The last two were hired. There hadn't been enough men in the family to make a team. Uncle Mitch, Howard's brother, had a bad back and was unable to carry. He slid into the pew now, his face a mask. The bearers, with the long inlaid wooden box with flowers dripping over its lid, passed by. Although what she'd known as a father was in that box, no shiver came up Joan's spine. The anaesthetic of ceremony had done its work. A strangling sound came up Joan's throat and that was all.

She tried to follow the service, but she seemed only to be able to hear the phrases she expected, the sonorous clichés. "In my father's house are many mansions." She resented the transposition, one father to another. She had not escaped one childhood to embrace a longer one; she was not a believer.

With zeal, the minister took up his lines. He spoke of Howard's perfectionism, his steady habits, his devotion to family. He said something about his taking the light and going up to bed, leaving us alone with the embers so long as they lasted. Joan gagged. He was like a stripper doing tricks to make his audience believe they were feeling something. His sluttish attitudes of devotion, submission, and pleading were calculated to evoke people's love, to make them howl. Joan wondered what the minister felt, as his practised phrases hit the spot and sighing, sobbing, and clasping of hands began to spread through the small chapel. Joan had learned disgust for people by watching them fall for her act. Did he think them all fools? Or did he believe his own lip service, and believe too that an automatic response was better than nothing?

Beside Joan in the pew, Martha's hands rubbed drily against each other. She sat with her head bowed, her chin resting in a froth of gold ruffles from her blouse. It was impossible to imagine what she was thinking. Her grey suit looked like stone; her hat cupped her hair so that it, too, was like carving. Feeling eyes on her, she lifted her head and smiled at Joan. It was a radiant smile, as if she had died and gone to heaven already, as if the anvil stroke of this grief had galvanized and raised her glowing.

It occurred to Joan that her mother was taking tranquillizers.

Strangely, the idea moved her. She would have had to go to their doctor, an old friend, and ask for them. An admission of need. Martha had loved Howard. Joan had never thought of that before. She had seen them as adversaries, their forces locked in battle to break her, Joan's, will. But that was the arrogance of a child. She had always been on the outside. Inside had been the secret and powerful bond of two ordinary people.

Finally the coffin was raised up and carried out. "O death, where is thy sting, O grave, where is thy victory," intoned the minister cheerfully. He was in the last minutes of his role. When he lowered his hands, the coffin would go to the crematorium and the relatives to their grief. It was done, and the finale came: the mourners filed slowly out of the chapel into brilliant sun looking purged and fresh.

That day the weather had turned from spring into high summer. Surely it was too early for the air to be this sweet, the trees to be in their full jollity? The sun felt almost hot, and patches of heat crossed Joan's way as she headed resolutely away from the crowd of handshakers to the limousine. She felt silly, as if she had been up against a wall to be shot, but the minister had pulled a trigger and instead of solemn death, out had fluttered a harmless little banner covered with words.

Back in Howard's house, the staircase loomed portentously behind human backs which were filling the front hall. Up there and along the hall he had had his attack. "I can't breathe, I can't breathe," he'd said. Joan's own breastbone began to heave. There were people standing all over the pale blue rug with its pattern of vines and roses. They were drinking sherry and speaking in soft voices. Out of the midst rose an occasional, very subdued rill of sympathy. These were the Sinceres and those they had married, uncles, cousins, second cousins, none of whom she'd seen for decades. There was an ancient aunt standing alone in a corner, let out from her old-age home to bury her nephew some twenty years younger than herself. She saw Joan and was unable to suppress a jubilant smile.

"Auntie!"

"You never come to see me. Do you know my place across the river?"

"I don't live here any more, Auntie."

"Oh, I know that, I know. We've just all had to learn to get along without you."

"Are you well, Auntie?"

"Not at all, dear, not at all." She smiled and patted Joan's shoulder. "Why are you wearing that dress? Is that the only one you have?"

"Just about."

Joan moved forward, fighting an irrational anger building in her chest. She could see into the dining-room. On the table there was salad, cold roast beef and a tray of radishes cut to look like roses. Joan helped herself to a glass of sherry and stood behind one of the clumps of people, unable to join their talk, hating the trill of their voices. She spun to avoid a cousin and left the room, turned into the hall and entered her father's den.

Here there was no one. The books on their shelves insulated the room and made it silent. There was his blotter, with notes to himself tucked around the edges, there his worn armchair where he would sit at night with the television on but the sound turned down because he hated noise. He let his head drop back and sat in the flickering light, that was all. There were his travel guides, for vacations to come in retirement, and everywhere, photographs in their frames.

Martha as a young woman, with her hair in a French roll. Martha holding a baby up over her head, wearing a jubilant smile. Joan at three, riding on her grandfather's shoulder. Grandfather, long dead, held captive there with his grimacing twenty-five-pound load. Joan at seven, her hair in braids. The view out the back window, of fences, the tops of trees, and the edge of the river bank. Martha in an evening dress. Joan standing on point in a red tutu, her long arms over her head. She had always hated being photographed by her father. Every special moment had been ruined when he dragged out his equipment and people started fussing with their hair. But he had been trying to say something as he focussed those lenses. Trying to stop time, hold on, make them all stay the way he put them.

You should be flattered, her mother always told her. He loves to photograph you. It had been his way of speaking to her, and she had fought it all the way. She could feel her father still in this room, smell him still, that mixture of old wool sweaters that had been in the cedar chest, aromatic tobacco and something else, something acrid, maybe a fluid he used in the studio. It was possible to remain angry with him, standing there with his odour alive in her nostrils. But as she backed to the door, it faded, and she knew he was gone forever.

She'd thought that before. She'd thought her father was gone forever when she went to London. Her parents were only over to see her twice in those dozen years. Twice, politely and carefully avoiding what she was. Twice to regard her as an aberration, a problem, a trial.

"If you're not going back to ballet, then are you sure you want to dance? Isn't this kind of work a bit unstable?"

"There's always work. What you mean is it's not respectable."

"Have you thought of teaching?"

"No, Mother, it's not for me."

"I can't see how you do it in these night-clubs, it's such a waste, with your training."

"Mother, you don't understand. It's burlesque, it's recognized, it's something people do." And then a lie. "It's not as if I go out on a ramp in some basement and spread myself so men can stare up my—"

"Joan, don't speak to your mother that way."

"Well, she has one, too."

"Joan!"

"I can look after myself."

"You've said that to me since you were five years old. I shouldn't have believed you then; I probably shouldn't believe you now. But what can I do? What can we do, dear?"

"What can I do, Mother? I don't want to work in a bank.

It's not normal, standing all the time." It was what she always said; it was what everyone said. Working in a bank was the ultimate civilian activity. Nobody's legs should have to survive it.

"You're lazy, is that it?" Her mother looked quizzically at Joan, seeking the decay of morals, the decay of breeding. She saw nothing. Who could have seen anything in Joan's face those days? Defence. Stubbornness. And a little pleasure at the pain she was causing.

Her father had paced. That time they were in the lobby of a big hotel, having tea. He wouldn't sit at the table, but kept walking by the window, looking across Park Lane. "We've lost her, Martha, don't keep on. We lost her long ago."

"Don't be melodramatic dear. She's still our Joan. We'll get her back."

"You talk about me as if I were a dog! Look, just go home and wait. If I can't make it here I'll be back. Then you can have what you want, a failure for a daughter."

Why had she said that, then? She couldn't bear her parents' lack of faith. They thought this kind of life left a permanent mark, like a tattoo. Dirty, decadent woman, their eyes said, you have allowed men's eyes to roam you lustfully. You have used your talent, your God-given body— your God-damned body, would perhaps be more honest— to do this bad thing. Her parents were not religious but there was some racial memory of puritanism there.

As they'd walked out of the pink and pearl-coloured tea-room two Arabs had eyed her appreciatively from the confines of their burnouses. Her parents had held on to each other and walked bent over as if experiencing inner pain. Walking behind them, Joan felt like a six-year-old. Banished yet bound; apologetic, fearful, determined to be bad. She didn't know what she was punishing them for, except for being parents. She could not tolerate being the meek third party, the witness to their unity, to their joined, neutered sexuality.

Her father had taken her aside at the door. His face was very stiff and his lips moved as if they were frozen. "I don't agree with your mother," he said. "I don't expect you back. As long as you keep up this kind of thing, you're not my daughter."

Of all their partings, that had been the real one. He had wanted to disown her. Maybe he didn't mean what he said; maybe he regretted it later. But she hung on to that bitter moment. Even though she saw him again and smiled, and even kissed him, she let him know that she remembered. In a perverse way it pleased her. Let him deny her, she had done him one better. She had disowned her own daughter. It was her secret way of hurting him back, to take that away from him. Joan was not his daughter and Sara was not his granddaughter either, and that was the bitter end of it.

Joan rejoined the party. She had never got the hang of these conversations, and the thought that all of these relatives were curious about her was daunting. They watched her; one man with a rumpled suit and no chin hovered near her. She considered telling him that for her grief, she would rather run around a fire pit, jumping and chanting mumbo-jumbo or dance barefoot on stones in a rain storm tearing her garments, than pass the time of day with the likes of him. Perhaps they could all get drunk on this sherry and throw their arms around one another, these restrained, right-thinking people. They were not a close family. They just held on tightly.

She took a sip from her funnel-shaped glass. Everything was hidden in this house, every rumpled sheet, every bit of used clothing, every sign of human habitation was cleaned, pressed, tucked out of sight. She wished she would burst wide open on the pale blue rug and the brocade upholstered chairs, splattering the still-life oils of fruit bowls and the white-painted oak newel post at the foot of those damn stairs with her blood.

With the air of a tragedian and a sheaf of papers in her hand, Aunt Beth took the floor. She turned around twice, like a dog looking for a spot. Coffee cups clattered to their saucers and the family waited. Aunt Beth patted her hair; she was going to make an announcement.

"Sinceres, you have all come to us today to share our grief, and I thank you."

Murmurs. Martha fidgeted.

"We are not only saying goodbye to Howard, but to the family name. It is sad that Mitch and I had no children, and as Howard only had a daughter—" Only a daughter. That was Joan. "—and she is not married ... this is the end of the line. That is why what I have to show you is doubly unfortunate, doubly an outrage." Beth's neck muscles stood out of their wrinkles in her passion. She passed out the papers. Joan reached for one, knowing as she did exactly what it was. There, Xeroxed on good white stock, was the newspaper article STRIPPER PACKS WALLOP. The stark black reproduction was a further abstraction of the photograph even than the shades of grey that had first appeared in newsprint. In this Joan looked like an aging statue, full of cracks and sunken with weather. Written across the page in red felt pen was, "Can you let this happen to our name?"

"Oh Beth, really. I don't think this is the time," said Martha wearily.

"I have struggled with my anger and with my sense of propriety on this one," cried Beth, "and the former won."

Rustling the papers, people read the story and glanced at each other.

"Is this Joan? I don't think I recognize her."

"Beth," said Uncle Mitch, "this is uncalled for."

"I must speak my mind. She's dragging the family name, my name, Howard's name, through the mud, that's what she's doing, using it to make herself famous, putting her picture in the papers—"

"I know enough about papers to know that Joan didn't put that there herself," said Martha.

"She's dangerous. She's violent. And furthermore that's what we will be remembered for. People will come up to me and say are you related to—" Spittle, tiny bubbles of venom had gathered at the corners of Aunt Beth's mouth.

She licked them back quickly and looked around for support.

"It's a publicity stunt, that's what it is. Down east they do that kind of thing. I've heard of it."

No one was looking at Joan. She was third person, although present: a familiar situation.

"It's a *sin*, that's what it is. Taking off her clothes in these places, Lord knows what else—"

"Beth, that is enough," said Mitch. He took her by the arm and removed her from her spot in the middle of the room. She was still talking, but she had lost her audience. The Sinceres were not religious, they never had been; it was one of the family oddities. That was one reason the funeral was so awkward: there were no believers in after-life. To say the word *sin* was to embarrass them. While they looked askance at Joan for wearing a sexy costume and getting her picture in the newspaper, she was wronging civilized people, not God. Invoking God was going a bit far.

With Aunt Beth out of the way eyes turned naturally to Joan. She felt a cold draft, despite the sun on her shoulders. This room was some place she'd lived in a dream. All the others wore proper clothing and she was naked. Unprotected. Under scrutiny. She felt cold, but exhilarated. Public denunciation was in some ways a relief.

"It's true," she said, laughing a little. "I dance and take my clothes off for money."

The faces expected an explanation.

"Do you want to know what it feels like? It feels like work. I'm not selling myself, I'm just showing off. That's show business. Like everyone's work, with a few additional hassles." In this family they ought to bow down before employment: utility was their religion.

The faces continued to examine her. They were Sinceres, each with traits reminiscent of her father—the hair here, the ruddy cheeks, the thick torso, the crinkly eyes. He had died but his view of her lived on in them. If she had thought that she could in some way reclaim him by acting in his image, by being courageous, silent, uncorruptible, she gave up then. It was not possible.

"You could at least use a stage name," someone suggested timidly.

"I don't need an alibi, I like my name."

Martha caught Joan's eye and gave a confused smile. She wanted to help, but she seemed too genteel even to come to grips with the exchange. She crumpled the paper. "This is the kind of thing that goes out in the garbage the day after it's published and is forgotten forever."

"I told Beth she was making too much of it," said Mitch. "She's the one who's giving it publicity."

"Everyone's making speeches," complained Auntie. "Where's the coffee?"

More coffee was served, and then cakes. Aunt Beth subsided into snivels and the rest of the Sinceres went out the door backwards, shaking hands without looking in each other's eyes.

The next morning Martha drove Joan back to the airport.

"Do you think Aunt Beth will get over this?"

"We'll never know," said Martha. "She wouldn't talk about it now, not to our faces."

"Oh."

"You're sure you've got to get back?"

"There's my dog, you know. And I've got to look for a new job. I lost the old one."

The sensitive subject of work dangled in mid-air, and in the pause, threatened to drop. At the last moment, Martha caught it.

"Are you thinking of a change, Joan?"

Today, to her mother, she couldn't gild the story. "I'm desperate for one." She drew in her breath. "I have an appointment," she said, letting her voice drag vaguely, "about an acting job." Oh how she was building this house of lies; one day she would be living in it. "I sent her a résumé." That at least was true.

"I wish you luck," said Martha. The straight line had given away, after the funeral, to the old triangle. It was as if the three of them were there, Howard, Martha, and Joan, stuck in position, solid as a wedge. They might not understand one another, they might not approve of what they knew, but they were always there. Even with Howard gone, the relationships would continue; his memory held the spot.

"Mother, what are you going to do?"

"The same, only on my own. Run the shop, hire someone to do the photography."

"Can you manage? Are you all right?" It was safe to ask now. They were at the airport.

Martha sniffed. "It's as if someone has taken a hammer and knocked off an arm and a leg. But I can't feel anything. I'll be all right. Working will help."

"You barely cried."

"You were the same. Are you going to come out and visit sometime? Get some time off? You might look up some of your old friends. I know that Lindsay Reed married and is living on the south side somewhere."

"If I can, Mother, it depends. You should come down east."

"I might. I'd have to get things settled first."

But already things were settling, as if there'd been no change of state. Martha would live with Howard's death by herself.

"I didn't ask you about this charge you've had."

"I got a lawyer. Alex Rennick, remember him?"

"Of course. He always liked you." Martha brightened a little, at the mention of someone she knew. It gave her courage to ask further. "And this new man friend you mentioned. Will he be good to you?"

"I don't know, Mother."

"Oh Joan, what's going to become of you?"

They kissed goodbye in front of the check-in desk. Joan pressed her face into the side of her mother's neck and stepped back. "I could ask the same of you," she said.

"Oh, I'll be all right," said Martha, her chin quivering.

CHAPTER NINE

When Joan arrived home in Toronto, it was dark. She took the bus to Union Station and the subway from there to Dundas. At the corner of Yonge and Dundas, waiting for the streetcar going west, she thought she saw Joe. He was in one of the pin-ball arcades, bent over the machine in profile to the street, the head of a medieval king on the body of a thief. He had his hands on the sides of the machine and was throwing his weight against it, trying to nudge the ball out of some trap.

His hair-line was farther back, but then she'd last seen Joe twelve years ago. She fled out of the light at the open door of the arcade. When the car came, she went straight to the back and calmed herself. It couldn't have been him. She had imagined the likeness, because the fortune-teller had mentioned his name. "That's over," she had said to the fortune-teller.

"Over, but not finished."

She walked from the car stop to her apartment, dropped her bag, and took Rudy out for a walk. The darkness was violet. The stars were faint through streaks of cloud. The street lights on Joan's block were hidden by the chestnut trees, their new, wide leaves shaped like hands, and the fat white torches held erect. The moon was young, very thin, hanging over the cavern of Bay Street. Looking down that way she could see the CN Tower, winking from its height as if it were a great joke on the city. She passed the Chinese man in front of his empty-looking grocery shop. There were half a dozen crates piled outside the door, cartons of mysterious vegetables and tins without labels.

The city garbage truck, gleaming white and going too fast, careened around the corner. Three men in coveralls sprang off the back fender, shouting and laughing. The truck pulled to the curb in front of a pile of garbage bags and the air brakes exploded in gasps.

"Want some?" said one of the men, swinging a bag in front of his buddy's face.

The retreating round back of the truck had yellow lights. With its curved lip over the bin, it looked like a furious snail creeping along the edge of the street, ingesting the inhabitants' leavings. Joan wanted the silence back. Her night alone had a clarity; it was in her control. Now that she had escaped her family she wished to remain unmolested by humankind for a time. She would reconstruct her bubble where she was safe from pain and insult, beginning tonight with a long sleep.

"Hey there, yoo-hoo."

The hairs stood up on Joan's arms. Rudy lifted his nose from the concrete pillar that attracted him, and sniffed the wind. They couldn't see anyone.

"Yoo-hoo, dearie, I'm over here."

In the shade of a rickety wooden arbour raised like a comic valentine over the walk to an empty house, down under a bush, in the darkness, there was a darker lump. In front of the lump were two feet. Rudy braced his front legs, tensed so that his tail shivered, pointed his chin at the feet and let go.

"Rudy, stop that. *Stop* that! It's only the bag lady."

The ankles, as Joan came up on them, were like blocks, thick and stiffly extended. The feet were still, shapeless, toes pointing to the sky. The rubber soles were worn through on the bottom, with some kind of stuffing showing around the edges. Newspaper, probably.

"Excuse me, are you all right?" The bag lady must have a name, but Joan didn't know it. "I'm sorry I didn't get your name."

"It's Mrs. Poole, dear. One minute please. I'll be with you in a minute."

The voice was servile and demanding at once, that of a long-entrenched parlour maid.

"What are you doing down in there?"

"This is my seat," said the bag lady, her head still in shadow. "It's a very nice place to sit. But I have the feeling it may get damp tonight. It's time I was moving on. Help me, would you dear?" The bag lady was irritated to have to even ask for help. Those who came along behind her had a duty to look after her carcass.

Stepping forward, Joan suddenly remembered the knife on her doorstep, it seemed like weeks ago, when she'd left for Edmonton. She hesitated. Rudy had gone right up to the feet, his frame trembling as he smelled them. The woman must present a fantasy of odours from her journeys among the trash cans—garbage that the dog was forbidden to touch—such a depth of odour, layers of her own and others for years back. Was she friend or foe? Rudy was unable to give an opinion.

Joan pushed open the little gate and saw the bag lady. She sat in the shade of the bush, her pram beside her. Her grey hair stuck out of her headscarf; newspapers sprouted around her hips like leaves on a lettuce. A streak of moonlight fell across her face and into her lap. She smiled brightly at Joan: she looked quite mad.

"Help me up. I must get over to the subway station."

"Oh, of course." Joan leaned over and caught the woman under the arms. She pulled. The bag lady must be made of straw; she weighed almost nothing. Perhaps her stuffing would fall out, perhaps she would break. Joan set her on her feet on the sidewalk. The feet wobbled and then held. The bag lady reached for her pram. She said nothing about her baby tonight. Joan almost laughed for having been afraid. This woman could never be dangerous.

"Getting old," said Mrs. Poole. "It's the bones, you know. They feel everything."

The two of them began to walk, the bag lady pushing the pram and Joan following. If she hadn't come along, Mrs. Poole would have lain in the dirt all night, and tomorrow the bones would have felt older yet.

"Which subway do you take?"

Mrs. Poole smiled. A mischievous smile, showing two

long, thin teeth with curves on the sides, where they had
been pressed up against other teeth no longer present.

"I don't take one at all. That's where I sleep. My friend
and I."

They walked on. Rudy pranced ahead and pranced
back, a cloud of movement in the darkness, only his white
collar showing in the light fall from the lamp-posts. They
passed bicycles leaning against steps, great padlocks and
chains holding them down. In the dark passage between
two houses an old man stirred. There was the bench
where the Chinese ladies sat, in front of the chiropractor's
office. The neighbourhood was only three blocks wide,
and it barely held together, with the old, the foreign, and
the antedated hippies. The bag lady with her sack of
discards gave it a certain coherence.

"Who is your friend?"

"My friend Marie. She used to work in Rosedale."

Joan didn't want to know any more, and the bag lady fell
into a cunning silence. She wasn't about to give away her
secrets about hiding places, ways of getting warm. Perhaps
she thought Joan might be a rival.

When they reached the red and white TTC sign, Mrs.
Poole leaned even further onto the handle of the pram and
flashed a crafty smile. She was thinking ahead to her
folded newspapers, and warmth.

"There's Marie."

Joan couldn't see anyone.

"Good night, then."

"Good night." She did not look back to Joan; already she
had forgotten the act of kindness. But she said, as she
went off, "That man will be waiting for you."

Joan walked home more quickly. She wanted to feel safe in
her bubble, to forget the outside; but events were conspir-
ing to defeat her. She turned the corner of her street
imagining the stairs going up, the key in the lock, the
bedroom with its pink light. Rudy would go straight to his
bowl and start crunching kibble, since he rarely ate when

she was away. Her reappearance would turn him into a
night eater, and he would want to be let out early in the
morning. There were days like that, when he turned the
clock around.

These were concerns she was contented with. Small,
familiar. Enough to occupy her without posing a threat.

But what had the bag lady meant, "That man would be
waiting"? For a minute she'd thought she was referring to
Joe, or the man who looked like Joe, but there was no
connection. The bag lady would never have seen Joe; she
wouldn't know anything about him. David, she must have
meant. Tonight she didn't want to think of David. The idea
of knowing anyone intimately was oppressive.

David was ordinary. He was like her relatives. There
was a word for people like that. Dancers called them
civilians. A civilian was anyone who didn't live on the line,
who hid in the securities of normal life. Why had it never
struck her before that David was a civilian? She'd been
blinded for a time, by his enthusiasm, his cleverness. But
it was so obvious. He had civilian clothes, a civilian job.
He even walked like a civilian, springy, tense, with a tight
ass. Being a civilian, he must be looking for a civilian
lady-friend. Perhaps he was plotting to turn her into an
ordinary lady.

Oh, she could see it now. She'd be standing by the
refrigerator telling him not to hug her because she was
looking for the whipping cream. She wouldn't find it, so
she'd close the door and run down to the supermarket.
She'd have to listen to his stories when he came home
from work and cluck her lips without expressing an opinion.

A civilian's life would be so predictable, so circum-
scribed. Joan had always wanted to believe that anything
might come along. That couldn't end, just because she was
thirty. Oh, she'd accepted the fact that she would cross a
line some day—maybe when she was forty, or fifty—and
after that she would no longer be a footloose dancer, but
would have become a refugee, fleeing her past, moving
from spot to spot ahead of the bouncers, all of her possessions lost or destroyed or rolled in plastic and carried at

her side. Still, she'd rather be a bag lady than a civilian. She had got through this far with only a few regrets, and she expected no solution to her life. She wasn't going to let David have her.

All this she told herself, and then she saw David's car idling in front of her house. She realized that she had worked up a frenzy over him, the way he stalked her, the way he was insinuating himself.

He stood up in the lee of his car door, as always.

"David." His eyes stood out in the darkness; he looked strange. She realized that he'd been growing a beard. The bottom half of his face had disappeared.

"Don't sound so surprised. I said I'd meet you tonight."

"Did you?"

He stepped out of the car and walked up to her. She did not open her arms. He stooped to pet Rudy. "Was the funeral that bad?"

"It was what you'd expect."

"I've got something to tell you."

"I'm not sure I'm in the mood." She was evading his arm, searching in her bag for her keys. She found them, and jiggled them in her right hand.

"Come on. It's something nice. I've been thinking a lot." He tickled her underarm, trying to jolly her up. "Is anything wrong?"

"Nothing."

"Yes, something is."

"I'm probably just tired."

"Why don't you tell me about it? Shall I come up with you?"

"No."

She had said that far too quickly. The moist edges of his eyes hardened. The eager look slipped down his face.

"You should let me help you. I want to."

"It's late and I'm tired, all right?"

"O.K., O.K., I heard you, Joan."

They stood apart trying to stare one another down. Then David put both his hands on her shoulders. "Listen, Joan, what I wanted to tell you was that I got a friend's farmhouse in the country for a few days. Do you want to come?"

Just like a civilian. He had such a bad sense of timing. "It would be good for you. For us."

"You're such a jerk, David. I can't, not now." She dodged his arms, his weight on her shoulders. She put her hand on the doorknob.

"Come on, listen. I've decided something. I've decided that I love you."

"Oh, God."

"Joan, I said I loved you."

"Well, I never asked you to."

"*What?*" His voice was rising. Hers too.

"Saying that kind of thing, it's just to make you feel good, you know, just to make you feel like a hero." Now his eyes were turning red around the rim, with the strain; she had a moment of pity. "Look David, I'm just not up to this discussion. I'm going in. Come on, Rudy."

"Hey, what's happening?" He reached for her again, twisting her shoulders so that she faced him. "I mean all I said was—"

"Don't!" she shrieked. She tried to control herself. He dropped his hands and it was easier. "No. Look, it's just a bad time for me. I've got to get my life together, get another job, something. I'm sorry if I hurt your feelings."

"You should be." He had backed off: now he was leaning on his car, arms folded.

"No, really I am. That was horrible of me. It's nice, David, what you said."

"Nice?"

"Really nice."

"Yeah, well, I take it back. I don't even know why I said it. I just got into a strange frame of mind while you were away. Now that you're here I can see it would never work. You won't let anyone near you. I'm fed up. I've got to get going, Joan."

She veered around like a kite being reeled in. "You're going? Aren't you coming up?"

"I thought you wanted to be alone."

"But you came here and disturbed me. Now I want to talk."

"Bye." He walked around the car. He was going to get in and drive away, leaving the street emptier than ever after his intrusion.

"Is that all you're going to say, 'bye'?"

"Take care."

"Is it all you can say, seriously? If it is David, I don't ever want to talk to you again."

"See ya."

"I said, is that all you can say?" She had her feet apart and her hands on her hips. Rudy was quivering at her knees. She had a desperate need to have David do her will. He shrugged.

"This is ridiculous. First you tell me to get lost, and then you won't let me say goodbye."

"Don't leave like this. I mean it, David."

"You blow up at me, you call me a jerk because I invite you for a holiday, you laugh when—well, never mind, and then, *then* you expect me to stick around. You know what I think? Joan, I think you're crazy. You only want the impossible."

"That's not crazy," said Joan, surprised into calm for a second at their first real difference of opinion. "It's what everyone wants."

"Anyway, I'm going," said David, missing the point. "Bye."

"If that's all you can say—" Joan leaned across the windshield. She was swept with blood through her head and chest, and the blood pounded in her ears. The way he said *bye* enraged her. He *couldn't* leave. She was furious, more furious than she could remember being for years. He started the car. She slammed her palm hard on the windshield, and shouted.

"I'll never speak to you again. Ever. Got it? You *jerk*. You civilian. You don't know anything about me. You never did anything right with me. Not even in bed. So just fuck off, why don't you?"

He put the car in forward; it began to roll.

She pounded the hood with her fist and then fell back from it. He gunned the car. She ran alongside and kicked the door. The tail lights winked. That was it; he was gone.

Joan stood on the street, let down, her rage unsatisfied. She felt sad. She felt also someone was watching her. Sure enough, there was the Frenchman on his veranda with a cigarette. She filled her lungs with air.

"Fuck off!"

He didn't move, didn't say a word. Joan pounded her leg with her fist. She growled like a dog. Damn David! Why had he gone away? He was never there when she wanted him. Now she'd never see him again. It was stupid. Stupid, stupid; she started spitting tears. He was a stupid man who never knew what to do. Just as well, he was gone. At least she didn't have to worry about his trying to make her a civilian. She turned to the door, but then she saw the headlights.

His car came around the block. It slowed in front of her. David leaned over and rolled down the window.

"Want a lift?"

She did. "Sure."

"Get in. We're all going on a holiday."

She opened the door; Rudy jumped over the seat into the back. As she got in she waved goodbye to the Frenchman. Then she leaned over to hug David. His beard had passed the painfully rough stage: it felt almost soft against her face.

THE FARMHOUSE WAS white frame with two gables and a wide porch set low on the ground. It was surrounded by crumpled fields; the trees in their new leaf rimmed the road leading to the mail-box. Here and there were the tall riggings of dead Dutch elms. Very little moved in the landscape, sometimes only a far away herd of cows nudging themselves from one pasture to another. It was too early for bugs; the utter quiet seemed to come up from the earth itself.

They were one hundred miles from Toronto, ten miles

from the general store where they'd bought their food, two miles from the T-intersection where they turned down the road and five hundred yards up the muddy driveway from the road. No one was going to come here. The bed was covered with an old quilt made in tiny triangles. Joan could feel them with her fingertips in the dark; she could run a jagged path along their edges. She heard Rudy wiggle himself to a sleeping place under the bed. David was still and hot beside her. There was sleep within sleep here. The first sleep was sinking, losing herself.

Now, in the middle of the night, Joan woke. They could make love and it would be effortless.

She touched him, exploring. He smiled, but didn't open his eyes. She felt all the breath inside her stirring. She had been naked so often before with men but this time in the deep darkness she felt luminous; her skin flickered like a candle. She pushed back the quilt and moved to kiss David.

There were pulses in his throat and in his groin; she pressed her mouth on them wherever she found them. She felt that she was creating him with her desire, as he began to move. He took her hips in his hands and she touched him. He had not been this hard, this supple, this demanding before. She was moulding him in her hand. Her limbs strained to wrap around him but first she needed to be touched. They lay side by side. She stretched, long, and tilted her breasts to his lips, bringing his hand down her belly. He pulled at her until she was tingling. She wanted so much for him to enter her that she groaned.

The round head of his penis prodded her thigh, her stomach, her pubic hair. Everywhere the opening happened. In the heart, in the mouth, the knees, the labia. He lifted himself between her legs, still lying beside her. The entry was slow and long. She had begun to gasp, her stomach to contract, before he was fully inside. He pressed himself up against her pubic bone and waited until she had subsided. Then he pulled out of her and began to enter again. He was sweating; she could feel the moisture spring out of the small of his back. His hips thrusting against her made her body wide and flat, like a bowl; it changed her whole geography. They had become something other than the two of them.

She turned on top of him, crouched on her hands and knees and became a snail shell, slowly lapping up his skin. Then she stretched flat on his stomach. They passed through wonder and became greedy. There were caverns not filled, points not met. They threw their weight into each other, crashing at the wall of each other's bones. David's chest was running with sweat; Joan was slipping from his hips. They saw each other through half-closed eyes. They hadn't spoken. All of the things people say while making love, inadequate before, were now utterly useless. But the rhythm quickened; David seemed to swell. "I can't—" "Please, now—" The great and timely climaxes were met, first his and then finally, hers. And then they collapsed, twisting and gripping and moaning, faces pressed into hair, hands into wet crevices.

The second sleep was oblivion. Long after light had entered the room they at last woke, rose, cooked, ate, drank coffee. They dressed, and still under the spell, went to investigate the barn. There was nothing in there but stripes of light from holes in the roof, and an old tractor. The farm was not worked; not even chickens or pigs shared their home.

David had brought a few strands of hay; he put some in a bottle of water in the kitchen. Already he said, he would have paramoecia in the bottle. Joan could see nothing but strands of grass, with tiny bubbles of air on their surfaces, magnified underwater. He told Joan he had a surprise. He went out to the car and brought in a black box, his microscope. He put some of the water from his bottle on a glass slide and set the piece of glass under the microscope. He showed Joan how to look through the eyepiece: the first problem was to avoid your eyelashes. Then you focussed with one eye.

There was a world floodlit in the eyepiece. A languid, decentralized suburban kind of world where many little stations sailed, equal in distance from one another, peaceable. Paramoecium was there, David said, fuzzy with irregular patches of hair, like an old sock pulled over a light bulb for darning.

David had also brought a book. In it there were pictures of paramoecia, taken with an electron microscope. The pictures told a story. Paramoecium drifted in the water, propelled by its cilia. Another organism approached it. This one looked like an onion, with hairs around one end, like a stem. The enemy was called didinium. Didinium was not deterred by the little harpoons that paramoecium sent out to fend off dangerous neighbours. Didinium had its own little harpoons and they were better. Paramoecium was setting off tiny explosions lasting a thousandth of a second, driving its own missiles. The victor floated to its prey, opened its whiskered mouth, and took the other cell, as big as itself, within its own walls.

War. All of this was happening, too tiny for her to see. It looked so regulated, exquisite, as if it took place to music. The invisible beat of the cilia, the slow drift of the organisms, the deadly fusion, the silent devouring. An inner-space ballet.

David read aloud a part about the paramoecium, in memory of his and Joan's first meeting.

Their astonishing complexity of structure and behaviour is exemplified by *Paramoecium*, the most famous and thoroughly studied member of the phylum. . . . Paramoecia usually reproduce by cell division. But an elaborate form of sexual behaviour called Conjugation occurs when the two paramoecia line up tightly against each other and fuse in the oral region of the body. (Fig. 24). During the next several hours there is an extensive reorganization and exchange of nuclear material. The macro-nuclei break up and disappear. Each of the micro-nuclei divides and one of the two daughter nuclei migrates over to the other cell, where it fuses with its counterpart. The exchange is perfectly reciprocal—each of the two paramoecia gives and receives an equal amount of genetic material. The two organisms now pull away and depart, having been genetically refreshed.

The book had a photo of the two slipper cells pressed together, side by side, their walls crossing into each other's centre. There was finality in it, peace. For the first time in her life Joan sensed that such a peace might be within her.

DURING THE SECOND long night at the farm, they listened to music. Delibes, Mozart, Randy Newman. Joan lay against David's chest and imagined that she danced with a man. Their hands touched while she stood on point and turned. He pulled her hand above her head, stopping the spin and suspending her there. She arched her back, extending her leg behind her until she was tight as a bow about to shoot an arrow into the ground. He placed his hands on her waist and folded her down over her own knee, twisting her toward him until she was curled around his waist, a hand around a stake. He bent his knees and when there was a plateau on his thighs she shot out lengthwise, lying over him. She bent and was lifted, leapt and was caught: the hands reached out toward hers. Hers were the risks, his the obligations. This man—catcher, stabilizer—had skills no one could describe. He manipulated her back and inner thighs, her waist and upper arms, his hands and hers crossing over each other and pressing and lifting. He did it so well you could hardly tell he was doing it.

Joan experimented with her day-dream. She took herself out of it, so that there was just empty space and the male dancer's hands. The hands continued their complicated magic: it looked as if they were tossing a salad.

The hands were beautiful. She could almost feel the palms against the nerves in her back, the fingers stretching around the side of her waist. Did she still hope she'd find such hands?

*   *   *

After class the girls went to the *barre* and wiped their faces with towels. They looked like marionettes with their painted faces and improbable, tight limbs turned out at the joints. They wore black eye-liner and crusty lines of mascara on the lashes and under the lower lids. They seemed to have no lips, no cheeks; their hair was painted to their scalps. In daylight they looked exhausted and stringy, like old women. But at night or under spotlights they looked like twelve-year-olds, staving off adulthood.

In the canteen the boys ate meat, potatoes, and gravy; the girls picked up an apple or maybe a cheese sandwich because they had to watch their weight. Their conversation was silly.

"He fancies you."

"Oh, come off, how do you know?"

"He does, too."

"He's a queer, don't you know?"

"He's got a disease."

"What's that?"

"He's a homosexual."

There had been one particular boy who fancied her. She remembered they had sat together somewhere, staring at a wall. They were somewhere where the light was grey, as if reflected off stone. He had his hands under her sweater. There was music playing, something sacred, a procession-al. The music coiled on and his hands pressed harder on her breast. Now he had his hand in her pants.

"Is there somewhere we can go?"

"No."

They took off their shoes and socks. There was a carpet that tickled their feet. They began to dance, using lifts they'd learned together, positions they had only aspired to before this. They didn't look at each other.

"Are you hot?"

The music ended and then it began again, piano this time. Standing there eye to eye, they undressed. It was very risky, Joan recalled. Her sweater went over her head with a pop. She kept on her brassière and undid the waistband of her skirt, letting it drop to the floor and then stepping out of it. She had on the woollen bloomers that her mother had bought for her; he wore jockey shorts.

There was a place on his thigh where she could put her foot: the muscle filled her arch. He balanced her, plotting the weight instinctively. She was being handled, but she could see the strength in the passive role. It was she who guided his guidance, she who ruled. At the end the boy lay on the carpet, very still. There was a record spinning, its needle gone into the paper. It had been illusion. They got dressed and left: London was out there somewhere. That boy was around again, but they never touched. They were always in the studio, working.

"You're too emotional," Madam said to her. "You're putting too much feeling into it. Only the soloist can do that."

The old choreographer seemed to understand her problem. He had picked her in the first week; he often watched her from the sidelines. He gave her perhaps ten words a month, but he made Joan feel special. "You won't do it to yourself, will you?" he would say, drawing her by the elbow away from the other girls. "You won't make yourself sexless."

But Madam told her the opposite. First she was to relax, to give in; then she was to control herself. When she gave up on feeling and just did the steps, Madam would turn to her after the tenth try and say, "Now. *Dance* it." She was expected to turn on the passion then, the sparkling eyes, the toss of the neck. It was false.

But they all acted, all the time. Joan learned how to be a tease. She would get up to leave the canteen and trail her woollies past the boys' faces. She would open her eyes wide and make fish kisses behind their backs in class, to make the other girls laugh.

"Joan, you should be careful." Arlene spoke in the darkness, lying still on the other side of the room in her narrow bed.

"Why?"

"Because they're watching you and they won't take you seriously if you keep on. You're really good. You could go all the way. Everyone knows it. But you're always acting up."

"I'm bored."

"I'm not."

"No, you wouldn't be, would you, you suck."

How horrid she'd been to Arlene, how unspeakably horrid. "Don't I have the right to have fun?" she insisted.

"Who said anything about rights? I came here to work. Didn't you?"

"I don't know."

What did Arlene care anyway, thought Joan. She should be happy. Joan's fall would be her rise. Now she supposed Arlene was going to be loyal, to show that she cared more about Joan than she did about herself, just to prove she was a better person.

"Nobody but you thinks I'm that good, anyway. I'm too tall and they're always telling me to tone down."

"You're not too tall for a soloist. And you have to work harder."

But working harder was the hitch. It had come clear to Joan at last that inspiration was cheap. Even the shortest, mousiest girl in the class could do three times the number of *pirouettes* that she could, just because she worked steadily.

"We have a saying in our profession," Madam said to Joan one day, drily. "If you do it once, you can do it twice. Joan, that was very nice. But I want you to repeat it. This time make it technique, not accident. Otherwise, out the door."

As the others stood along the *barre*, Joan leapt back and forth in front. She had done the *jetés* well once, but she didn't know how it had happened. She couldn't do it twice. Her body wouldn't work when pushed like that. Back and forth. Madam didn't say a word. The other girls watched. Back and forth. After five minutes Joan broke into tears.

Madam pointed to the door. "Come back when you're under control."

Joan sobbed in the white hallway. Her legs were shaking and she was damp with sweat. She could see the road through the filthy windows, the stream of traffic squealing to a stop at the traffic light. Where was home from here? If she started by walking to the tube, how long would it take her to get there? She could go by train to the airport and by airplane to Toronto, then to Edmonton. She had no money, but her father might wire some. She'd have to wait hours, maybe days. Then she would be back where the sky was crystal and the air had not been inhaled and exhaled three times before it got to her, where the voices weren't piercing and stingy.

She pictured the airport at home: she would step down the ramp into the cold night, and be caught in the swirling beacon light from the top of the terminal building. She would look to her parents taller, more disciplined, sadder. She would be a tragic figure. But she would have given up. She would have gone back to being called for breakfast, to reproaches when she left for dance class. And the girls from her year would all be gone, some to university, some to Las Vegas, others to bungalows where they would have babies and get fat. Home wasn't big enough for her now.

Five minutes later, Joan was on her way out the door of the school. She had taken her hair down from the bun and back-combed it so that it came out around her ears. She had put on blue eye-shadow up to her eyebrows and white lipstick. She felt wonderful. She was on her way to play the pin-ball machines in Leicester Square.

She picked up a Pakistani boy. They had a bitter cup of coffee together at a snack shop. Then they slid down from their stools and walked out. They stood in front of lurid movie posters where women dangled before the jaws of lions. They walked on and kissed. There was no place for them to go. He lived with friends: the bed-sit she shared with Arlene would not do either.

"I know a bloke with a flat on Berwick Street. Many times he asks me to visit him there." The boy said visit like *wisit*. He pulled a piece of paper out of his wallet. The name was written in black ink. Joe Langelli. 157 Berwick. Upstairs.

"Who is this guy?"

The crumpled bit of paper looked as if it was torn from a school scribbler. The name thrilled her.

"Wery nice bloke, wery friendly man. Plays music in the Roundhouse pub. I meet him many times. One time I give him money so he didn't have to go to jail."

157 Berwick had a wooden door painted grey, stuck between a curiosity shop and the entrance to the Cardinal Club. It opened to a push: inside there was a low, dark room with a stone floor. The building must have been centuries old. The light from the street ran along the stones ahead, narrowing to a slit as the door swung shut behind them. In the dimness, Joan and the boy walked toward the wooden stairs. Joan's skin was tingling.

"Shouldn't you call up?"

"Joe there?"

There was no answer.

The steps were wooden and worn thin in the middle, like cakes of soap. They climbed and turned and climbed again, and then they saw a door with a light under it.

"Call again."

"Joe?"

There was the sound of a violin playing, slowly, rasping.

"He's there."

The stairs behind them were so dark that even if they'd wanted to they couldn't have gone back down. They knocked. They waited for a break in the music and knocked again. Heels cracked on the floor and the door burst open. A tall, broad-shouldered man stood there. He stared at them for a full minute, eyebrows high and nostrils flaring. He had a wide forehead and hollow cheeks, a moustache and waving beard. He looked like Jesus Christ in smouldering rage.

The face blazed at them and they shrank. This had been a terrible mistake. They must get away. Then slowly the face changed. The eyebrows came down and the mouth widened in its nest of hair; the icy blue eyes crinkled at the sides. The face folded in on itself. Then it exploded again, this time in laughter.

"Well, well, what have we here? Let me see. Let me guess. Little Raj has found himself a tart down on the street and he wants to see if Joe will lend him the flat. My, my, my. Come on in and let me have a look at you."

The room was long; the windows at the front so grimy that the other side of the street was barely visible. There was a circle of chairs and an old couch near the window. Behind them in a narrow alcove was a table and what seemed to be a kitchen. On all surfaces were empty bottles.

Having invited them in, Joe seemed immediately to forget Joan and the boy. He sat on a chair, his feet apart, the high heels of his cowboy boots sticking out the bottom of his jeans to drum on the floor. He picked up the violin again and began to play. It was nerve music, wild music: she wanted to let her head roll back; she wanted to sling her skirt over her head and howl.

"You like that?" He stood up, came over to Joan and took a fistful of her hair. "You feel like letting loose?"

She began to blush. Joe grinned.

"You're not that shy."

"Are you American?"

"Born in St. Louis, Missouri. Left there for New York City but I haven't been back there for ten years now. You're Irish."

"I am not."

"Now don't get haughty. I don't care what you are. You've got a funny lilt to your voice, that's all. What's your name?"

"Joan."

"Well, then this here's Joan's Waltz." He lifted his bow. "While you're up," he said, "get the bottle of wine down from the cupboard back there. There'll be three glasses somewhere, might have to wash them."

She did what she was told.

The Pakistani boy danced in slow, inward turns while Joe leaned over his violin and wove back and forth with the rhythms of his bowing. Joan flew around the dirty flat, stamping her boots. She put her skirt on her head and shrieked, and didn't care who was watching. Between tunes, they drank silently, looking at each other over the kitchen glasses, daring more energy out of the afternoon. No one said, "Isn't this marvellous?" or "Can we meet again?" Joan's Waltz went on, a hoarse voice calling her.

When the wine was drunk, Joe put down his violin.

"Well, I'll leave you to it." Abruptly he stood, reached for a jacket on a peg, and swung toward the door. Joan could feel the heat a foot away from her face; her hair was stuck to her temples. To get a red face is not ladylike, her mother said. She did not want to be ladylike.

"You're leaving us. You don't have to."

He looked at her fast, as if in anger. She held her chin up: the flashing eyes weren't going to mow her down this time.

"You can come again," he said.

His heels were gunshots going down the stairs. When he was gone, it was quiet. The red and yellow lights of Soho glowed through the dirty window. Inside there was a brass lamp with a shade made of woollen tassels. The bulb cast an orange glow. The boy opened his eyes when Joan pulled him to bed. She kissed them shut. She was just as glad she didn't know who he was.

Ten days later she climbed the soap-cake stairs at 157 Berwick to see Joe Langelli again. She was fearless. It was a state she would come to recognize in her life: every few years she had a day, an hour only, sometimes, when she had no nerves. At those times she could have jumped out a third floor window without hurting herself, dashed through a flaming car wreck, called up the queen on the telephone. She felt that nothing could stop her. Moments like these, she did things that changed the course of her life, and sometimes she was sorry after.

She hadn't been able to get Joe Langelli out of her thoughts. He was almost old, a wild, scruffy character who probably had dirty hands and got drunk, the kind of man they'd have stopped to stare at on Edmonton streets. And yet she felt as if he were kin.

She knocked at the door. It was silent on the other side. No music played, no bottles clinked. But someone was in there. She could feel quiet, heavy movements on the other side of the door. Perhaps he was dressing. It was four o'clock in the afternoon and Joan had just come from *pas de deux* class.

She knocked again. The movement ceased. He must be listening. She knocked again. There was a thump and a curse and another thump. Were people in there fighting? Suddenly the door opened and Joe stood in front of her. His chest was naked and his lower half was wrapped in a sheet. Joan looked straight at his breastbone. He had the most amazing rug of dark hair on his chest: it covered an area from his collar-bone to the bottom of his ribs, an almost perfect square with a tiny peak of hair at the bottom pointing down toward the navel. Then she looked at his face. Again, he looked furious. His eyes flared and the lips behind his moustache were open in an O.

"Well I'll be damned. The little dancer."

"Joan."

"Yes, Joan of Joan's Waltz. What do you want?"

She didn't know what she wanted. She just stood there.

"It's good to see you, Joan. But I'm a little occupied just now."

She nodded. He started to laugh.

"Come on, it's not that bad. Do you want to wait for me? Tell you what, sit down on the front step and I'll see you in half an hour."

"It doesn't matter. I can go away. I only came because, because, you said—"

"I said, did I, Joan?"

Joan could tell he hadn't remembered. She didn't care.

"You said to come back and see you."

"Sit downstairs on the step. I'll be down in a while."

There was only one thin step and it was very dirty. She didn't feel like sitting there and anyway if she did she'd be propositioned, she knew that much by now. She walked to the end of the street and looked down. There was a bookstore there, where she liked to go to browse through old costume sketches, but she was afraid if she went out of sight of Joe's doorway, she'd miss him. She crossed the street and bought a bun and then stood in front of a porn shop: the man inside called good afternoon. She finished the bun and then reached into her bag for a tissue. She sorted things out, rolling her tights over, putting a few loose pins in their box, trying to look occupied while she kept an eye on Joe's doorway.

In fifteen minutes the wooden door opened and a woman came out. She had long, frizzy red hair and a fringed shawl and she was painted as if she were a cancan girl in a Toulouse-Lautrec poster. As the door fell shut behind her she put one hand on her skirt and twisted it violently around her waist, as if it had been on backwards. Then she stooped to buckle a shoe. She set her sights on Joan at the bottom of the street and marched toward her, swinging a carpet bag.

Joan held her ground, prepared for an attack, but the woman passed without giving her a glance. "God damned son of a bitch bastard," she said. "Damn his soul." And she was gone. Joan registered that she had wrinkles in her neck.

Now she took a deep breath and waited. She could feel the cold breeze where the woman had passed her, and feel too the thrill that she was gone and now the coast was clear.

In minutes, the door opened again. Joe's head poked out. He looked down at the step as if he expected to see Joan lying there like a parcel. Then he looked up and down the street. Finally he came out into the full light and stood in the centre of the sidewalk, his hands on his hips.

Joan stepped forward and began to walk toward him, enjoying the power, the equality. He had come out to meet her.

"How old are you?" he said aggressively when she was within fifteen feet.

"Eighteen." Almost.

"I'm thirty-three."

Christ was the only man of that age she could compare him to. His face was a great, wide-browed shield but instead of that simpy, marked look that Christ had in pictures, Joe had what her mother would have called a lean and hungry look.

"You don't look thirty-three." At thirty-three most dancers were looking for a retirement home. It sounded to Joan like an awful age, the end of the road. Still, Joe gave it a new cachet.

"What did you come to see me for?"

"To hear my song." She had stopped a few feet away from him. "But maybe I should go. Your girl-friend's mad."

Joe smiled. "She's not mad. She's insane, and I like her that way."

Joan smiled back, entering the betrayal. "What were you doing when I knocked?" If he could use his worldliness, she could use her innocence.

He grinned wide, and ignored the question. "Now that you've interrupted me, you might as well come up." He put his arm around her back and turned her toward the door. She jumped from the touch of his hand. It turned the blood around in her veins so that it began to trace a new route. She could have rolled up that arm and into his chest in a minute. But she held herself stiff. You *might as well* come up, he'd said. There was always some sort of insult involved.

SINCE THAT DAY she'd said his name over and over. Joe Langelli, Joe Langelli, as if it were a charm. But there was nothing magical about Joe. He was almost incidental; he was the occasion and not the cause. Her flood had come over him when he opened the gates; it had poured on in tears until his traces were washed from her face, from her skin, emptied from the inside of her. He had seemed so kind at first. He had taught her how to make love. He had loved her. It was true, she still believed it, despite everything. She had to believe it.

That day he asked her if she wanted tea. He made the tea sloppily in a big brown pot that he set on the floor. They had poured it out into two cups, but never drunk it. He sat in the chair across from her stool and leaned back.

"Why are you sitting 'way over there?"

"Me?" She'd been tripped up at first by the way he turned things around. It was he who had gone across the room and sat far away, but it was she who got up and walked across to him, timidly, embarrassed, her stomach quaking.

He was sunk in a large, deep old armchair in the centre of the room. Behind it was the dangling wool of the lampshade and the distant river of neon across the street. London was so dirty, there was black dust on everything, and drafts, cool air travelling in flat sheets across the floor. She had sat on his lap. His arms came out and clasped tightly over her back and around her waist. They were long ropes; they went around her almost twice. And he had rocked her for a long time, before she turned to face him and they kissed.

His lips were sweet and purple inside the circle of beard and moustache. He held her tightly against him for the longest time. When her breath began to come quickly, her breast pressing against his, he let his arms expand to give her room. That had been the first metamorphosis. The slow, barely shaped creature of her passion began to move outward, drawing force from what had previously been dreams. If he had moved a muscle it would have retreated, dissolved. But he didn't.

The hot place where she sat on his lap began to expand to fill the air around them; it came back in waves. Joan's legs slipped down his, stretching to the floor. She had to pull him off the chair to lie on the floor. She lay atop his long body moving only to adjust more closely to him. She found the hard place, the place below his belt buckle that reached back to her. Clothes went, seeming to crumble between their hot skin like so many dry leaves. Then there were circles, all through her. She was made of circles, containing him.

By men's definition there were two kinds of women. The kind of woman a man left for another and the kind of woman a man could not afford to lose, a keeper. Joan had accepted Joe's definition from the beginning: she was no keeper. Joe had abandoned her, and therefore set her in limbo, a woman always to be left.

So she thought. Now it baffled her to see David trying so hard to please her. The second day at the farm he took her for a walk. He pointed out the trees—oak, beech, maple and elm, and told her how to tell which was which. When it got dark he taught her how to walk without seeing, how to stand still while the eyes adjusted, and then pick a spot a few feet ahead on the ground, staring at it until it grew light enough to be clear, and then moving forward, a few steps at a time.

Joe had done all he did to her by sitting still. He didn't move from his spot; he didn't even seem to exist outside of that third-floor flat with its tasselled lampshade and saggy chair. After the first day he never even came down the street to meet her. Occasionally they went together down to the Roundhouse for a pint, or for a Chinese dinner, but that was all. He said goodbye when she left without asking her to return. But she did return. Joan made herself take responsibility for it all; above all she despised the role of the victim.

But maybe she was the victim. In the peace of the country, the idea crept into her thoughts. It was as if her calendar had flipped around again after a dozen years to the same season, and she had a second chance to see it.

Nearly every day she went to see Joe. Usually she couldn't stay for long, because she had to get back home or to a class. She met a few of his friends when they chanced by; she even met the red-haired lady, who regarded her with scorn. Joan never asked what Joe did when she wasn't there. It seemed to her impossible that he could have repeated with some other woman the extravagant motions he made with her. To Joan, their love-making was a devouring and absolutely original thing.

He was her private gymnasium: she had the run of his body. She found the root of the muscles in the small of his back, and the cords that popped up in the front of his thighs when he bent his knees. The patterns of hair on his chest and back were as familiar as the map of the world, but making love with Joe was never quite the same today as it had been yesterday. Every day the exchange became more detailed, more complex, more powerful. Two ambassadors of foreign states met, each speaking in his own tongue. They engaged in orgies of sound and gesture, excited, not understanding. But so driven were they to match on all points that they continued their frenzied efforts until the two tongues became one.

Fascination with Joe carried Joan in a trance through her final winter and spring at the school. Her training was nearly over, and a kind of peace descended. There was a special light that came into the rehearsal rooms in April. Bright, but never yellow, a silver green, pure as the smallest new leaves. In the light, the rehearsal rooms were like paintboxes, a square of solid white with high windows letting in smaller squares of white pastels. The *barres* along the sides were grey lines; the dancers brush strokes here and there around the floor, always moving, leaving their shadows behind them again and again, only to be covered up by the light. For hours at a time they worked, their knitted leg warmers drooping to their knees, wisps of hair escaping their nets. There were scuffles, small groans of frustration and sometimes a voice rose, commanding silence down the floor.

One worked to an absolute standard, setting a small goal such as eight *fouettés* and making their perfection the only god for a morning, returning the next day to find that, if the goal were not achieved, one might still count oneself a fraction closer. For the first time in her life Joan understood what consumed other dancers. She walked into the studio in her disguise of rubber warm-up pants, wrap-around sweater and headband, one of the many soldiers dedicated to this mass expression. She worked until her legs glowed and then burned, until sweat had run and dried and run again. It was a sustained and patient search for ecstacy, the pleasure coming to the surface in knots and circles, the climax possibly never to arrive.

And after dancing she had Joe. The weight and grit of sex filled her; it seemed to be a search completed. Then she would go home and lie in bed across from the silent Arlene. Finished her work and her play, still and pristine in her flannel night-gown, images would fly past Joan's eyes. We are pliers, interlocking; we are a team of horses, pulling; we snap open and shut like jaw-bones. We leap in and out of focus like flames. We, always we, but the partner's face was blurred. It was I, and a shadow.

She had been at the ballet school eighteen months, two full terms. She had not been home and she had not seen her parents. Her life outside ballet, such as it had been, had dried up. She was one of a dozen trained young bodies, striving for pliancy, for submissiveness, for anything that would further her hopes. She and the other girls looked out through the dark holes of their eye make-up like nocturnal animals in some Canadian forest. She was no longer a virgin. She had forgotten that she was lonely, homesick and uncomfortable most of the time, that she rarely ate a hot meal. Homesickness had become restlessness.

Then, the girls had known each other so well that they could recognize the back of a neck, an ankle, an arm a block away. But now the faces would not return in memory, only the voices were there, piping insistent voices like the voices of ghost children demanding their due. They all sat in the canteen, their hair in nets, staring into plates of cooked carrot.

"Have you seen Arlene?"

"I thought she went down to the BBC. Didn't you know?

They're doing a special on students graduating from the school. Aren't you in it?"

"No." A shock of violent jealousy. The others had known for a week and no one had told her: Arlene hadn't said a word.

Joan stretched out on the bench, playing the fool. She put her head in Frankie's lap.

"I'm tired."

"Did you get left out of the show?"

"Nobody loves me, Frankie."

"Frankie loves you, he does."

"But Frankie, you're a fag."

"I know sugar, isn't it awful?"

Four girls had been chosen to go straight into the company from the upper school: Arlene, Joan, Dido, and Nessa. Joan's invitation was the only one with a rider on it: she had to watch her behaviour or she'd be out. Instead of feeling grateful, as she was expected to, she felt insulted. Dido and Nessa were beating their feet under the table, practising the rhythm of a *ronde de jambe* exercise they'd been given that day.

"You're obsessed persons," observed Joan. "You all go mad at the end of the term here. You go right off the deep end."

"But Frankie's all right, isn't he?" Frankie cooed like a pigeon.

"I went on an eating binge last night," confided Dido.

"What'd you eat?"

"Pizza, crisps, cake, ice cream, the lot." Gloom was on her face.

Madam's assistant came into the room. "Dido, dear?"

"Yes, Gwenyth?"

"May I speak to you?"

She drew Dido aside, but not so far aside that the others couldn't hear plainly.

"It seems that Arlene is ill and can't make it to the BBC taping."

Dido's eyes opened, becoming more innocent. "Oh,

poor Arlene," she murmured. She drew her breath in. The other girls at the table held theirs also.

"I wonder if you could get your things together and we'll send you down in a taxi."

"Yes, Gwenyth, of course. Is Arlene going to be all right?"

"I think it's just a flu."

"That's good."

Dido sat still until Gwenyth had reached the stairs. As soon as she disappeared, she turned to the table, put her hands over her ears and shrieked.

"Wow! Did you hear? Arlene's sick! Fantastic. I get to do it!"

The cooked carrot made Joan sick. The smoke from Frankie's cigarette made her sick. She wanted to fall asleep. The girls who had not been chosen sat at the next table: they were depressed all the time. Their lives had been shaped for this, and now the shape had drawn to a stopping point.

"Why didn't anyone warn us? I should have quit a year ago."

"Come with me, we'll arrange auditions for the musical comedies."

"I'm sick of dancing. I'm going to be a clerk in Woolworth's. I'm too old to learn anything else." Too old at eighteen; there was a wretchedness about dancers they'd never noticed before; even their heroines, Sibley, Seymour, Ulanova. They were too soon old and too late schmart, as the wall plaque had said in Miss Levy's studio.

Joan went down to Soho to see Joe. As she came up the stairs she saw that his door was ajar. Smoke was winding around the woven lampshade. Again she felt nauseous. There were three other men in there with him; they were all playing cards. Joe didn't like her coming in when his friends were there. He said they thought she was too young and stupid. But that evening she braved it, sauntering across the room and throwing her bag down on his bed, raising her brows at the men. They said nothing.

Exaggerating her ballet walk, heels in, toes out, she

went down to the kitchen where she rummaged for a glass and poured herself a little beer. She acted as if she lived there. Probably Joe's other women—she had come to believe more and more that he had other women—did the same. Joe was so rude. Still, she felt privileged beyond imagination when the door closed on the others and he finally turned a smile on her.

"Did you want something?"

"Did I chase your friends away?"

He shrugged.

"Do you want me to go?"

"Come here, you little minx."

Joe collected Joan's limbs into his arms and squeezed her into a knot on his lap. Then he began to bite her neck, her shoulders, her arms. She pushed him backwards on the couch and sat over him, looking down at his face. He still looked like Christ to her, but a cunning Christ, with sharp lines around his mouth under that moustache. Christ looking down from the cross with a wink and a come-hither look: Christ demanding his carnal dues.

Looking at him that minute she realized what was wrong with her. This thing that had been wrong with her for weeks, even as she lost herself in rehearsals for the school show, and dozed with a sick stomach over the canteen table. She had been crazy not to realize: she was pregnant.

Joe had never asked her if she was doing anything about it; he had never offered to do anything himself. Every time she went upstairs to his room she found him there, waiting but pretending not to wait, affecting this lack of need for her. He took her like he did then, peeling her clothing off, and humming to himself. She should have known this would happen. Maybe she had known. He undid her pants and then he forced himself inside her, twisting her this way and that and bobbing her on his lap, teasing her all the time with words she hadn't heard before, and only heard again in the basement rooms of sleazy night-spots, the haunts that were then collecting in her future.

Afterwards, she washed her hands at the kitchen sink. To go to the toilet was difficult there; it was down a narrow hallway past another door where sometimes an old man sat, and the room itself was freezing, with a grate open to the back alley. Joe picked up a guitar. They never spoke, after. They rarely spoke before. Joan was angry.

"When was the last time you washed these glasses? It's disgusting."

"Get me a beer, will you?"

"I said it's disgusting in here."

"You said that, did you? Well why not do a little clean-up then?"

"I'm not the maid."

"You're not the maid." He put down the guitar and held out his arms again. "There's never been any maids around here." He laughed, gently. He just didn't think much, Joe. He beckoned her.

"Joe do you know what happened today?"

He buried his head in her chest. "Ballerinas have no tits," he said.

"You don't even care."

"Are you going to turn into an infant?"

"You don't care."

He groaned and pushed her away. "Don't get demanding, Joan. I've heard all this before. Don't act like all women act."

"I've never done this before," she said haughtily. "I've never had a lover before. Don't compare me, I don't like it."

That made him laugh. Joe had a merciless laugh. His eyes folded and his mouth split wide across his face and the sound came out high, with a lot of breath in it, like a big bird on a branch leaning down and looking at the world, finding it worthless. He had to catch his breath. "Joan, you're marvellous."

"I've got to go home. Arlene's sick."

On the way home Joan cried on the tube. No one looked at her and she could see her face in the window. She made herself cry, thinking about being kidnapped and

Joe having to run through the streets calling for her.
Madam and Miss Levy and others, her parents too, would
stand over the body when he found it. She imagined the
sight, a stabbed, fallen Joan. Finally the spectacle of her
dripping nose in the scum of the train window made her
stop. She wiped it on her scarf.

Arlene was in bed with the lights out. There was half a
bowl of soup on the table and the room was stifling hot.

"Are you awake?"

"Mmmmmm."

"You missed the BBC thing?"

"Mmmmmm."

"What's the matter?"

"Sick."

"Sick in what place?"

Arlene took the covers off her face. "I don't know.
Everything aches." All Joan could see in the dark was the
faint light of eyes and teeth.

"Did they call the doctor?"

"No. I'll be O.K. tomorrow."

"Arlene, are you faking?"

She didn't answer. Joan went and kneeled by the side of
her friend's bed. She touched her hair.

"Arlene, why?"

Silence. Then Arlene spoke in a normal voice. "Who
went?"

"Dido."

"You're kidding. I thought they'd send you. They should
have."

"Hah! My name is mud around there. Arlene, is that
why you stayed home?"

Arlene sobbed. "I don't know. I didn't want to go
myself. I thought it should be you. I really am sick. Now
that we're really going to do it, be in the company and be
real dancers, I'm too scared."

Arlene recovered in a day, but Joan felt worse. Her face
was even paler than usual. She was hungry but food made
her sick. First of all she had stopped eating meat; when

she saw it her mouth watered and she felt like vomiting. Then butter and milk had to go; finally all she could eat was thin soup and fruit. Two days before the school show she fainted in the canteen. The girls made a joke of it and said she was trying to get attention. But she fainted again the next day at the top of the stairs. She saw someone coming a long way away and cried "Help!", hanging onto the bannister and struggling not to go down on her knees. She woke up like a cliché, with her head on someone's knees. She had no idea where she was: the dome overhead with clouds in it, the white rail of the staircase, the echo from the hallway all suggested heaven's gate. Eventually she realized that she was still in the world, but couldn't recognize the land mass. Around her voices asked what was wrong with Joan.

She regarded the pregnancy as a miracle: it was a command, a human inevitability that swept her up. For that, she was grateful: it took her out of the category of dancers lost to civilian life. The girls were all at risk of pregnancy. They claimed that *pliés* and splits broke their hymens early. That rupture was like tearing a sheet off a work of art; they had to let their bodies be free. Most of them were smart about it. Those who had no weight problems were on the pill. Some had diaphragms. Some made their boy-friends use condoms. There was plastic wrap if condoms weren't around; there was Coca-Cola for a douche. A few unlucky ones had been through abortions already. But mostly, they watched out for themselves. Only Joan was different. She was as she always had been, wildly careless, throwing her body around and trying to get love back.

"This is not entirely unexpected then, Joan, if I understand you correctly?" Madam looked only slightly pink from her grand fury: her small feet were still neatly crossed at the ankle.

"I knew it would happen eventually."

Madam pressed her lips into a ferocious little bun. Her hand sat on the desk like a wary mouse: her feet twitched under her chair as if they wanted to get up and race, pulling their chariot with them. Joan could hear her father's voice, speaking about Miss Levy. "The trouble with these fanatics is they won't leave the rest of us alone." Joan dipped her head to hide a smile. Madam let her decisive feet take her over to the window. Her toe tapped steadily.

"How many hours do you suppose we've spent on you here? How many corrections have we given you, bringing you along, Joan? Our time is very precious. We are in the business of producing artists, Joan. We can't possibly make do with girls who are so *wilful*, so *spiteful*, so *undisciplined*. I mean to say, Joan, you've hurt me very badly."

"I'm sorry, Madam."

"You are a beautiful girl, although a trifle tall. You are an exceptionally talented girl, a sweet girl, really, when you can be bothered. That's why we've had you this far, that's why we've given you a *chance* to get into the company." Madam's speech was like a volley from the troops. Some words were meant to fall short but the rest were to hit hard deep in the lines. "I don't even know what I'd do with you if you were mine."

"Yes, Madam."

"May I ask you if you have any idea of what you want? Will you be marrying your young man?"

"Not exactly."

Madam looked relieved.

"I thought I'd continue dancing for a while. I'm not too fat yet." In fact, Joan had lost weight. She was under one hundred pounds for the first time in years. "Couldn't I?"

"Frankly, Joan, I simply don't know what to say to you."

"Until it shows."

"Joan, you aren't thinking ahead! What are you going to do about this pregnancy?"

Madam's toe hesitated in its rhythmic taps.

"I'm not going to do anything about it."

Tap, tap, tap.

"Then I can't keep you here."

"Can I go in the show?"

"Tonight and tomorrow, and that's the end."

"Thank you, Madam."

Joan got up to leave. She noticed how much taller she was than Madam. Their bodies angled against each other as she turned to the door. Madam looked back at her desk, her papers, her pretend children. As Joan left the office she heard a growl of frustration from the tombs of Madam's lungs, but she had no pity. She had no fear, either. She would prevail. There would be no kitchen-table abortion for her, no injected salt solution, no rushing home in pain waiting for the world to fall out of her womb. There would be something else instead. This starved little belly would swell and make itself dominate. She would forget all about dancing.

She'd got a job in Selfridges. It was hard on her legs, as everyone said it would be. At five months she couldn't get her knees together and her breasts were long as eggplants. At eight months she was sitting on the sofa bed in the big kitchen at the back of a house of refuge. The resident girls wore cotton house wraps and hair rollers; they had a tiny pale blue portable record-player that sat on a chair, like a special guest. St. Barnabus House, at 1 Greek Street, was an old Georgian home; the girls were the lucky ones who had the proper references to get in. It was Madam who got Joan in after she couldn't work any more. Joan would be there until she had the child and maybe a little after, depending, the matrons said, on how she behaved. They all thought Joan was crazy. Joan wasn't really angry that Madam had interfered now because Joan had got her way. When it was over Joan would escape.

"Why don't you dance for us?"

"We don't have the right music."

"How about the Stones?"

It was 1968. Less than a mile away, Carnaby Street welcomed the world. You wore your miniskirt and listened to the music that led you down the yellow brick road.

"I can't do ballet to the Stones. Oh well, all right. 'Jumping Jack Flash' is O.K."

The other crazy girls with their pasty faces wanted to learn how to do ballet. They were always dancing togeth-

er, always holding hands. When the record went on, the
blonde began to dance with the refrigerator door. She held
the handle as it swung open, and crooned to herself with
her chin up. Her free hand drew little figure eights in the
air. The blonde had been sent down from the juvenile-
detention home where she'd been kept for five years after
trying to murder one of the dons in her boarding school
when she was fourteen. She said it had been a prank. Now
her parents wouldn't have her; the social workers were
trying to find her a job before they let her loose.

Joan felt superior to the girls here. She was a profes-
sional; all of this was part of a plan. When the pregnancy
was done she'd get her body back, she'd get a job dancing
in Soho. Already before she went into the hostel, she'd
looked at the ads in show-business magazines. *Wanted,
girl dancers to play slaves in "Aladdin." Minimum, 5'6"*.
For once, her height would be an advantage. Meantime,
she got up and did a few *pliés* and *tendus*. The girls cooed.

Upstairs in the rococo plaster in the parlour were the
faces of the Lord Mayors of London; in the back yard was
a tree that Dickens named, or sat under, or something; the
last mulberry tree in Soho. It was like the English to stand
a nice lady in a woollen suit with strands of pearls at the
door to usher tourists through the house.

"Yoo-hoo girls, please turn the music down. I have some
guests coming through," cried the dowager guide.

"Coming through girls, turn the music down, please."
In her voice was the petulant whine, "What will they
think?" She had already shown the tourists the famous
spiral staircase and the faces in the plaster. Down here the
doors were shut to all the bedrooms but you had to pass
the kitchen to get to the back staircase and the yard.
There was no way of avoiding the sight of the girls. Joan
could hear the pearls of her voice dropping words off the
string—drop, drop, drop down the halls. She could hear
the footsteps following hesitantly and the appreciative
murmurs. When the steps reached the door, she turned
the record-player up to a blast.

Jumping Jack flash, it's a gas, gas, gas.

The girls were all up and dancing, rubbing hips with one another, making cow eyes and waving their arms above their heads. Joan stood in the glory of her ballooning smock and began to dance. She did *bourrées* down the centre of the room: the opera-house stage had not seen better.

Three people stopped in the doorway, the guide and two tourists, a couple in their early fifties, American or Canadian, they could have easily been people Joan knew, friends of her parents, her parents even, but they weren't. The girls went on dancing, fully engrossed and outrageous. The blonde slid up and down the refrigerator door. Joan did the dying swan, elbows lifting and dropping, head lying along the top of the arm, horizontal, as if it had been pulled out of its socket. She remembered some great ballerina, Beriosova, it was, saying "Misery is in the elbows." The elbows fluttered, they melted, there were no bones in those elbows. It was as if someone took Joan's hands and shook them hard, and the ripples were sent violently back into the shoulders. How she hated art, hated it for what it had done to her.

"Excuse me girls if we could just, excuse us could you please. . . ."

The guide and her followers worked their way through the fray as the record came to an end. When the tourists were out of sight, everyone went back to a chair to pick off nail polish. The other girls thought Joan was pretty good.

When a child is already given away, the mother is not supposed to see it. They told her it was a girl. It hurt more than seemed possible. As she'd meant it to. The world she'd made passed through her and out, as if it were excrement. The baby was a nothing, she thought. A not-seen, not-known thing, a tearing out, a gaping wound. A nothing from a nothing: her own true daughter.

In the hospital room, Joan fell into her old habit of holding her hand up to the light and making shapes of it. She had been saying a little poem from A.A. Milne that her mother used to read to her.

Halfway down the stairs
is a stair where I sit
there isn't any other stair
quite like it.
I'm not at the bottom
I'm not at the top
so this is the stair
where I always stop.

The matron's face wore a look of raw, dripping guilt. The baby's new parents had come to take her. Joan didn't even know who they were: later she learned they'd called the baby Sara. The putative father, as the matron called Joe, had been against her having the child. He hadn't wanted to see Joan any more when she went ahead. At first she'd gone to Berwick Street and cried and begged and ended up making love with him. But finally she'd stopped. The putative father had not been notified of the birth. Nor had Joan's parents, who thought she had dropped out of ballet school because she couldn't get into the company; they were still expecting her to come home. It was all over and done with, the pregnancy. It was astonishing how easy it had been, to give another being life for no reason.

Joan's stomach retracted minute by minute. Immediately, she would dedicate herself to the repair of her body. It was all she had now, her only love.

THE THIRD DAY of the farm holiday came in an explosion of hot sun and green. The kitchen moved with shadows of the trees as David made scrambled eggs at noon. Joan watched him. He looked different. He was sharp faced and when he was dressed, he appeared thin. Now, in shorts, he looked much bigger. His body was heavy boned with large muscles that protruded on his calves, arms and back. He moved constantly, and his eyes moved too, always sharply. At night he would sleep absolutely still, like some peasant, she thought, who had laboured all day. And now, in the morning, he had a quality of separateness. It made her want to go over to the wood stove and touch him, be sure he was still with her.

Perhaps that was what was meant by being an intellectual. David didn't look effete: his knees didn't knock and his chest wasn't concave. But perhaps he was one, perhaps this way he occupied space was the proof. He had a presence apart from what you saw. His mind stalked the room where he stood. She could ask him now what he was thinking and he would have an answer. He would be thinking about the sound flames make, or heat convection, or even a line of poetry.

"You should keep that beard short," she said, "if you're determined to have it. You don't want to look like a hermit."

He padded over and poured coffee in her cup, resting his hand on the back of her neck. His hands and feet were wide, like planes, and very clever: they could manoeuvre among rocks and on a sloping earthen hill, the fingers would tap the keys of a tiny calculator and make her nipples stand up by lightly brushing them. Joan moulded her hands around the warm cup. She had not dared to imagine their holiday would be this way.

The owner of the farm was a friend of David's and David had been there many times before. He knew how to turn on the pump for water and how to keep the wood stove going. Today he would get the canoe and put it into the lake. "We'll paddle all the way to the rock cliffs," he said, "and climb to the top."

After breakfast they went out. The heat of the sun broke on Joan's skin and David joked about her night-club tan. She saw that David knew how to move in the country; it was different from the way you moved in the city. There Joan stepped out aggressively; here she was timid. But David paddled a canoe the same way he walked, with assurance that he had a right to what lay ahead. She had never noticed his grace before. It was not the standard sort of grace, because he was angular and not beautiful, but his body had a quality that moved her. He moved with care, with affection for the life around him. He showed her things, the marks of beaver teeth on saplings, and the larvae of insects lying on the surface of the water. Even Rudy knew more about the country than Joan did: he chased a racoon up a tree, where it sat fat and furry, eyes narrowed down at them.

The lake they were on was long and thin. They paddled along the edge as he taught her how to lean into the paddle and make her back do the work. He showed her where the lily-pads would bloom, and how to see submerged rocks by looking through sun-glasses. When she was paddling they pulled into the shallows and talked. He wanted to know all about her past, and about the reasons she did things. She had seen her life as a series of things done to her but he kept asking her why, why did you go, why did you quit, assuming that she had choices.

The rock David loved most of all protruded out of the side of the hill next to the lake and rose thirty feet. It was a forceful, monument-shaped rock. They climbed the hill beside it, cutting back and forth across its face at the upper reaches and finally arriving at the top. On its smooth, brown-and-black top they sat cross-legged looking at the water, thirty feet below. The water was ruffled on the surface, and you could not see what lay beneath it. Another canoe went by, close to the shore. The man in it did not see Joan and David. When the canoe had passed, they took their shirts off to feel the sun and eventually, very carefully on the hard ground, made love.

They paddled home slowly—against the current, worn out. Joan's shins and the tops of her feet hurt from kneeling in the canoe. Behind her, David sang voyageur songs to keep up their spirits. At the farmhouse they dropped into wicker rockers on the porch, with beer.

"Now I've shown you all my tricks," he said. "Will you take me?"

"Some performance," she said.

She was engaged by the things he brought forward to her as if on a plate—his laughter, his beautiful voice, his familiarity with the woods, his relaxation. He rubbed her shins and they watched the sun begin to fall. It was their last day at the farm. In the morning they would leave; by noon he would be at work in Toronto. She had not imagined what she would do when she got back. She did not want to think of all her losses: they had been obscured for the three days.

Joan wanted to do something for David. He had been kind, wanting to win her. The idea made her vaguely uncomfortable. She felt as if she should do something in return.

"Why do you want to make me happy?"

"Don't you think I know what kind of person you are? I recognize you, Joan. It's a good idea for us to be together."

She thought about that one for awhile; she wasn't sure she deserved David. He brought her a glass of wine before bed and they sat on the edge of the coverlet, rubbing their sore muscles. He was humming under his breath. "I love showing you things."

"Why?"

"You're so suggestible—it all surprises you so."

"I thought I was jaded."

"Jaded? No, you just think you are."

Joan lay under the coverlet, knowing it was for the last time. Falling in love with David was making her remember falling out of love with Joe. In retrospect what she felt about her first love affair was a sense of bewilderment, that it had ever been, and that once it had come into being it had ended as it had. The passion was groundless, without a home, without a name. She'd spent twelve years since it had ended holding her breath against its coming again. It seemed that something slid apart inside her, like the two parts of an egg whose shell had been broken. She was no longer innocent, as she had been yesterday, holding together her heart after a painful first love. She had leapt from that into age, and had become complex.

It was her old dream in reverse. Instead of pushing the fragments back together, she presided over the separation, offering up her fragile pieces. Nothing would ever be quite so clear again but nothing would be quite as painful either. She could love someone who offered her real things, forward motion, life in the world. It would be the same as deciding to grow.

David was beside her, not sleeping yet. The two of them were of the same oil, burning in separate vessels. She didn't know what he was thinking, but she turned to him and at the same moment he reached across the gap to her.

CHAPTER TEN

David was in his office, his mind jangling with the faint rings of telephones that reverberated through the old building. So many wires, so many circuits. He had had insomnia for three days, ever since he got back from the farm. Too much peace made him unfit for his life. What he wanted today was a temporary lobotomy, just for a day or two, so that he could relax and get some sleep. Instead he fished in his pocket for change and went downstairs to get a cup of coffee.

It spilled over the side of the hard, rippled plastic and burned his fingers as he made his way up the stairs again. "God-awful brew," he murmured to himself. He made it back to his office without bumping into anyone, which was fortunate. If he had, he would probably have started a fight: he was mad at just about everyone he knew.

He wiped the cup with Kleenex to remove the stickiness and sat at his desk. He turned the cup between his thumb and fingers and looked not out the window but straight at the wall. The wall was covered floor to ceiling with shelves; on the shelves were packed flat, square boxes. Inside each box was a tape, wound tightly around itself; on each shiny tape was a voice, or many voices, talking on and on, giving out information. The wall reminded David of his mind.

David was full of information. It was beautifully ar-

ranged inside on vast numbers of plastic-coated wires
coded and strung over pin-heads of gold and silver: his
brain was as neat as a microprocessor. He was not a
computer, however, because he had no plug. With a plug
he could have been disconnected and he would forget it
all, clear the memory and start again. He envied machines; they were organized and predictable. His mind
only *looked* organized. It wasn't really. For one thing it had
associations with information that was not officially on file,
links to his tear-ducts, his sweat-glands, his stomach, his
balls. For another thing, it did not always work.

Now it would not stop spinning, would not let consciousness go, not from one inch of him. He had buzzing
nerves, bad digestion, and he was tense. He didn't know
why but today he stood tense and especially he walked
tense, the muscles of his seat pulled up tight, tucked
under, his legs perforce swinging a little out to the side.
He seemed to be on the balls of his feet a lot, swaying,
like an antenna, like rabbits' ears.

Rabbits' ears, that was it: he could practically feel
himself quivering. He tried to understand this failure to
relax. It seemed to him that he was on guard against
information, stiffened against the speed at which it tried to
get through him. There was so much information—the
book-review pages listed new packages of it every day and
especially on Saturdays, and then Sunday there was more,
people writing commentary on what other people were
writing about. He greeted printed information with the
combined exhilaration and despair with which an addict
would greet a new supply of drugs. Experts were interviewed
on air, reporters flew into Iran, professors dug things up in
the Urals, analysts on Bay Street made predictions, and it
was his job to attend to this, absorb it, file it, pass it on,
put it in context.

It was too much. He had to resist. If David opened his
circuits and ceased to be an exchange in the information
flight, would it not sear through him, blasting the connec-
tors? And what would he be then? A forest after the fire,

babbling like a homeless animal? Or perhaps like a new-born sprite, unblemished, with pale white, unseeing eyes.

He could do that, let the stress wipe out his brain, and then retire to a pure life in the country. The three days with Joan had opened him up, sensitized him, made him ready. That was all very well but they'd have to come back. Would this affair play in Toronto? He doubted it. They both had their problems. She had her temper, her court case, and no job. He had his overwrought brain and his job, which he was avoiding just now.

There were more and more of these moments of inactivity at work. Up and down the halls people were committing little assassinations in order to get what they wanted. The dragons at the top were deciding even now who would be fried at the mouth of the cave and who would be next in line. He didn't particularly care. His job, he decided, was for callous young men and cynical old ones. At present he was neither. He was in between. His ability to simplify, reduce and distort—yes, he had to say distort—had begun to leave him.

And in the future? He could become an administrator, be kicked upstairs. The offer had been made and would likely be made again. If he went there he would have to give up on his precious information and settle for the routing of it. He would be standing back, not feeling the current, not knowing what it meant, only seeing that it passed through the proper terminals. The Terminal Man, that would be him. *Terminal*. He did not like the sound of that.

If not management, then he could hang in as an announcer. He would become increasingly helpless, passed over, not respected, vain, leaning on the admiration of an unseen audience. No, he had better find another job. Leave this one for young men, old men, and inexplicable women like Ellen.

Ellen hovered in the doorway of the next office. She was wearing a dress of some fabric which was both fuzzy and stretchy, like a housecoat should be. The dress was strapless; it strained across her bosom; she had a jacket tacked on her shoulders as an afterthought. People said terrible things about Ellen. He could never figure out whether she deserved them, or whether those who said the things were jealous of her corporate power.

For instance, Ellen had recently been to Mexico where, it was said, she'd been raped. "Funny thing," Charlie remarked when telling David the story, "she was wearing the same strapless sunsuit she'd been wearing when she was raped in Portugal." It was also said about Ellen that she had hated her late mother so much that, after the cremation, she'd taken her ashes and thrown them down the toilet. Perhaps it was an apocryphal story.

Right now Ellen was dealing with the public-relations department: there had been protests lodged against a program she intended to run.

"I'm not going to reschedule it and I'm not going to cancel it, tell them that. I'll meet them after it's been aired to hear their complaints. No, I haven't got time tonight."

Mumble, mumble, came the voice from the office beyond.

"Look, Rod, I've got a child and I've got to get home. I'll make it after the thing has been aired." Ellen didn't hesitate to use her marriage and motherhood when it came in handy, when she was refusing to compromise, reminding her opposition that it was a woman in the holiest of roles they were crossing. But, two minutes later, as she approached David's desk, she did not emanate matronliness.

"Boy, do you look bad. Can I cheer you up?" She sat on the corner of his desk and leaned over to peck his cheek.

"Useless day, Ellen, a useless day. I'm not cut out for it."

"That's what we all love about you. You're not."

"Got to get out doing something. I'm going to rot in here."

"Let's have a drink."

"I thought you had to get home."

"That's for them. For you, I've got time for a drink."

Later that evening David was supposed to go to see Joan; she was performing in some kind of benefit because the strippers were trying to unionize. He didn't see why she should get involved if she'd truly given up performing, but she said she wanted to support the principle. He'd never yet seen her dance. Come to think, he'd like to have a drink first, to prepare himself.

"O.K., Ellen, you're on."

He packed his scripts back in his desk drawer with a sense of adventure. Some things he just knew he wasn't supposed to do. This was one. He could tell by the sly smile that wanted to break out of the side of his mouth. Three weeks ago Ellen was a pest to avoid; now he was flirting with her. Bad David, he thought, grinning. It made him feel better already.

JOAN PICKED UP her dressing-gown from the hook on the back of the bedroom door. Her first move of the day was out to the kitchen to put the kettle on. The pilot light was still out and now even her camp flint had given up the ghost. She reached for the box of kitchen matches to light the gas. STRIKE ANYWHERE, the box said. An open invitation.

Sometimes she had a narrative voice in her head, speaking in the third person. "She was a good girl but she became a stripper," the voice suggested. It was her personal justifier. "No," interrupted Joan, "I became a stripper." "Yes, but it was all their fault," said the justifier. They—the justifier called the rest of the world "they" —they had taught her not to say I. Say us, say you, so it's for him or him. Your "I" is not what is wanted. But now it was different. David wanted her to say I. She wanted to say I herself. I kicked a man and I have to go to court. I want to find a new job.

She struck the match. There had been complicity in her act, in her life. The hand that undressed her was her own hand. The hand that seduced her was her own hand. She was ravagee and ravager. She watched the blue ring of flame and placed the kettle over it. But it was time to stop laying blame. Something had to happen soon.

The weeks of idleness had emptied her bank account and the old manager had been looking nervous when she went in to see him. When she came back from the country she'd found another threat, this time a rusty hammer, on her doorstep. And yet tonight, as if she could afford to give it away free, she was going to dance in a benefit. She wanted a new idea for her act.

She sat at the kitchen table, her fingers filtering through the magazines there, seeking distraction. She picked up a magazine that David must have left. She flipped the pages. It seemed that these days sociologists were studying victimology. It was a new theory: there were individuals who had been burgled three dozen times in five years, for instance. Sometimes they got beaten with the butt of a gun. It happened to them in their houses, at their offices, in their cars, when it didn't happen to anyone else around them. This was the sort of puzzle that really turned on the social scientist. Eureka! They had been wasting their time looking at criminals: criminals were only behaving as expected.

But the victims: what was it these unfortunates were doing wrong? How did they spark the crime, bring it down upon them like a lightning-rod brings down the bolt? It turned out, the scientists said, that these victims *wanted* to be burgled. They had been scrawny kids with glasses and the only attention they got was an occasional cuff. They needed affection. even if it consisted only of a rude frisking. There were babies, the article said, who invited battering just by the look on their faces. The victims needed involvement; they needed to have a relationship with their oppressor. So they co-operated, bringing criminal and victim together in an ecstatic little mugging. There might be an act in that, Joan thought.

As the water dripped through the coffee filter, she put her foot on the kitchen counter and stretched her hamstring. The muscles were bunching: it had been three weeks since she'd danced.

The telephone rang.

Joan looked at it balefully. All of the calls were harassment;

the only reason she ever picked it up any more was that it might be one of the few people in her life she felt like talking to. Arlene. David. One of the girls organizing the benefit. She hoped it was David. David had been weird since they'd come back from the country.

"Hello."

"Joan Sincere? This is Johanna, at Characters." The voice was warm, overpowering. Joan felt instantly pale and breathless. "I got your stuff in the mail."

"Oh good."

"You look like everything I've heard about you."

She's heard? thought Joan. Do people talk about me?

"I'd like to meet you, Joan. I can't say before seeing you that I can take you on, but there is a project coming up. I see you have no straight acting experience."

Here it came: Joan swallowed and delivered the bad news.

"I might as well tell you I'm terrified to talk."

"I'm suspecting you've got other things going for you." An ambiguous laugh, or was Joan too sensitive? Somehow this woman made Joan feel different than the others did. "You can break that. A good voice coach, a different way of breathing. Oh it's nothing big, what I could try you in. Just a little film that's being made locally. But the director was in, and happened to see your picture on my desk."

The new picture, one that David had taken. It was the first time she'd posed without dance gear, as her natural self. She'd been afraid to look at the print, she'd felt so undisguised before his camera. Someone had liked her picture! "Wow," said Joan, for want of something more profound to say.

"Why don't you come in, and we'll meet, anyway."

Afterwards Joan wondered if simply by wanting it so much, by telling people about it, she was making this all come true. If she was, she'd keep on with it; if she could invent a future this far, she could surely bring it all the way.

TONIGHT. STRIPFEST. TORONTO'S FINEST BURLESQUE ARTISTS IN NON-STOP PERFORMANCES IN SUPPORT OF THE

NEW US—United Strippers. SEE SUGAR BUSH, UNITY DRAW-
SON, JOAN SINCERE many many more. SUPPORT OUR UNION.

Inside, Candy was grinning at her. At least that squab-
ble was forgotten.

"Gonna be a big crowd tonight, honey. You gonna bust
anyone up?"

"Haven't decided."

The room was already three-quarters full. A dancer Joan
had never seen before was on stage, and in the audience
were men, women—different types from usual. They looked
like feminists, maybe union people, a few other performers.
She wedged her way into the dressing-room. It was filled
with clothes and bags; some of the other women in the
audience must be strippers waiting for their turn to perform, Joan decided. There was no room for them backstage, that was for sure.

It was her first performance since the assault, and she
was getting the itch. Damn it, she was happy. Happy for
no reason, happy because she was in love and she was
going to do something she knew how to do well, and
happy to be among friends. She had a feeling it was going
to be a good night. She'd brought a case full of crazy stuff
to wear that she'd picked up on Queen Street that afternoon, but she wasn't going to be on until much later. She
went out in her jeans to watch the show.

She sat alone at a table watching the waitresses circulate
with drinks, and the light turn slowly in the ceiling.
Herbie came toward her.

"What are you doing here? This do isn't for management: there's girls at the door collecting three dollars a
head for the union." She hadn't forgotten that Herbie was
the scum who'd called the cops on her.

He smiled affably.

"Looks like you're going to do well tonight, they're still
coming in. How're ya feeling, Joan?"

"Surprised. To see you here."

"You know I'm all in favour of raising the standards in
the profession, Joan."

The doorway to the street was blocking up with the

torsos of men. The Stripfest had become such a curiosity that people who didn't support them were coming out anyway. Either that, or Joan had underestimated the sympathy of audiences. The tables were nearly all full. A man came up and asked to sit at Joan's table.

"Drink?" he said.

"No thanks."

She looked away from him. Candy was on stage, doing one of her "sophisticated" routines. She came out in a little-girl outfit, a pinafore with matching ruffled pantaloons under it. She had a ragdoll with her, identically dressed. First she stripped her doll. It had pubic hair drawn on its cloth body.

The man beside Joan leaned over again. "Hard work, isn't it?" he said sarcastically.

Joan got up and walked out to the hallway. She pressed her knee against her chest, one leg and then the other. The concrete floor of the place was chilling her legs. Gina and Candy laughed at the way Joan molly-coddled her legs. They crashed around in high heels without thinking about tendon damage. But Joan had seen too many ruined bodies in her life. "Take care of it, it's the only one you get," the old choreographer used to say. Press, press, first one leg up, and then the other. She placed one foot behind her and leaned forward to stretch the back.

Candy flew past behind her, down to a beige G-string, clutching her discarded ruffles, on the way to the dressing-room. The master of ceremonies was back at the mike. He was talking about working conditions. Stages too small, dressing-rooms dirty, demands to do illegal acts. Some cheered, some hissed. She went back to her seat. Gina was on next. Gina did a frenzied routine to Rod Stewart, gyrating against the mirror with her mouth pressed in an astonished O. Joan walked back to her seat hoping the man had got her message.

The bar man came around, selling French fries.

"Aren't the girls great? Each one is better than the last." He looked at Joan and the silent man. "Are you folks having a nice time? It's for the union, you know. They work their guts out and they don't make much. They're tired of this bullshit too. They're human, eh?"

The man beside Joan grunted.

Joan bought a box of chips and soaked them in vinegar. She was glad that David was coming. The audience was hot and when you got this many girls together, competition made them go wild.

Stripping had changed a lot in the past eight years, since Joan had begun. There were rules about stripping, just the way there were rules about ballet. For instance, there was a whole range of things no self-respecting stripper would do. Chair acts, bottle acts, "dirty acts" as the girls called them, like faking orgasm. They had taste, and they didn't want to have it dictated to them.

That was what was wrong with the morality regulations. It used to be there were signs up in the dressing-rooms of the clubs, saying what was allowed.

If you should lose a pastie, cover yourself and go off-stage. No one even wore pasties any more, but the signs were remembered fondly. *All panties must have a two-inch strip of opaque material up the back.* Different cities had different taboos. Topless had been fine in London but G-strings obligatory, except in the peekaboo parlours where a man paid five pounds to stand behind a glass and watch a nude woman move around in a case. In Toronto you could be topless or bottomless but never both. Girls had been busted for nudity if they got caught without bra and G-string. But they could take one and then the other off in sequence, as long as they changed off-stage. It ruined the dramatic structure but saved your ass, the girls said, if you took it all off but the G-string, then repaired to the hallway to replace your bra and came out for the final pantie drop.

It all had to do with what turned people on. The rules were precise: they'd been made by experts. You could be sure if you broke a rule you would hit whatever worked.

Anything forbidden, that's what turned them on. If she ever thought stripping was liberated, she'd learned by now. She could tell you more about restrictions and re-

pression than you'd ever want to know: it was her stock
and trade. And they liked a little abuse thrown in, too.
From the publicity angle, it looked like her best move in
years had been to kick a guy in the jaw.

"The girls are being modest tonight," the emcee said.
"They don't want to have to take their G-strings off when
it's against the law."

Some cheered; some booed. Joan didn't see anything
wrong with nudity herself. The trouble was that men
couldn't handle it. The moment the last stitch was off they
turned into animals.

At nine, the place couldn't hold any more. Maxima X
was on stage. She was a beautiful black woman who loved
to dance disco and hated to take her clothes off. She was
tight and quivering like a wire. She had sparkles in her
cleavage and inner thighs, and she looked in the mirror
without seeing the audience. When a man got too close to
the stage she shouted, "Get down!" without missing a
step.

At the end of her act someone yelled, "Let's have Joan
Sincere!"

There was a lot of cheering. Why were they cheering?
Were they on her side, or did they just think that a feisty
stripper was camp?

Maxima gave Joan a dirty look when she came off stage.

"Joan Sincere's coming up right away," said the emcee.
"But first we've got your favourite, a real crowd pleaser,
the very lovely dancer and revolutionary thinker, Miss
Polly Anna."

Polly was an intellectual; she came on in a blue sun-
dress with white gloves and a straw hat. To a scratchy
record of "After the Ball Is Over" she mimed a courtship
with an invisible man, dodging and shying away, then
rubbing up against him like a cat. She was fair and
delicate: she kept blowing her hair out of the corner of her
mouth. She lay on the stage floor with her dress pulled up
and mimed trying to get a man's hand out of her pants, as
the relationship with the phantom progressed. She let
"him" take them off once, but quickly stood up and pulled

her dress back to rights. Then she had a tantrum with real tears, little fists, twisting and throwing herself around, pursing her lips and putting her finger in her babyish mouth. She wanted the audience to heckle her. "Tell me no! I won't!" she shouted. "Don't make me! Make me!" When they began to shout, "Take it off," she smiled radiantly. She brought a little white rug onto the stage and lay on it to take off the rest of her clothes. Once down to her G-string she turned aggressive. She ended up scrubbing the floor with her panties, shouting "Women's work!" The audience was roaring, except for one man in front who'd been rebuked for reaching up to touch Maxima, who stared bitterly into his beer.

It was nine-thirty; Joan had to perform after the break. She'd searched the doorway for David's face and hadn't seen it. She got up to change. The shows tonight were reminding her of what stripping had been about, for her, when she'd first begun. Knowing, witty, a way of saying what you felt, an all-purpose metaphor. She wanted to do well.

As she stepped out of her jeans the door burst open behind her. That was the trouble with being a stripper: no one ever figured you wanted privacy when you were dressing. Herbie never knocked.

"There's a man out here says he knows you."

"Oh yeah? What's his name?"

"I don't know. Blond, thin, blue eyes."

"Tell him I'll talk to him after, I'm just about to go on."

The door closed behind Herbie, and she brought out her costume.

That morning she'd had the idea she would come as a terrorist. She'd gone down to Queen Street and bought a pair of black cotton pants for practitioners of martial arts—they had a draw-string waist and puffy legs—and an army camouflage shirt. She'd found an ancient pair of Kodiac boots abandoned in a shoemaker's store and filled them with socks: she tucked the pants into the top of the boots. She had borrowed an ammunition belt from the military-antiques store and the owner had donated a couple of hand grenades to hang from it. Then she'd gone to a toy store and found that you could buy a surprisingly real-looking machine gun. She'd splurged on it. The final touch was a black wool balaclava with red rims around the eyes that covered her hair and head and only left holes to see and breathe.

She went out the door, signalled for her music, and waited for the follow spot to pick her up. Violent punk noise blasted from her tape. She drew in her chin and backed up the steps to the stage, then she spun around, strafing them with her gun. There were gasps, even a few screams. She laughed, stamped, screamed, and shot more rounds. When the audience stopped screaming she threw up her hands as if she'd been caught, dropping her gun.

"Take my arms, I wanna lose them, take my lips, I'll never use them," sang Willie Nelson, as Joan took her gun strap over her head and offered it. She pursed her lips through the hole in the balaclava. *"Take my lips, I'll never use them . . . you took a part of what once was my heart so why not take all of me?"*

The music broke off again into screeches and percussion. She ripped off her balaclava, letting her hair tumble free. She loosened the ammunition belt and held it on either side of her hips, drawing it over her buttocks, with mock sensuality, and finally pulled it up in the air like a prize. Then she dropped it.

As the drums pounded on, she sat on the stage and began, laboriously, to unknot and unlace her heavy boots. Now laughter was turning into rhythmic clapping. Once she got them undone, she threw each boot up in the air and heard it thump. Then she began to draw the thick socks down her leg, slowly, inch by inch, as she had done so many times with her silk stockings. Socks off, she jumped up: barefoot and bare legged, she kicked and spat about the stage: she jumped as if on to some prey, and pummelled the air.

The music changed. She went romantic again, running her hands over her shoulders and chest in the army shirt, inside the draw-string waist of her pants. *Regulation Three:*

Once you have started to remove your clothing you cannot touch your body with your hands. She picked up her gun from where it lay on the stage; and began to dance with it. *You cannot bump a prop.* She used the end of the machine gun to pop the buttons on her shirt, then took the shirt off and swung it overhead. Underneath she had a black lace bra. More laughter swept over her. She took the shirt and twisted it like a rope, then tied it to the chair and attempted to climb it. *You cannot run any article of clothing between your legs.* Abandoning that effort to escape, she became coy again, running her fingers down her bare arm, over her hips, pulling down the waist of her pants, giggling as she tickled herself. For the first time she looked out over the faces and saw David.

He was standing at the bar at the back. She was sure it was David: an alert went through her nerves. But he was standing with someone, a blonde woman. The blonde woman was virtually drizzling down his left arm.

"*So why not take all of me?*" crooned Willie. Finally, the combat music came back. Joan spun into a crouch, leaping into kicks, somersaults, splits, dragging herself on the floor as she battled an imaginary assailant. She was truly furious. How dare he? It was a flagrant insult, to bring another woman to watch her. That swine! She'd never, never speak to him again.

The music changed again. She got up slowly from the floor, dusted herself, and undid the draw-string of her pants. Slowly, deliberately, she pulled them down her hips and off her ankles, stepped on them, and threw them over the heads of the audience. *You cannot communicate with the audience, i.e., talking, noises, give-away items to patrons.* She felt deadly serious.

Now she wore a bra and bikini. She touched herself. Fingers had given her fun, fingers were friendly, fingers were tapping feet, exploring animals on her chest, drops of water on her belly. She could feel her skin tighten at their touch. She could feel the audience stop their laughter to suck in their breath. She was no longer their prisoner. She had caught them.

She slid around the stage in her black lace, covering herself with her hands, warming herself, fondling herself. Around and around she circled. She rotated her hips. Then she undid the snap on one side of her bikini. Pop. One tiny bit of air, under the constriction. The leg wanted out now, the skin wanted to feel the soft silk descending inch by inch. She sat on the chair and pulled her legs toward her, pressing her knees against her chest. She drew one leg up like an arrow, then the other. The bra undid in front. She snapped the hook loose and let the sides fall open. Her breasts bobbed free. She dropped the bra behind her. She felt the air settle on her as soon as the satin left her skin. Suddenly she was in a hurry. She popped the other side of her bikini and drew it away from her.

Now she was a pale, free body in the spotlight. She was round, lean, wearing only the tiny flesh-coloured G-string that filled the gaps, making her smooth, impenetrable. Hairless, seamless, an endless circle of flesh. She began to dance. She thought she could still see David's face, and it looked incongruous, like a surprise view of a relative in a sea of foreigners. A man was on his feet at the side of the stage. But she could see that he was no threat, his stance was worshipful rather than belligerent.

This was what it was supposed to be all about. This was the way it was meant to be, naked in the impersonality of the dance, with the crowd around cheering. In the little vortex of light and music and eyes she became all that she had aimed to be, hard as an atom and unreachable.

People were cheering, but Joan wasn't listening. She was listening to the music, letting herself go out and be dance. She was exposing more than skin now. She was showing something of her longing, something of her desire. This is I, she said. This is the scene of the battle, all that I have. This is I, this whirling flesh. But it is also not I. This is not to touch, not to take or to talk to. This is not just my body, but a ceremony.

WHEN IT WAS over she walked off stage without taking a bow. She changed, and went straight to the bar at the back. David was still there. Now the woman was standing two feet away from him. Joan walked up close and stared into his face.

"You finally made it."

"At least I saw your act."

"Yeah. And I saw yours."

He laughed nervously. "Joan, I'd like you to meet Ellen. Ellen works at the CBC."

"Hi, Joan. I've heard all about you. You were terrific."

Joan looked at her coldly. So they were going to try to bluff and get away with it, were they? "Glad you could make it. We got all types here tonight."

"So are you ready to go?" David said to Joan. He moved slightly away from Ellen.

"Yeah, I'm leaving. But there's more. Mr. Big is going to be on. Why don't you stay? It looks like you're having a great time, and I'll just go on home."

"Joan . . . ? Come on. Why not have a drink with us?" Ellen's eyes went back and forth between David and Joan. She made no sign to leave.

"Thanks, but I wouldn't want to intrude."

"We're only having a drink. Listen, it was a bad day at work and. . . ."

"Looks like you've had a lot of drinks. Naw, I'll be off. You're a shit, David."

"I—what?"

"You're a shit and I hate you. I can't stand the sight of you."

David took Joan's arm and led her away from Ellen. "For Christ's sake, she's just the woman in the next office, and she asked me, what could I do, I can't be *rude* . . ."

"You can't? You finally come to see me and bring someone else—that's not rude, that's unforgivable."

"Now wait a minute, don't tell me what I can and can't do—"

She threw off his arm. "What you can do is go stuff yourself. Go to bed with her, do whatever you want only don't hang around me any more. This time I mean it."

She pushed her way past the far tables and out the door. She did mean it. She never wanted to see him again.

CHAPTER ELEVEN

Joan got off the subway at Yonge and Queen and headed toward Old City Hall where the trial was to be. As she pressed through the crowd a man touched her arm. "God bless you, my child," he said. He tried to give her a pamphlet.

She shook her elbow to lift off his hand, and then regretted it. Someone had better wish her well today, even if it was only a religious fanatic. She was going to her trial alone. She hadn't told any of her friends the date, not wanting the shame of an audience. Only Alex Rennick would be on her side.

The courthouse stood on a little rise on the north side of Queen Street. Its pinkish stone recently cleaned, it had a face like a baked oatmeal cookie, stodgy and respectable. Approaching it, you had to pass the cenotaph, where you were instructed to remember the dead. Joan climbed the central steps to the building. Over the tall wooden doors was a rim of stone gargoyles, contorted, froggish faces apparently being strangled by a stone vine that wound among them.

On the brass door handle PUSH was written in ornate script. Joan pushed. The centre hall was studded with columns that met the ceiling in an eruption of gold froth. She stood and looked around. No opportunity to intimidate had been spared: there was marble everywhere except on the floor, which was mapped out in mosaic tiles like a series of parlour carpets. The space opened around her like a great clap, leaving her suspended in it. Voices echoed high up in the spaces but they seemed to have separated long ago from the people passing underneath.

Joan stopped to look at a map to find out where she had to go to find Courtroom 24. Up, and around to the left, then down the hall.

She passed several policemen in their blue suits with silver buttons and their snappy little blue hats. The policemen were in charge here; the rest of the people in the courthouse followed a descending order of being. Those were lawyers in their pin-striped suits, with their neat little beards and soft eyes; here but really a little above it all, independent, choosing sides. Loud-voiced men with their hands in their pockets, talking fast, worked for the Crown and bargained for people's futures. Women with notebooks were social workers or maybe reporters. And the rest, slouched on wooden benches with evasive eyes, black or Indian or old or young, were the accused.

Ahead of her she saw a bundle of clothes on the bench, feet sticking out, long matted white hair half-hidden. This man didn't have to be accused, he was already guilty—homeless, drunk, old. He'd found himself the safest place: if anyone wanted to arrest him now they wouldn't have to take him far.

She was one of the accused.

She didn't feel like herself. Alex had said something to her over the telephone yesterday. "I don't exactly know how to put this, Joan, but it can make quite a bit of difference, how you appear in court. You know, if you can look sympathetic to the judge. So if you could dress a little, well, like a lady, you know what I mean?"

"No army shorts with twelve buckles? No sleeveless halter tops?" She'd show him she could dress like a respectable person. That morning she had put her hair back in the old ballet bun at the nape of the neck, and had worn a white blouse with a white belt and a full red summer skirt. She'd put a sprig of red berries around the knot in her hair and kept the make-up down to mascara and lipstick. She wore white espadrilles that snapped around the ankles, and altogether, as she had looked in her hall mirror, she'd thought she looked convincingly proper.

But here, in these halls, she felt too red, like neon. She wished she'd worn something freer, something where she didn't feel tied up like a package.

She was standing at the receiving end of someone's cigarette smoke. She didn't smoke herself, but she wanted a cigarette suddenly, wanted to have one in her hands to stave off the miscasting, this gross mistake that was being practised on her. The benches outside Courtroom 24 held a complement of sulky teenagers in toppling high heels, probably up for soliciting. A black girl hung on the arm of a man with dreadlocks and a very thin old man sat erect as a robin at the end of the row. Joan peeked in the door.

"Recess," said the robin.

"Oh." She let go of the door and it shut, soundlessly.

She stood. People were gathering, several dozen of them. Where was Alex, for God's sake? People were looking at her.

And then he was striding down the hall toward her.

"Alex!"

He took her hand and squeezed it. He looked exactly like the other lawyers in the place.

"You look great, Joan. How do you feel?" Without stopping to hear, he ushered her into the courtroom.

It was a large room with high windows that showed the curved back of City Hall and a lot of sky. The judge's seat was raised; beside it, a small exposed box was the witness stand. An oak fence enclosed the two main positions, separating them from the rows of seats. As the waiting people filed in, Joan saw some lean to their neighbours and whisper.

The judge came in from a door at the front. He wore a black robe with a red collar and silver glasses with tinted lenses. Beside him on the desk was a huge jug of water, its significance nearly religious in the bare room. He sat.

Joan was so nervous that she began to see in patches, to hear in patches.

When her case was called, Alex stood up to introduce himself. The Crown was a tall, black-haired man with a long nose and abrasive voice. The Crown was the enemy in the Queen versus Joan Sincere, she knew that much. He called the policeman who arrested Joan. Joan looked at the policeman. She'd forgotten how pudgy his face was, and how childish the straight wisps of hair over his square forehead.

"And is she the woman you found in the dressing-room at the Coliseum that night?"

"Yes, she is."

"Could you point her out to the judge, please."

"That's her, there."

His blue arm rose up and the finger jabbed toward Joan. She stared straight ahead, permitting a prim smile on her lips.

"And what did she say to you when you called her from her dressing-room?"

"She said I should get stuffed. She said that the kick had been an accident and that Mr. Yorrick had been in her way."

"And then what happened?"

"I told her I was going to take her down to the station and ask her some questions."

"And did she come quietly?"

"She did."

"And what happened as she left the club?"

"The audience cheered her on, asking her to rough up the men a little more, something like that."

"Were you of the opinion that this form of attack was a habit with Miss Sincere?"

"Objection, Your Honour."

"Objection overruled. We want to establish what sort of show this was, Mr. Rennick."

"Yes, I was."

In a minute Alex stood up to cross-examine the policeman. Feet shuffled, shadows moved in the bright midday of the courtroom. Joan was remembering the night at the Coliseum. It was difficult to conjure the logic of that event away from the smoky basement where it had taken place; difficult to judge what people do in their night-clubs by rules of deduction. And too, the courtroom was so like a theatre. You had your costume, your lines, and the lines of others with which to establish a character. That was all. There was no background in here, no credible other world.

The Crown attorney had his turn again: this time he called the complainant. Mr. Yorrick was short and paunchy with closely curled hair that grew in a square from his ears across his brow. He had a fat, crumpled body and a fat, crumpled, pugnacious face. And he was madder than he ought to be, Joan thought, considering it had happened almost two months ago. He wore a righteous, wounded expression. He wasn't really a simple ignorant salesman from Hamilton who bore a grudge, he was every dumb loser who'd come on to her over ten years of this work. Ten years! How many thousands of leers? It was more than the spirit could tolerate. What she'd hated most about stripping was not how much you took off, but who you took it off for. Ten years! He was lucky he was still alive.

Joan didn't have to look hard to know him. Guys like this figured they could do anything they wanted with the girls. Put their hands anywhere, clutch, pinch, pry. They were like children. And when they were slapped down, when they were told No!, Not yours!, Don't touch!, Mummy doesn't like you!, their outrage turned to squalls and brooding silences. Oh, she knew his type. He said he was a sales representative for a household-products firm in Hamilton.

"Can you describe to us the events of the night of April twenty-fourth?"

"I went with some of my buddies to the Coliseum, oh, maybe eight or nine at night. We'd been working hard all day. We had a few beers and watched the girls dance."

"How many is a few?"

"I'd say six. I had six."

"Six? Are you a heavy drinker?"

"Sometimes I drink ten. I've been worse. I wasn't drunk, just feeling good."

"That's what they all say, buster." Joan began to mutter under her breath, so she didn't hear the next few questions.

"... I mean, I figured she was asking for it."

"Objection, Your Honour."

"Objection sustained."

"Carry on, please, without ascribing motives to the dancer, please."

"So she seemed to like it when the guys shouted things to her, I mean sorry, she was smiling and dancing faster and taking more off when we, you know, pitched in, like you know. So I got up and I figured I'd help her out a bit, my buddies were cheering for me and still yelling things, so I got up and I put my arms in the air like I wanted her to dance with me ..."

Bullshit, mouthed Joan. Like you wanted to wrestle with me.

"... soon's I got near to her she turned ugly and kicked me in the chin. I tell you she kicked me hard and next thing I knew I was lying on the ropes and bleeding and my buddies had to help me up. Now I got expensive dental work here ..."

"Tell me, Mr. Yorrick, was there any warning that she was going to kick out at you? Did she say anything? Did she tell you to get out of the way?"

"No she didn't."

"Were you of the opinion that the dancer saw your actions as threatening?"

"Hell no, she just kept right on."

Mr. Yorrick concluded by describing his injuries to the court. Joan stopped listening. She saw Alex get to his feet, swaggering, a pencil between two fingers, ready to pose something clever and catch this man.

"Mr. Yorrick, you said you'd had six beers since eight or nine o'clock. The so-called assault took place at eleven P.M. And you say you weren't drunk?"

"I was feeling good."

"Feeling good, inebriated, you mean?"

"A little."

"And could you tell me how you got to the dancer, what route you took?"

"I just stood up from the table and went straight ahead, it was only a few feet."

"You don't remember how you got there?"

"I just said."

"You said when you fell, you fell into the ropes. Was the area where Miss Sincere danced cordoned off in any way?"

"Oh yeah. I guess there were some ropes strung around it."

"But you don't remember climbing over them?"

"No."

"As a matter of fact, the stage was raised three feet and there were steps up to it. Did you climb the steps first, to get to her?"

"I don't know."

"You don't know? Come on, Mr. Yorrick. Think."

"I guess I must have," he said sulkily.

"Could it be that the six beers had slightly more effect than you imagined? If you don't remember exactly what you did, for instance?"

"Objection, Your Honour. I don't see the point of this. After all, the man was kicked. It's still an assault whether he was drunk or sober."

"Mr. Rennick?"

"I'm trying to establish, Your Honour, the degree of threat to the accused."

The judge pressed his lips together and looked irritated. He wanted to pronounce, to get to his part in the play. His silver hair and silver glasses gleamed in the sun. Their pinkish tint made him look like a fish.

"Very well, carry on."

"Thank you, Your Honour. Mr. Yorrick, you say your buddies were calling things out to the dancer. Do you by chance remember any of those things that were said?"

"Just the usual things you say."

"What usual things? Perhaps His Honour and I don't

frequent places like the Coliseum; perhaps we don't know what sort of things people like to say to the dancers."

"Objection."

"Overruled. Answer the question."

"Well, you might say take it off or something, but I don't remember anything special we were sayin' that night."

"Isn't it possible that you said something that offended Miss Sincere?"

"Objection."

"Overruled."

"Isn't it possible you told her to hurry up and take it all off?"

"I guess so."

"No 'I guess so's' here. Did you or didn't you?"

"I don't know."

"Isn't it possible you told her to come on over and show you her 'pussy'?"

"I don't know."

"Isn't that possible?"

"Yes."

"And isn't it possible you told her to come and sit on your face?"

"It's possible."

Mr. Yorrick's face was blank as Alex finished. Joan listened to the words that had enraged her with little more than curiosity now. To her mind they had composed a violence more shattering than the kick in the teeth. But now it seemed to her that such words, clipped or slurred, fuzzy or sharp, had surrounded her always. They were her environment. Like the hostile darts of the one-celled creatures under the microscope, they filled the spaces between the animals, keeping them apart, occasionally paralyzing their object.

"Does the Crown have any further witnesses?"

"Yes, Your Honour. I'd like to call Mr. Herbert Spanatakis."

Herbie! Joan looked up from her lap. She'd lost track of the proceedings; she had been examining the bright red crescents she'd cut in her palms with her finger-nails as she squeezed her fists. Freshly shaven, his hair wet and stuck to his scalp, Herbie was trying as hard as she was to put on a good face. But he was testifying for the prosecution, against her. Stinking creep! All the work she did for him, never missing a show, putting up with all the hassling just so he wouldn't have bad vibes in his place. She looked him straight in the face. He should be ashamed.

"Miss Sincere was a good dancer. I always only hired the prettiest anyway, I have the best dancers in my club. It is a very good club, very quiet, the right kind of people there, and I never had trouble until she came."

"What sort of trouble did she bring?"

"She was fighting with the other girls, always squabbling, something was wrong. Maybe she had personal problems. She didn't want to be friendly any more, no more drinks at the bar."

"Was she accustomed to drinking at the bar with the clients?"

"If I ask the girls to, they do."

"Tell me, if there was an obstruction in her path on stage would it be possible for Miss Sincere to change her steps in order to avoid it?"

"Objection. That's a question for the defendant. This man is her employer, he's not a dancer."

"Overruled."

"I can tell you this, if there's water on the stage, like once we had a spill, she could avoid that. Or if she dropped her skirt in the wrong place, she goes around that. I don't know why she couldn't have gone around that man."

The Crown attorney was smirking as Herbie stepped down. Alex had cross-examined him, but the feeling in the air didn't change: things were going against Joan. Alex came back to sit beside her before she went up to the witness stand. She had begun to shake.

"I'm too scared. I can't go up there."

"You've got to, Joan, unless you want to change your plea to guilty."

"I'm not guilty. But they're going to convict me anyway."

The word *convict* split her tongue. As she sat in the

courtroom, the whole incident had taken on an awful profundity. It was as if she'd plotted a murder and was caught. "Look, I'm just a run of the mill stripper trying to keep out of trouble. Here we are in a court of law talking about my choreography. When I kicked the guy I never thought it would come to this."

"Come on Joan, say your piece. I think there's even a few reporters here, it'll be good for you. Remember, I'll only ask you what we talked about. And don't worry about the Crown—I can handle him."

"Sure?"

"Sure."

She stood in the witness-box; the lawyers were in front of her and the judge on her right hand. She stared at the reporters and curiosity seekers. She swore on the Bible to tell the truth and then turned to Alex. She told him how she'd noticed that the man was very drunk, how she'd seen him looming on the stairs as she turned from a kick and how the shouts of the audience had confused her. She repeated the insults, hitting each word clean like a hammer hitting a nail, driving it home. There was silence in the court. She drew herself up taller. She didn't look at anyone but Alex. He paused and then continued questioning.

"And what did you think when you saw Mr. Yorrick on the stage and heard that remark?"

"I thought he was coming to grab me. I thought he was going to get in my way, and that I might fall, and that he'd go after me."

"And then what did you do?"

"Nothing out of the ordinary. I didn't stop dancing. I just kept on, with lots of force, so he couldn't get near me."

"And then?"

"He got in the way of my foot."

There was a trickle of laughter in the courtroom. Joan straightened her shoulders.

"Did you intend to kick him?"

"I didn't think about kicking him, I just wanted him to

move back. Then I was going to tell him to get off the stage."

"Is it normal for men to come on the stage while you're dancing?"

"Absolutely not."

"Why?"

"It's a rule, it's part of performance. You can't come up and touch the artist during her act. You could cause an injury. The distance is part of the act. Most girls wouldn't strip if someone came up on the dance floor."

The Crown attorney bounced up under Joan's nose for cross-examination. He had narrow eyes and down-turned cheeks. He asked her about her experiences in the past few years and then came to the point.

"Would you say, Miss Sincere, you've seen a lot of clubs, a lot of men in that time?"

"I'd say I've been in a lot of clubs, yes."

"And has it been your experience that they run these places like concert halls? Aren't there often raucous comments? And don't the men in the audience sometimes make advances, often successful, to—how shall I say—strike up an acquaintance with the stripper?"

"He was hardly trying to strike up an acquaintance."

The judge looked annoyed. "Answer the question, please!"

"Perhaps in some cases. Not in my experience, no."

The Crown pulled on the ends of his moustache as he composed the next question. "Miss Sincere, would you change your steps if there was a hole in the floor in front of you?"

"Of course. I'm not looking for accidents."

"You're not looking for accidents, and yet you made no attempt to avoid Mr. Yorrick. Instead, you went right on and 'put more force,' as you said, in your kick. If that's not an assault, I don't know what is."

"Objection! Your Honour, the Crown is giving his opinion."

"Sustained."

"It was not an assault. He was in my space. All I wanted was to do my job, and he got in the way."

"Miss Sincere, just answer the questions, please."

*   *   *

Joan stepped down with a buzz in her head not at all sure of what she'd said. She looked at Alex for reassurance, but there was no expression on his face as he stared at the judge.

"Do you have anyone else to call?"

"No."

"Very well."

The judge leaned forward and lifted his jug of water to fill the glass. He poured it and then sipped once before putting the glass down in exactly the same spot. The courtroom was silent, watching him as he turned in his seat to look out the window. He sat without moving, his eyes seeming to have been turned off behind his tinted lenses. Then he turned back to his desk and brought his regard to bear on the notes he'd taken. Joan resented his insistence on this suspense.

The onlookers were neither for nor against Joan, but curious, waiting to see how natural order would assert itself. It didn't matter what was decided, only that something be decided. When two people's rights conflicted, a line had to be set. He could not go thus far without interfering with her; she could not go that far without crossing him. The contest was about who got the most room; the one who was judged most powerful would have the most space.

Right now, lines seemed to be drawn far too close around Joan. She could barely move without being in the wrong. She sat stubbornly in her seat as a form of protest.

Finally the judge looked up. Looking over Joan's head, he began to talk. This time she didn't hear the words because she didn't need to hear the words. He had decided against her. He allowed as there had been some provocation. She heard that word provocation. But he regarded this as normal in the particular environment. He felt she'd chosen not to avoid the accident, and that it was her fault.

"Guilty as charged." The gavel clattered on the wooden desk.

Joan held her chin up and stared through the faces, using her old stripper's trick of letting her eyes go out of focus so that there were no faces out there, only a gluey pudding of eyes and mouths floating in the room.

A rustling sigh of gratified expectations went around the room.

Alex jumped to his feet immediately, asking for a pre-sentence report. The judge set a remand date for three weeks. As the courtroom door opened, the watchers formed lines to get out and moved away, nodding and chatting.

THE OLD CHOREOGRAPHER was the only one who'd seen Joan cry. He had patted her hand with his, a thick, heavy transparent pad with liver spots on it. "You're bloody," he said, "but the wounds aren't mortal." His white neck and the loose bob of his Adam's apple reminded her that he was old, old. The high, bald dome over his sad eyes was a chapel of wisdom.

"You'll find that all pain, no matter how bad it may seem, is the same pain. To break a treasured porcelain vase, to catch a bad case of sinus, to lose my wife to cancer is terrible, stunning. But it passes. It all passes."

"I'm being punished," Joan had sobbed. It was years ago, when she had to leave the ballet school.

Then the thin skin over his cheeks showed pink and his voice was angry. "Pain, we suffer," he said, lifting his hand from hers and bringing it down on the table. "But never let it be punishment."

She wondered what he would say today. Joan sat at the back of the bar in a Yonge Street club. The place was long and narrow, stretching away from the street: from where she sat the sidewalk and the people might just as well not exist. She had walked straight here from the courthouse, and had been drinking for hours. She was in the area of Yonge Street that had been devastated by the glass elephant of the Eaton Centre: these little independent places outside of the bubble maintained themselves wearily, defiantly, and Joan was drawn to them in sympathy.

She got up from her seat and went to the women's room. She looked at herself in the mirror. She had been crying. She did not look like the girl of eighteen who cried. Then, her face had been long and white and fearful. Now it was long and white and guilty, guilty as charged. Guilty of having a history. The eyes were no longer darkly rimmed with make-up. They didn't need to be because they had darkness in them. Some soil, some smudge, came from the whites of her eyes. And from the edges of her perfect nose—she always thought she'd been lucky with that nose—there were lines. Straight, deep lines in the flesh of her cheeks. Sour lines, lines of disappointment, canny lines. Lines that sliced the smoothness of her face like a knife slices wedges off a lemon.

Think on this guiltiness, Joan said to herself. Must I be punished? Have I been bad? It is true, I have lived on the edge, I have done ugly things, I have seen more ugly things, I have been what I don't like to remember being. And yet. She could not hate herself so easily. She looked further into the mirror. Long, silver-brown hair today in this braided bun at the nape of her neck. Parted in the centre, the hair was a smooth wrap to the oval face. Red finger-nails, tiger's-eye ring on one long slim finger, long neck held up very high. The bearing of a lady who knew the score, the bearing of a commercial lady.

The old choreographer had taught Joan that if she fixed her eye on the one ballet dancer in the middle of the second line on the left-hand side of the stage, she would not understand a thing about the dance. Even if she watched three of them in a row, turning, raising their legs in *arabesque* four times to the right and four times to the left and then running to form a circle around Princess Aurora, she would only get a glimmer of the general idea. To truly understand, she had to see the whole. Meaning lay not in any single movement or in any single dancer, but in the sign of the entire dance.

She had to know, in a ballet, that she was just a spit of energy, with little significance. Joan had walked out on that humility. When she started her new life, moving into a flat with the blonde from St. Barnabus house who might or might not have murdered the schoolmistress, she had first gone to theatrical agents and got jobs in pantomimes, in musicals. It had seemed that she controlled her own destiny utterly. Finally she settled on the clubs, because it was the easiest thing. She loved to do a solo act. Her baby finger became as important to the audience as she herself, perfectly schooled, had been in the back lines of the corps in "Sleeping Beauty." Her limbs were principal performers, each one. Her face, her breasts, her hips were stars. It had been a life in intense close-up.

Then, Joan created the world on her own terms. Suddenly it was that simple to say I am unique and therefore wonderful. Look at what I can do. She loved being looked at all over. She was happy all the time, like a pin-wheel carried high over the heads of a crowd. She wanted every one of those breezes, every breath that went up there. She had costumes and easy money. She celebrated both. She loved the late morning, waking up at eleven after a three o'clock night and doing her washing and ironing for the new day. In those days friends would pound on Joan's door and want breakfast, or supper, any hour of the day or night. She felt safe because she knew everyone in Soho. Even the bobby came up to have coffee with her. There were parties and parties. Screw the future, that was her motto. She was twenty. She knew that at thirty she'd be as good as dead, her breasts crestfallen and veined, the nipples hard and puckered, like the insides of old bottle caps, her stomach too white, the flesh settling like old whipped cream. At thirty she'd be used goods, but that had been a lifetime away.

What had she done that was bad, that she herself believed to be wrong? People thought strippers were hookers. In all those years Joan had only met one girl who hooked on the side. If you did six shows a day and your laundry and ironing, there wasn't time. But more important, if you took your clothes off for men you made sure they weren't going to touch you. You can only take so much exposure before you go crazy.

Hooking she had not done, but there was something else. Something ugly and fascinating, in the exchange between a stripper and an audience. Joan could watch and watch and still not see who was the sucker. A man sat on his bar stool like a king, revelling in the fact that this woman was offering herself to him. He could have her if he wanted, he muttered into his drink. But the stripper knew it was a pretence, that she was tantalizing him, drawing him on with no intention of slaking his desire. To her, lust was an acknowledgement of her power. And so they fenced, with eyes and jibes.

There were places where the girls walked around the tables and let men tuck rolled-up notes in their G-strings. She'd seen it done, yes, she'd done it herself.

She would swing her hips forward, drawing a half-circle in the air. The rhinestones of her G-string would wink. He would lean back in his chair, thrusting himself up as he reached in his back pocket for his wallet, find the bulging leather pouch and draw out a pound note. He would wave it in the air in front of her, beckoning her.

Then she would wiggle, come closer. He would lick his lips and reach forward.

Remembering, Joan lived the shame. He rolls the bill around his finger. See, the money is mine, he says. I am powerful. I *buy* you with this. I reach out and you are irresistibly drawn by this. I poke it into your costume, between your legs, poke it right inside you. You let me. *Meaning*, I am big and you are base.

There is a still moment when he deposits the money, stuffs it up, bending his finger as he does it. Then he withdraws his hand.

Instantly, everything changes. Like a trap shutting, the G-string moves back; the twinkle of the rhinestones dulls. She closes her mouth, her moist lips drying. Hah! she is saying. You were moved, you desired me enough to flash your money. But you've been tricked. I have the money and you have nothing. You haven't touched me, you aren't even real to me. The power is mine. By the end the G-string looks like an Indian money belt, bills lined up side by side along the edges of the pubic triangle, suggestive little rolls emptied of the finger that put them there but reminiscent of the exploratory poke, the cadged feel.

Joan could remember the shame as the fingers met her skin, the revolted flush that would fill her. There were places where men offered the stripper a Coke bottle and wanted her to use it. Chair legs, dogs, whatever. Joan had heard of it all and had seen most of it. She hadn't done it all. Not yet. She hadn't had to because she was still young enough and good-looking enough. She wasn't going to let herself go all the way down. Having the baby and giving it away was half-way down; taking tips like that was getting close to the bottom. She knew when to stop.

There had been times, when clapping was sparse, when Joan would pick up her clothes and walk off the stage saying "Spare me" to the hands still moving. When the audience didn't like her she began to hate them. Out there was nothing but a brainless, featureless mass. Oh, she remembered half a dozen of them—the biker who'd come to the edge of the stage in his black leather and thrown a glove at her feet; the bank clerk from Threadneedle Street who'd wept and sent flowers for a solid week trying to get her to date him. A few had talked to her, had been people. But the rest? Losers. Sad, spiteful, twisted losers. She would never think of them again, nor they of her.

When the bad feelings began to get to her, Joan protected herself with the rules, since rules were what she'd known. Don't walk home down the lane after dark. Don't go near the woods at the foot of the street because a hermit lives there. Don't sit beside a man on the bus. First home rules, then ballet rules. Don't look at your feet; don't let your hair loose; don't tense your neck. Old rules, gone now: when she made her own they were surprisingly similar. Get a good sleep at night; eat vitamins C, B, B_6, and kelp. Take a half a raw cucumber and drink carrot juice although you hate it. Exercise every day in the cramped flat or down on the sidewalk before the people come in the morning. Wash and fold your clothes at night.

She dressed flamboyantly, but she was always as neat as if it were the first day of school. The feather in her hair was fresh and fluffy, the paint on her toe-nails unchipped. Her tight T-shirts were clean and her high-heeled shoes in good repair. She liked buckles and ties on everything. She had a favourite shirt, an old Canadian boy scout shirt with epaulettes and a woodsman badge. She wore multibuckled military pants and vests and blazers over sweaters and T-shirts. She liked the feeling of having lots of things to undo, things to take off; it was the security of being in a game of poker with plenty of chips.

Over those years, Joan's face became longer, her jaw more pronounced, the crescent-shaped hollow in her cheeks deeper. She walked quickly, toes slightly turned out and heels tersely tapping, and carried a large bag on one shoulder. She looked like a woman who couldn't be interfered with, a woman who knew how to look after herself. Joan Sincere, stripper. Look don't touch. She was the only one who never used a stage name. As long as the rules were in place what did it matter if she danced in the "nud," as the English said. She was as cold as the brass effigies on top of the tombstones in Westminster Abbey. A man who wanted to lay her might as well have tried to take a rubbing. If the audiences wanted her to twirl her high heels on their noses, she would do that too.

She had begun to assume that because that was all the world she saw, it was all the world there was. After all, what was the difference between a little G-string and a little cocktail dress? Not many years went by before she began to see that even her civilian friends were liars and cheats. She watched them go through the streets of Soho and they looked like rats dressed in human clothing; little hands tucked into their coats, little fingers clutching ticket stubs and transit passes and paper sacks. They were clutching for dear life to their possessions with one hand and shoving the person ahead of them with the other hand.

She designated one night a year for regrets. It was February 8, the day of her daughter's birth. She went out, got stinking drunk, and talked to men in bars. She told them about her faraway home, her ballet, her baby, Joe.

Maybe the men looked at their watches, maybe they were even too drunk to understand, but they listened. It appealed to their sense of propriety that she should be guilty for her way of life, that she should have a tragedy behind her. Tears were shed nightly over the bar; who cared what they were for? Her tears taught them that one night, anyway, she was one of them, a loser herself.

Joan had taken it for kindness. It had been the only kindness she could take. None of the men had ever come back, and there had always been another to take his place. It was true what the fortune-teller had said; Joan had gone from man to man. She hadn't wanted to stop. She hadn't wanted to remember Joe, or to find him in another man. Two years after the child was born he came to her and asked her to come to his place, as if it didn't matter that he'd abandoned her when she needed him, as if nothing had changed. That was when Joan realized she hadn't gone all the way down. She still believed there could be a world between two people not like the one she lived in every day. She sent him away. And then she went on to the next man. It was true; she had been desperate for love. Each rejection, each aborted affair had been nothing but a demand for more.

At some point during those years, Arlene fell in love. The man was married; he played in the ballet orchestra and his wife was an actress. He was sour with a long thin nose and wore baggy grey suits. Arlene was in raptures. The tension in her body lifted; she seemed to move more lightly and to breathe more deeply. Soon she was bringing Joan all her cares about whether he would leave his wife, whether she would be allowed to meet his children, to cook his dinner, to keep him overnight. Joan asserted that this was merely evidence of Arlene's masochism.

Arlene had gone into the company, worked like a horse, and had got from the back row to the middle row. Joan was given to feeling sorry for her, thin, strained, sexless as she looked. Arlene came down to see Joan's act and said nothing. They would go for tea between shows. Sometimes after tea if there was time they would go over to the homeopath's on Bond Street and buy arnica and cupernicum, their favourite herbs for curing sore muscles. They also took tiny pellets containing arsenic to ward off colds. They did these things to preserve the past, neither of them willing to let it go, but neither of them sure, now, that the past could survive the present.

Joan began to wonder if she should quit. She didn't like it so much any more when people watched her. She had a violent temper; she drank too much. She was like the other women who'd been there a long time. She could bring them all back to her mind now, like a police line-up in their G-strings and their garters, their boas and their foolish slippers that ruined their feet. The gay women from Paris, the single mother whose nine-year-old son played in the dressing-room. If you didn't start stripping because you hated men, you soon learned. And then, because women were scared of you, you stopped liking them too.

She created a glass bubble for her protection, enclosing the space she could make her own. The barman went out and got her a taxi after her last show so that she could step right out the club door and into its shoe-box interior. The taxi was her glass carriage, her bullet-proof limousine, her trap. It would drive around three blocks and drop her at home. She didn't even have to take out her ear-plugs because she knew the fare.

Her rules had become stricter than any she'd left behind. She could hardly believe that other people touched, shared meals and a bed, trusted one another. She couldn't stand to be touched, not even by—especially not by—a lover. A hand on her body unleashed a nerve response and made her twitch. There had been too many hands, just as there had been too many eyes, and none of them belonged to anyone real. Men came like ghosts to her, wanting everything, leaving nothing but a damp chill.

And then something made Joan angry. It was just one more thing, but it dislodged her from Soho. Maybe it even turned her homeward. Arlene made a success at the Garden. She had a solo in a new ballet, five minutes on stage alone, and the critics raved. She was going to be promoted. She was going to do Giselle the next season; she had been asked to learn other leads. And suddenly her man decided he might leave his wife, that he should emigrate to Canada and get a new job. Arlene was going to give up dancing and go with him.

It had been easier to go down herself than to watch Arlene do it. Joan had shouted at her, cried, and begged her not to go. She'd worked so hard, she was on the edge of being a true star, the man wasn't worth it. Arlene just sat and wrung her hands. She said she couldn't live without him. Her resignation from the company had been accepted. She was moving to Toronto.

It hadn't been long after that that Joan finally decided she'd had enough, that she would move back to Canada, too, and start living again.

THE DRINK WAS gone, and so were the tears. It was nearly dinner time and Rudy would be wanting his walk. Joan picked up her purse. She would change her life, wouldn't she? She had hopes anyway. She'd gone to see Johanna, at Characters. The woman didn't need a last name, she was never anywhere else but at Characters. She was wonderful, enormously fat with red hair and freckles. She was, as David had said she would be, utterly frank in her assessment.

"The voice," she'd said, "is bad all right. You sound like someone with a hand around your throat. I bet you never learned to speak up for yourself."

Joan had stood in front of her, stunned by the observation. Maybe there was a hand choking her, a hand she'd never been able to escape from. She didn't feel insulted as she inevitably did with agents like Marty when they sized her up. "As for the rest," said Johanna, "VERY interesting.

You've got presence. I bet you know how to work an audience."

Joan had smiled, modestly. That she did.

"Listen," said Johanna. "This isn't going to be a fairy tale. It's not very often I take someone on and then find them work right away. Nothing's for sure," she said. "But you've got the equipment. Plug in the brain and we can do something with it."

She had smiled, brightly, and taken a phone call. Joan was dismissed.

Being an actress would be different, wouldn't it?

Anyway, she had other blessings to count. Rudy. Some good friends. David. Well maybe David. They'd not spoken since the fight at the benefit. Without noticing that she was doing it, Joan got two dimes from her wallet. She kept them between her thumb and forefinger as she pushed through the glass doors to the street. She wanted to talk to David. She wanted to tell someone she was convicted; she wanted to tell him he was forgiven. She turned up Yonge Street looking for a telephone booth.

There was one. Inside, without closing the door to the roar of the traffic, she put in her dime and pressed the buttons. Beep, beep, beep, BEEP, bee-bee-bee-bee——. Why was it that last number on push-button telephones always faltered? Perhaps it was just to show you how conditional this communication was. You might not make your connection, the service might be withdrawn at any moment. But it had rung through. Now she was embarrassed. You aren't speaking to David since he'd shown up with that other woman, remember, Joan?

"Local 2552, please."

She waited. And then he picked up the phone. "Hello?" It was a question, not a statement. A question like, why are you bugging me? But she wasn't going to lose her nerve now. The silence grew long. She looked out at the traffic. You could lose nerve at any time. In rush hour, for instance. You'd already dashed across the first two lanes only ten feet in front of the surge. You stood on the centre line, and faced the next two lanes still: cars rolled past so close behind you it lifted the hairs on your head, and so close in front of you they might roll over your toes, and suddenly you were terrified to move. You stood, fearing for life and feeling the thud already as you bounced off the hood of whatever car it was going to be. The longer you stood the greater was the danger.

"Hello?"

"Hi, David, it's me, Joan." Her voice was pathetic, asking for help.

CHAPTER TWELVE

David came out of the squash club at six-thirty. Charlie had wanted to stay for a beer in the lounge but David had to get going. Sitting in all that smoke, with the purple rug and the blue blare of the television, negated the benefits of the squash game for David. He liked to smash the ball around and outmanoeuvre Charlie, thudding, sweating, and swearing amongst the sound of racquets hitting the floor and the squeal of court shoes. And after the game he liked to sit in the whirlpool, his arms propped along the curb of the tiled bath, his back against the water outlet, his genitals bobbing softly under the water like the next guy's. Then he liked to shower, dress, and get out.

His eye strained for the yellow tag on his windshield that would have infuriated him. There wasn't one! Once again he had beaten the cops. He unlocked the door, pushed the seat down and threw his sports bag into the back seat. He felt good. He still hadn't decided what he was going to do about this latest development, but he felt good.

David hated decisions. He was thirty-six years old and so far he'd avoided most of them, waiting until one or another option became inevitable. He backed the car and pushed forward to get onto Adelaide Street. He was aware that men half his age had buckled down to life's more unpleasant necessities; to assembly lines, wives, children. He had had excuses: graduate school, no job, then temporary free-lance work that took all his energy. Once he got started on the six-month contracts it had been hard work to keep on top of things. He hadn't the time to develop anything meaningful in the social line.

It had not appealed to him, as it had appealed to other men he'd met along the way, to marry a woman who required little maintenance. One who would have gone along as baggage, who would cheerfully absorb the fits and starts in his life, smoothing it down, making it seem normal. Some of those women people married were brilliant illusionists. They made a home, set a table, chatted over cocktails, as if they were part of a real family. But the men operated, as ever, as if their wives were not even there. He thought it wasn't fair. He thought it probably wasn't even fun. He wanted no such illusionist wife.

But where did that leave him? It left him skipping out on affairs, dodging women who wanted him. Skittishness, which once he'd justified as a necessity, had now become a disease. He had security, maturity, time, money, no more excuses. He was lonely. Men friends were available for a game of squash, but neither he nor they wanted to be called upon by persons in need. He didn't like confessional conversation, especially confessional conversation among men, because they were usually so dishonest. He kept his own insecurities so tightly confidential that he barely conceded them to himself: this too was a survival technique that was wearing thin.

Today, for instance, he was prepared to admit that he'd been a jerk, taking Ellen to see Joan strip. The truth was, he'd been afraid to go on his own. He'd wanted something for his side: if Joan was going to have all those men admiring her, he'd show up with someone who wanted him. He hadn't considered that Joan would be humiliated by it. Nor had he considered that he would drink so much he'd give up on evading Ellen's advances. That had been stupider yet; he'd been prepared to junk the whole love affair with Joan, with all his vows and good intentions, for a night with someone else's wife. He felt terrible.

He wondered how he could make it up to Joan. Perhaps, he thought insanely, he should marry her. Perhaps that was still in the cards for him, that he would devour some life like hers. After all, he had been given, by virtue of his sex, this power, these assurances that he should do so. He imagined devouring Joan. Putting her in his bedroom, his kitchen, his dining-room. Causing her to stop working, of course, and giving her a weekly allowance. Having her serve roast beef to people he wanted to impress, her long hair dripping down over the serving tray as she placed the rolled, browned, juicing flesh in front of him. That sultry look of hers dampened with heat from the oven, an apron tying down the perfect breasts, wrenching in the small waist which was the only sign of frailty in her body. The waist growing thicker. Two children pulled up to the table. No.

The sun was shooting off the glass all around as it sunk behind the office towers. He shook the glaze from his eyes. He didn't know why he still conjured these images of the statistically normal family—mum, dad after work, two children, dog and cat also in residence. He'd just read somewhere that only seven per cent of the population lived that way. The truth was nobody lived that way any more. Nobody was "normal." Especially not Joan or David.

There had to be other solutions.

David had never thought his way of living was permanent. He never thought anything he did was permanent: he lived on short-term deadlines, just the way he prepared radio shows. Some might say he'd taken a "permanent" job at the CBC when he went on staff. Having a permanent job didn't mean, he reasoned at the time, that you had to stay on but that you could stay on. However he saw that "could" was just as bad as "had to." Worse, in fact. You could stay even if you did a lousy job, even if you became an alcoholic, even if you were certifiably insane, as were, in David's opinion, certain members of the administration.

This "could" had become a threat to his manhood.

However, only this week he had done something about it. Something he was proud of. He had gone to the executive producer of his section. He was quite a young man, not much older than David. He wore white socks and loafers with tassels on them.

"I'd like to have a word with you."

"Most certainly." The man had got up immediately and shut the door behind David.

"Is there something I can help you with? A problem?"

"Frankly, I haven't got enough work to keep myself interested."

Charlie had told David this would be a suicide move. "They'll think you're a traitor; they'll take your budget away, they'll take the door off your office and partition it for secretaries," Charlie had warned. But David couldn't stand the waste of time any more. He figured it was better now than later, if he was going to leave his job.

But the risk had paid off in a way he hadn't expected.

"I appreciate your mentioning that, David. There's going to have to be some changes made around there. I don't mind telling you your name is being tossed around for the new position in programming. What would you say to that?"

David had said no to it. Charlie thought that too was madness. "Once you've turned down advancement your stock will drop," he said. "They hate being refused. You'll never be offered anything again." David went back to the executive producer and suggested a new show. It would be a show on the future, and David would talk to people with discoveries, predictions, options. The executive producer liked the idea. Together they would work out a proposal and a budget; there was a good chance they'd get approval. Maybe it wasn't a big thing, but it cheered David immensely. That solution had been so much closer to the problem than he'd imagined.

He finally came to University Avenue and turned north. He looked at the convex glass at the back of the windshield of the car in front of him, and listened to the traffic report on commercial radio, enjoying the thought of that helicopter monitoring the bottle-necks and accident sites around the city. His mind, like the traffic, turned, started, and then stopped. He forced it ahead a little.

He'd been doing some bedroom reading about invertebrates in the weeks since he'd seen Joan. When two individuals of the particular species he was studying were placed in close contact, the smaller of the two chose to disintegrate. He was not destroyed, this small individual (or she, as it might have been), but merely made the choice to avoid competition and release her own death mechanism. To dismantle herself.

He had found this a sobering observation. Perhaps it was a relief to know that little invertebrates did not suffer aggression from big ones. To say they were victims of outright hostility would have been too simple. Their own humble self-destruction was crueler. There was a warning in that. David thought that for one of his shows he might begin to put together a list of the lessons taught by microscopic creatures. Parables of the Paramoecium, something like that.

The cars loosened themselves from their tangle at University and Dundas, and began to speed and weave, trying to get the thirty feet ahead of the next one, a distance that seemed to the driver like freedom, David supposed. He had a problem to face before he went much farther. It was that curious telephone call from Joan.

That last time he'd seen her she'd screamed at him and told him never to try to see her again. Granted, he had acted badly. But still. He'd spent days telling himself the whole affair was a ghastly mistake. He'd almost convinced himself. Now she had called up in trouble asking for sympathy. He had been cool, fraternal. He had said he was willing to meet her, and had hung up the telephone as he did after all conversations with her, ruffled by the winds in her voice. Had he responded properly? He never knew whether he had got his responses together fast enough to give her what she wanted. There was so little notice given between the "I love you's" and the "Fuck off's" he didn't see how anyone could collect their wits fast enough to deal with her.

She had said she needed to see him. How did he feel about that? Elated, he'd have to admit. He'd trounced Charlie six nothing right after the call. Once, he'd made a promise to love her and make it work. Maybe he'd tried too hard, too fast. In any case, he'd made a stupid mistake. She'd let him know about it, but now, she was giving him a second chance. They could make of it who knew what, something abnormal, but wonderful. So why was he dilly-dallying along trying to treat the matter with the scientific method?

He was at Queen's Park, heading north. He pulled to the curb at a spot which clearly said NO PARKING, 9 A.M. to 9 P.M. He got out and locked the car. There was a florist's shop on Wellesley. If he was going to declare himself to a felon he wanted to hang out a white flag first.

JOAN WAS WALKING Rudy in Queen's Park. It was seven o'clock at night and the sky was a distant, vibrant blue, set deep as if to give more room, in its final moments, to a brilliant day. Nearby, the stone of the government buildings reflected the street lights; the tall pillars of downtown clustered in the south and east. They were black, and punched out all over with white holes where the lights were. Toronto, which had seemed so grey and sprawling, so dead after London, had crept into Joan's imagination. She loved its frankness on a clear night. She scanned the skyline: The Westin in white, Britannica in red, the Bay.

Rudy was chasing squirrels. He saw one half-way between two tree trunks, its curved tail quivering upright as it picked through the grass for something—a nut? A chocolate wrapper? The dog flew at it, stretching flat in the air between bounds. Things looked hopeless for the squirrel. But somehow, in the last split second, the little rodent sensed its doom, flicked its tail, and in one instant leapt impossibly to the nearest tree, there to run up the trunk and chatter in outrage. Meanwhile, having narrowly escaped bashing his brains out on the tree trunk, Rudy pranced below, considering himself victorious.

David had called the dog her psychic projectile.

It was true she enjoyed watching the chase. In her view the squirrels were too fat and needed the exercise. But tonight she put her head down and pushed her hands deep in her pockets. The park was oval and surrounded by a river of cars. Long beams of headlights ran into each other and formed a swirl of brilliance as they went round and round the circle: some of the cars bleeding off north, some bleeding off south, some east. People walked in the shadows under the trees, university students, government clerks, teenagers in track suits. Joan thought she was probably the only criminal there.

She went along the path that crossed the park diagonally to the central hill where King Edward stood on his horse. Passing the king, she stopped at a bench. Rudy came and sat beside her, leaning his head on her knee.

"Come on, run. This walk is for you, dog." She shut her mouth suddenly. Maybe she was crazy. How long ago had she started saying complete sentences to her dog?

He wouldn't walk while she was sitting, so Joan stood up and continued north. A wind came through the leaves and the shadows began to cross every which way on the ground, blending and darkening until the grass was all black. She felt a desolation that even David wouldn't fill, were he to come. He said he would come over tonight. But tonight wasn't soon enough. She had wanted someone then. She wanted someone now.

"Have you got a light?"

A man stepped away from the trunk of a tree. He was about five feet from her, tall, with a beard and a cowboy hat. He wore a leather jacket, open. She'd seen him somewhere before. At the pin-ball arcade. He looked like Joe.

"No, I'm sorry, I haven't."

He stepped toward her, tentatively, as if there were something else he wanted to ask. Sensing danger, Joan took a few steps back. Her instinct was to run. He took another step toward her. A shaft of yellow light from a distant street lamp fell between them.

"It's Joan, right?"

She peered into his face. The wide cheekbones, the deep, blazing eyes. Joe. Joe, ten years later. As soon as she admitted it, she realized she'd known all along that he was around; she'd felt a ghost on her trail.

"Joe Langelli. What on earth...."

"Got a light?"

"No." She stood a minute. She was irrationally afraid.

He held a cigarette in the air between them, cocking his head to look at the too-white glimmer of the little cylinder. His beard was longer than it had been and more pointed. His hat covered the hair-line but it looked as if his forehead were higher. Joe must be—she ran it through her head—he must be forty-six now.

"What are you doing here?"

"You walk the dog pretty near every day around here, don't you?"

She was silent. He'd always answered a question with a question, it was one of his tricks. It was uncanny how, as her old lover materialized in front of her, his memory sprang up as instantly. It was more intact than the man himself, from the looks of it.

"I mean in Canada."

"Driftin'."

"When did you leave England?"

"Oh, three-four years ago. Couldn't stand it any more. Yeah, so I went back to America and got into the old circuit...." Joe was the kind of man you didn't ask about employment or income. He always claimed he played with a group of musicians. You didn't want to know any more.

As she looked at Joe the words of Mr. Darling, horrid little genius Mr. Darling, came to her mind. Desperado. Joe was a desperado, he'd said. Strange as the word had seemed, it suited him.

"Well, I'm in a rush—" Joan had a feeling that she had to get home.

"Know where you live there on Baldwin."

"You do? How?"

"Just know." He rolled the cigarette once more through his fingers and then put it back in his breast pocket. "Saw your picture in the paper."

"Oh that." Joan had begun to shake. This was too creepy.

"Went by where you used to work, but you ain't been there for a while."

"No." The feeling that she had to get away was increasing. It was unlike Joe to show such interest, to have the persistence to find her. Finding her must have been an obsession. That told her she was in trouble.

They stood in the near darkness. He pushed the hat back on his head, and eyed her. It was true what she'd expected, his hair-line had receded. His face was off balance now. He didn't look like Christ or a medieval king. He looked—shifty. Mean and shifty. She stood there, three feet away from him, waiting to be released. She knew she couldn't bolt. Rudy stood at her knee, still, seeming to listen. He hadn't growled, but he hadn't decided Joe was harmless yet either.

"Turned into a good-looking woman, Joan. Knew you would." He put his head back and laughed, forced laughter. "You were quite a kid, couldn't believe it at the time." He laughed some more.

He was so cruel. In her heart she heard her younger self crying. "Don't compare me! I've never done this before." What a quagmire she'd chosen for her maiden voyage.

The darkness deepened. Joan stood stiffly. She wondered if Joe were going to mention the child. Sara. He'd had no part of it, he probably barely remembered. Of course he wouldn't. He was despicable. But he could say anything now because it was over. Over and finished, Mr. Darling. Joe had found her one day too late; this morning's guilty charge had closed the book on the part of her that was vulnerable to him.

She had an idea now of what Joe wanted. He wanted it not to be finished. He wanted to see if he could get a response, if she would cry, beg, shout, tangle with him. She decided she wasn't going to.

"What do you want?"

He pushed his hat further back. He had always been able to read her thoughts. She saw him register that he couldn't get at her any more. He couldn't make her break. He wouldn't humble himself to try, then. Now he was going to pretend it was only idleness that had led him to her. "Just curious, that's all."

They stood a while longer. Joan shrugged. "Satisfied?"

He shrugged. He turned as if to go.

"Yup."

And everything spun around backwards. He'd made as if to go and then instead he had bent and dodged toward her, crashing into her right side, grabbing her leather purse where it hung from her shoulder. At first she thought crazily that the gesture was meant as an embrace. Then the tackle knocked her off balance; she hung onto her purse strap, spinning in a circle as she tried to keep her feet. Her mind registered what was going on: it had finally happened. The fear that had followed Joan through the streets of large cities, fear of strange men materializing out of the darkness, fear of the sudden crack on the head, the hand on the shoulder, the fist under the ribs: the fear had been fulfilled. She was being attacked.

She had always imagined she would fight back. Now without thinking, she began to fight back. She clung to her purse as if it were a cord keeping her from a plunge to the abyss. Joe swung his right arm and punched her in the jaw, hard. She heard her teeth crunch. She heard Rudy barking, as if from afar. She clung to her purse. (What was in it? Practically nothing. A hairbrush, a mirror, a lipstick, a wallet with five dollars and her address book.) Joe pulled back, just as hard. It seemed he really wanted that purse. It was the only thing he could get from her.

Except for Rudy's barking, the park was altogether silent. Why didn't the dog bite him, for God's sake? Suddenly there was a lightness: the strap was slack in Joan's hands. She staggered, her arms at her sides, an open

target. Now that her purse was gone, she was sure she was
going to be killed. After all those dark alleys she'd passed
in Soho, all those strangers she'd feared and avoided, here
in front of the legislature of Ontario she was undoubtedly
going to get the shit kicked out of her by her old boy-
friend.

Joe took three steps to the trees.

"Bastard," she shouted.

She couldn't see him any more: the park had drunk it all
in. Even the shadows were absorbed in the leafy blotter.
Rudy was jumping at her knees. She bent over, putting
her arms around his barrel chest, pressing her cheek into
his fur. She cried and then laughed at the same time. She
was relieved: it was the last thing Joe could ever do to her.
It was the rock bottom.

Footsteps stopped by her ear.

"You all right, miss?"

"Oh yeah, yeah, I'm O.K." She lifted her face and wiped
the tears off it. One side had no feeling. "Someone just
snatched my purse."

"He get it?"

"Yeah. He's gone, though," she added quickly. She held
up the strap, giggling a little. "There was nothing in it."

"You hurt?"

"Just here." She saw that she was speaking to a man in a
pin-striped suit. "He hit me."

"You should call the police. I don't see a phone. Wait—
do you live near here?"

"Not f-far." An involuntary intake of breath made her
shudder.

"I don't have a car or I'd drive you. Here, let's get a
cab."

The man offered an elbow. Joan's limbs were aching
everywhere as if she'd just caught a bad case of the flu.
Rudy hung apologetically at her knees, growling at her
rescuer.

"Honestly, Rudy, you're worse than useless."

"Pardon me?"

"My dog." She must be crazy, giggling. Still talking to Rudy in complete sentences.

"You must be in shock, a little."

They made their way to Wellesley Street, she and her amputated purse strap, the three-piece suit man, and Rudy. The rush hour was over and the traffic had lessened. The beams of light from a car swept singly around the circle, like a beacon.

"I can get a cab myself."

"No, no. You don't want to stand here alone."

"Really, I know how—" she began testily. She stopped herself. She did not want to stand there alone. She leaned on the well-pressed suit and hiccupped softly. He got a cab and gave her five dollars to get home. He wouldn't listen to her promises to pay it back, either, but he gave her his card. She was thinking how lucky it was that at least she had her keys in her coat pocket.

THERE WAS A knock on the door. Joan was lying on her bed. She got up slowly and went to the door.

"Joan?"

She put her good cheek against the wood, and listened.

"David?"

"It's me."

"David?" she said again. She didn't want to open the door.

"Let me in, O.K.?"

"Listen, I had a bit of an accident."

"Come on, Joan, open the door."

"I look awful." She didn't really know that because she'd been afraid to look in the mirror. But she felt awful.

"Let me in, you idiot."

The door opened and a bush of cosmos—yellow and white —advanced with the legs of a man. She started to laugh again.

"Until Great Birnam wood to high Dunsinane..."

"Look David, I've had a bad day. First the cops got me and then the robbers."

"... Macbeth shall never vanquisht be."

He put the flowers on the table and turned to look at

her face. She told him about the punch in the ribs and about the way she'd hung on to her purse.

"How did he get up close to you?"

"He just stepped out from behind a tree." She looked David in the eye and smiled, numbly; she could only feel one cheek.

"Looks like you'll have a bruise. But you were brave, guarding your money."

"I didn't have any money."

He reached out his arms. She let them circle her, and then turned away from him, holding his hands very tight under her ribs, where her stomach still clutched convulsively. She doubled herself over the hands, pressing them harder into herself, wanting them to go right to her spine. She could still feel the shock of Joe's hard fist in her cheek. She'd heard women talk about the feel of going from one man to another in the space of an hour. The touch of one man, they said, was almost indistinguishable from the touch of another, and if you weren't careful you got them mixed up. One man's hands seemed to be any man's. She hiccupped. This is what you got when you let men near you: they hurt your body and then came back to comfort it. But David wasn't Joe. David had hurt her, but not like that. She had to let him near her, had to risk the hurt, had to trust again that he wouldn't do it.

"Poor Joan." He hung on tight. "Lucky you called me."

"That was before."

"You must have seen it coming."

"Don't say that."

His hands on her waist tried to turn her around. She resisted. He put them on her ribs, twisting, bringing her to face him. She turned, put her arms around his neck and reached up with her face to warm in his breath, his mouth. In the middle of the kiss she began to laugh and cry again.

"I can't believe I wanted my purse so much. There's nothing in it. Just my hairbrush and five dollars."

"Reflex."

"He punched me and I still held on. I got the strap."

David let her go. He walked to the kitchen table where the strap lay and picked it up. "Did you look at this? It's been sliced clean. He had a knife. Or a scalpel, something very sharp."

"Did he?"

"Look."

"No." She looked out the window. Somewhere in the city Joe was drinking her five dollars. So he had a knife. Knife. The knife at the door. The hammer. The phone calls. It all made sense. She spoke very softly. "It was just a purse."

"What do you mean?"

"At first, I thought I was being raped or something. But then I fought back. It was like being freed from a nightmare when you're being chased and you can't move: I fought him."

"You're tough, Joan."

"Hardly. I think I'm hysterical."

"Let me fix you up."

David bathed her cheek, examined her teeth and worked her jaw up and down to see that nothing was broken. It was as if she had a golf ball in the side of her mouth: the bruise had started to come up like a great pouch, the edges of it rippling purple. It pulled her already crooked mouth into a tight slant, and stretched her lips into a comical loop on the right side. Joan looked in the mirror: the face was a maniac's, you expected a drool to come out of that swollen corner.

"And it's going to get worse," said David cheerfully. "It'll end up all the colours that you can think of."

"What am I going to do? I've got to work. I'm out of money. What can I do with a face like this?"

"It'll go down in a week or so. After that, make-up will cover most of it. Look, just think of this as a holiday."

"I've had a holiday."

"A break before your new career as an actress."

"With this face?"

David leaned into the square of light from the mirror and kissed the left side of her mouth: even there, it hurt.

"You're a winner, Joan. It's written. Maybe not so soon as you'd like, but you'll get there. I can help you with money for a while. And something else."

"What?"

"You should call the police."

"No."

"Yes. He had a knife."

"No. I can't."

"You can't? Because you're mad at the cops? Look Joan, this guy is dangerous. The next lady might not fight back."

"Dangerous? I don't think so."

"A scalpel, remember."

"He won't do it again. It was a special case. He'll go back to picking pockets in bars."

David looked at her in the mirror. She stared straight back at him. She knew what she said was true: Joe wasn't dangerous to anyone but her.

"Sounds like he's a friend of yours."

"He was."

David's face withdrew from the mirror.

She waited, holding her breath. Please let David understand. Joe wasn't going to come back and what he did was for her, not for anyone else. What had Mr. Darling said? The taker loses and the loser wins a hundredfold? Please understand, David. His voice came from the corner of the kitchen, muffled.

"Just promise me, Joan, that you're not putting yourself in danger."

"I promise."

"Then I won't ask."

At last she was lying down in bed again. Without speaking of it, David and she had forgotten their estrangement. She let him mother her, take off her shoes, and then her socks, unbuckle her jeans and pull them over her hips and off. She sat up while he gently pulled her T-shirt over her head, shielding her sore chest. Then she lay back again. He sat on the bed beside her.

"How do you feel?"

"Wonderful."

She closed her eyes. She could feel him sitting there, his hand on her stomach. It was quiet and very dark, and they were both still. It seemed that a very long time passed, and that the time dwelled there between them, that they contained it. The time and the space that was them grew like a bubble blown large: it was warm and there was room to move inside it. In the darkness David stood, and got onto the bed.

He kneeled over her, one leg on either side of her body. What he did was so right it seemed hardly to have happened. He lifted her panties over the swell of her hips and brought them down. His hands moved lightly over her hip-bones into the hollow of her pelvis, over the top of the mound to the crevice where the rivers began. She moved a hand to the back of his neck and then gave in to the eddy.

Words began to toss up like slats from the craft they'd been riding in. Their words of anger, words of love, tentative testing words, falsifications, defences. Words without order, up and up the words tossed, letters dropping like matches, sounds snapping off in mid-air. Here was his hand, his mouth, her body, rushing toward the horseshoe falls. What would be left when it all happened, when the end came and the water peeled down as thin as skin?

Silence was left.

Stillness was left.

David moved, then. Before she lost consciousness, she felt him take off his clothes. Then he lay down beside her and they slept.

CHAPTER THIRTEEN

David had a chicken roasting in the oven. He was chopping Chinese vegetables from the market to fry in a wok. There was a bottle of wine open on the kitchen table. The refrigerator was full of food instead of pill bottles. The discarded leaves of the cabbage, the gleam of the white plates, the single stem of iris in a jar on the table: these things had a peculiar brightness. Just looking at them, Joan could see that something was happening. The long gloom was leaving. She had been mourning for so many weeks now that she had forgotten what light offered.

Her cheek was fading down to yellow from the purple, at last, after three weeks. David was talking facts as he chopped. He had been reading about termites. Facts excited him. It was not the termites, but the facts of the termites. Joan supposed that was what it meant to be intellectual. The termites stood for something else. She loved to listen to him.

"Tell me what you think of when I mention a colony of ants."

"Yech."

"You don't like them? You know they're tremendously intelligent."

"That's why they follow each other into little tins of Ant Trap and die."

"As a matter of fact, yes. Ants are social insects. Did you know that they have no option, when isolated, but to die?"

The telephone rang.

"You answer it." Joan was still afraid of the door, the street, the telephone bell. She wanted to be in hiding a little while longer. She had been so happy.

"Me? It's your house." But David let it ring one more time and then picked up the receiver.

"Miss Sincere's residence."

In the pause, Joan could hear the high timbre of a female voice. She was relieved. She'd never yet had an obscene call from a female, although she supposed there would be a first one day.

"Who's calling, please?"

David put his hand over the mouthpiece. "It's Arlene."

Arlene. She hadn't spoken to Arlene since the trial. David had never even met her oldest friend. That was how neglectful Joan had been. It hit Joan with a small twinge, like the flick of a tiny whip. She reached for the telephone.

"Hi, there." She got on the stool and waved David away. He went back to his vegetables.

"Was that him?" Arlene's voice was shrill and possessive.

"Him? Oh yeah, that was my cook."

"Since when did you get a cook?"

"Since I decided to go into the movies."

"Really, are you going into the movies? You never tell me anything. Seriously, is that the boy-friend you've been talking about?"

"Maybe and yes. Anything else you want to know?"

"Well, you sound a lot better than you were the last time I talked to you." Arlene sniffed. Her voice was trailing off, her interest in the matters surrounding Joan dying as she remembered herself. She gulped. "Listen, Joan."

"What's happening?"

"It's so awful I can hardly tell you."

"Why are you crying? Where are you? I hear traffic. Is something wrong?" It was dawning on Joan that the tone in Arlene's voice did not have to do with her, Joan, but with Arlene, a person with her own problems. It was an easy enough idea to grasp, now that it hove into reach of her understanding, but not one which Joan had reached before. Crack, crack, crack went the bubble that enclosed her, threatening to open wide any minute. But Joan held the edges together and peered out, cautious to the end. Arlene must be in trouble, why else would she be calling? And how would Arlene's trouble affect Joan here, sitting in her lovely kitchen with David, looking forward to dinner?

"I'm leaving him."

"You aren't." There had been so many times, years ago, when Joan had begged Arlene to ditch her husband. But Arlene would never do it. Now that she suggested it, Joan was alarmed.

"I am. I've had it. I can't let him do this to me any more. I'm through. It's over, we've killed whatever we had. I just can't go back. . . ." Her voice was cracking.

"Where are you? Where is he?"

"He's at home with the kids. I'm on the Danforth, at the phone booth." Her voice cracked again, this time into silence. Joan could just see Arlene, her thin shoulders hunched behind the folding glass door, cradling the receiver to her breasts and peering behind to see if her enraged husband was on his way to catch her.

"What are you going to do? I mean, Arlene, are you sure you've thought this through?"

"Thought? God, have you ever tried to think when he's waving a kid's baseball bat at you and screaming? He told me—the fortune-teller, remember?—that one day the problems would outweigh the good things. Well they have. I mean, I'm gone. Gone. Right out of there. I mean it."

"O.K., Arlene, O.K."

"He came home and the house was dirty and the kids were fighting and he said he was sick of me, he said he was going to leave until I got it all in order, and so he went out and got drunk and then came back and started after me with the bat. . . ."

"Oh, God, stop crying, Arlene, stop it for a minute." These domestic battles filled Joan with dread. Imagine being beaten up, not for passion, but for bad housekeeping. Unthinkable.

"I'm not going back."

"What have you got with you?"

"My purse, that's all. A few dollars and my bank-book."

"You'd better come over."

The telephone crackled and spit: Arlene was wiping her nose right over the receiver.

Joan sighed. "Arlene?"

"Yeah?"

"You coming over?"

"Yeah."

"O.K. The street door is unlocked. I'll be waiting for you. See you in a few minutes."

David was stirring his vegetables. He looked studiously uninterested but his ears were red. He had ears like a bat. He'd probably say bats didn't have ears or something.

"She's leaving her husband and his kids."

"For good?"

"I don't know. She's coming here."

"I'd better go."

"No, stay, we'll have our dinner with three."

"O.K., and then I'll go, leave you alone to defame men. How come you never call them by their names? It's just one pronoun after another—*he* did this, *he* did that. . . ."

The wooden spoon clacked on the side of the wok a little angrily. Joan reached for him from behind, taking the spoon out of his hand, laying it on the counter, pulling him toward her. He turned and they stood facing, arms wrapping around each other's backs, necks, heads. Again, light seemed to strike the room. Joan stood in the radiance. Had she overdosed on home cooking? What was this feeling?

ARLENE CAME UP the stairs and Rudy skated at her, barking. But suddenly he came to a halt, leaning back on his haunches, perceiving someone in pain. He went to lean on her legs. Arlene was still crying, her face pulled into itself in the centre, tears squeezing out, a four-year-old face.

"Oh Joan, I feel so awful, I feel so terrible," she said, the words slurred, her breath coming suddenly, as a laugh followed the sob.

Joan reached out her arms. Arlene stepped into the hall and the two embraced, big sobbing hugs, both of them half retching with emotion. "I'm sorry, you poor thing . . . it's been so long since. . . . you never called. . . ."

"And I never called when I. . . ."

"You wouldn't have told me if. . . ."

"But I didn't know. . . ."

They teetered, patting each other's backs. David took one look and fled past them down the hall to the living-room. Joan sat Arlene in a chair, found a box of Kleenex and pulled out a handful for herself. Why do I ever feel alone? she was asking herself. Here I am with my oldest ally in my own kitchen.

"Where'd you get that bruise?"

"Oh, it's a long story. I'll tell you some day. A guy tried to snatch my purse when I was walking Rudy in the park."

"Does it hurt? Did he get it?"

"Not any more. Yes, he did. But how about you? Did he hit you?"

"He didn't get that close."

David was so right. The endless he, no names required.

When Arlene stopped crying, Joan set out white plates with blue lines on them. David and the two women ate as if they were three friends on a summer night with nothing to worry about, as if Joan weren't going to court for sentencing the next day and Arlene not on the lam from her husband. Now the wine bottle stood empty, the shallow green interior reflecting a ghoulish dead light. David excused himself. Joan looked at the table. Napkins crumpled, plates greasy, the picked bones of a chicken a centre-piece. The artifice of her seclusion seemed more obvious than ever.

David left them alone for the evening.

"Coffee?"

"Got anything stronger?"

"You never touch spirits, Arlene."

"He never wanted me to."

They started drinking gin at ten o'clock. For the first hour Arlene detailed the crimes of her husband and his rum offspring. After the gin, they switched back to wine and Joan described how she had fallen in love, and how her life had seemed to get on track again. Then they switched back to Arlene's plans to go back to teaching ballet. Would Joan get the part in the film, and if she did, was it going to be a porn film? It had never occurred to Joan. Thinking of it, she realized that certain ambiguities were going to stay with her, even though she'd quit stripping.

Rather drunk, but still thirsty, they searched out a couple of bottles of beer and kept going. They sped through stale gossip about friends they never saw any more. They even got back to their old speculations that

Miss Levy was a lesbian. A question Joan had never asked before came to her lips.

"Remember the day you stayed in bed and didn't do the BBC show? Were you really sick?"

"No."

"Were you scared to go?"

"Oh, no."

"Then why?"

"I wanted you to do it. I always thought you were so much better than me. You'd have looked better on T.V."

"You're crazy."

"I was, a bit."

"Look what became of me."

"And me."

Their towering ambitions seemed very funny, all of a sudden. Over the years it had been made obvious that becoming famous ballerinas had been the least of their worries. They had grown down to normal, their pride smeared on the paving stones of the last few years.

By one o'clock in the morning Joan and Arlene were both leaning back on the cushions, boneless with alcohol, swearing tearfully that the other was the most important person in their lives. How long, how true their friendship had been, how loyal they were to each other, more loyal only to their infernal selves. Finally Joan staggered to the hall to get sheets for Arlene to use on the sofa which would be her bed. When she came back, her friend was horizontal already, unconscious, glutted with tears and memory.

Arlene lay on her back, her neck exposed. Her throat had two tiny lines around it, as if someone had wound a thread tightly around its narrow circumference, twice, and held the ends. Her mouth was open, the jagged, slightly protruding teeth the same as ever, a reminder of her imperfect start. Her legs were bare, the skirt pushed up over her knees, the clogs she'd worn dropped at the foot of the sofa.

One foot hung in the air just over the edge. The foot was like a hardened calloused hand, the hand of a workman—

thick, lumpy square toes at the end and an instep curled and lined with bulging veins. The ankle was thin. Her tendons were still drawn up as sharp as bowstrings and her calf muscles were round and hard like apples under the skin, shortening her legs so they looked like dwarf legs. This was the disguise of grace: it dwelt there, had spoken there, and could still be evoked, even with this worn and dirty apparatus.

Joan dropped the sheet over Arlene. Then she sat and turned out the light, tucking her legs under herself in the rocking-chair, the light of a street lamp outside the window falling in a prism on the floor beside her.

Here, only last week, she had tried to explain herself to the parole officer. The lady had skinny legs that she crossed and recrossed in front of her like a set of carving tools. She'd had black hair done in some kind of roll and big stupid glasses magnifying her eyes. Joan felt this woman had been sent to infuriate her, to test her patience. "I'm trying to help you," said the woman. "I'm going to do what I can for you." And Joan had looked at the sunken white cheeks under that pink glass and thought hah! You'll help me like a cannibal helps a missionary. Your livelihood depends on me. Without my guts you've got no job.

Thinking of the parole officer made Joan think of all her betrayers. Joe. Convicted, no mercy recommended. Arlene. Arlene, acquitted, always. Parents. Well, parents, guilty with extenuating circumstances, sentence suspended.

David. David had not betrayed her significantly. Yet, she added, out of habit.

The average relationship, David had told her, lasted seven years. The average house-plant lasted two. That begonia that had flourished in her window since she'd arrived more than a year ago now wanted to die. And it would not die without expressing its pain. It had begun by dropping its leaves as small reproaches and then turned brown at the tips of the remaining ones. It refused to put out new shoots; it choked on its own dried foliage and it withered. Why? It stood in the same window, received the same sun, the same water as always. It simply did not want to live there any more.

Joan had lasted twelve years in London. And then suddenly her favourite paths through crazy Soho streets, her favourite stools in the espresso bars, the wooden steps of the old flats in Covent Garden where her friends lived all became unbearable. Joan had come as a kid, Joan had been redesigned there, into this commercial lady with long nails and rings, and now it had come to an end.

She used to play the pin-ball machines in Leicester Square, at the end, thinking of the tangle of agents, managers, old boy-friends, those who she had thought of as friends at the time. They were all like the posts on the gangplank down which she shot her ball, posts against which she bumped once, bumped twice, rang a few bells, scored some points. Her mistake had been to think it was human contact when it was only gravity and rebounds.

Her last flat had been on Albany: Soho was getting too expensive. The flat was small; one wall had been covered in mirror to make the room feel bigger. It had been noisy too. Trucks came down the street at night like roaring jungle animals, and she would wake up in her bed expecting to see their tracks on the covers. Across the street there had been a military station. Northern Ireland was acting up: a soldier had stood there with a gun all hours of day and night. To Joan it had been a threat, not a protection.

You could buy ear-plugs at the chemist's down the road, ninety-five pence for six sets. Joan began to wear them almost constantly. She lived in the snail shell that was her head, with her ear turned inward, awash in inner seas. She floated undisturbed by voices and traffic: the telephone sounded like a fairy tinkle. If someone wanted to speak to her, she would reluctantly pull out one of the plugs, a scowl on her face to hear the roar that came from the unstoppered world. Because it did seem that it was the world she corked, rather than herself: that was the extent of the illusion.

After Arlene decided to quit the company and give up dancing, it was time for Joan to go home too. To go home as a failure, as she'd promised. But she wouldn't go to her parents' territory. She'd go to Toronto: Arlene was there, and she said it was all right.

And here she was, sitting in a dark living-room. She'd been trying the whole year to begin her life again. She had a nice apartment, a dog, a boy-friend. She was already part civilian; all she needed was a proper job. But would any job done by Joan Sincere be proper? Being apart rested within her; she needed only to abandon her shame in it, and live.

A phrase from a popular song came back to her: Misspent passion.

It was the story of her life. Misspent Passion. She rather liked it. The words came up in the air of the room like puffs left by a sky writer, fat, spreading letters in white along her grey walls. All that frenzy. All that desperate searching. Searching without touching, in the wrong directions, the wrong country, with the wrong people. She'd never stopped trying nonetheless.

And I've never been sorry, either, Joan pleaded to the words on the ceiling. Well, almost never. There was Sara. Sara the offspring of misspent passion. She supposed she was the very proof that it was all necessary. We are all the products of such mistakes. But don't say mistake, the old choreographer would have told her. Don't say you're wrong, say you're learning. Make use of it.

Miss Spent-Passion of Edmonton, London and Toronto. Not spent, either, but spending. Never spent, ready to try again. Miss Spend-Passion carries on. And what she has been disappears, expands, and refracts in the air until it is only something done with mirrors, only the light.

She looked down at the palm of her hand. Other people had things to show for their lives. They were surrounded by their things, comforted and shored up by them. From the lee of their things, they reached out occasionally and shared with others, shared joy and the admiration of their achievements. But mostly they were devoted to their things. Joan had very few things. These tacky chairs, that

record collection, the turntable. The white bed like a
boat. Things had not arranged themselves around her. She
had the palm of this hand, a foot like that one of Arlene's.
That which could provide no shelter. And as well, this
aching baggage of memory.

THE DAWN WAS shimmering, gold and blue, the kind of
blue that would fade later as the sun diffused in the
smoggy air. But at nine-thirty the blue was full, mature,
exultant. The door of the milk store was shut, an un-
opened plastic bag of newspapers parked in front of it. The
bent figure of the Chinese man who ran the store came
along the sidewalk: he was late this morning.

"Nice dog," he said, beaming and beaming. He said
that every time he saw Rudy. Rudy responded by sniffing
him suspiciously.

After that, Baldwin Street was empty. Joan walked in
silence, smiling at the sidewalk in front of her. She had not
gone to bed the night before, but had fallen asleep in the
living-room. She still wore the pink halter dress she'd
worn at dinner.

Rudy had met a friend. He was jumping fish jumps in
circles around the legs of the bag lady. Joan said good
morning, and noticed that the bag lady no longer looked
sinister. She walked around the block and then turned
toward home. When she opened the street door she could
smell coffee. David and Arlene were making breakfast.

She saw them sitting together at the kitchen table.
Yesterday they'd never met: now they were friends. Lives
can come together without warning—and fragments can
make sense.

The strange brightness of the night before had returned.
It was almost painful. Outside the window there were only
the browning spears left over from the chestnut blossoms,
and clusters of glossy oval leaves. The green of the leaves
illuminated the room. The mole on David's cheek, the
rattle of newspaper pages he turned, the sight of Arlene's

hands on the table, all of these small things were perilously heightened.

"Do you want milk in your coffee?"

"Yes."

The milk jug stood on the kitchen table, pale blue on the hard yellow.

Joan picked up the jug and watched the white stream leap from the blue point of china. It was so beautiful tears came to her eyes.

"Do you know what happens when strange termites are placed together in a group?"

"No, what?"

"They make friends. They begin to touch each other with their antennae. That makes their metabolism speed up and their wing muscles grow stronger. The group creates energy. It's the touching that's the key. They can't function if they're not touched. Isn't that something? But when they are touched, they become tied to the group. Their body acts as part of the group and their aspirations become the group's aspirations. And you know what's most interesting about that? Listen to this. It's not the touching that makes the change in them. It's the being touched. Passive." David sat back, a triumphant look on his face.

"Are you trying to tell us something?"

"I just told you."

"David, sometimes you're boring," said Joan.

David's face was cool, like water in a brook; pretty, but not welcoming. He was not at first a warm man, but he was a clear one. Sometimes there would be a stroke of sun and you could see right to the bottom. Joan got up and went to sit on his lap. He wrapped his arms around her waist, and his fingers dug into the soft parts of either side of her back. She had a tremulous feeling, as if she were ready to burst. Surface tension, David said, kept a droplet of water in one rounded mass, kept it quivering like that.

She went to do her hair, slowly and carefully. She braided it in corn rows from the hair-line to the crown and then let the ends spray up into the air, a cockscomb. She looked at her profile with a second mirror: her head shape, that long, ancient dome, pleased her. She went to her costume bags and rummaged. She wanted to be sure she felt like herself today in court. She decided upon her red and silver Mexican skirt and the mirrored Afghani vest with tassels.

Outside the courtroom she parted from David and Arlene: they'd be sitting in the spectators' seats.

"Break a leg."

"*Merde*."

Rennick blanched at the sight of her.

"How did you make out with the probation officer?"

"I've met her type before, only she ran a delinquent home in London."

"So you do have a history."

It was the same courtroom, the same judge, and possibly the same crowd of faintly curious onlookers. Alex and Joan slid into seats in one of the rows of pews half-way back. Joan was full of a shattering calm, that curious blankness she could get before a performance. She didn't want to plan it, she just wanted to stay in this suspense until the moment when she was called upon.

"What's her name? Sincere, is it? Have we got the pre-sentence report?"

"Yes, Your Honour, it's right here. It was just brought down this morning."

A man stood in front of the judge and passed him a sheaf of papers with a clip on top.

"Is Miss Sincere in the court? Has she read the pre-sentence report?" From the weight of his look, it seemed that the judge wanted to ask her something far more fundamental: he wanted to ask her if she was prepared to meet her maker.

"No, she hasn't."

"Why hasn't she read it?"

"There's only one copy, Your Honour."

"Well, give it to her. Miss Sincere, read that, and then we'll hear your case."

Alex carried the papers to Joan. She took them and glanced at the first few lines. Then she turned and walked back through the little wooden gate to where the spectators sat. She wanted to read it sitting down.

The court was silent. The judge turned to the side and looked out the window: already the blue sky had turned milky. Arlene and David sat side by side, intent on Joan's face. Alex had gone back to the table at the front. The fluorescent lights buzzed as Joan read on. Voices sounded, but they were far away.

"Is everyone here for number eight, Palozzi?"

"I appear for Mr. Palozzi, sir, may I check the hallway to see if he's here yet?"

"If he is, we'll hear him while we wait."

Someone walked out the door. Then he came back in. Joan read on.

"He's not there, Your Honour."

"Fine, we'll wait."

"Miss Sincere?"

"I represent Miss Sincere. The name is Rennick."

"Ask your client if she's finished reading."

Alex's feet came up beside her bench. "You ready?"

Joan looked up. Her heart was pounding. She was full of a powerful anger: she could have pushed him over.

"Alex, I'm going to do this myself. I'll trade you places." She stood up. She felt tall, very tall. She put her hand on his chest, pushing past him. She walked through the wooden gate to the bullpen.

The judge smiled strangely. "Are you Miss Sincere?"

"Yes."

"Are you going to speak for yourself now?"

"Yes, I am."

The judge lifted one hand and let it fall. It was O.K. with him. "Have you read the report? Is there anything you dispute? Is it correct?"

"Correct? Well, I suppose. But I dispute the whole damn thing."

Joan jabbed her heel into the floor, her toe raised to the side, one hand on her hip. Like Joe, the report came one day too late. She had not made a difficult peace with herself only to go to court and agree to this kind of smear. She shook the papers in front of the judge. "You can't be serious. Come on, this report is full of crap, Mr. Judge."

The judge sat forward and opened his mouth, but she took a quick breath and went on.

"I mean, I'm Joan Sincere and I'm reading here about some woman who's got my name, my address, my history, too. But she's not me, I tell you. She's not anybody. She's not even human, she's a file, she's a PROBLEM."

Joan swung her head around. She could see David and Arlene frozen in their seats. She experimented with movement, taking a few steps forward, turning her body back toward the judge. It was happening: she could work the old magic, but with words. The hand Johanna had said was around her throat was loosening. She could feel her windpipe expand, freed. She opened her chest; her head filled up with air and power. She was talking.

"I know you legal types. You think I'm a crook, you think I'm a nobody. Well, you should do something. You go down to a club any day of the week and you'll learn one thing. Any stripper's worth ten of her audience. You can see that even reading this lousy report made by some chick with her legs crossed twice. You know what I think when I read this? I think, hey, this woman has guts. I think, man, this Joan Sincere's at least sticking to her guns."

"Miss Sincere, be aware that we're indulging you. Would you please make your point?"

"People say to me look, Joan, don't take this personally, it's just the law. But I believe in taking things personally. You can't separate me from what I do. I'm putting myself on the line. I've done it all my life, whether I stripped or not. And you know what I think about you? I think you don't even know what that means. If I took away your little pedestal there and the desk you're hiding behind, where would you be? Is there a man inside that robe? If you take off that red collar and then the suit and tie—"

The judge brought his hand down sharply.

"—what will we see?" She was moving fast across the court to get away from the officer. She could see someone in the audience taking notes; she loved it.

"About this report. The way I read it you're likely to go easy on me if I say I'm sorry. Well, by my rules I haven't done a thing wrong. But I don't make the rules here. You make them and you oughta know whether I broke them or I didn't. So don't give me this 'moral weakness,' this 'borderline existence,' this 'give her a chance' stuff. That's bullshit. I'm not going to a psychiatrist. I'm not sorry, and I'm not going to reform."

"Miss Sincere, if you'll excuse me." The judge had become dry and clever. She could tell he was shaken. He knew she had the audience, with her hair standing around her head like a cloud of gnats and her flashing vest a competition for his robes. She had the audience but he had the power. This was only case seven on the morning's list: he could dispense with her.

"The pre-sentence report suggests lenience. A suspended sentence, a probation perhaps. You've convinced me that it is wrong. You've been convicted of assault, and in one minute you're going to be charged with contempt. I'm going to fine you four hundred dollars or thirty days."

"I'm not paying any fine."

"All right, thirty days in jail, to begin immediately. Case dismissed." He banged the gavel.

THERE WAS NOISE around her. The policeman had her by the arm. She was trembling, but the surface tension was gone. She hung like the drop of water ready to fall from the eaves, weak, heavy. She was going to jail. She looked over her shoulder to David. He stood with Arlene, at the wooden fence, leaning toward her. Arlene looked as if she were going to cry. David raised his fist in the air: he was no civilian.

"Look after the dog!" She began to shake violently. She could feel the air, the small breezes in the room as people moved, their voices rising. She felt as if she'd just stepped from a vacuum into an atmosphere. An atmosphere where the best and the worst happened at once. She had learned how to talk; it had taken her life thus far to find the words to come to her own defence. And having learned, she was going to jail. She almost giggled. The drop of water was plummeting, that dizzying heavy fall down to who knows where. The bitterness came with joy, the pride with pain. She felt peeled raw. She was going to jail, making an exit on the policeman's arm as a camera popped. It was just like the night when the whole thing had started. But this time David and Arlene were there, her friends were with her. She could still see them as she was led away down the hall.

ABOUT THE AUTHOR

KATHERINE GOVIER was born in Edmonton, Alberta. She graduated in 1970 from the University of Alberta, where she studied Canadian literature under Rudy Wiebe and Dorothy Livesay.

In 1972 Govier completed her M.A. in English at Toronto's York University. She spent the next few years working at various part-time jobs before earning a steady income as a freelance journalist. Her articles have been published in some of Canada's finest newspapers and magazines, including *Saturday Night, Miss Chatelaine, Weekend, Quest, The Globe and Mail* and *Toronto Life.* As well, her short stories have appeared in *Canadian Forum, Descant* and other literary journals.

Katherine Govier is the author of the acclaimed *Random Descent,* which was published in 1979.

SEAL BOOKS

Offers you a list of outstanding fiction, non-fiction and classics of Canadian literature in paperback by Canadian authors, available at all good bookstores throughout Canada.

The Mark of Canadian Bestsellers   SB-7